SHE SLAMMED ON THE ⋯⋯⋯⋯⋯⋯⋯⋯⋯⋯⋯ ᴅ.
Somehow her brain functioned to take care of little ⋯⋯⋯⋯⋯ᴛn
off the ignition, take out the key, pull open the door. She was
shaking in the late evening heat. An earlier rain and rising temperatures caused mist to spiral up from the pavement. She ran
through it, looking frantically right, left, back over her shoulder.

The dark. She'd nearly forgotten there were things that hid
in the dark.

The noise level rose as she pushed open the doors. The fluorescent lights dazzled her eyes. She continued to run, knowing
only that she was terrified and someone, anyone, had to listen.

She raced along the hallway, her heart beating a hard tattoo.
A dozen or more phones were ringing. Someone cursed in a low,
continual stream. She saw the doors marked Homicide and bit
back a sob.

He was kicked back at his desk, one foot resting on a torn
blotter, a phone tucked between his shoulder and ear. A Styrofoam cup of coffee was halfway to his lips.

"Please help me," she said, collapsing into the chair facing
him. "Someone's trying to kill me."

—from *Public Secrets*

# PUBLIC SECRETS

••••

*A Novel*

*Nora Roberts*

BANTAM
NEW YORK

2022 Bantam Books Mass Market Edition

Copyright © 1990 by Nora Roberts

Published in the United States by Bantam Books,
an imprint of Random House, a division of
Penguin Random House LLC, New York.

BANTAM BOOKS is a registered trademark and the B colophon is a
trademark of Penguin Random House LLC.

Originally published in the United States by Bantam Books,
an imprint of Random House, a division of
Penguin Random House LLC, in 1990.

ISBN 978-0-553-28578-9
Ebook ISBN 978-0-307-56811-3

Cover design: Derek Walls
Cover image: © Darlo Issa Amade/Shutterstock (bridge),
© Thammanoon Khamchalee/Shutterstock (clouds)

Printed in the United States of America

randomhousebooks.com

56  58  60  62  64  63  61  59  57

Bantam Books mass market edition: September 2022

*For my first hero, my father*

# PUBLIC SECRETS

# Prologue

♦ ♦ ♦ ♦

Los Angeles, 1990

SHE SLAMMED ON the brakes, ramming hard into the curb. The radio continued to blare. She pressed both hands against her mouth to hold back hysterical laughter. A blast from the past, the disk jockey had called it. A blast from her past. Devastation was still rocking.

Somehow her brain functioned to take care of little matters: turn off the ignition, take out the key, pull open the door. She was shaking in the late evening heat. An earlier rain and rising temperatures caused mist to spiral up from the pavement. She ran through it, looking frantically right, left, back over her shoulder.

The dark. She'd nearly forgotten there were things that hid in the dark.

The noise level rose as she pushed open the doors. The fluorescent lights dazzled her eyes. She continued to run, knowing only that she was terrified and someone, anyone, had to listen.

She raced along the hallway, her heart beating a hard tattoo. A dozen or more phones were ringing; voices merged and mixed in complaints, shouts, questions. Someone cursed in a low, continual stream. She saw the doors marked Homicide and bit back a sob.

He was kicked back at his desk, one foot resting on a torn blotter, a phone tucked between his shoulder and ear. A Styrofoam cup of coffee was halfway to his lips.

"Please help me," she said, collapsing into the chair facing him. "Someone's trying to kill me."

# *Chapter One*

♦ ♦ ♦ ♦

London, 1967

*T*HE FIRST TIME Emma met her father, she was nearly three years old. She knew what he looked like because her mother kept pictures of him, meticulously cut from newspapers and glossy magazines, on every surface in their cramped three-room flat. Jane Palmer had a habit of carrying her daughter, Emma, from picture to picture hanging on the water-stained walls and sitting on the dusty scarred furniture and telling her of the glorious love affair that had bloomed between herself and Brian McAvoy, lead singer for the hot rock group, Devastation. The more Jane drank, the greater that love became.

Emma understood only parts of what she was told. She knew that the man in the pictures was important, that he and his band had played for the queen. She had learned to recognize his voice when his songs came on the radio, or when her mother put one of the 45s she collected on the record player.

Emma liked his voice, and what she would learn later was called its faint Irish lilt.

Some of the neighbors tut-tutted about the poor little girl upstairs with a mother who had a fondness for the gin bottle and a vicious temper. There were times they heard Jane's shrill curses and Emma's sobbing wails. Their lips would firm and knowing looks would pass between the ladies as they shook out their rugs or hung up the weekly wash.

In the early days of the summer of 1967, the summer of love, they shook their heads when they heard the little girl's cries through the open window of the Palmer flat. Most agreed that young Jane Palmer didn't deserve such a sweet-faced child, but they murmured only among themselves. No one in that part of London would dream of reporting such a matter to the authorities.

Of course, Emma didn't understand terms like alcoholism or emotional illness, but even though she was only three she was an expert on gauging her mother's moods. She knew the days her mother would laugh and cuddle, the days she would scold and slap. When the atmosphere in the flat was particularly heavy, Emma would take her stuffed black dog, Charlie, crawl under the cabinet beneath the kitchen sink, and in the dark and damp, wait out her mother's temper.

On some days, she wasn't quick enough.

"Hold still, do, Emma." Jane dragged the brush through Emma's pale blond hair. With her teeth gritted, she resisted the urge to whack the back of it across her daughter's rump. She wasn't going to lose her temper today, not today. "I'm going to make you pretty. You want to be especially pretty today, don't you?"

Emma didn't care very much about looking pretty, not when her mother's brush strokes were hurting her scalp and the new pink dress was scratchy with starch. She continued to wriggle on the stool as Jane tried to tie her flyaway curls back with a ribbon.

"I said hold still." Emma squealed when Jane dug hard fingers into the nape of her neck. "Nobody loves a dirty, nasty girl." After two long breaths, Jane relaxed her grip. She didn't want to put bruises on the child. She loved her, really. And bruises would look bad, very bad, to Brian if he noticed them.

After dragging her from the stool, Jane kept a firm hand on Emma's shoulder. "Take that sulky look off your face, my girl." But she was pleased with the results. Emma, with her wispy blond curls and big blue eyes, looked like a pampered little princess. "Look here." Jane's hands were gentle again as she turned Emma to the mirror. "Don't you look nice?"

Emma's mouth moved stubbornly into a pout as she studied herself in the spotted glass. Her voice mirrored her mother's cockney and had a trace of a childish lisp. "Itchy."

"A lady has to be uncomfortable if she wants a man to think she's beautiful." Jane's own slimming black corset was biting into her flesh.

"Why?"

"Because that's part of a woman's job." She turned, examining first one side, then the other in the mirror. The dark blue dress was flattering to her full curves, making the most of her generous breasts. Brian had always liked her breasts, she thought, and felt a quick, sexual pull.

God, no one ever before or since had matched him in bed. There was a hunger in him, a wild hunger he hid so well under his cool and cocky exterior. She had known him since childhood, had been his on-again, off-again lover for more than ten years. No one knew better what Brian was capable of when fully aroused.

She allowed herself to fantasize, just for a moment, what it would be like when he peeled the dress away, when his eyes roamed over her, when his slender, musician's fingers unhooked the frilly corset.

They'd been good together, she remembered as she felt herself go damp. They would be good together again.

Bringing herself back, she picked up the brush and smoothed her hair. She had spent the last of the grocery money at the hairdresser's getting her shoulder-length straight hair colored to match Emma's. Turning her head, she watched it sway from side to side. After today, she wouldn't have to worry about money ever again.

Her lips were carefully painted a pale, pale pink—the same shade she had seen on supermodel Jane Asher's recent *Vogue* cover. Nervous, she picked up her black liner and added more definition near the corner of each eye.

Fascinated, Emma watched her mother. Today she smelled of Tigress cologne instead of gin. Tentatively, Emma reached out for the lipstick tube. Her hand was slapped away.

"Keep your hands off my things." She gave Emma's finger an extra slap. "Haven't I told you never to touch my things?"

Emma nodded. Her eyes had already filmed over.

"And don't start that bawling. I don't want him seeing you for the first time with your eyes all red and your face puffy. He should have been here already." There was an edge to Jane's voice now, one that had Emma moving cautiously out of range. "If he doesn't come soon . . ." She trailed off, going over her options as she studied herself in the glass.

She had always been a big girl, but had never run to fat. True, the dress was a little snug, but she strained against it in interesting places. Skinny might be in fashion, but she knew men preferred round, curvy women when the lights went out. She'd been making her living off her body long enough to be sure of it.

Her confidence built as she looked herself over and she fancied she resembled the pale, sulky-faced models who were the rage in London. She wasn't wise enough to note that the new color job was unflattering or that the arrow-straight hair made the angles of her face boxy and harsh. She wanted to be in tune. She always had.

"He probably didn't believe me. Didn't want to. Men never want their children." She shrugged. Her father had never wanted her—not until her breasts had begun to develop. "You remember that, Emma girl." She cast a considering eye over Emma. "Men don't want babies. They only want a woman for one thing, and you'll find out what that is soon enough. When they're done, they're done, and you're left with a big stomach and a broken heart."

She picked up a cigarette and began to smoke it in quick, jerky puffs as she paced. She wished it was grass, sweet, calming grass, but she'd spent her drug money on Emma's new dress. The sacrifices a mother made.

"Well, he may not want you, but after one look he won't be able to deny you're his." Eyes narrowed against the smoke, she studied her daughter. There was another tug, almost maternal. The little tyke was certainly pretty as a picture when she was cleaned up. "You're the goddamn image of him, Emma luv. The papers say he's going to marry that Wilson slut—old money and fancy manners—but we'll see, we'll just see about that. He'll come back to me. I always knew he'd come back." She stubbed the cigarette in a chipped ashtray and left it smoldering. She needed a drink—just one taste of gin to calm her nerves. "You sit on the bed," she ordered. "Sit right there and keep quiet. Mess with any of my stuff, and you'll be sorry."

She had two drinks before she heard the knock on the door. Her heart began to pound. Like most drunks, she felt more attractive, more in control, once she'd had the liquor. She smoothed down her hair, fixed what she thought was a sultry smile on her face, and opened the door.

He was beautiful. For a moment in the streaming summer sunlight, she saw only him, tall and slender, his wavy blond hair and full, serious mouth giving him the look of a poet or an apostle. As nearly as she was able, she loved.

"Brian. So nice of you to drop by." Her smile faded immediately when she saw the two men behind him. "Traveling in a pack these days, Bri?"

He wasn't in the mood. He was carrying around a simmering rage at being trapped into seeing Jane again and put the bulk of the blame on his manager and his fiancée. Now that he was here, he intended to get out again as quickly as possible.

"You remember, Johnno." Brian stepped inside. The smell, gin, sweat, and grease from yesterday's dinner, reminded him uncomfortably of his own childhood.

"Sure." Jane nodded briefly to the tall, gangly bass player. He was wearing a diamond on his pinky and sported a dark, fluffy beard. "Come up in the world, haven't we, Johnno?"

He glanced around the dingy flat. "Some of us."

"This is Pete Page, our manager."

"Miss Palmer." Smooth, thirtyish, Pete offered a white-toothed smile and a manicured hand.

"I've heard all about you." She laid her hand in his, back up, an invitation to lift it to his lips. He released it. "You made our boys stars."

"I opened a few doors."

"Performing for the queen, playing on the telly. Got a new album on the charts and a big American tour coming up." She looked back at Brian. His hair fell nearly to his shoulders. His face was thin and pale and sensitive. Reproductions of it were gracing teenagers' walls on both sides of the Atlantic as his second album, *Complete Devastation*, bulleted up the charts. "Got everything you wanted."

Damned if he'd let her make him feel guilty because he'd made something of himself. "That's right."

"Some of us get more than they want." She tossed her long hair back. The paint on the swingy gold balls she wore at her ears was chipped and peeling. She smiled again, posing a moment. At twenty-four she was a year older than Brian, and considered herself much more savvy. "I'd offer tea, but I wasn't expecting a party."

"We didn't come for tea." Brian stuck his hands in the wide pockets of his low-riding jeans. The sulky look he'd worn throughout the drive over had hardened. True, he was young, but he'd grown up tough. He had no intention of letting this old, gin-soaked loner make trouble for him. "I didn't call the law this time, Jane. That's for old time's sake. If you keep ringing, keep writing with all your threats and blackmail, believe me I will."

Her heavily lined eyes narrowed. "You want to put the bobbies on me, you go right ahead, my lad. We'll see how all your little fans and their stick-in-the-mud parents like reading about how you got me pregnant. About how you deserted me and your poor little baby girl while you're rolling in money and living high. How would that go over, Mr. Page? Think you could get Bri and the boys another royal command performance?"

"Miss Palmer." Pete's voice was smooth and calm. He'd already spent hours considering the ins and outs of the situation. One glance told him he'd wasted his time. The answer here would be money. "I'm sure you don't want to air your personal business in the press. Nor do I think you should imply desertion when there was none."

"Ooh. Is he your manager, Brian, or your blinking solicitor?"

"You weren't pregnant when I left you."

"Didn't know I was pregnant!" she shouted and gripped Brian's black leather vest. "It was two months later when I found out for sure. You were gone by then. I didn't know where to find you. I could have gotten rid of it." She clung harder when Brian started to pry her hands off. "I knew people who could have fixed it for me, but I was scared, more scared of that than of having it."

"So she had a kid." Johnno sat on the arm of a chair and pulled out a Gauloise which he lit with a heavy gold lighter. In the past two years he'd gotten very comfortable with expensive habits. "That don't mean it was yours, Bri."

"It's his, you freaking fag."

"My, my." Unperturbed, Johnno drew on the cigarette, then blew the smoke lightly but directly into her face. "Quite the lady, aren't we?"

"Back off, Johnno." Pete's voice remained low and calm. "Miss Palmer, we're here to settle this whole matter quietly."

And that, she thought, was her ace in the hole. "I'll just bet you'd like to keep it quiet. You know I wasn't with anybody else back then, Brian." She leaned into him, letting her breasts press and flatten against his chest. "You remember that Christmas, the last Christmas we were together. We got high and a little crazy. We never used anything. Emma, she'll be three next September."

He remembered, though he wished he didn't. He'd been nineteen and full of music and rage. Someone had brought cocaine and after he'd snorted for the first time he'd felt like a thoroughbred stud. Quivering to fuck.

"So you had a baby and you think she's mine. Why did you wait until now to tell me about her?"

"I told you I couldn't find you at first." Jane moistened her lips and wished she'd had just one more drink. She didn't think it would be wise to tell him she'd enjoyed playing the martyr for a while, the poor, unwed mother, all alone. And there'd been a man or two along the way to ease the road.

"I went on this program, they have them for girls who get in trouble. I thought maybe I'd give her away, you know, for adoption. After I had her, I couldn't, because she looked just like you. I thought if I gave her up, you'd find out about it and get mad at me. I was afraid you wouldn't give me another chance."

She started to cry, big fat tears that smeared her heavy makeup. They were uglier, and more disturbing, because they were sincere. "I always knew you'd come back, Brian. I started hearing your songs on the radio, seeing posters of you in the record store. You were on your way. I always knew you'd make it, but, Jesus, I never knew you'd be so big. I started thinking—"

"I'll bet you did," Johnno murmured.

"I started thinking," she said between her teeth. "That you'd want to know about the kid. I went back to your old place, but you'd moved and nobody would tell me where. But I thought about you every day. Look."

Taking his arm she pointed to the pictures she'd crowded on the walls of the flat. "I cut out everything I could find about you and saved it."

He looked at himself reproduced a dozen times. His stomach turned. "Jesus."

"I called your record company, and I even went there, but they treated me like I was nobody. I told them I was the mother of Brian McAvoy's baby daughter, and they had me tossed out." She didn't add that she'd been drunk and had attacked the receptionist. "I started reading about you and Beverly Wilson, and I got desperate. I knew she couldn't mean anything to you, not after what we had. But I had to talk to you somehow."

"Calling Bev's flat and raving like a maniac wasn't the best way to go about it."

"I had to talk to you, to make you listen. You don't know what it's like, Bri, worrying about how to pay the rent, whether you've got enough for food. I can't buy pretty dresses anymore or go out at night."

"Is money what you want?"

She hesitated just an instant too long. "I want you, Bri, I always have."

Johnno tapped out his cigarette in the base of a plastic plant. "You know, Bri, there's been a lot of talk about this kid, but I don't see any sign of her." He rose, and in a habitual gesture, shook back his gleaming mop of dark hair. "Ready to split?"

Jane sent him a vicious look. "Emma's in the bedroom. And I'm not having all of your troop in there. This is between Brian and me."

Johnno grinned at her. "You always did your best work in the bedroom, didn't you, luv?" Their eyes held for a moment, the disgust they had always felt for each other clear. "Bri, she was a first-rate whore once upon a time, but she's second-rate now. Can we get on?"

"You bloody queer." Jane leaped at him before Brian caught her around the waist. "You wouldn't know what to do with a real woman if she bit you on the dick."

He continued to grin, but his eyes frosted over. "Care to give it a shot, dearie?"

"Always could count on you to keep things running smoothly, Johnno," Brian muttered as he twisted Jane around in his arms. "You said this business was with me, then keep it with me. I'll have a look at the girl."

"Not them two." She snarled at Johnno as he shrugged and pulled out another cigarette. "Just you. I want to keep it private."

"Fine. Wait here." He kept his hand on Jane's arm as she walked to the bedroom. It was empty. "I'm tired of the game, Jane."

"She's hiding. All these people put her off, that's all. Emma! Come here to your mam right now." Jane dropped to her knees beside the bed, then scrambled up to search through the narrow closet. "She's probably in the loo." Rushing out, she pulled open a door off the hallway.

"Brian." Johnno signaled from the kitchen doorway. "Something here you might want to see." He held up a glass, toasting Jane. "You don't mind if I have a drink, do you, luv? The bottle was open." He jerked the thumb of his free hand toward the cabinet under the sink.

The stale scent was stronger there, old liquor, ripening garbage, molding rags. Brian's shoes stuck to the linoleum as he crossed to the cupboard, then crouched. He pulled open the door and peered inside.

He couldn't see the girl clearly, only that she was hunched back in the corner, her blond hair in her eyes and something black hugged in her arms. He felt his stomach turn over, but tried to smile.

"Hello there."

Emma buried her face in the furry black bundle she held.

"Nasty little brat. I'll teach you to hide from me." Jane started to make a grab, but a look from Brian stopped her. He held out a hand and smiled again.

"I don't think I can fit in there with you. Would you mind coming out a minute?" He saw her peep up over her folded arms. "No one's going to hurt you."

He had such a nice voice, Emma thought, soft and pretty like music. He was smiling at her. The light through the kitchen window was on his hair, making the deep, rich blond shine. Like an angel's hair. She giggled, then crawled out.

Her new dress was smeared and spotted. Her wispy baby hair was damp from a leak under the sink. She smiled, showing little white teeth with a crooked inciser. Brian ran his tongue over a similar one in his own mouth. When her lips curved, a dimple winked at the left corner of her mouth, a twin of his. Eyes as deep and blue as his own stared back at him.

"I fixed her up real nice." There was a whine in Jane's voice now. The smell of the gin was making her mouth water, but she was afraid to pour a glass. "And I told her it was important to stay tidy. Didn't I tell you to stay tidy, Emma? I'll wash her up." She grabbed Emma's arm hard enough to make the girl jump.

"Let her be."

"I was only going to—"

"Let her be," Brian repeated, his voice flat and dull and threatening. If he hadn't been staring at her still, Emma might have dashed under the sink again. His child. For a moment he could only continue to stare at her, his head light and his stomach fisted. "Hello, Emma." There was a sweetness in his tone now, one women fell in love with. "What have you got there?"

"Charlie. My doggie." She held the stuffed toy out for Brian to examine.

"And a very nice one." He had an urge to touch her, to brush his hand over her skin, but held back. "Do you know who I am?"

"From the pictures." Too young to resist impulses, she reached out to touch his face. "Pretty."

Johnno laughed and swallowed some gin. "Leave it to a female."

Ignoring him, Brian tugged on Emma's damp curls. "You're pretty, too."

He talked nonsense to her, watching her closely. His knees were like jelly, and his stomach tightened and loosened like fingers snapping to a beat. Her dimple deepened as she laughed. It was like watching himself. It would have been easier to deny it, and a great deal more convenient, but impossible. Whether he had meant to or not, he had made her. But guidance didn't come along with acceptance.

He rose and turned to Pete. "We'd better get to rehearsal."

"You're leaving?" Jane dashed forward to block his path. "Just like that? You only have to look at her to see."

"I know what I see." He felt a pang of guilt as Emma inched back toward the cupboard. "I need time to think."

"No, no! You'll walk out like before. You're only thinking of yourself, like always. What's best for Brian, what's best for Brian's career. I won't be left back anymore." He had nearly reached the door when she snatched up Emma and raced after him. "If you go, I'll kill myself."

He paused long enough to look back. It was a familiar refrain. He could have set it to music. "That stopped working a long time ago."

"And her." Desperate, she flung out the threat, then let it hang as they both considered it. The arm she had banded around Emma's waist tightened until the girl began to scream.

He felt a bubble of panic as the child's, his child's screams bounced off the walls. "Let her go, Jane. You're hurting her."

"What do you care?" Jane was sobbing now, her voice rising

higher and higher to drown out her daughter's. "You're walking out."

"No I'm not. I need a little time to think this through."

"Time so your fancy manager can make up a story, you mean." She was breathing fast, gripping the struggling Emma with both arms. "You're going to do right by me, Brian."

His hands had balled into fists at his sides. "Put her down."

"I'll kill her." She said it more calmly this time, having centered on it. "I'll slit her throat, I swear it, and then my own. Can you live with that, Brian?"

"She's bluffing," Johnno muttered, but his palms were sweating.

"I've got nothing to lose. Do you think I want to live like this? Raising a brat all on my own, having the neighbors gossip about me? Never being able to go out and have fun anymore. You think about it, Bri, think about what the papers will do when I call in the story. I'll tell them everything right before I kill us both."

"Miss Palmer." Peter held up a soothing hand. "I give you my word we'll come to an arrangement that suits everyone."

"Let Johnno take Emma into the kitchen, Jane. We'll talk." Brian took a careful step toward her. "We'll find a way to do what's best for everyone."

"I only want you to come back."

"I'm not going anywhere." Braced, he watched her grip relax. "We'll talk." He signaled Johnno with a slight nod of the head. "We'll talk it all through. Why don't we sit down?"

Reluctantly, Johnno pried the girl from her mother. A fastidious man, he wrinkled his nose a little at the grime she'd accumulated under the sink, but carried her into the kitchen. When she continued to cry, he sat down with Emma on his lap and patted her head.

"Come on now, cutie, give over. Johnno won't let anything bad happen to you." He jiggled her, trying to think what his mother might have done. "Want a biscuit?"

Damp-eyed, hiccuping, she nodded.

He jiggled some more. Under the tears and dirt, he decided she was a taking little thing. And a McAvoy, he admitted with a sigh. A McAvoy through and through. "Got any we can pinch?"

She smiled then, and pointed to a high cupboard.

Thirty minutes later, they were finishing up the plate of

biscuits and the sweet tea he'd brewed. Brian watched them from the kitchen doorway as Johnno made faces so that Emma giggled. When the chips were down, Brian thought, you could always depend on Johnno.

Going in, Brian ran a hand down his daughter's hair. "Emma, would you like to ride in my car?"

She licked crumbs from her lips. "With Johnno?"

"Yeah, with Johnno."

"I'm a hit." Johnno popped the last biscuit into his mouth.

"I'd like you to stay with me, Emma, in my new house."

"Bri—"

He cut Johnno off, lifting a hand palm up. "It's a nice house, and you could have your own room."

"I have to?"

"I'm your da, Emma, and I'd like you to live with me. You could try it, and if you're not happy, we'll think of something else."

Emma studied him, her full bottom lip pushed out in a pout. She was used to his face, but it was different somehow from the pictures. She didn't know or care why. His voice made her feel good, safe.

"Is my mam coming?"

"No."

Her eyes filled, but she picked up her battered black dog and hugged it close. "Is Charlie?"

"Sure." Brian held out his arms, and lifted her.

"Hope you know what you're doing, son."

Brian sent him a look over Emma's head. "So do I."

# Chapter Two

♦ ♦ ♦ ♦

$\mathcal{E}$MMA HAD HER first look at the big stone house from the front seat of the silver Jag. She was sorry that Johnno, with his funny beard, was gone, but the man from the pictures let her push buttons on the dash. He wasn't smiling anymore, but he didn't scold. He smelled nice. The car smelled nice. She pushed Charlie's nose into the seat and babbled to herself.

The house looked enormous to her with its arching windows and curvy turrets. It was stone, weathered gray, and all the windows were made up of diamond shapes. The lawn around it was thick and green, and there was a scent of flowers. She grinned, bouncing with excitement.

"Castle."

He smiled now. "Yeah, I thought so, too. When I was little I wanted to live in a house like this. My da—your grandda—used to work in the garden here." When he wasn't passed out drunk, Brian added to himself.

"Is he here?"

"No, he's in Ireland." In a little cottage Brian had bought with money Pete had advanced him a year before. He stopped the car at the front entrance, realizing he would have to make some calls before the story hit the papers. "You'll meet him someday, and your aunts and uncles, your cousins." He gathered her up, amazed and baffled at how easily she cuddled against him. "You have a family now, Emma."

When he walked inside, still carrying her, he heard Bev's light, quick voice.

"I think the blue, the plain blue. I can't live with all these flowers growing on the walls. And those beastly hangings have to go. It's like a cave in here. I want white, white and blue."

He turned into the parlor doorway and saw her sitting on the floor, dozens of sample books and swatches around her. Part of the wallpaper had already been stripped, part of the replastering was finished. Bev preferred tackling a single job from a dozen angles.

She looked so small and sweet sitting amid the rubble. Her dark cap of hair was cut short and straight to angle down toward her chin. Big gold hoops glinted at her ears. Her eyes were exotic, both in shape and color. They were long-lidded with gold lights flecked in pale sea-green. She was still tanned from the weekend they had spent in the Bahamas. He knew exactly how her skin would feel, how it would smell.

She had a small triangular-shaped face, and a small angular body. No one looking at her sitting cross-legged in snug checked pants and a tidy white shirt would suspect she was two months pregnant.

Brian shifted his daughter in his arms and wondered how his pregnant lover would react.

"Bev."

"Brian, I didn't hear you." She turned, half rising, then went still. "Oh." Her color drained as she stared at the child in his arms. Recovering quickly, she stood and signaled to two decorators who were bickering over samples. "Brian and I want to discuss our choices a little more. I'll call you by the end of the week."

She hurried them out, making promises, flattering. When she closed the door on them, she took a deep breath, holding a hand over the baby growing inside her.

"This is Emma."

Bev forced a smile. "Hello, Emma."

" 'Lo." Suddenly shy, she buried her face in Brian's neck.

"Emma, would you like to watch the telly for a while?" Brian gave her bottom a reassuring pat. When she only shrugged, he went on, desperately cheerful. "There's a nice big one in this room over here. You and Charlie can sit on the sofa."

"I have to pee," she whispered.

"Oh, well . . ."

Bev blew her bangs out of her eyes. If she hadn't felt so much like crying, she might have laughed. "I'll take her."

But Emma clung tighter to Brian's neck. "I guess I'm elected." He took her to the powder room across the hall, sent Bev a helpless look, then closed the door. "Do you, ah . . ." He trailed off when Emma pulled down her panties and sat.

"I don't wet my pants," she said matter-of-factly. "Mam says only stupid, nasty girls do."

"You're a big girl," he said, stifling a fresh flow of rage. "Very pretty and very smart."

Finished, she struggled back into her panties. "Can you watch the telly?"

"In a little while. I need to talk to Bev. She's a very nice lady," he added as he lifted her up to the sink. "She lives with me, too."

Emma played with the running water a moment. "Does she hit?"

"No." He pulled her into his arms, holding tight. "No one's going to hit you again. I promise."

Torn, he carried her out, past Bev, to a sitting room with a cushy sofa and a big console television. He switched it on, settled on a loud comedy show, and said, "I'll be back soon."

Emma watched him walk out, relieved when he left the door open.

"Maybe we'd better go in here." Bev gestured to the parlor. Inside, she sat on the floor again and began poking at samples. "It seems Jane wasn't lying."

"No. She's mine."

"I can see that, Bri. She looks so much like you it's scary." She felt tears well up and hated herself.

"Oh Christ, Bev."

"No, don't," she said when he started to slip an arm around her. "I need a minute. It's a shock."

"It was one for me, too." He lit a cigarette, drew hard. "You know why I broke things off with Jane."

"You said it felt like she could eat you alive."

"She wasn't stable, Bev. Even when we were kids, she was never quite right."

She couldn't look at him, not yet. She reminded herself that it had been she who had pressured him into seeing Jane again, into finding out the truth about the child. Folding her hands in her lap, Bev stared into the dusty marble fireplace. "You've known her a long time."

"She was the first girl I ever slept with. I was barely thirteen." He rubbed his hands over his eyes, wishing it wasn't so easy to remember. "My father would get drunk, go on one of his famous rages before he passed out. I'd hide out in the cellar of the flat. One day Jane was there, like she was waiting. Before I knew it, she was on top of me."

"You don't have to go into all this, Bri."

"I want you to know." He took his time, drawing in smoke, letting it out. "We seemed a lot alike, Jane and I. Somebody was always fighting at her house, too. There was never enough money. Then when I started getting interested in music, I spent more time with that than her. She went crazy. She threatened me, threatened herself. I kept away from her.

"Then not long after the guys and I got together, when we were struggling so hard to get a break, she showed up again. We were playing in dives, barely making enough for food. I guess it was because she was someone I knew, someone who knew me. Mostly it was because I was an asshole."

Bev sniffled, gave a watery laugh. "You're still an asshole."

"Yeah. We got back together, almost a year. Toward the end she was outrageous, trying to start trouble between me and the others. She'd break up rehearsals, make scenes. She even came to the club and went after one of the girls in the audience. Afterward, she'd cry and beg me to forgive her. It got to the point where it stopped being easier to say, sure, fine, forget it. She said she'd kill herself when I broke it off with her. We'd just hooked up with Pete and had a series of gigs in France and Germany. He was working on the first record deal. We got out of London, and I put her out of my mind. I didn't know she was pregnant, Bev. I hadn't even thought of her in over three years. If I could go back—" He broke off, thinking of the child in the next room with her crooked tooth and little dimple. "I don't know what I'd do."

Bev drew up her knees and leaned over them. She was a young, practical woman from a stable family. It was still difficult for her to understand poverty and pain, though those were the very things in Brian's background that had drawn her to him.

"I guess it's more to the point what you're going to do now."

"I've already done it." He stubbed out the cigarette in a

nineteenth-century porcelain bowl. Bev didn't bother to mention it.

"What have you done, Bri?"

"I've taken Emma. She's mine. She's going to live with me."

"I see." She took a cigarette. She'd cut out drinking and her dabbling with drugs since her pregnancy, but tobacco was a harder habit to break. "You didn't think we should talk it over? The last I heard we were going to be married in a few days."

"Are going to be." He took her by the shoulders then, shaking her, afraid that she, like so many others, would turn away from him. "Goddammit, Bev, I wanted to talk to you. I couldn't." He released her to spring up and kick at the sample books. "I walked into that filthy, stinking flat intending to do no more than threaten Jane if she didn't stop harassing us. She was exactly the same, screaming one minute, pleading the next. She said Emma was in the bedroom, but she wasn't there. She was hiding." He pressed the heels of his hands against his eyes. "Jesus, Bev, I found the kid hiding under the sink like a frightened animal."

"Oh God." Bev dropped her head on her knees.

"Jane was going to beat her—she was going to beat that tiny little girl because she was frightened. When I saw her . . . Bev, look at me. Please. When I saw her, I saw myself. Can you understand?"

"I want to." She shook her head, still fighting tears. "No, I don't. I want things to be the way they were when you left this morning."

"Do you think I should have walked out on her?"

"No. Yes." She pressed her fisted hands on each side of her head. "I don't know. We should have talked. We could have arranged some sort of settlement."

He knelt beside her to take her hands. "I was going to leave, drive around a little and think before I came home to talk to you. Jane said she'd kill herself."

"Oh, Bri."

"I might have handled that. I think I was furious enough to egg her on. But then, she said she'd kill Emma, too."

Bev pressed a hand against her stomach, over the child that was growing inside her, a child that was already beautifully real to her. "No. Oh no, she couldn't have meant it."

"She did." He tightened his grip on her hands. "Whether

she would have followed through, I don't know. But at that moment, she meant it. I couldn't leave Emma there, Bev. I couldn't have left a stranger's child there."

"No." She took her hands from his to lift them to his face. Her Brian, she thought. Her sweet, caring Brian. "You couldn't have. How did you get her away from Jane?"

"She agreed," Brian said shortly. "Pete's having documents drawn up so it will all be legal."

"Bri." Her hands firmed on his cheeks. She was in love, but she wasn't blind. "How?"

"I wrote her a check for a hundred thousand pounds. In the agreement she'll get twenty-five thousand a year every year until Emma reaches twenty-one."

Bev let her hands drop away. "Christ, Brian. You bought that baby?"

"You can't buy what's already yours." He bit off the words because it made him feel dirty. "I gave Jane enough to be sure she would stay away from Emma, from us." He laid a hand on her stomach. "From ours. Listen to me. There's going to be press, some of it will be ugly. I'm asking you to stick with me, ride it out. And to give Emma a chance."

"Where would I go?"

"Bev—"

She shook her head. She would stick with him, but she needed a little time yet. "I've been reading a lot of books lately. I'm pretty sure you shouldn't leave a toddler alone for this long."

"Right. I'll go take a look."

"We'll take a look."

She was still on the sofa, her arms curled tight around Charlie. The blare of the television didn't disturb her as she slept. There were tears drying on her cheeks. Seeing them, Bev's heart broke a little.

"I guess we'd better get the decorators busy on a bedroom upstairs."

♦ ♦ ♦ ♦

*E*MMA LAY IN the bed between fresh soft sheets and kept her eyes tightly closed. She knew if she opened them, it would be dark. There were things that hid in the dark.

She kept a hammerlock on Charlie's neck and listened. Sometimes the things made swishing noises.

She couldn't hear them now, but she knew they were waiting. Waiting for her to open her eyes. A whimper escaped and she bit her lip. Mam always got mad if she cried at night. Mam would come in and shake her hard, tell her she was stupid and a baby. The things would slink under the bed or into the corners while her mam was there.

Emma buried her face in Charlie's familiar, stale-smelling fur.

She remembered that she was in a different place. The place where the man from the pictures lived. Some of the fear vanished in curiosity. He said she could call him Da. That was a funny name. Keeping her eyes closed, she tried it, murmuring it into the dark like a chant.

They had eaten fish and chips in the kitchen with the dark-haired lady. There had been music. It seemed music played in the house all the time. Whenever the Da man spoke, it sounded like music.

The lady had seemed unhappy even when she had smiled. Emma wondered if the lady was going to wait until they were alone before she hit.

He'd given her a bath. Emma remembered that he'd had a funny look on his face, but his hands hadn't pinched and he hadn't gotten much soap in her eyes. He asked about her bruises, and she had told him what her mam had warned her to say if anyone asked. She was clumsy. She fell down.

Emma had seen the angry look come into his eyes, but he hadn't smacked her.

He'd given her a shirt to wear, and she had giggled because it had come all the way to her toes.

The lady had come with him when he had put her in bed. She'd sat on the edge and smiled when he had told a story about castles and princesses.

But they had been gone when she'd awakened. They'd been gone and the room was dark. She was afraid. Afraid the things would get her, snap their big teeth, eat her. She was afraid her mam would come and slap her because she wasn't home in her own bed.

What was that? She was sure she had heard a whispering noise in the corner. Breathing through her teeth, she opened one eye. The shadows shifted, towering, reaching. Muffling her sobs against Charlie, Emma tried to make herself smaller, so small she couldn't be seen, couldn't be eaten by all the ugly, squishy things that hid in the dark. Her mam had sent them because she'd gone with the man in the pictures.

The terror built so that she was shuddering, sweating. It burst out of her in one high wail as she scrambled out of bed and stumbled into the hallway. Something crashed.

She lay sprawled, clutching the dog and waiting for the worst.

Lights came on. They made her blink. The old fear dissolved in a new one as she heard voices. Emma scooted back against the wall and sat frozen, staring at the shards of china from the vase she'd broken.

They would beat her. Send her away. Shut her up in a dark room to be eaten.

"Emma?" Still dazed with sleep, floating a bit on the joint he'd smoked before he and Bev had made love, Brian walked toward her. She curled into herself, bracing for the blow. "Are you all right?"

"They broke it," she told him, hoping to save herself.

"They?"

"The dark things. Mam sent them to get me."

"Oh, Emma." He dropped his cheek to the top of her head.

"Brian, what—" Still belting her robe, Bev rushed out. She saw what was left of her Dresden vase, gave a little sigh, then crossed to them, avoiding the shards. "Is she hurt?"

"I don't think so. She's terrified."

"Let's have a look." She took Emma's hand. It was fisted, her arm taut as a wire. "Emma." Her voice had firmed, but there was no meanness in it. Cautious, Emma lifted her head. "Did you hurt yourself?"

Still wary, Emma pointed to her knee. There were a few drops of blood on the white T-shirt. Bev lifted the hem. It was a long scratch, but shallow. Still, she imagined most children would have wailed over it. Perhaps Emma didn't because it was nothing compared to the bruises Brian had found on the girl when he'd bathed her. In a gesture more automatic than maternal, Bev lowered her head to kiss the hurt. When she saw Emma's mouth drop open in shock, her heart was lost.

"All right, sweetie, we'll take care of it." She picked Emma up and nuzzled her neck.

"There are things in the dark," Emma whispered.

"Your daddy will chase them away. Won't you, Bri?"

The Irish in him, or perhaps the drug, made him weepy when he looked at the woman he loved holding his child. "Sure. I'll chop them up and toss them out."

"After you do, you'd better sweep this up," Bev told him.

Emma spent the night, the first of her new life, snuggled with her family in a big brass bed.

# Chapter Three

• • • •

$\mathcal{A}$S SHE HAD every day for nine days, Emma sat on the big window seat in the front parlor and looked through the mullioned glass. She stared beyond the edges of the garden with its nodding foxglove and bushy columbine to the long graveled drive. And waited.

Her bruises were fading, but she hadn't noticed. No one in the big new house had hit her. Yet. She'd been given tea every day, and presents of sugar plums and china dolls from the friends who came and went so casually in her father's house.

It was all very confusing for Emma. She was given a bath every day, even if she hadn't been playing in the dirt, and clean-smelling clothes to wear. No one called her a stupid baby because she was frightened of the dark. The lamp with the pink shade was turned on in her room every night, and there were little rosebuds on the walls. The monsters hardly ever came into her new room.

She was afraid to like it, because she was sure her mam would be coming soon to take her away again.

Bev had driven her in the pretty car to go shopping in a big store with bright clothes and beautiful smells. She had bought bags and boxes of things for Emma. Emma liked a pink organdy dress with a frilly skirt the best. She'd felt like a princess when she'd worn it the day her da and Bev had been married. She'd had shiny black shoes with little straps as well, and white tights. No one had scolded when she'd smudged the knees.

The wedding had seemed very strange and solemn to Emma,

with everyone standing out in the garden and the sun fighting off clouds. One of the men everyone called Stevie had worn a long white shirt and baggy white pants. He'd sung in a husky voice while strumming a glossy white guitar. Emma had thought he was an angel, but when she'd asked Johnno, he'd only laughed.

Bev had worn a circle of flowers in her hair and a flowing multicolored dress that had swept her ankles. To Emma, she was the most beautiful woman in the world. For the first time in her young life, she had been struck by true envy. To be beautiful, and grown-up, and standing beside Da. She'd never be afraid again, or hungry again. And like the girls in the fairy tales Brian was so fond of, she would be happy ever after.

When the rain had started, they had gone inside to have cake and champagne in a room with fabric books and flowers and fresh paint. More guitars had been played and people had sung along and laughed. Beautiful women, in slim short skirts or flowing cotton dresses, had roamed the house. Some of them had cooed over her or patted her head, but for the most part she'd been left to herself.

No one noticed that she'd had three pieces of cake and smeared icing on the collar of her new dress. There had been no other little girls to play with, and Emma was too young to be dazzled by the names and faces of the luminaries of the music business who had wandered through the house. Bored, a little queasy from cake, she'd gone off to bed, lulled by the sounds from the party.

Later, she'd woken. Restless, she had dragged Charlie out of bed to go downstairs. But the heavy scent of pot smoke had stopped her. She was familiar with it, too familiar. Like the stink of gin, the sweet scent of marijuana was firmly linked in her mind with her mother, and the shakings and beatings that had come whenever Jane had crashed from her highs.

Miserable, she had huddled on the steps, cooing reassurances to Charlie. If her mam was here now, she would take her away. Emma had known she would never again wear the pretty pink dress, or hear her da's voice, or go into the big, bright stores with Bev.

She'd cringed when she heard the footsteps on the stairs, and waited for the worst.

"Hello there, Emma luv." Soaring, at peace with the world, Brian had dropped down beside her. "What're you doing?"

"Nothing." She'd curled tighter over the stuffed dog. She made herself small, very small. If they couldn't see you, they couldn't hurt you.

"It's quite the party." Leaning back on his elbows, he'd grinned at the ceiling. Never in his wildest fantasies had he believed he would one day entertain giants like McCartney, Jagger, Daltrey, in his own house. And his wedding, too. Good Christ, he was married. A married man with a gold ring on his finger.

Tapping his bare foot to the beat of the music that crashed its way up the stairs, he'd studied the ring. No going back, he'd thought comfortably. He was Catholic enough, and idealistic enough to believe that now that the deed was done, it was forever.

It was one of the biggest days of his life, he'd thought as he'd fumbled in his shirt pocket for the pack of cigarettes he'd left downstairs. One of the biggest, he'd thought again with a sigh. And if his father had been too drunk or too lazy to pick up the bloody tickets he'd sent to Ireland, what did it matter? Brian had all the family he needed right here.

He'd pushed thoughts of yesterdays out of his mind. From now on there would only be tomorrows. A lifetime of them.

"How about it, Emma? Want to go down and dance at your da's wedding?"

She'd kept her shoulders rounded and barely shook her head. The smoke twining mystically in the air had made her temples throb.

"Want some cake?" He had reached out to give her hair a gentle tug, but she'd cringed away. "What's this?" Baffled, he'd patted her shoulder.

Already queasy, Emma's stomach had rolled with a combination of terror and too many sweets. After one hiccup, she'd lost her cake and tea all over her father's lap. Wretched, she managed a single moan before curling back over Charlie. As she lay too sick to defend herself from the beating she was certain was coming, he'd begun to laugh.

"Well, I imagine you're feeling a good bit better." Too high to be disgusted, he'd staggered to his feet then held out a hand. "Let's get cleaned up."

To Emma's amazement there had been no beating, no cruel pinches or sudden smacks. Instead he had stripped them both down to the skin in the bathroom, then hauled her into the shower. He'd even sung as the water had poured over them, something about drunken sailors that had made her forget to be sick.

When they were both bundled in towels, he had woven his way to her room to slip her into bed. His hair had been wet and sleek around his face as he'd fallen over the foot of the bed. Within seconds, he'd been snoring.

Cautious, Emma had crawled out from under the covers to sit beside him. Gathering her courage, she'd leaned over and pressed a damp kiss to his cheek. In love for the first time, she had tucked Charlie under Brian's limp arm, and gone quietly to sleep.

Then he had gone away. Only days after the wedding the big car had come, and two men had carried out luggage. He had kissed her and had promised to bring her a present. Emma had only been able to watch wordlessly as he'd ridden away, and out of her life. She hadn't believed he was coming back, even when she heard his voice over the phone. Bev said he was in America where girls screamed every time they saw him, and people bought his records almost as fast as they were made.

But while he was gone, there wasn't as much music in the house, and sometimes Bev cried.

Emma remembered Jane crying, and the smacks and shoves that had usually accompanied the tears. So she waited, but Bev never hit her, not even at night when the workmen were gone and they were all alone in the big house.

Day after day, Emma would cuddle up on the window seat with Charlie and watch. She liked to pretend that the long, black car was cruising down the drive, and when it stopped and the door opened, her da came out.

Each day when it didn't come, she became more certain it never would. He had left because he didn't like her, didn't want her. Because she was a nuisance and bloody stupid. She waited for Bev to go away too, and leave her alone in the big house. Then her mam would come.

◆ ◆ ◆ ◆

WHAT WENT ON IN the girl's mind? Bev wondered. From the doorway she watched as Emma sat in her now habitual position on the window seat. The child could sit for hours, patient as an old woman. It was rare for her to play with anything except the ratty old stuffed dog she'd brought with her. It was rarer still for her to ask for anything.

She'd been in their lives now for almost a month, and Bev was a long way from resolving her feelings.

Only a few weeks before, her plans had been perfectly laid. She wanted Brian to succeed, certainly. But more, she wanted to make a home and family with him.

She'd been raised in the Church of England, in a calm, upper-middle-class family. Morals, responsibilities, and image had been important parts of her upbringing. She'd been given a good, solid education with the idea that she would make a sensible marriage and raise solid, sensible children.

She had never rebelled, mostly because it had never occurred to her to rebel. Until Brian.

She knew that although her parents had come to the wedding, they would never completely forgive her for moving in with Brian and living with him before marriage. Nor would they ever comprehend why she had chosen to marry an Irish musician who not only questioned authority but wrote songs defying it.

There had been no doubt that they had been appalled and baffled by Brian's illegitimate child, and their daughter's acceptance of her. Yet, what could she do? The child existed.

Bev loved her parents. A part of her would always desperately want their approval. But she loved Brian more, so much more that it was sometimes terrifying. And the child was his. Whatever she had wanted, whatever her plans had been, that meant the child was now hers as well.

It was difficult to look at Emma and not feel something. She wasn't a child who faded into the woodwork no matter how quiet and unobtrusive she tried to be. It was her looks, certainly. Those same elegantly angelic looks of her father. More, it was that sense of innocence, an innocence that was in itself a miracle considering how the child had lived the first three years of her life. An innocence, and an acceptance, Bev thought. She knew if she walked into the room right now, shouting, slapping, Emma would tolerate the abuse with barely a whimper. That struck Bev as more tragic than the miserable poverty she'd been saved from.

Brian's child. Instinctively Bev laid a hand over the life she carried. She'd wanted so desperately to give Brian his first child. That wasn't to be. Yet every time she felt resentment, she had only to look at Emma for it to fade. How could she resent someone so utterly vulnerable? Still she couldn't bring herself to love, not as unquestioningly, as automatically, as Brian loved.

She didn't want to love, Bev admitted. This was another woman's child, a link that would forever remind her of Brian's intimacy with someone else. Five years ago or ten, it didn't matter. As long as there was Emma, Jane would be a part of their lives.

Brian had been the first man she'd slept with, and though she had known when they'd become involved that there had been others for him, it had been easy to block it out, to tell herself that their coming together had been an initiation for them both.

Dammit, why had he had to leave now, when everything was in upheaval? There was this child slipping around the house like a shadow. There were workmen hammering and sawing hour after hour. And there was the press. It was as ugly as Brian had warned her it would be, with headlines screaming his name, and hers, and Jane's. How she hated, how she detested, seeing her picture and Jane's on the same page of a paper. How she loathed those nasty, gloating little stories about new wives and old lovers.

It didn't fade quickly, as she had prayed it would. There was speculation and questions about the most personal areas of her life. She was Mrs. Brian McAvoy now, and public property. She had told herself countless times that because marrying Brian was what she wanted most, she would be able to tolerate the public dissections, the lack of freedom, the smirking headlines.

And she would. Somehow. But when he was away like this, thousands of miles away, she wondered how she could bear a lifetime of being photographed and hounded, of running away from microphones, of wearing wigs and sunglasses to do something as ordinary as buy shoes. She wondered if Brian would ever understand how humiliating it was for her to see something as intimate as her pregnancy splashed in headlines for strangers to read over their morning tea.

She couldn't laugh at the stories when he wasn't with her, and she couldn't ignore them. So she rarely left the house when he was gone. In less than two weeks, the home she had envisioned for them with its cozy rooms and sunny windows had become a prison. One she shared with Brian's child.

But she was enough her parents' daughter to know her duty, and to execute it unwaveringly.

"Emma." Bev fixed a bright smile on her face as Emma turned. "I thought you might be ready for your tea."

There was nothing Emma recognized quicker or distrusted more than a false smile. "I'm not hungry," she said and gripped Charlie tighter.

"I guess I'm not, either." If they were stuck there together, Bev decided, at least they could talk to each other. "It's hard to have a nice tea with all the hammering going on." Taking the step, she sat on the window seat beside Emma. "This is a nice spot. I think I should plant more roses, though. Don't you?"

Emma's lip poked out a little as she moved her shoulders.

"We had a lovely garden when I was a girl," Bev continued desperately. "I used to love to go out in the summer with a book and listen to the bees hum. Sometimes I wouldn't read at all, but just dream. It's funny, the first time I heard Brian's voice, I was in the garden."

"Did he live with you?"

She had Emma's attention now, Bev thought. It only took a mention of Brian's name. "No. It was over the radio. It was their first single—'Shadowland.' It went . . . 'At night, midnight, when shadows hug the moon.' " Bev started the tune in her soft lilt, then stopped when Emma picked it up in a clear, surprisingly strong alto.

" 'And the land is hot and still, breathless I wait for you.' "

"Yes, that's the one." Without realizing it, Bev reached out to stroke Emma's hair. "I felt he was singing it just for me. I'm sure every girl did."

Emma said nothing for a moment, remembering how her mother had played it over and over on the record player, drinking and weeping while the words had echoed around the flat. "Did you like him because he sang the song?"

"Yes. But after I met him, I liked him much more."

"Why did he go away?"

"His music, his work." Bev glanced down to see Emma's big eyes shiny with tears. Here was kinship, where she hadn't wanted or expected it. "Oh, Emma, I miss him too, but he'll be home in a few weeks."

"What if he doesn't come back?"

It was foolish, but Bev sometimes woke with that same awful fear in the middle of the night. "Of course he will. A man like Brian needs people to listen to his music, and he needs to be there while they do. He'll often go away, but he'll always come back. He loves you, and he loves me." As much for comfort as to comfort, she took Emma's hand. "And there's one more thing. Do you know where babies come from?"

"Men stick them in ladies, but then they don't want them."

Bev broke off an oath. She could cheerfully have throttled Jane at that moment. Although Bev's own mother had always been reserved, unable to speak of intimacy in more than a vague fashion, Bev firmly believed in openness. "Men and women who love each other make babies together, and most of the time they both want them very much. I have a baby right here." She pressed Emma's hand against her stomach. "Your father's baby. When it's born, it will be your brother or sister."

After a moment's hesitation, Emma slid her hand over Bev's stomach. She didn't see how there could be a baby in there. Mrs. Perkins across the alley had had a big bloated belly before little Donald had come.

"Where is it?"

"Inside. It's very, very small now. It has almost six months more to grow before it's time for it to come out."

"Will it like me?"

"I think so. Brian will be its da just like he's your da."

Enchanted, Emma began to stroke Bev's stomach as she sometimes stroked Charlie. "I'll take good care of the baby. No one will hurt it."

"No, no one will hurt it." With a sigh, Bev slipped an arm around Emma's shoulders and looked out toward the hedgerow. This time Emma didn't inch away, but sat still, fascinated, one hand over Bev's stomach.

"I'm a little afraid of being a mum, Emma. Maybe you can let me practice on you."

After a deep breath, Bev stood up, bringing Emma with her. "We're going to start right now. Let's go up and put on your pretty pink dress. We're going out to tea." The hell with reporters, the hell with starers and gawkers. "We're going to make ourselves into the two prettiest ladies in London and have our tea at the Ritz."

◆ ◆ ◆ ◆

FOR EMMA IT was the beginning of her first relationship with another female that wasn't based on fear or intimidation.

Over the following days, they shopped at Harrods, walked in Green Park, and lunched at the Savoy. Bev ignored the photographers who snapped them. When she discovered Emma's love of beautiful materials and bright colors, she indulged them shamelessly. Within two weeks, the little girl who had come to her with only the shirt on her back had a closet bulging with clothes.

But at night the loneliness crept back, when each lay in bed pining for the same man.

Emma's longings were more direct. She wanted Brian to come back because he made her feel good. Love wasn't something she'd learned to define or agonize over.

But Bev agonized. She worried that he would grow tired of her, that he would find someone more in step with the world he lived in. She missed the good, strong sex they shared. It was so easy to believe he would always love her, always be with her during that calm drugging time after love and before sleep. But now, alone in the big brass bed, she would wonder if he filled up his loneliness with women as well as music.

The sky was just beginning to lighten when the phone rang. Bev groped for it on the third ring. "Yes." She cleared her throat. "Hello."

"Bev." Brian's voice was urgent.

Instantly awake, she shot up in bed. "Bri. What is it? What's happened?"

"Nothing. Everything. We're a smash, Bev." There was a dazed and dashing edge to his laughter. "Every night the crowds get bigger. They've had to double security to keep the girls from flinging themselves on stage. It's wild, Bev. Insane. Tonight one of them grabbed Stevie's sleeve as we were making the dash for the limo. Ripped his coat clean off. The press is calling us vanguards of the second wave of the British invasion. Vanguards."

Sinking back onto the pillows, Bev struggled to drum up enthusiasm. "That's wonderful, Brian. There've been some snippets on the telly here, but not much to go by."

"It's like being a gladiator, standing there onstage and listening to the roars." He didn't think he could explain, even to her, the thrill and the terror. "I think even Pete was impressed."

Bev smiled thinking of his pragmatic, business-first-and-last manager. "Then you must be something."

"Yeah." He drew on the joint he had lit to extend the high. "I wish you were here."

She heard the background noises, loud music, male and female laughter mixed with it. "So do I."

"Then come." He pushed away a blonde, half naked and glazed-eyed, who tried to crawl into his lap. "Pack a bag and fly over."

"What?"

"I mean it. It's not half as good as it would be if you were here." Across the room a brunette, nearly six feet tall, slowly stripped. Stevie, the lead guitarist, popped a Quaalude like rock candy. "Look, I know we talked about it and decided it was best for you to stay home, but we were wrong. You need to be here, with me."

She felt tears well in her eyes even as laughter bubbled. "You want me to come to America?"

"As soon as you can. You can meet us in New York in—shit. Johnno, when are we in New York?"

Sprawled on a couch, Johnno poured the last of the Jim Beam. "Where the fuck are we now?"

"Never mind." Brian rubbed his tired eyes and tried to concentrate. His mind was bloaty with booze and smoke. "I'll get Pete to work out the details. Just pack."

She was already out of bed. "What should I do with Emma?"

"Bring her, too." On a burst of family feeling, Brian grinned at the blonde. "Pete will figure out how to get her a passport. Someone will call you this afternoon and tell you what to do. Christ, I miss you, Bev."

"I miss you, too. We'll be there as soon as we can. I love you, Bri, more than anything."

"I love you. Talk to you soon."

Moody and restless, Brian reached for the brandy bottle the moment he'd hung up. He wanted her with him now, not a day from now, not an hour from now. Just listening to her voice had him hard and hurting.

She had sounded just as she had on the night he'd met her, shy, a little hesitant. She'd been so sweetly out of place in the smoky pub where his band had been playing. Yet even with the shyness, there had been something so solid, so true about her. He hadn't been able to get her out of his mind, not that night, not any night since.

He lifted the brandy and drank deeply. It seemed as though the brunette and Stevie weren't going to bother to move to the privacy of one of the bedrooms to have sex. The blonde had given up on Johnno and was rubbing her long, limber body against P.M., their drummer.

Half amused, half envious, Brian drank again. P.M. was barely twenty-one, his face still round and youthful with its sprinkle of acne on the chin. He looked both appalled and delighted as the blonde slid down to bury her face in his lap.

Brian closed his eyes, and with music filling his head, fell asleep.

He dreamed of Bev, and the first night they had spent together. Sitting cross-legged on the floor of his flat, talking earnestly, about music, about poetry. Yeats and Byron and Browning. Dreamily passing a joint back and forth. He'd had no idea it had been her first encounter with drugs. Just as he'd had no idea, until he had slipped into her, there on the floor with the candles guttering in their own wax, that it was her first encounter with sex.

She'd wept a little. Instead of making him feel guilty, her tears had brought out feelings of protectiveness. He'd fallen completely, and somehow poetically, in love. That had been more than a year ago, but he had never been with another woman during that time. Whenever the temptation came strongly, he would see Bev's face.

The marriage had been for her, and the child, his child, she carried. He didn't believe in marriage, the foolishness of a contract on love, but he didn't feel trapped. For the first time since his miserable childhood, he had something more than music to comfort and excite him.

*I love you more than anything.*

No, he couldn't say that to her with the ease and honesty she could say it to him. He probably would never be able to say that to her. But he did love, and where he loved, he was loyal.

"Come on, my lad." Barely rousing him, Johnno dragged Brian to his feet. "It's bed for you."

"Bev's coming, Johnno."

Brow lifted, Johnno glanced over his shoulder at the tangle of bodies. "So's everyone else."

"She'll meet us in New York." With a half-laugh, Brian slung a rubbery arm around Johnno's neck. "We're going to New York, Johnno. New fucking York. Because we're the best."

"That's dandy, isn't it?" Grunting only a little, Johnno

dumped Brian on the bed. "Sleep it off, Bri. We've got to go through the whole bloody business again tomorrow."

"Got to wake Pete," Brian mumbled as Johnno pulled off his shoes. "Passport for Emma. Tickets. I have to do the right thing by her."

"You will." Weaving a little, courtesy of the Jim Beam, Johnno studied his newly purchased Swiss watch. He didn't imagine Pete was going to appreciate being awakened, but he staggered off to do the deed.

# Chapter Four

· · · ·

$O$N HER FIRST transatlantic flight, Emma traveled first class. And was miserably sick. She could not, as Bev periodically urged her, look out at the pretty clouds or page through any of the colorful picture books Bev had stuffed into her carry-on bag. Even empty, Emma's stomach pitched and rolled. She was vaguely aware of Bev's helpless little hand pats and the stewardess's soothing voice.

It didn't matter that she had a new outfit with a short, bright red skirt and a flowered fussy blouse. It didn't matter that she'd been promised a ride to the top of the Empire State Building. The nausea was so unrelenting that it no longer mattered that she was going to see her father.

By the time the plane banked over JFK airport, she was too weak to stand. Frazzled, Bev carried her through the gate. After clearing customs, she nearly gave way to tears when she spotted Pete.

In his impeccable Savile Row suit, he took a long look at the pasty-faced child and the edgy woman. "Rough trip?"

Instead of tears, Bev found laughter bursting through. "Oh no. It was a delight from start to finish. Where's Brian?"

"He wanted to come, but I had to veto it." He took Bev's carry-on bag, then her arm. "The lads can't even open a window for a breath of air without causing mass hysteria."

"And you love it."

He grinned, steering her toward the exit of the terminal.

"Optimist that I am, I never expected this. Brian's going to be a very rich man, Bev. We're all going to be rich."

"Money doesn't come first with Bri."

"No, but I can't see him kicking it out of his way as it comes pouring in. Come on, I've got a car waiting."

She shifted Emma, but the girl only moaned and hung limply in Bev's arms. "The bags."

"They'll be delivered to the hotel." He shuffled her out of the terminal. "There are plenty of pictures of you in the fan mags, too."

It was a white Mercedes limo, as big as a boat. At Bev's puzzled look, Pete grinned again.

"As long as you're married to a king, luv, you might as well travel in style."

Saying nothing, Bev settled back and lit a cigarette. She hoped it was the long, miserable flight that made her feel so out of place and hollow. Between her and Pete, Emma curled on the seat and sweatily slept through her first limo ride.

Pete didn't pause in the lobby at the Waldorf but rushed them through and onto an elevator. He wasn't sure if he was relieved or disappointed that their luck had held. A mob scene at the airport or on the street in front of the hotel would have been inconvenient, but it would have made great copy. And copy sold records.

"I've got you a two-bedroom suite." The extra expense bothered his practical soul, but he justified it by knowing that Bev's presence would make Brian more cooperative, and more creative. And it wouldn't hurt for the press to know that Brian's family was traveling with him. If he couldn't promote Brian as a sexy single man, he could promote him as a loving husband and father. Whatever worked.

"We're all on the same floor," he went on. "And security's very tight. In Washington, D.C., two teenage girls managed to get into Stevie's room in a maid's cart."

"Sounds like a laugh a minute."

He only shrugged, remembering that Stevie had been drunk enough to appreciate the girls' offers. The guitarist had rationalized that two sixteen-year-olds equaled one thirty-two-year-old. That had made them into one older woman.

"The lads have some interviews scheduled today, then the *Sullivan* show tomorrow."

"Brian didn't say where we were going next."

"Philadelphia, then Detroit, Chicago, St. Louis—"

"Never mind." Bev heaved a long, grateful sigh as the elevator doors opened. The hell with where they were going. She was here now. It didn't matter a damn that she was enormously tired or that her arms ached from carrying the sleeping Emma. She was here, and could all but feel Brian's energy in the air.

"Just as well," Pete said as he pulled out a key. "You've a couple of hours before the boys' interview. It's with some new mag that'll publish its first issue later this year. *Rolling Stone.*"

She took the key, pleased that he was sensitive enough not to intrude on the two hours he'd given her with Brian. "Thanks, Pete. I'll make sure he's ready for it."

The moment she opened the door, Brian came racing out of the adjoining bedroom to sweep both her and Emma into his arms. "Thank Christ," he murmured, raining kisses over Bev's face. He took the limp, drowsy Emma. "What's wrong here?"

"Nothing now." Bev dragged her free hands through her hair. "She was dreadfully sick on the plane. Hardly slept. I think she'll do fine once she's tucked up."

"Right then. Don't move." He carried Emma into the second bedroom. She stirred only once as he slipped her between the sheets.

"Da?"

"Yes." It still rocked him. "You sleep now awhile. Everything's fine."

Comforted by the sound of his voice, she took it on faith, and drifted to sleep again.

He automatically left the door ajar, then just stood and looked at Bev. She was pale with fatigue, the shadows under her eyes making them huge and dark. Love welled up in him, stronger, needier than any he'd ever known. Saying nothing, he crossed to her, picked her up in his arms and carried her to his bed.

He didn't have words, though he was a man always filled with them. Words to poetry, poetry to lyrics. Later he would be filled with them, reams of words, flowing through him, all stemming from this, what might have been his most precious hour with her.

She was, in that hour, so completely his.

The radio beside the bed was on, as was the television at the foot of it. He'd chased away the silence of his rooms with voices. When he touched her, she was all the music he needed.

So he savored. He undressed her slowly, watching her, absorbing her. The shudder of traffic outside the window—later he would remember it in bases and trebles. The small, yielding sounds she made were pitched low in countermelody. He could even hear the whispering song of his hands gliding over her skin.

There was sunlight pouring through the window, and the big, soft bed yielding under them.

Her body was already changing, subtly, with the life growing in it. He spread his hand over her rounded stomach, amazed, dazzled, humbled. Reverently he lowered his lips to her flesh.

It was foolish, he thought, but he felt like a soldier returning from war, covered with scars and medals. Perhaps not so foolish. The arena in which he'd fought and won wasn't one he could take her to. She would always wait for him. It was in her eyes, in her arms as they tenderly enfolded him. That promise and patience was on her lips as they opened for his. Her passion was always steadier than his, less selfish, balancing his edgier and more dangerous urges. With her he felt more of a man, less of a symbol in a world that seemed so hungry for symbols.

When he slipped inside of her, he spoke at last, saying her name on a long, fluid sigh of gratitude and hope.

Later, when she lay half dozing under the tangled sheets, Brian sat at the foot of the bed in his underwear. She was sated with sex, but his mind was in overdrive. Everything he'd ever wanted, ever dreamed of, was at his fingertips.

"Pete had film taken of the Atlanta concert. Jesus, it was wild, Bev. Not just the fans screaming, though there was plenty of that. Sometimes you could hardly hear yourself sing for the noise. It was like, I don't know, being on the runway of an airport with planes taking off all around, but mixed with the noisy ones were people who were really into it, just listening, you know. Sometimes you could see through the lights and the pot smoke, and there'd be a face. You could sing just for that one face. Then Stevie would go into a riff, like in 'Undercover,' and they'd go wild again. It was like, I don't know, like great sex."

"Sorry I didn't applaud."

Laughing, he tugged on her ankle. "I'm so glad you're here. This summer is special. You can feel it in the air, see it in people's faces. And we're part of it. We're never going back, Bev."

She tensed, watching him. "To London?"

"No." He was half impatient, half amused by her literal mind. "To the way things were. Begging to play in some grimy pub, grateful if we got free beer and chips for pay. Christ, Bev, we're in New York, and after tomorrow millions of people will have heard us. And it's going to matter. We're going to matter. It's all I've ever wanted."

She sat up to take his hands. "You've always mattered, Bri."

"No. I was just one more scruffy singer. Not anymore, Bev. And never again. People listen. The money's going to make it possible for us to experiment a bit—do more than the boy-girl rock. There's a war going on, Bev. A whole generation's in upheaval. We can be their voices."

She didn't understand big, sweeping dreams, but it had been his idealism that had attracted her from the beginning. "Just don't leave me behind."

"I couldn't." He meant it sincerely, completely. "I'm going to give you the best, Bev. You and the baby. I swear it. I've got to get dressed." He kissed both her hands, then shook back his tousled hair. "Pete's really high about us being in the first issue of this new mag that'll come out in November." He tossed her a tie-dyed T-shirt. "Come on."

"I thought I'd stay in here."

"Bev . . ." They'd been through all this before. "You're my wife. People want to know about you, about us." He bit back annoyance when she simply sat, running the shirt through her hands. "If we give them a little, they won't hound us for so much." When he said it, he believed it. "It's especially important because of Emma. I want everyone to see that we've made ourselves into a family."

"A family should be a private thing."

"Maybe. But the stories about Emma are already out there." He'd seen them, dozens of them, labeling Emma as a love child. There could be worse things, he mused, since Emma hadn't been made out of anything remotely resembling love. It was his other child, he thought as he laid a gentle hand on Bev's stomach again, who had been made of love. "I need you with me on this."

Hating it, she climbed out of bed and began to dress.

Twenty minutes later, she answered a knock on the door. "Johnno."

He gave Bev a quick grin. "I knew you couldn't stay away from me." Swooping her into an exaggerated dip, he kissed her. As she laughed, he looked over her head to where Brian was coming through the doorway. "Ah well, he's found us out. We'd better come clean."

"Where'd you get that ridiculous hat?" was all Brian said.

After setting Bev back on her feet, Johnno straightened the floppy white fedora. "Like it? It's a happening."

"Makes you look like a pimp," Brian commented before he walked to the bar.

"There. I knew I'd made the right choice. Nearly cost me my life, but I managed to break out of here and do some shopping on Fifth Avenue. I'll have one of those, luv." He nodded to the whiskey Brian was pouring.

"You went out?" Brian stood with the bottle in one hand and a glass in the other.

"Sunglasses, a flowered tunic . . ." He wrinkled his nose. "And love beads. Worked nicely as far as disguises go, until I tried to get back in. Lost the love beads." He helped himself to the glass Brian held. With a pleased sigh, he flopped on the couch. "This is the place for me, Brian, my lad. I *am* New York."

"Pete will have your head if he finds you went out on your own."

"Bugger Pete," Johnno said cheerfully. "Though he's not precisely my style." Grinning, he downed the whiskey. "So, where's the little brat?"

"She's sleeping." Bev picked up a cigarette.

Brian answered the next knock. Stevie strolled in, and after an absent nod to Bev headed straight to the bar. P.M. followed, and looking a little pale, dropped into a chair.

"Word from Pete is we'll do the interview here," he said. "He'll be bringing the reporter along. Where'd you get the hat?" he asked Johnno.

"It's a long, sad story, son." Glancing over, he spotted Emma standing at the crack in her bedroom door. "Don't look now, but we've company. Hello there, prune face."

She giggled a little, but didn't come in. At the moment, her eyes were all for Brian.

He crossed over and, picking her up, patted her bottom. "Emma. How does it feel to be an international traveler?"

She thought she'd dreamed it, that one moment where he'd

tucked her in bed and kissed her cheek. But it wasn't a dream, because he was there, smiling at her, his voice making all the nastiness in her stomach disappear.

"I'm hungry," she said and offered him a huge grin.

"I'm not surprised." He kissed the dimple at the corner of her mouth. "How about some chocolate cake?"

"Soup," Bev put in.

"Cake and soup," he amended. "And some nice tea."

He set her down to go to the phone and ring room service.

"Come over here, Emma. I have something for you." Johnno patted the cushion beside him. She hesitated. Her mother had often said just that. And the something had been a smack. But Johnno was smiling a true smile. When she settled beside him, he took a small, clear plastic egg from his pocket. Inside was a toy ring with a gaudy red stone.

Emma gave a little gasp as he put it in her hand. Speechless, she turned the egg this way and that, watching the ring slide from side to side.

It had been a careless thing, Johnno thought. A machine that took American quarters, and he'd had change left after his speedy shopping spree. More touched than he wanted the others to see, he opened the egg for her, then slipped the ring on her finger.

"There. We're engaged."

Emma beamed at the ring, then at him. "Can I sit on your lap?"

"All right then." He leaned close to her ear. "But if you wet your pants, the engagement's off."

She laughed, settled on his lap, and began to play with her ring.

"First my wife, then my daughter," Brian commented.

"You'd only have to worry if you had a son." Stevie tossed off the words as easily as he tossed off the drink. Then wished he'd cut off his tongue. "Sorry," he muttered as the room fell silent. "Hangover. Puts me in a filthy mood."

At the knock on the door, Johnno gave a lazy shrug. "Better put on that famous smile, son. It's show time."

Johnno was angry, but hid it well as the young, bearded reporter sat down with them. They had no idea what it was like, he thought. None of them, save Brian who had gone to school with him, had befriended him. The names he'd been called—fag, pussy, queer. They had hurt a great deal more than the occasional beatings he'd taken. Johnno knew he would have had his face smashed into a pulp more than once if it hadn't been for Brian's ready fists and loyalty.

They had been drawn together, two ten-year-old boys with drunken fathers. Poverty wasn't uncommon in London's east end, and there were always toughs ready to break an arm for pence. There were ways of escaping. For both him and Brian, the escape had been music.

Elvis, Chuck Berry, Muddy Waters. They would pool whatever money they could earn or steal to buy those precious 45s. At twelve, they'd collaborated on their first song—a really poor one, Johnno remembered now, lots of moon/June rhymes set to a three-chord rhythm they'd pounded out on their battered guitar. They'd traded a pint of Brian's father's gin for that guitar, and Brian had taken an ugly beating. But they'd made music, such as it was.

Johnno had been nearly sixteen before he realized what he was. He'd sweated over it, wept over it, pounded himself into any girl who would have him to turn his fate around. But sweat, tears, and sex hadn't changed him.

Finally it had been Brian who had helped him to accept. They'd been drinking, late at night, in the basement of Brian's flat. This time, Johnno had pinched whiskey from his father. The stench of garbage had been rank as they sat with a candle between them, passing the bottle back and forth. On the dented portable record player, Roy Orbison had been soaring with "Only the Lonely." Johnno's confession had come out with drunken weeping and wild threats of suicide.

"I'm nothing, and I'll never be nothing else. Living like a bleeding pig." He'd guzzled whiskey. "My old man stinking up the room and Mum whining and nagging and never doing nothing to make it change. My sister's working the streets and my little brother's been arrested twice this month."

"It's up to us to get out of it," Brian said with boozy philosophy. With his eyes half closed he listened to Orbison. He wanted to sing like that, with that otherworldly melancholy. "We've got to make a difference for ourselves, Johnno. And we will."

"Difference. I can't make it any different. Not unless I kill myself. Maybe I will. Maybe I'll just do it and be done with it."

"What the bloody hell are you talking about?" Brian searched in their crumpled pack of Pall Malls and found one.

"I'm queer." Johnno dropped his head on his folded arms and wept.

"Queer?" Brian paused with the match an inch from the tip of the cigarette. "Come on, Johnno. Don't be daft."

"I said I'm queer." His voice rose as he lifted his tear-stained, desperate face to Brian. "I like boys. I'm a freaking, flaming fag."

Though he was shaken, the drink was enough of a cushion to make him open-minded. "You sure?"

"Why the bloody hell would I say it if I wasn't sure? The only reason I could make it with Alice Ridgeway was because I was thinking of her brother."

Now that was disgusting, Brian thought, but kept his feelings to himself. They'd been friends for more than six years, had stood up for each other, lied for each other, had shared dreams and secrets. Brian struck another match, lit the cigarette, and pondered.

"Well, I suppose if you're made that way, then you're made that way. Nothing to slit your wrists over."

"You're not queer."

"No." He fervently hoped not—and vowed to spend the next few weeks proving it to himself with every girl he could charm into spreading her legs. No, he wasn't queer, he assured himself. The sexual acrobatics he'd experienced with Jane Palmer should have been a good indication of his preferences. Thinking of her, he hardened and shifted his legs. It wasn't the time to get horny, but to think of Johnno's problem.

"Lots of people are queer," he said. "Like literary people and artists and such. We're musicians, so you could think of it as part of your creative soul."

"That's shit," Johnno mumbled, but wiped his dripping nose.

"Maybe, but it's better than slitting your wrists. I'd have to find a new partner."

With a ghost of a smile, Johnno picked up the bottle again. "Are we still partners, then?"

"Sure." Brian passed the cigarette. "As long as I don't start making you hot and bothered."

And that had been the end of it.

When Johnno took a lover, he took him discreetly, and never discussed it. His sexual preference was common knowledge within the band, but for his own privacy, and at Pete's insistence, he cultivated an image of a heterosexual stud. For the most part, it amused him.

There were regrets, though he hated to acknowledge them. It came to him now, as he bounced Emma on his lap, that he would never have a child of his own.

And with frustration, he was forced to admit, as he watched Brian slip an arm around Bev, that the one man he truly loved would never be his lover.

# Chapter Five

• • • •

EMMA WAS DAZZLED by New York. After a late breakfast where Brian indulged her with strawberry jam and sugary pastries, she was left in Bev's hands. It didn't worry her, not this time. Her da was going to be on the telly that night, and he'd promised that she could go to the place where the telly pictures were made and watch.

In the meantime, she and Bev drove around the city in the big white car. She giggled at the blond wig and big round sunglasses Bev wore. Though Bev didn't smile much at first, Emma's excitement soon distracted her. Emma liked watching the people rush along the sidewalks, jostling each other, streaming across intersections while horns blared. There were women in short skirts and high heels, their bouffant hairdos as steady as carved stones. There were others in denim and sandals, with their manes of hair hanging straight as rain down their backs. On the corners there were vendors selling hot dogs and soft drinks and ice cream which the pedestrians snapped up as the temperature soared outside the cool cocoon of the limo. There was a nervy aggression to the traffic that Emma didn't understand but enjoyed.

Unruffled, and proper in his tan uniform and stiff-brimmed hat, the driver pulled to the curb. He didn't think much of music himself, unless it was Frank Sinatra or Rosemary Clooney, but he was sure his two teenagers would go wild when he brought them home autographs at the end of his two-day job.

"Here we are, ma'am."

"Oh." A little dazed, Bev stared out the window.

"The Empire State Building," he explained with a gesture toward the doors. "Would you like me to pick you up in an hour?"

"An hour, yes." Bev took Emma's hand firmly in hers when the driver opened the door. "Come on, Emma. Devastation's not going to the top alone."

There was a long, winding line, with wailing babies and whining children. They started at the end, two bodyguards silently falling in behind, and were soon swallowed up. A group of French students filed in seconds later, all carrying Macy's shopping bags and talking in their fast, flowing language. Amid the mix of perfume, sweat, and wet diapers, Emma caught the dreamy aroma of pot. No one else seemed to notice or care. They were shuffled onto an elevator.

Long, stuffy minutes later, they were led off to wait again. She didn't mind. As long as her hand was firmly caught in Bev's, she could crane her neck and look at all the people. Bald heads, floppy hats, scraggly beards. When her neck got tired, she switched to shoes. Rope sandals, shiny wing tips, snowy white sneakers, and black pumps. Some people shuffled their feet, others tapped, a few shifted from side to side, but hardly a one was still.

When she grew tired of that, she just listened to the voices. She heard a group of girls arguing nearby. As teenagers, they had Emma's immediate envy.

"Stevie Nimmons is the cutest," one of the girls insisted. "He's got big brown eyes and that groovy moustache."

"Brian McAvoy," another corrected. "He's really fab." To prove her point, she took a photo, cut from a fan magazine, out of her madras purse. A communal sigh went up as the girls crowded around it. "Every time I look at it, I just about die."

They squealed, were glared at, then muffled giggles with their hands.

Both pleased and baffled, Emma looked up at Bev. "Those girls are talking about Da."

"Ssh." Bev was amused enough to want to relay the story to Brian, but she was also aware that she was wearing the wig and sunglasses for a reason. "I know they are, but we have to keep who we are a secret."

"Why?"

"I'll explain later," she said, relieved when their turn at the elevators arrived.

Emma's eyes widened when her ears popped as they had on the airplane. For a moment she was terrified that she would be sick again. She bit her lip, closed her eyes, and wished desperately for her da.

She wished she hadn't come. She wished she'd brought Charlie for comfort. And she prayed, as fervently as a three-year-old could, that she wouldn't lose her wonderful breakfast all over her shiny new shoes.

Then the doors opened, and the dreadful swaying motion stopped. Everyone was laughing and talking and crowding out. Obeying Bev's tug on her hand, she kept close to her while still fighting the nausea.

There was a big stand with shelves of bright souvenirs, and wide, wide windows where she could see the sky and the spread of buildings that was Manhattan. Dumbfounded, she stood still while people swarmed around them. Sickness passed into wonder.

"It's something to see, isn't it, Emma?"

"Is it the world?"

Though she was as amazed as Emma, she laughed. "No. Only a small part of it. Come on then, let's go out."

The wind barreled over them, sending Emma's skirts flying up as she staggered back. But the sensation excited rather than frightened as Bev, laughing again, plucked her up.

"We're on top of the world, Emma."

As they looked over the high wall, Emma felt her stomach do playful little leaps and bounces. It was all spread out below, the crisscross of streets in the canyons made by the buildings, the tiny cars and buses that looked like toys. Everything ran so straight and true.

When Bev put a coin in a box, she looked through the telescope, but she preferred her own view, through her own eyes.

"Can we live here?"

Bev fiddled with the telescope until she focused on the Statue of Liberty. "Here, in New York?"

"Here. On top."

"No one lives here, Emma."

"Why not?"

"Because it's a tourist attraction," she answered absently.

"And one of the wonders of the world, I think. You can't live in a wonder."

But Emma looked out over the high wall and thought that she could.

♦ ♦ ♦ ♦

THE TELEVISION STUDIO didn't impress Emma. It didn't look as pretty or as big as it did onscreen. The people were ordinary. She did like the cameras, though. They were big and bulky, and the people behind them seemed important. She wondered if looking through one of the cameras was like looking through the telescope on the Empire State Building.

Before she could ask Bev, a skinny man began talking in a loud voice. It was the oddest American accent she'd heard yet. She couldn't understand half of what he said, but she caught the word "Devastation." Then came the explosion of screams.

After the first shock, Emma stopped cringing into Bev's skirts and leaned out. Though she didn't understand the screaming, she realized it wasn't a bad sound. It was a good, young noise that bulleted off the walls and slammed off the ceilings. It made her grin, though Bev's hand trembled lightly in hers.

She liked the way her father moved across the stage, prancing and strutting as his voice, strong and clear, merged with Johnno's, then Stevie's. His hair glowed gold under the bright lights. She was a child, and easily recognized magic.

As long as she lived she would hold this picture in her mind, and her heart, of four young men standing onstage, drenched in light, in luck, and in music.

♦ ♦ ♦ ♦

THREE THOUSAND MILES away, Jane sat in her new flat. There was a pint of Gilbey's and an ounce of Colombian Gold on the table beside her. She'd lit candles, dozens of them, using those and the drugs to mellow her mood. Brian's clear tenor played on her stereo.

She'd moved into Chelsea with the money she'd taken from Brian. There were young people there, musicians and poets and artists, and the ones who followed them. She thought she would find another Brian in Chelsea. An idealist with a beautiful face and clever hands.

She could pop off to the pubs whenever she liked, listen to the music, pick out a likely companion for the night.

She had a six-room flat with shiny new furniture in every room. Her closets bulged with clothes from fashionable boutiques. On her finger was a fat diamond ring she'd bought the week before when she'd been feeling blue. She was already bored with it.

She had thought that one hundred thousand pounds was all the money in the world. She ran one hand down the silk robe she wore, pleased, very pleased with its sinuous feel. She'd soon discovered that large amounts were as easily spent as small ones. She still had enough to last her awhile, but it hadn't taken long for her to realize she'd sold Emma cheap.

He'd have paid twice as much, she thought as she nursed her gin. More than twice, no matter how much the bastard Pete had frowned and muttered. Brian had wanted Emma. He had a soft spot for children. She'd known it, but, she thought in disgust, hadn't been clever enough to exploit it.

A lousy twenty-five thousand a year. How was she supposed to live on that, she wondered.

A little bleary with gin, she rolled a sloppy joint.

She still took in a john now and then, but that was as much for the company as the extra cash. She'd had no idea she would miss Emma. As the weeks passed the concept of motherhood took on new, emotional meanings.

She'd given birth. She'd changed nasty nappies. She'd spent her hard-earned money on food and clothes. Now the little brat probably didn't remember she existed.

She'd hire a solicitor. She'd hire the best with Brian's money. There was justice in that. There wasn't a court in the country that wouldn't see that a child belonged with her mother. She'd get Emma back. Or better, she'd get twice as much money.

Once she'd bled them a bit, Brian and his snotty new wife wouldn't forget her. No one would forget her, not the stinking press, not the stupid public, or her own little brat.

With this thought dangling in her mind, she brought out her cache of Methedrine and prepared to go flying.

# Chapter Six

• • • •

 $E$ MMA COULDN'T WAIT much longer. There was a nasty sleet falling outside, but she continued to press her face against the window to try to see through it.

They would be coming soon. Johnno had said so. She was wise enough to know that if she asked him how soon again he'd snarl at her. But she couldn't wait. After her nose grew cold, she stepped back to dance from one foot to another. Her da was coming home, with Bev, and her new baby brother. Darren. Her brother's name was Darren. She tried the name out to herself in a whisper. Just the sound of it made her smile.

Nothing in her life had ever been so huge, so important as having a brother. He would be her own, and he would need her to tend to him, to look out for him. She'd been practicing for weeks and weeks on the dolls that now filled her room.

She knew you had to hold their heads ever so carefully, or they fell way back and broke off. Sometimes babies woke in the middle of the night, crying for milk. She wouldn't mind, Emma thought. She rubbed her own flat chest and wondered if Darren would find milk there.

They hadn't let her go to the hospital to see him. That had upset her so that for the first time since she had come to her new home, Emma had hidden in a closet. She was still angry about it, but she knew it mattered very little to adults if children were angry.

Weary of standing, she sat on the window seat to pet Charlie and wait.

She tried to think of other things. Her time in America. Humming to herself, Emma let herself picture all the things she'd seen. There had been the big silver arch in St. Louis. There had been the lake in Chicago that had seemed as big as the ocean to her. And Hollywood. She'd liked the big white sign, and remembering it, tried to picture all the letters.

Her father had played at a huge theater there right outside. They had called it a bowl. She had thought that strange, but it had been fun to listen to the cheers and screams rising on the open air.

She'd celebrated her birthday, her third birthday, in Hollywood. Everyone had come to eat the white cake with the little silver balls on top.

They had gotten into a plane almost every day. And every day it had scared her, but she'd been able to battle back the sickness. There had been a lot of people with them. Roadies her father called them. Which seemed silly since they were so often in the air, and not on any road at all.

She'd liked the hotels best, with room service and new beds almost every night. She'd liked looking out the window at new places and new people every morning.

With a yawn, she settled back with the dog snuggled under her arm.

When they went to a hotel again, Darren could go with them. Everyone would love him.

Watching the sleet made her sleepy. And she thought of Christmas. It had been the first she'd ever had with a stocking hanging from the mantel with her name on it. Under the tree they had decorated had been stacks and stacks of presents. Toys and games and dolls in pretty dresses. They'd all played Snakes and Ladders in the afternoon. Even Stevie. He'd pretended to cheat to make her laugh, then had taken her on a screaming piggyback ride through the house.

Afterward her father had carved a big Christmas goose. When gluttony had made her sleepy, she had curled up in front of the fire and had listened to the music.

It had been the best day of her life. The very best. Until this one. The sound of a car roused her. Pressing her face against the window again she peered out. With a screech, she leaped off the seat.

"Johnno! Johnno! They're here." She went flying down the

hallway, her shoes clattering on the wood floor that had been painstakingly refinished and polished.

"Hold on." Johnno stopped scribbling the lyrics that had been playing in his head to catch her on the run. "Who's here?"

"My da and Bev and my baby."

"Your baby, is it?" He tugged on her nose, then turned to Stevie who was experimenting with chords at the piano. "Shall we go welcome the newest McAvoy?"

"Be right along."

"I'm coming." P.M. stuffed the last of a tea cake into his mouth before he rose from the floor. "Wonder if they managed to get out of the hospital without being mobbed."

"The precautions Pete took makes James Bond look like a piker. Two decoy limos, twenty burly guards, and the final escape in a florist truck." With a laugh, he started down the hall with Emma in tow. "Fame makes beggars of us, Emma luv, and don't you forget."

She didn't care about fame or beggars or anything else. She only wanted to see her brother. The moment the door opened, she pulled her sweaty hand from Johnno's and shot down the hall.

"Let me see him," she demanded.

Brian bent over, shifting the blanket from the bundle in his arms. For Emma, the first sight of her brother was love. Unconditional, all-encompassing. It was so much more than anything she'd expected.

He wasn't a doll. Even as he slept she could see the gentle flutter of his dark lashes. His mouth was small and moist, his skin thin and delicately pale. He wore a little blue cap over his head, but her father had told her that he had hair as dark as Bev's. His hand was curled in a fist, and she touched it, gently, with her fingertips. Warmth, and the faintest of movements.

Love burst through her like light.

"What do you think?" Brian asked her.

"Darren." She said the name softly, savoring it. "He's the most beautiful baby in the world."

"Got that pretty McAvoy face," Johnno murmured, feeling foolishly sentimental. "Nice job, Bev."

"Thanks." And she was glad it was done. None of the books she had read had prepared her for the exquisite, draining pain of childbirth. She was proud to have brought her son into the world naturally, though it had been touch and go during those last hours. Now she wanted nothing more than to settle down and be a mother.

"The doctor doesn't want Bev on her feet much for the next few days," Brian began. "Do you want to go up and rest?"

"The last thing I want is to get into another bed."

"Come on in and sit then, and Uncle Johnno will fix you a nice cup."

"Beautiful."

"I'll go up and put the baby down." Brian grinned at the way P.M. stood back and gawked. "He doesn't bite, old man. He doesn't have teeth."

P.M. grinned and stuffed his hands in his pockets. "Just don't ask me to touch him for a while."

"Entertain Bev. She really had a rough go of it. We've got a nurse coming in this afternoon, but I don't want her doing anything strenuous in the meantime."

"That I can handle." He wandered back toward the parlor.

"We'll put the baby to sleep," Emma announced and kept one hand on the edge of the blanket. "I can show you how."

They started up the stairs with Emma leading the way.

The nursery had been finished with frilly white curtains and rainbows painted on the pale blue walls. The bassinet had a skirt of snowy Irish lace dotted with satin ribbons of pink and blue. An old-fashioned pram stood in the corner guarded by a six-foot teddy bear. An antique rocker waited by the window.

Emma stood beside the bassinet as her father laid Darren down. Once the little cap was removed, she reached in to carefully stroke his downy black hair.

"Will he wake up soon?"

"I don't know. I get the feeling babies are pretty unpredictable." Brian crouched down beside her. "We have to be very careful with him, Emma. He's so helpless, you see."

"I won't let anything happen to him, not ever." She put her hand on her father's shoulder and watched the baby sleep.

◆ ◆ ◆ ◆

*E*MMA WASN'T SURE she liked Miss Wallingsford. The young nurse had pretty red hair and nice gray eyes, but she rarely allowed Emma to touch baby Darren. Bev had interviewed dozens of applicants, and was well satisfied with Alice Wallingsford. She was twenty-five, of good family, and had excellent references and a pleasing manner.

In the first months after Darren's birth, Bev was so tired and moody Alice's services became invaluable. More, she was another woman to talk with about things like teething, breast-feeding, and diets. Bev was as determined to gain back her willowy figure as she was to be a good mother. With Brian closed up writing songs with Johnno, or in meetings with Pete about the next recording, she struggled to make the home she wanted so badly for them.

She listened when he spoke of things like war in Asia, race riots in America, but her world centered on whether the sun would shine warm enough to take Darren for a stroll. She taught herself how to bake bread and tried her hand at knitting, while Brian wrote songs, and spoke out against war and bigotry.

As her body returned to normal, her mind eased. For Bev, this was the sweetest time of her life. Her son was chubbily healthy, and her husband treated her like a princess in bed.

With Darren at her breast and Emma at her feet, she rocked in the chair by the nursery window. There had been rain that morning, but the sun was out now, and bright. She thought that by afternoon she could take the baby and Emma for a walk in the park.

"I'm going to put him down now, Emma." Bev shifted her blouse to cover her breast. "He's fast asleep."

"Can I hold him when he wakes up?"

"Yes, but only when I'm with you."

"Miss Wallingsford never lets me hold him."

"She's just being cautious." Bev smoothed the blanket over Darren before she stepped back. He was nearly five months old now, she thought. Already she couldn't imagine her life without him. "Let's go down and see about baking a nice cake. Your da loves chocolate cake."

Knowing she had to be satisfied with that, Emma followed her out. Alice paused in the hallway, holding fresh linens for the nursery.

"He should sleep awhile, Alice," Bev told her. "His tummy's full."

"Yes, ma'am."

"Emma and I will be in the kitchen."

An hour later, when they'd taken the cake out to cool, the

front door slammed. "Your da must be home early." Bev automatically fluffed her hair before she hurried out of the kitchen to greet him. "Bri, I didn't expect you until . . . what's wrong?"

He was dead pale, his eyes red-rimmed and bleary. He shook his head as if to clear it as Bev held out her hands to him. "They've shot him."

"What?" Her fingers clamped down hard on his. "Who? Shot who?"

"Kennedy. Robert Kennedy. They've killed him."

"Oh my God. Oh sweet God." She could only stand and stare, horrified. She remembered when the American president had been killed, and the shocked world had mourned. Now his brother, his bright, young brother.

"We were rehearsing for the album," Brian began. "Pete came in. He'd heard it on the radio. None of us believed it, not until we'd heard it ourselves. Goddammit, Bev, just a few months ago it was King, and now this. What's happening to the world?"

"Mr. McAvoy . . ." Alice started down the stairs, her face as white as her apron. "Is it true? Are you certain?"

"Yes. It should be just a nightmare, but it's true."

"Oh, that poor family." Alice wrung her apron in her hands. "That poor mother."

"He was a good man," Brian managed. "He would have been their next president. He would have stopped that bloody war, I know it."

It disturbed Emma to see tears in her father's eyes. The adults were much too involved with their own grief to notice her. She didn't know anyone named Kennedy, but she was sorry he was dead. She wondered if he had been a friend of her da's. Maybe he'd been a soldier in the war her father always talked about.

"Alice, fix some tea. Please," Bev murmured as she led Brian toward the parlor.

"What kind of a world have we brought our children into? When will they understand, Bev? When will they finally understand?"

Emma went upstairs to sit with Darren and leave the adults to their tears and tea.

They found her there, in the nursery, an hour later. She was singing one of the lullabies Bev often sang at bedtime while she rocked Darren.

Panicked, Bev started in, only to have Brian catch her arm. "No, they're fine. Can't you see?" It eased some of the rawness inside him to watch them. Emma rocked with her feet dangling far from the floor, and the baby carefully supported in her arms.

Emma looked up and smiled beautifully. "He was crying, but he's happy now. He smiled at me." She leaned over to kiss his cheek as he gurgled. "He loves me, don't you, Darren?"

"Yes, he loves you." Brian moved over to kneel in front of the rocker and wrap his arms around both of them. "Thank God for all of you," he said as he held out a hand for Bev. "I think I'd go mad without you."

◆ ◆ ◆ ◆

*B*RIAN KEPT HIS family closer during the next weeks. Whenever possible, he worked at home, and even toyed with the idea of adding a recording studio onto the house. The war in Southeast Asia preyed on his mind. The horrible and useless fighting in his homeland of Ireland tore at him. His records soared up the chart, but the satisfaction that had rushed through him in the early days paled. He used his music both as a projection of his feelings and a buffer against the worst of them. His need for family kept him level.

They were sanity, he was certain.

It was Bev who gave him the idea to take Emma to the recording studio. They were about to lay the first tracks for their third album. An album Brian considered even more important than their debut. This time, he had to prove that Devastation wasn't a fluke, nor a pale imitation that was clinging to the coattails of groups like the Beatles and Rolling Stones. He had to prove to himself that the magic, which had dimmed so during that last year, would still be there.

He wanted something unique, a sound distinctively their own. He'd shuffled aside a dozen solid rock numbers he and Johnno had written. They could wait. Despite Pete's objections, the rest of the group was behind him in his decision to pepper the cuts with political statements, down-and-dirty rebel rock, and Irish folk songs. Electric guitars and penny whistles.

When Emma walked into the studio, she had no notion she

was being allowed to witness the making of music history. To her, she was spending the day with her da and his mates. It seemed like an enormous game to her, the equipment, the instruments, the tall glass room. She sat in a big swivel chair, sipping a Coke straight from the bottle.

"Don't you think the tyke's going to get a bit bored?" Johnno asked as he fiddled with the electric organ. He wore two rings now, the diamond on one pinky and a fat sapphire on the other.

"If we can't entertain one little girl, we'd best pack it in." Brian adjusted the strap of his guitar. "Anyway, I want to keep her close awhile. Jane's making noise again."

"Bitch," Johnno said mildly, then picked up a glass of Coke liberally laced with rum.

"She won't get anywhere this time either, but it's a nuisance." He cast a quick look at Emma and saw she was occupied with talking to Charlie. "She's trying to say she was tricked into signing the papers. Pete's handling it."

"She just wants more money."

With a grim smile, Brian nodded. "She won't get more out of Pete. Or out of me. Let's have a sound check here."

"Hello there, Emmy luv." Stevie stopped beside her to poke a finger into her belly. "You auditioning for the band?"

"I'm going to watch." She stared up at him, fascinated by the gold hoop he now wore in his ear.

"That's fine, then. We always do better with an audience. Tell me something, Emmy." He bent down close, whispering. "Truth and nothing but. Who's the best of this lot here?"

It had become a standard game by this time. Knowing the rules, Emma looked up, then down, then side to side. Hunching her shoulders, she bellowed, "Da!"

It earned her a snort of disgust and a lot of tickled ribs. Struggling not to wet her pants, she squirmed to the back of the chair.

"It's illegal in this country to brainwash children," Stevie said as he joined Brian.

"The kid has taste."

"Right, all bad." He took his Martin out of its case and ran loving fingers down the neck. "What's on first?"

"We'll lay down the instrumentals on 'Outcry.'"

"Saving the best for first." With a nod, Stevie sped through some experimental chords. "Let's get to work, mates."

Of the four, Stevie was the only one who had grown up with real money, in a true house with a garden and two live-in servants. He was used to the finer things, expected them and was easily bored with them. He'd fallen in love with the guitar, and had made his proper parents rue the day they had given it to him.

At fifteen, he'd formed his own band. Stevie and the Rousers. It had lasted six months before bitter infighting had broken it up. Undaunted, he'd formed another, then another. His natural, flashy talent with the guitar had drawn many hopefuls to him. But then they'd looked to him for leadership that he'd been innately incapable of providing.

He'd come across Brian and Johnno at a party in Soho, one of those candlelit, smoke-and-incense-choked gatherings his parents were terrified of. He'd been attracted immediately to Brian's intensity about music, and Johnno's caustic, careless wit. For the first time in his life, Stevie had joined instead of formed. He'd followed Brian's lead with relief.

There had been lean days, grubbing in pubs begging for a chance to play. There had been heady days spent writing songs and creating music. There had been women, gloriously sweaty acres of them ready to fall on their backs for a fair-haired man with a guitar in his hand.

There had been Sylvie, the girl he had met on their first gig in Amsterdam. Pretty, round-cheeked Sylvie with her broken English and guileless eyes. They'd made love like maniacs in a filthy little room where the roof leaked and the windows were coated with grime. He'd fallen in love, as much as he believed himself capable. He'd even entertained ideas about bringing her back to London with him, setting up house in some cramped cold-water flat.

But Sylvie had gotten pregnant.

He remembered when she'd told him, her face pale and her eyes full of hope and fear. He hadn't wanted children. Good Christ, he'd only been twenty. His music had come first, had had to. And if his parents had discovered he'd fathered a child with a Dutch cocktail waitress . . . It had been lowering to realize that no matter how far he'd run, how much he'd protested, what his parents thought had still mattered so much.

Pete had arranged for an abortion, discreetly, expensively. Sylvie, with the tears flowing down her cheeks, had done what he'd asked. Once she had, she had walked out of his life. Until she had gone, Stevie hadn't realized he'd loved her even more than he'd believed himself capable.

He didn't want to think of it, hated to remember it, and her. But just lately it had begun preying on his mind. It probably had to do with Emma, he thought as he glanced over and saw her sitting flushed and delighted in her swivel chair. His child, whatever it had been, would have been about her age now.

The day in the studio was fun for Emma. So much fun her only regret was that Darren wasn't there to share it. Watching her father and his friends play now was different from seeing them in the theaters and auditoriums across America. There was a different energy here. She didn't understand it, but she felt it.

On tour, Emma had begun to see them as a unit, like a body with four heads. The picture that made in her mind made her laugh to herself, but it seemed a true one. Today, they argued, and swore, joked or just sat silently during playbacks. She didn't know the meaning of the technical terms being tossed back and forth—didn't need to. She amused herself when they huddled together, or was amused by them when they took a moment to tease her. She ate gobs of greasy chips and bloated her belly with Cokes.

During a break she sat on P.M.'s lap and bashed away at the drums. She said her name into one of the mikes and heard her voice echo through the room. With a spare drumstick in her hand, she dozed in the swivel chair, her head pillowed on the faithful Charlie. And she awoke to her father's voice, soaring in a ballad of tragic love.

Spellbound she watched, rubbing the sleep from her eyes and yawning into Charlie's fur. Her heart was too young to be touched by the lyrics. But the sound reached her. She would never hear the song again without remembering the moment when she'd awakened to hear his voice filling her head. Filling the world.

When he had finished, she forgot that she was supposed to be quiet. Bouncing on the chair, she clapped her hands together. "Da!"

In the engineering booth, Pete swore, but Brian held up a hand. "Leave that on." With a laugh, he turned to Emma. "Leave it on," he repeated as he held out his arms to her. When she reached them, he tossed her into the air. "What do you think, Emma? I've just made you a star."

# Chapter Seven

♦ ♦ ♦ ♦

$\mathcal{I}$F BRIAN'S FAITH in man had been shaken in 1968 with the assassination of Martin Luther King, then Robert Kennedy, it was expanded during the summer of 1969 with Woodstock. It was a celebration for him of youth and music, of love and brotherhood. It symbolized the chance to turn around the year of bloodshed and war, of riots and discontent. He knew, as he stood onstage and looked out at the sea of bodies, that he would never do anything so huge or so memorable again.

Even as it thrilled him to be there, to leave his mark, it left him by turns depressed and terrified that the decade, and its spirit, were ending.

He rushed through his three days in upstate New York at a fever pitch of emotional and creative energy, fueled by the atmosphere, heightened by the drugs that were as handy as popcorn at a Saturday matinee, and pushed by his own fears about where success had taken him. He spent an entire night alone in the trailer the band used, composing for a marathon fourteen-hour stint while cocaine stormed through his system. On one illuminating afternoon he sat in the woods with Stevie, listening to the music and the cheers of four hundred thousand. With the help of LSD he saw whole universes created in a maple leaf.

Brian embraced Woodstock, the concept of it, the reality of it. His only regret was that nothing he had said had persuaded Bev to come with them. She was, once again, waiting for him. This time she waited in the house they had bought in the Hollywood hills. Brian's love affair with America was just beginning, and his second American tour felt like a homecoming. It was the year of the rock festival, a phenomenon Brian saw as demonstrating the strength of rock culture.

He wanted, needed, to recapture that towering high of excitement when success had been new, when the band, the unit of them, had been like one electric force smashing through the world of music and public recognition. Over the past year, he had sensed that electricity, that unity, slipping away like the sixties themselves. He'd felt it forge again at Woodstock.

When they boarded the plane, leaving the faithful at Woodstock behind, Brian fell into an exhausted sleep. Beside him, Stevie carelessly popped a couple of barbiturates and zoned out. Johnno settled back to play poker with some of the road crew. Only P.M. sat restlessly by the window.

He wanted to remember everything. It annoyed him that unlike Brian, he saw beneath the symbolism and statement of the festival to the miserable conditions. The mud, the garbage, the lack of proper sanitary facilities. The music, good Christ, the music had been wonderful, almost unbearably so, but often, too often, he'd felt the audience had been too blissed out to notice.

Still, even someone as pragmatic and simple as P.M. had felt the sense of commitment and unity. Of peace—a peaceful trio of days with four hundred thousand living as family. But there had also been dirt, prolific and heedless sex, and a careless abundance of drugs.

Drugs frightened him. He couldn't admit it, not even to the men he considered his brothers. Drugs made him sick or silly or put him to sleep. He took them only when he saw no graceful way not to. He was in turn amazed and appalled at the cheerfulness with which Brian and Stevie experimented with whatever came their way. And he was more than a little frightened by the ease with which Stevie was quietly, and consistently, shooting smack into his veins.

Johnno was more particular about what he pumped into his system, but Johnno's personality was so strong no one would laugh at him for refusing to indulge in acid or speed or snow.

P.M. knew personality wasn't his strong point. He wasn't even a musician, not like the others. Oh, he knew he could hold his own with any drummer out there. He was good, damn good. But he couldn't write music, couldn't read it. His mind didn't run to poetry or political statements.

He wasn't handsome. Even now, at twenty-three, he was plagued by occasional outbreaks of pimples.

Despite what he considered his many disadvantages, he was part of one of the biggest, most successful rock groups in the world. He had friends, good and true ones, who would stand for him. In two years, he had earned more money than he had ever expected to make in the whole of his life.

And he was careful with it. P.M.'s father ran a small repair shop in London. He knew about business and books. Of the four he was the only one who ever asked Pete questions about expenses and profits. He was certainly the only one who bothered to read any of the forms or contracts they signed.

Having money pleased him, not only because he could send checks home—a kind of tangible proof to his doubting parents that he could succeed. It pleased him to have it jingling in his pocket.

He hadn't grown up as poor as Johnno and Brian, but he'd been a long way from knowing the comforts of Stevie's childhood.

Now they were on their way to Texas. Another festival in a year crammed with them. He didn't mind really. After that, it would be another performance in another city. They were all blurring together, the months, the stages. Yet he didn't want it to stop. When it did, he was desperately afraid he would sink back to obscurity.

He knew that when the summer was well and truly over, they would head to California, to Hollywood. For a few weeks, they would live among the movie stars. And for a few weeks, he thought with twinges of guilt and pleasure, he would be close to Bev. The only person P.M. loved more than Brian was Brian's wife.

◆ ◆ ◆

EMMA SET UP the lettered blocks. She was very proud of the fact that she was learning to read and spell, and was determined to teach Darren. "E-M-M-A," she said, tapping each block in turn. "Emma. Say 'Emma.'"

"Ma!" Laughing, Darren pushed the blocks into a jumbled pile. "Ma Ma."

"*Em*-ma." But she leaned over to kiss him. "Here's an easy one." She set up two blocks. "D-A. Da."

"Da. Da, Da, Da!" Delighted with himself, Darren climbed onto his sturdy legs to race to the doorway and look for Brian.

"No, Da's not there now, but Mum's in the kitchen. We're having a big party tonight, to celebrate the new album being finished. We'll be going home to England soon."

She was looking forward to it, though she liked the house in America just as much as the castle outside of London. For more than a year she and her family had flown back and forth over the ocean as casually as other families drove across town.

She had turned six in the autumn of 1970, and had a proper British tutor, at Bev's insistence. When they settled back in England again, she knew she would go to school with others her age. The idea was both frightening and wonderful.

"When we get back home, I'm going to learn lots more, and teach you everything." As she spoke, she piled the blocks into a neat tower. "Look, here's your name. The best name. Darren."

On a cry of glee, he pranced back to crouch and study the letters. "D, A, Z, L, M, N, O, P." After sending Emma a wicked smile, he swooped his arm through it. Blocks crashed and tumbled. "Darren!" he shouted. "Darren McAvoy."

"You can say that well enough, can't you, boy-o?" In three years, the flow and cadence of her voice had come to mirror Brian's. She smiled as she began to build something a little more intricate for him to demolish.

He was the light of her life, her little brother with his dark thick hair and laughing sea-green eyes. At two, he had the face of a Botticelli cherub and the energy of a demon. He'd done everything early, crawling weeks before the baby books had warned Bev to expect it.

His face had been on the cover of *Newsweek*, *Photoplay*, and *Rolling Stone*. The world had an ongoing love affair with Darren McAvoy. He had the blood of Irish peasants and staunch British conservatives in his veins, but he was a prince. No matter how careful Bev was, the paparazzi managed to snap new pictures of him on a weekly basis. And the fans clamored for more.

They sent him truckloads of toys which Bev meticulously shipped off to hospitals and orphanages. Offers poured in for endorsements. Baby food, a line of children's clothing, a chain of toy stores. They were unilaterally refused. Through all the attention and adulation, Darren remained a happy, healthy toddler, who was currently enjoying, with relish, his terrible twos. If he had known about the attention, no doubt he would have cheerfully agreed he deserved it.

"This is the castle," Emma told him as she arranged blocks. "And you're the king."

"I'm the king." He plopped down to bounce on his padded bottom.

"Yes. King Darren the First."

"First," he repeated. He knew very well the meaning of that word, and enjoyed being put there. "Darren's first."

"You're a very good king and kind to all the animals." She pulled the ever faithful Charlie closer. Dutifully, Darren bent to give him a wet kiss. "And here are all your good and courageous knights." Meticulously she set up dolls and stuffed toys. "There's Da and Johnno, Stevie and P.M. And here's Pete. He's, ah . . . prime minister. This is the beautiful Lady Beverly." Pleased, Emma posed her favored ballerina doll.

"Mum." Darren kissed the doll in turn. "Mum's pretty."

"She's the prettiest lady in the world. There's a horrible witch after her, who locked her in a tower." Emma had a vague image of her own mother, but it passed quickly. "All the knights go out to save her." Making galloping noises, she pushed the toys toward the doll. "But only Sir Da can break the spell."

"Sir Da." The combination of words struck Darren as so funny he rolled and smashed the castle.

"Well, if you're going to go around knocking down your own castle, I give up."

"Ma." Darren wrapped his arms around her and squeezed. "My Ma Ma. Let's play farm."

"All right, but we have to pick up the blocks or prissy Miss Wallingsford will come in and say we're noisy, messy children."

"Pissy. Pissy. Pissy."

"Darren." Emma clapped both hands over her mouth and giggled. "Don't say that."

Because it made her laugh, he said it again, at the top of his voice.

"What a word to come out of a nursery." Not sure if she should be amused or stern, Bev stopped in the doorway.

"He means prissy," Emma explained.

"I see." Bev held out her arms as Darren ran to her. "That's a very important *r*, my lad. And what are you two up to?"

"We were playing castle, but Darren liked knocking it down better."

"Darren the Destructor." Bev nuzzled against his neck until he squealed with laughter. His little legs locked around her so that she could hold him in his favorite position. Upside down.

She hadn't known it was possible to love so much. Even the passion she felt for Brian paled beside the love she felt for her son. He gave back without even knowing he was giving. It was simply there, a hug, a kiss, or a smile. Always at the right time. He was the best and brightest part of her life.

"Here now, go help your sister tidy up the blocks."

"I can do it."

After setting Darren down, Bev smiled at Emma. "He has to learn to pick up his own messes, Emma. However much you and I would like to do for him always."

She watched them together, the delicate, fair-headed girl and the dark, sturdy boy. Emma was a neat, well-mannered child who no longer hid in closets. Brian had made a difference for her. And Bev hoped she herself had had a hand in forming Emma into the bright, cheerful child she was today. But it was Darren, she knew, who had truly tipped the scales. In her devotion to him, Emma forgot to be frightened, she forgot to be shy. In turn, Darren loved her completely.

Even as a baby, he had stopped crying more quickly if Emma soothed him. Each day the bond between them only strengthened.

Bev had been pleased the day a few months before when Emma had begun to call her Mum. It was a rare thing for her to look at Emma and think of her as Jane's child now. She didn't, couldn't, feel for Emma the fierce almost desperate love she felt for Darren, but the love she did feel was warm and steady.

Because he liked the clattering they made, Darren dropped the blocks back in their box. "D," he said, holding his favorite letter over the opening. "Dog, drum, Darren!" He let it fly, satisfied when his letter made the most noise. Certain he'd done his duty, he hopped on his red and white rocking horse and headed west.

"We were going to play farm." Emma took the big Fisher-Price barn and silo off the shelf. It only took the word "farm" to have Darren leaping off his horse. He dragged off the top to shake the animals and round-faced people out of the silo.

"Let's go, let's go," he chanted while his still clumsy fingers struggled to set the white plastic fence pieces straight.

Emma steadied his hand before she glanced up at Bev. "Can you play, too?"

She had a million things to do, Bev thought, with all the people Brian had asked over that evening. In a few hours, the house would be full. It always seemed to be full, as if Brian were afraid to spend a few hours in his own company. What he was running from, she didn't know, and doubted that he did.

When we get back to London, she thought. Everything would click into place again when they got home.

She looked down at the children, her children. And laughed.

"I'd love to play."

An hour later Brian found them as the turkey rug which stood in for the cornfield was plowed under by a fleet of Tonka trucks. Before he could speak, Emma was scrambling up.

"Da's home." She rushed forward, ending on a bound, sure that his arms would be there to catch her.

He scooped her up, planting a noisy kiss on her cheek before sweeping his free arm around Darren. "Give us a big one," he told Darren, then staggered as the boy pressed a hard, wet kiss on his chin. Hefting them both, Brian stepped around the white plastic fences and stubby figures spread around the floor.

"Farming again?"

"It's Darren's favorite." Bev waited for him to sit, then grinned. Brian was always at his best in the circle of his family. "I'm afraid you've just plopped down smack in the manure pile."

"Oh?" He leaned over to pull her against him. "Wouldn't be the first time I've sat in shit."

"Shit," Darren repeated, his diction perfect.

"Good going," Bev murmured.

Brian only grinned and tickled his son's ribs. "So what's the plan?"

She settled back as Darren wiggled out of Brian's hold to sit in her lap. "We're plowing under the corn since we've decided to plant soybeans."

"Very wise. Quite the gentleman farmer, aren't you, old man?" He poked a finger into Darren's pudgy stomach. "We'll have to take that trip to Ireland. Then you can ride on a real tractor."

"Let's go. Let's go." Darren bounced on Bev's lap, chanting his favorite phrase.

"Darren can't ride on a tractor until he's bigger," Emma said, sedately folding her hands over her knee.

"Quite right." With a smile, Bev nodded toward Brian. "Just like he can't use the cricket bat or the bicycle someone bought him."

"Women," Brian said to Darren. "They don't understand macho stuff."

"Pissy," Darren recited, pleased with his new word.

"I beg your pardon?" Brian managed over a laugh.

"Don't ask." After a quick hug, Bev set Darren aside. "Let's clean up this business so we can go have our tea."

"Excellent idea." Brian sprung up and grabbed Bev's hand. "Emma, you're in charge, luv. Mum and I have something to do before tea."

"Brian—"

"Miss Wallingsford's just downstairs." He continued to pull Bev from the room. "Don't forget to wash up."

"Brian, the nursery's in a shambles."

"Emma'll take care of it. She's tidy as a pin." He pulled Bev into the bedroom. "Besides, she likes to."

"Even so, I—" She caught his hands as he started to tug off her T-shirt. "Bri, we can't do this now. I've a million things to see to."

"And this is top of the list." He closed his mouth over hers, pleased when her halfhearted struggles ceased.

"It was top of the list last night," she murmured, running her hands down to his hips. "And again this morning."

"It's always top of the list." He unhooked her jeans.

It amazed him how small, how firm she was. After two children. No, one child, he reminded himself. He often forgot, perhaps deliberately, that she hadn't given birth to Emma. No matter how familiar her body became, touching her like this took him back to their first nights together.

They'd come a long way from a two-room flat with a single creaky bed. They owned a pair of homes now, in two countries, but the sex was as strong and sweet as it had been when he had had nothing in his pockets but desperate hopes and shiny dreams.

They rolled over the bed, limbs tangled, mouths growing

hungrier. As she rose over him, he watched her aching pleasure reflected on her face.

She'd changed so little. Her hair swung to her shoulders now, sleek and straight. Her skin was milk pale, delicately flushed from the passion that heated it. Pushing up, he circled her breasts with slow, whispery kisses. When her head fell back, he sucked greedily, excited by the small, helpless sounds she made.

With Bev, he wanted the beauty. With Bev, he found it.

Gripping her hips, he lifted her up and onto him, letting her set the pace. Letting her take him exactly where he wanted to go.

♦ ♦ ♦

NAKED, SHE STRETCHED, then curled up against him. With her eyes half closed she could see the sun pouring through the windows. She wanted to pretend it was morning, some lazy morning, when they could stay just as they were for hours.

"I didn't think I'd like staying here this time, for all these months while you recorded. But it's been wonderful."

"We can stay a bit longer." His energy was beginning to build, as it always did after making love with her. "We could take a few weeks, lie around, go to Disneyland again."

"Darren already thinks it's his own personal amusement park."

"Then we'll have to build him one." He rolled over, propping himself on his elbow. "Bev, I had a quick meeting with Pete before I came home. 'Outcry' has gone platinum."

"Oh, Bri. That's marvelous."

"It's more than marvelous. I was right." He pulled her by the shoulders until she sat beside him. "People are listening, really listening. 'Outcry' has become like an anthem for the antiwar movement. It's making a difference." He didn't hear the faint desperation in his voice, the desperation of a man trying to convince himself. "We're going to release another single from the album. 'Love Lost,' I think, though Pete's muttering about it not being commercial enough."

"It's so sad."

"That's the point." The words snapped out, and he bit off the impatient rest to continue more calmly. "I'd like to pipe it into Parliament and the Pentagon and the U.N., all those places where the smug, fat bastards make decisions. We need to do something, Bev. If people listen to me because I have hit records, then I have to make sure I have something important to say."

◆ ◆ ◆ ◆

IN THE PENTHOUSE he'd rented in the heart of L.A., Pete Page sat at his desk and considered the possibilities. Like Brian, he was delighted with "Outcry" 's success. With him it was a matter of sales generated more than social conscience. But that's what they paid him for.

As he had predicted only three years before, Brian and the others were very rich. He was going to see to it that they all became a great deal richer.

Their music was sterling. He had known that since he'd listened to their first demo six years before. It had been a little rough, a little raw, and exactly the right sound for its time. He had already managed two other groups to solid record contracts, but Devastation had been his chance for glory.

He had needed them. They had needed him. He'd gone on the road with them, sat in dives, hustled record producers, called in all of his markers. It had paid off far beyond his initial expectations. But his expectations were flexible. He wanted more for them. He wanted more for himself.

The band, individually and as a group, was beginning to worry him. They wandered off on their own too much these days, Johnno with his frequent trips to New York, Stevie spending weeks at a time God knew where. P.M. was always within arm's reach, but he was taken up in an affair with some ambitious starlet. Pete no longer believed it was a fling. There was Brian, of course, spouting antiwar politics at the drop of a hat.

They were a band, dammit, a rock-and-roll band, and what they did separately affected what they did as a group. What they did as a group affected their sales. Already they were backing off planning a tour after the new album was released.

He wasn't going to see them cracked down the middle as the Beatles had been.

After a deep breath, he settled back to think about them, as they had been, and as they were.

It pleased him to see Johnno's collection of cars. The Bentley, the Rolls, the Ferrari. There was one thing about Johnno, Pete thought with a small smile. The man knew how to enjoy money. He'd nearly stopped worrying that Johnno's sexual preferences would leak. Over the years Pete had gained a strong respect for Johnno's intelligence, common sense, and talent.

No, he didn't have to worry about Johnno, Pete decided as he glanced over the papers on his desk. He was one who could keep his private affairs private. And the public loved him for his outlandish outfits and glib tongue.

Then there was Stevie. The drugs were a bit of a problem. It wasn't affecting his performance, yet, but he had noticed that Stevie's mood swings were wider and more frequent. He'd been stoned during the last two recording sessions, and even Brian, no slouch in the drug department himself, had been annoyed.

Yes, he'd have to keep his eye on Stevie.

P.M. was as dependable as a sunrise. It was true that Pete was by turns amused and irked that the drummer pored over every word in a contract. But the boy was investing his money well, and earned Pete's respect there. It had also been a surprise, a pleasant and profitable one, when the girls took so giddily to his homely face. Where Pete had once worried that P.M. would prove the weak link, he had turned out to be one of the strongest.

Brian. Pete poured himself two fingers of Chivas Regal, sat back in his overstuffed leather chair and considered. Brian was, without doubt, the heart and soul of the group. He was the creative drive, the conscience.

It had been fortunate that the business with Emma hadn't set them back. Pete had worried about it, then had been delighted when the whole affair had generated sympathy, and record sales. True, Pete still had to cross swords with Jane Palmer from time to time, but the mess had never put a dent in the group's popularity. Nor had Brian's marriage. It had frustrated Pete that he hadn't been able to portray the group as four young, single men. But Brian's family life had turned into a bounty of press.

The pity was the peace rallies, the speeches. Brian's affection for the Students for a Democratic Society, his outspoken support of American draft dodgers. They'd nearly had the cover of *Time* before Brian had popped off with a few ill-chosen criticisms of the Chicago Seven trial.

Pete understood the power of the press, how one careless statement could have the masses, the record-buying masses, turning against you. John Lennon had opened his own can of worms a few years earlier with an offhand, sarcastic comment about the

Beatles being bigger than Jesus. Brian had come close, too close, to making the same mistake.

He was entitled to his politics, of course, Pete thought as he sipped his whiskey. But there was a point where personal beliefs and public success parted ways. Between Stevie's enchantment with drugs and Brian's idealism, there was bound to be a disaster.

There were ways to avoid it, of course, and he had already begun to consider a few. He needed the public to see Stevie not just as a drugged-out rocker, but as an extraordinary musician. He needed them to see Brian as not only a peacenik but a devoted father.

With the right balance of images, not only the youth would be buying records and magazines but their parents as well.

# Chapter Eight

◆ ◆ ◆ ◆

THEY STAYED IN California another two weeks, basking in long, lazy days, making love in the afternoon, giving all-night parties. There were midweek trips to Disneyland in careful disguises. The photographers Pete hired to record the outings were so discreet Bev never noticed them.

She decided to throw out her birth control pills, and Brian wrote love songs.

As the time to go back to England drew near, the group made peace within themselves, and set up an informal headquarters in Brian's hillside home.

"We should all go." Johnno carelessly passed his turn on the bong. "*Hair* was the first important musical for our generation. A rock musical." He liked the phrase, the grandeur of it. Already he was turning over ideas for one. He hoped, when they returned to London, he and Brian could put together a musical that would outdo *Hair*, and the Who's current success, *Tommy*.

"We can lay over in New York a couple of days," he continued, "see the play, raise some hell, then head back to London."

"Do they really strip naked?" Stevie wanted to know.

"Right down to the buff, son. That should be worth the price of a ticket."

"We should go." Mellowed from the company and smoke, Brian rested his head on Bev's knee. He'd already stayed in one place longer than he liked, and the idea of New York appealed. "For the music and the statement."

"You go for the statement." Stevie grinned. "I'll go for the naked birds."

"We'll get Pete to fix it up. What do you say, Bev?"

She didn't like New York, but she could see Brian's mind was set. And she didn't want to spoil the easy, peaceful mood of the last weeks. "It'll be fun. Maybe we can take Darren and Emma to the zoo and through Central Park before we fly home."

◆ ◆ ◆ ◆

EMMA WAS THRILLED. She remembered her first trip to New York well, the big bed in the hotel room, the soaring thrill of standing on top of the world, the glorious rides on the carousel in Central Park. She wanted to share all of that with Darren.

She tried to explain all the wonders of it to him as they prepared for the trip. As Alice Wallingsford packed up the nursery, she kept Darren out of mischief with his favored farm.

"Moo cow," he said, holding up the black spotted white piece from the set. "Want to see a moo cow."

"I don't think we'll see a moo cow, but we'll see lions at the zoo." She made a roar that had him squealing.

"You're getting him too excited, Emma," Alice said automatically. "And it's nearly bedtime."

Emma just rolled her eyes as Darren danced around her. He was wearing his Oshkosh overalls and little red Keds. For Emma's approval, he struggled to do a sloppy somersault.

"All that energy." Alice clucked her tongue, though in truth she was charmed by the boy. "I don't see how we'll get him to sleep tonight."

"Don't pack Charlie," Emma put in before Alice could drop the stuffed dog into a packing box. "He has to ride on the plane with me."

With a sigh, Alice set the worn dog aside. "He needs a good washing. I don't want you sneaking him into the baby's crib anymore, Emma."

"I love Charlie," Darren announced and tried another somersault. He landed heavily on his Playskool tool bench, but instead of crying, picked up the wooden hammer to play a tattoo on the colored pegs. "I love Charlie," he sang to his own rhythm.

"Be that as it may, sweet thing, he's getting a bit smelly. I don't want germs in the bed with my baby."

Darren sent her a sunny smile. "I love germs."

"It's a heartbreaker you are." Alice picked him up to bounce him on her hip. "Now Alice is going to give you a nice bath before bed, with bubbles. Emma, don't leave those pieces spread about," she added as she paused in the doorway. "You can have your bath as soon as Darren's finished. Then you can go down and say good night to your parents."

"Yes, ma'am." She waited until Alice was out of sight before she got up to get Charlie. He did not smell, she thought as she buried her face in his fur. And she would put him in Darren's crib, because Charlie watched over him when she was sleeping.

♦ ♦ ♦ ♦

"*I* REALLY WISH you hadn't asked all those people over tonight." Bev fluffed the pillows on the couch, though she knew such niceties were a waste of time.

"We have to say goodbye, don't we?" He put on a Jimi Hendrix album because it reminded him that though the artist was dead, the music lived on. "Besides, once we're back in London, we're back to work in a big way. I want to relax while I can."

"How can we relax with a hundred people milling about the house?"

"Bev. It's our last night."

She opened her mouth again, then closed it when Alice ushered the children in. "There's my boy." She scooped Darren up on the fly before she winked at Emma. "Is Charlie ready for his trip?" She knew and sympathized with Emma's unease with planes and smoothed a hand over the girl's hair.

"He's just a little nervous. He'll be all right with me."

"Of course he will." She pressed a kiss on the delicate area between Darren's ear and throat. "Already bathed?" She'd wanted to take care of that evening chore herself. There was nothing Bev liked better than to play with Darren in the tub, smoothing the soapy cloth over his pale, shiny skin.

"All washed and ready for bed," Alice put in. "They've just come to say good night before I tuck them up."

"I'll do that, Alice. With all the confusion today, I've hardly seen the children."

"All right, ma'am. I'll finish the packing."

"Da." Emma gave Brian her shy little smile. "Can we have a story? Please."

What he'd planned to do was roll a joint of good grass and listen to music. But he had a hard time resisting that smile, or his son's bright, bubbly laughter.

He went upstairs with his family, leaving Hendrix wailing.

It took two stories before Darren's eyes began to droop. He fought sleep as he fought all sedentary activities. He wanted to be doing, to be running or laughing or turning somersaults. Most of all, he wanted to be the brave young knight his father spoke of. He wanted to take up the shining magic sword and slay dragons.

He yawned and, cozied between his mother's breasts, began to doze. He could smell Emma, and went off to sleep happy that she was nearby.

He didn't wake when Bev lifted him into his crib. Darren slept the way he did everything. With a full heart. She tucked the satin-bordered blue blanket around his shoulders and tried not to think that he would soon be too big for a crib.

"He's so beautiful." Unable to resist, Bev stroked her fingers across his warm cheek.

With Emma's head resting on his shoulder, Brian looked down at his son. "When he's like this, it's hard to believe he can tear a room apart single-handed."

With a soft laugh, Bev slipped an arm around Brian's waist. "He uses both hands."

"And his feet."

"I've never known anyone who loves life as much. When I look at him, I realize I have everything I've ever wanted. I can see him a year from now, five years from now. It makes the idea of growing older pleasant somehow."

"Rock stars don't get old." He frowned, and for the first time Bev heard a trace of sarcasm, or was it disillusionment, in his voice. "They OD or start playing Vegas in white suits."

"Not you, Bri." She tightened her arm around his waist. "Ten years from now, you'll still be on top."

"Yeah. Well, if I ever buy a white suit with sequins, kick me in the ass."

"With the greatest pleasure." She kissed him, lifting a hand to his cheek to soothe as she might with one of the children. "Let's put Emma down."

"I want to do right by them, Bev." Shifting Emma, he started down the hall to her room. "By them, and you."

"You are doing right."

"The world's so fucked up. I used to think if we made it, really made it, people would listen to what we had to say. That it would make a difference. Now I don't know."

"What's wrong, Bri?"

"I don't know." He laid Emma down, wishing he could put his finger on the reason for the restless dissatisfaction he'd begun to feel. "A couple of years ago, when things really started to break for us, I thought it was fab. All those girls screaming, our pictures in all the mags, our music on every radio."

"It's what you wanted."

"It was, is. I don't know. How can they hear what we're trying to say, what difference does it make how good we are, if they scream through every bloody concert? We're just a commodity, an image Pete's polished up to sell records. I hate that." He stuffed his frustrated fists in his pockets. "Sometimes I think we should go back to where we started—the pubs where people listened or danced when we played. When we could reach them. I don't know." He passed a hand through his hair. "I guess I didn't realize how much fun we were having then. But you can't go back."

"I didn't know you felt this way. Why didn't you tell me?"

"I didn't know myself really. It's just that I don't feel like Brian McAvoy anymore." How could he explain that the feeling he'd revived at Woodstock had stubbornly faded in the year following it? "I didn't know how frustrating it would be not to be able to go out and have a drink with the lads, or sit on the beach without people swarming around, wanting a piece."

"You could stop. You could pull back and write."

"I can't stop." He looked down at Emma, sleeping peacefully. "I have to record, I have to perform. Every time I'm on-stage or in the studio, I know, deep down, that this is what I want to do. Need to do. But the rest of it . . . The rest of it sucks, and I didn't know it would. Maybe it's Hendrix and Joplin dying the way they did. Such a waste. Then the Beatles breaking up. It's like the end of something, and I haven't finished."

"Not the end." She laid a hand on his shoulder, automatically kneading the tense muscles. "Just a change."

"If we're not moving forward, we're moving back, don't you see?" But he knew she couldn't, and tried to put his feelings into more understandable words. "Maybe it's Pete pressuring us to tour again, or talking Stevie into sitting in with other groups in studio sessions, and doing that movie score. All I know is, it's not just the four of us getting together and playing from the heart anymore. It's image and bloody marketing, it's brokers and tax shelters."

Emma rolled over, murmuring.

"And I guess it's worrying about Emma going to school, and Darren going off one day. What's it going to be like for them? Will people start picking at them, wanting pieces of them because of what I am? I don't want them to have the filthy childhood I did, but am I doing any better by them, making them a part of something that's gotten bigger than all of us? And hungrier."

"You think too much." She turned to take his face in her hands. "That's what I love most about you. The children are fine. You've only got to look at them to see. Maybe their childhood isn't normal, but they're happy. We're going to keep them happy, and safe. Whatever you are, whoever you are, you're their da. We'll work out the rest."

"I love you, Bev. I must be daft, worrying about all this. We've got everything." He brought her closer, to rest his head on her hair. He wished he could understand why everything had turned out to be too much.

◆ ◆ ◆ ◆

$B$RIAN'S DISCONTENT VANISHED after a couple of joints. The house was full of people Brian felt understood him, what he wanted to do, where he wanted to go. The music was loud, the drugs were plentiful and varied. Snow, grass, Turkish hash, speed, bennies. The grinding, soul-wrenching rock of Janis Joplin poured out as his guests took their pick. He wanted to listen to her, again and again, to hear her belt out "Ball and Chain." Somehow it helped him grab onto the fact that he was alive, he still had a chance to make it matter.

He watched Stevie dance with a redhead in a purple miniskirt. Stevie didn't worry about being a figurehead or turning into a poster for some girl's wall, Brian mused as he washed down pretzels with smooth Irish whiskey. Stevie gleefully jumped from woman to woman without a care in his head. Of course, he was stoned most of the time. With a half-laugh, Brian picked another joint out of the bowl and decided it was time to get stoned himself.

From across the room, Johnno watched Brian settle back. Distancing himself, Johnno reflected as he chose a Gauloise over grass. It had been happening more and more recently. Perhaps because Johnno was closest to Brian, he had been the only one to notice. He thought now that the only time Brian seemed truly in tune was when the two of them sat down to write. Melody, countermelody, phrases, bridges.

He knew Brian had been upset by the deaths of Hendrix and Joplin. So had he. In its way, it had been as devastating as the Kennedy assassinations. People were supposed to grow old and decrepit before they died. But though he'd been shaken, he hadn't mourned as Brian was mourning. Then, Brian always cared more, needed more.

Like Brian, he glanced over at Stevie. He didn't like what he saw. It didn't matter a damn if Stevie screwed every woman on the continent, though he felt it lacked a certain finesse. It was the drugs, and the fact that Stevie was rapidly losing control over them, that concerned Johnno. He didn't care for the image they were beginning to project. The stoned-out rockers.

Shifting his gaze, he looked at P.M. There was a bit of a problem there as well. Oh, not with drugs. Poor old P.M. could barely function after one toke. It was the busty blond bimbo that had attached herself to the drummer two months before. P.M. didn't appear to be making any attempt to shake her off.

Johnno watched her now, the long-faced, sloe-eyed blonde— all legs and tits in a tight red dress. She wasn't as softheaded as she made out to be, Johnno mused. She was sharp as a tack, and knew how to play the tune P.M. wanted to hear. If they didn't watch themselves, she'd get him to marry her. And she wouldn't stay quietly in the background like Bev. No, not this one.

The three of them, in their separate ways, were on the verge of destroying the group. And nothing mattered more to Johnno.

◆ ◆ ◆ ◆

WHEN EMMA WOKE, the floor was vibrating with the bass from the stereo. She lay quietly a moment listening, trying as she did from time to time to recognize the song from the beat alone.

She'd gotten used to the parties. Her da liked to have people around. Lots of music, lots of laughing. When she was older, she would go to parties, too.

Bev always made sure the house was very clean before the guests arrived. That was silly, really, Emma thought. In the morning, the house was a terrible mess with smelly glasses and overflowing ashtrays. More often than not a few of the guests would be sprawled over the sofas and chairs amid the clutter.

Emma wondered what it would be like to sit up all night, talking, laughing, listening to music. When you were grown-up, no one told you when you had to go to bed, or have a bath.

With a sigh, she rolled over on her back. The music was faster now. She could feel the driving bass pulse in the walls. And something else. Footsteps, coming down the hall. Emma thought. Miss Wallingsford. She prepared to close her eyes and feign sleep when another thought occurred to her. Perhaps it was Da or Mum passing through to check on her and Darren. If it was, she could pretend to have just woken, then she could persuade them to tell her about the party.

But the footsteps passed by. She sat up clutching Charlie. She'd wanted company, even if only for a moment or two. She wanted to talk about the party, or the trip to New York. She wanted to know what song was playing. She sat a moment, a small, sleepy child in a pink nightgown, bathed by the cheerful glow of a Mickey Mouse night-light.

She thought she heard Darren crying. Straightening, she strained to listen. She was certain she heard Darren's cranky tears over the pulse of the music. Automatically she climbed out of bed, tucking Charlie under one arm. She would sit with Darren until he quieted, and leave Charlie to watch over him through the rest of the night.

The hallway was dark, which surprised her. A light always burned there in case Emma had to use the bathroom during the night. She had a bad moment at the doorway, imagining the things that lurked in the shadowy corners. She wanted to stay in her room with the grinning Mickey.

Then Darren let out a yowling cry.

There was nothing in the corners, Emma told herself as she started down the dark hallway. There was nothing there at all. No monsters, no ghosts, no squishy or slithering things.

It was the Beatles playing now.

Emma wet her lips. Just the dark, just the dark, she told herself. Her eyes had adjusted to the dark by the time she'd reached Darren's door. It was closed. That was wrong, too. His door was always left open so he could be heard easily when awakened.

She reached out, then jumped as she thought she heard something move behind her. Heart pumping, she turned to scan the dark hallway. Shifting shadows towered into nameless monsters, making sweat break out on her brow and back.

Nothing there, nothing there, she told herself, and Darren was crying his lungs out.

She turned the knob and pushed the door open.

"Come together," Lennon sang. "Over me."

There were two men in the room. One was holding Darren, struggling to keep him still while the baby screamed in fear and anger. The other had something in his hand, something that the light from the giraffe lamp on the dresser caused to glint.

"What are you doing?"

The man whirled at her voice. He wasn't a doctor, Emma thought as she made out the needle in his hand. She recognized him, and knew he wasn't a doctor. And Darren wasn't sick.

The other man swore, a short spurt of ugly words, while he fought to keep Darren from wriggling out of his arms.

"Emma," the man she knew said in a calm, friendly voice. He smiled. It was a false smile, an angry smile. She noted it, and that he still held the needle as he stepped toward her. She turned and ran.

Behind her she heard Darren call out. *"Ma!"*

Sobbing, she raced down the hall. There were monsters, her panicked mind taunted. There were monsters and things with snappy teeth in the shadows. They were coming after her now.

He nearly caught the trailing edge of her nightgown. Swearing, he dove for her. His hand skimmed over her ankle, slid off. She yelped as though she'd been scalded. As she reached the top of the stairs, she screamed for her father, shrieking his name over and over again.

Then her legs tangled. She tumbled down the flight of stairs.

In the kitchen, someone sat on the counter and ordered fifty pizzas. Shaking her head, Bev checked the freezer for ice. No one used more ice than Americans. As an afterthought, she dropped a cube in her warming wine. When in Rome, she decided, then turned toward the door.

She met Brian on the threshold.

Grinning, he hooked an arm around her waist and gave her a long, lazy kiss. "Hi."

"Hi." Still holding the wine, she linked her hands behind his neck. "Bri."

"Hmm?"

"Who are all these people?"

He laughed, nuzzling into her neck. "You've got me." The scent of her had him hardening. Moving to the sinuous beat of the Lennon/McCartney number, he brought her against him. "What do you say we take a trip upstairs and leave them the rest of the house."

"That's rude." But she moved against him. "Wicked, rude, and the best idea I've heard in hours."

"Well, then . . ." He made a halfhearted attempt to pick her up, sent them both teetering. Wine spilled cool down his back as Bev giggled. "Maybe you can carry me," he said, then heard Emma scream.

He rammed into a small table as he turned. Dizzy from drugs and booze, he stumbled, righted himself, and rushed into the foyer. There were people already gathered. Pushing through them, he saw her crumpled at the foot of the steps.

"Emma. My God." He was terrified to touch her. There was blood at the corner of her mouth. With one trembling finger, he wiped it away. He looked up into a sea of faces, a blur of color, all unrecognizable. His stomach clenched, then tried to heave itself into his throat.

"Call an ambulance," he managed, then bent over her again.

"Don't move her." Bev's face was chalk-white as she knelt beside him. "I don't think you're supposed to move her. We need a blanket." Some quick-witted soul was already thrusting a daisy afghan into her hands. "She'll be all right, Bri." Carefully, Bev smoothed the blanket over her. "She'll be just fine."

He closed his eyes, shook his head to clear it. But when he opened them again, Emma was still lying, dead-white, on the floor. There was too much noise. The music echoing off the ceilings, the voices murmuring, muttering all around. He felt a hand on his shoulder. A quick, reassuring squeeze.

"Ambulance is on the way," P.M. told him. "Hold on, Bri."

"Get them out," he whispered. He looked up and into Johnno's shocked, pale face. "Get them out of here."

With a nod, Johnno began to urge people along. The door was open, the night bright with floodlights and headlights when they heard the wail of the sirens.

"I'm going to go up," Bev said calmly. "Tell Alice what's happened, check on Darren. We'll go to the hospital with her. She's going to be fine, Brian. I know it."

He could only nod and stare down at Emma's still, pale face. He couldn't leave her. If he had dared, he would have gone into the bathroom, stuck a finger down his throat, and tried to rid his body of some of the chemicals he'd pumped into it that night.

It was all like a dream, he thought, a floaty, unhappy dream. Until he looked at Emma's face. Then it was real, much too real.

The *Abbey Road* album was still playing, the sly cut about murder. Maxwell's silver hammer was coming down.

"Bri." Johnno put a hand on his arm. "Move back now, so they can tend to her."

"What?"

"Move back." Gently Johnno eased him to his feet. "They need to have a look at her."

Dazed, Brian watched the ambulance attendants move in and crouch over his daughter. "She must have fallen all the way down the stairs."

"She'll be all right." Johnno sent a helpless look toward P.M. as they flanked Brian. "Little girls are tougher than they look."

"That's right." A bit unsteady on his feet, Stevie stood behind Brian with both hands on his shoulders. "Our Emma won't let a tumble down the stairs hold her up for long."

"We'll go to the hospital with you." Pete moved over to join them. Together they watched as Emma was carefully lifted onto a stretcher.

Upstairs, Bev screamed . . . and screamed and screamed, until the sound filled every corner of the house.

# *Chapter Nine*

· · · ·

$L$OU KESSELRING SNORED like a wounded elephant. If he indulged in a beer before bed, he snored like two wounded elephants. His wife of seventeen years coped with the nightly event by wearing earplugs. Lou knew Marge loved him in her own steady, no-nonsense way, and he considered himself fortunate and smart for not sleeping with her before marriage. He was honest, but had kept this one little secret. By the time she'd discovered it, he'd had his ring on her finger.

He was really rattling the shingles tonight. It had been nearly thirty-six hours since he'd slept in his own bed. Now that the Calarmi case was closed, he was going to enjoy not only a good night's sleep but a whole weekend of sloth.

He actually dreamed about puttering around the yard, pruning roses, playing a bit of catch with his son. They'd barbecue some burgers on the grill and Marge would make her potato salad.

He'd had to kill a man twelve hours before. It wasn't the first time, though, thank God, it was still a rare occurrence. Whenever his work took him that far, he needed, badly, the ordinary, the everyday. Potato salad and charred burgers, the feel of his wife's firm body against his during the night. His son's laughter.

He was a cop. A good one. In the six years he'd been with Homicide, this was only the second time he'd had to discharge his weapon. Like most of his colleagues he knew that law enforcement consisted of days of monotony—legwork, paperwork, phone calls. And moments, split seconds, of terror.

He also knew, as a cop, that he would see things, touch things, experience things that most of the world was unaware of —murder, ghetto wars, back-alley knifings, blood, gore, waste.

Lou was aware, but he didn't dream of his work. He was forty, and had never, since picking up his badge at the age of twenty-four, brought his work home.

But sometimes it followed him.

He rolled over, breaking off in mid-snore as the phone rang. Instinctively he reached out, and with his eyes still closed, rattled the receiver off the hook.

"Yeah. Kesselring."

"Lieutenant. It's Bester."

"What the fuck do you want?" He knew he was safe using what Marge called the F word since his wife had her earplugs in.

"Sorry to wake you up, but we've got an incident. You know McAvoy, Brian McAvoy, the singer?"

"McAvoy?" He scrubbed his hand over his face, fighting to wake up.

"Devastation. The rock group."

"Yeah, yeah. Right." He wasn't much on rock himself— unless it was Presley or the Everly Brothers. "What happened? Some kids turn up the music too loud and cook their brains?"

"Somebody killed his little boy. Looks like it might have been a bungled kidnapping."

"Ah, shit." Awake now, Lou switched on the light. "Give me the address."

The light woke Marge. She glanced over, saw Lou sitting naked on the side of the bed and scrawling on a pad. Without complaint, she got up, tucked her arms into her cotton robe, and went down to make him coffee.

♦ ♦ ♦

*L*OU FOUND BRIAN at the hospital. He wasn't certain what he'd been expecting. He'd seen Brian a few times, in newspapers, or television, when the singer had spoken out against the war. A peacenik they called him. Lou didn't think too much of the bunch that went around getting stoned and growing their hair ass-long and passing out flowers on street corners. But he wasn't sure he thought much of the war, either. He'd lost a brother in Korea, and his sister's boy had left for Vietnam three months before.

But it wasn't McAvoy's politics, or his hairstyle, that concerned Lou now.

He paused, studying Brian, who was sprawled on a flower-patterned chair. Looked younger in person, Lou decided. Young, a little too thin, and oddly pretty for a man. Brian had that dazed, dream-struck look that came with shock. There were others in the room, and smoke billowed up from a number of ashtrays.

Mechanically Brian put a cigarette to his lips, drew in, set it down again, blew out.

"Mr. McAvoy."

Repeating the routine with the cigarette, Brian glanced up. He saw a tall, leanly built man with dark hair carefully combed back from a long, sleepy face. He wore a suit, a gray one, and a conservative tie of nearly the same shade against a crisp white shirt. His black shoes were glossy, his nails neatly trimmed, and there was a slight nick on his chin where he'd cut himself shaving.

Odd the things you notice, Brian thought as he pulled on the cigarette again.

"Yes."

"I'm Lieutenant Kesselring." He took out his shield, but Brian continued to look at his face, not the ID. "I need to ask you some questions."

"Can't this wait, Lieutenant?" Pete Page took a long, hard look at the identification. "Mr. McAvoy's not in any shape to deal with this now."

"It would help us all if we got the preliminaries over with." Lou sat. After replacing his badge, he spread his hands on his knees. "I'm sorry, Mr. McAvoy. I don't want to add to your grief. I want to find out who's responsible for this."

Brian lit a cigarette from the butt of another and said nothing.

"What can you tell me about what happened tonight?"

"They killed Darren. My little boy. The took him out of his crib, and left him on the floor."

Sick at heart, Johnno snatched up his Styrofoam cup of coffee and turned away. Lou reached in his pocket for his pad and freshly sharpened pencil.

"Do you know of anyone who might have wanted to harm the boy?"

"No. Everyone loves Darren. He's so bright and funny." Brian's throat locked up, and he looked around blindly for his own cup.

"I know this is difficult. Can you tell me about tonight?"

"We had a party. We were all going to New York tomorrow, and we had a party."

"I'd like a list of the guests."

"I don't know. Bev might . . ." He trailed off, remembering that Bev was in a room down the hall, heavily sedated.

"We should be able to put together a fairly accurate list between us," Pete put in. He tried to drink more coffee, but it was burning a hole in his gut. "But you can be sure that no one Brian invited to his home would have done this."

Lou intended to find out. "Did you know everyone at the party, Mr. McAvoy?"

"I don't know. Probably not." He rested his elbows on his knees a moment to rub the heels of his hands hard against his eyes. The pain was the closest he could get to comfort. "Friends and friends of friends, and like that. You open the door and people come. It just happens."

Lou nodded as if he understood. He remembered the parties Marge planned. The careful guest lists, RSVPs, the detailed checks and rechecks of food. Their fifteenth-anniversary party had been planned as meticulously as a state dinner.

"We'll work on the list," Lou decided. "Your daughter, Emma, is it?"

"Yes, Emma."

"She was upstairs during the party."

"Yes. Asleep." His babies, tucked away, safe and sound. "They were both asleep."

"In the same room?"

"No, they have separate rooms. Alice Wallingsford, our nanny, was upstairs with them."

"Yes." He'd already had the report that the nanny had been found bound, gagged, and terrified in her own bed. "And the little girl fell down the steps?"

Brian's hand jerked spasmodically on his cup, his fingers pushing through the Styrofoam. Coffee spilled out the holes and onto the floor. "I heard her call me. I was coming out of the kitchen with Bev." He remembered, clear as a bell, that quick, norny kiss they'd shared before the scream. "We ran in, and she was on the floor at the foot of the steps."

"I saw her fall." P.M. blinked his red-rimmed eyes. "I looked up and she was tumbling down. It all happened so fast."

"You said she screamed." Lou looked back at P.M. "Did she scream before she fell, or after?"

"I . . . before. Yes, that was why I happened to look up. She called out, then seemed to lose her balance."

Lou noted it down. He'd have to talk to the little girl. "I hope she wasn't badly hurt."

"The doctors." Brian's cigarette had burned down to the filter. Dropping it in the ashtray, he switched to the inch of cold, bitter coffee that was left in the mangled cup. "They haven't come out again. They haven't told me. I can't lose her, too." The coffee spilled as his hand began to shake. Johnno sat beside him.

"Emma's tough. Kids take tumbles all the time." He sent Lou a vicious look. "Can't you leave him alone?"

"Just a few more questions." He was used to vicious looks. "Your wife, Mr. McAvoy, she found your son?"

"Yes. She went upstairs after we heard the ambulance. She wanted to check on . . . She wanted to be sure, you see, that he hadn't woke up. I heard her screaming, screaming, screaming. And I ran. When I got into Darren's room, she was sitting on the floor with him, holding him. And screaming. They had to give her something to put her out."

"Mr. McAvoy, have there been any threats against you, your wife, or your children?"

"No."

"Nothing?"

"No. Well, there's some hate mail from time to time. Political stuff mostly. Pete has it screened."

"We'd like to see everything that's come in for the last six months."

"That's quite a bundle of mail, Lieutenant," Pete told him.

"We'll manage."

Brian ignored them both and rose as the doctor came in. "Emma," was all he said. All he could say.

"She's sleeping. She has a concussion, a broken arm, and some bruised ribs, but no internal injuries."

"She's going to be all right."

"She'll need to be watched carefully for the next few days, but yes, the outlook is very good."

He cried then, as he hadn't been able to when he'd seen his son's lifeless body, as he'd been incapable of doing when they'd taken his family from him and left him in the green-walled waiting room. Hot tears poured through his fingers as he covered his face.

Quietly, Lou closed his notebook and, motioning to the doctor, stepped into the hall. "I'm Lieutenant Kesselring. Homicide." Again, Lou flashed his ID. "When will I be able to talk to the little girl?"

"Not for a day, perhaps two."

"I need to question her as soon as possible." He took out a card and handed it to the doctor. "If you'd call me as soon as she's able to talk. The wife, Beverly McAvoy?"

"Sedated. Ten or twelve hours before she should come around. Even then I won't guarantee she'll be able to talk, or that I'll be willing to allow it."

"Just call." He glanced back toward the waiting room. "I've got a son of my own, Doctor."

◆ ◆ ◆ ◆

$\mathcal{E}$MMA HAD TERRIBLE dreams. She wanted to call out for her da, for her mum, but it was as though a hand were closed over her mouth, over her eyes. Great weights seemed to press her down and down.

The baby was crying. The sound echoed in the room, in her head, until it seemed as though Darren were inside her mind, screaming to get out. She wanted to go to him, had to—but there were two-headed snakes and snarling, snapping *things* with black, dripping fangs all around her bed. Each time she tried to climb out they lunged at her, hissing, spitting, grinning.

If she stayed in bed, she'd be safe. But Darren was calling for her.

She had to be brave, brave enough to run to the door. When she did, the snakes disappeared. Beneath her feet the floor felt alive, moving, pulsing. She looked back over her shoulder. It was just her room, with toys and dolls tidily on the shelves, with Mickey Mouse smiling cheerfully. As she watched the smile turned into a leer.

She raced into the hall, into the dark.

There was music. The shadows seemed to dance to it. There were sounds. Breathing, heavy, wet breathing, snarls and the movement of something dry and slithering on the wood. As she ran toward the sounds of Darren's cries, she felt the hot breath on her arms, the quick nasty nips at her ankles.

It was locked. She pulled and pounded on the door as her brother's screams rose higher, only to be drowned out by the music. Under her small fists, the door dissolved. She saw the man, but there was no face. She saw only the glint of his eyes, the gleam of his teeth.

He started toward her, and she was more afraid of him than of the snakes and monsters, the teeth and the claws. Blind with fear, she ran, with Darren's screams rising behind her.

Then she was falling, falling into a dark pit. She heard a sound, like a twig snapping, and tried to scream out at the agony. But she could only fall silently, endlessly, helplessly, with the music and her brother's cries echoing in her head.

When she awoke, it was bright. There were no dolls on the shelves. No shelves at all, just blank walls. At first she wondered if she was in a hotel. She tried to remember, but as she did, the aching began—the hot, dull aching that seemed to throb everywhere at once. Moaning against it, she turned her head.

Her father was sleeping in a chair. His head was back, turned a bit to the side. Beneath the stubble of his beard his face was pale. In his lap, his hands were clenched into fists.

"Da."

Already on the edge of sleep, he woke quickly. He saw her lying against the white hospital sheets, her eyes wide and a little afraid. The tears welled up again, clogging his throat, burning his eyes. He fought them with what little strength he had left.

"Emma." He went to her, sitting on the edge of the bed and pressing his exhausted face against her throat.

She started to put her arm around him, but it was weighed down with the white plaster cast. That had the fear bubbling quick again. She could hear in her mind the sound of that dry snap, the screaming pain that had followed.

It hadn't been a dream—and if it had been real, then the rest . . .

"Where's Darren?"

She would ask that first, Brian thought as he squeezed his eyes tightly shut. How could he tell her? How could he tell her what he had yet to understand or believe himself? She was only a child. His only child.

"Emma." He kissed her cheek, her temple, her forehead, as if somehow that would ease the pain, for both of them. He took her hand. "Do you remember when I told you a story about angels, about how they live in heaven?"

"They fly and play music and never hurt each other."

Oh, he was clever, Brian thought bitterly, so clever to have woven such a pretty tale. "Yes, that's right. Sometimes special people become angels." He reached far back for his Catholic faith and found it weighed heavily on his shoulders. "Sometimes God loves these people so much he wants them with him up in heaven. That's where Darren is now. He's an angel in heaven."

"No." For the first time since she had crawled out from beneath the dirty sink over three years before, she pushed away from her father. "I don't want him to be an angel."

"Neither do I."

"Tell God to send him back," she said furiously. "Right now."

"I can't." The tears were coming again; he couldn't stop them. "He's gone, Emma."

"Then I'll go to heaven too, and take care of him."

"No." Fear clutched in his gut, drying his tears. His fingers dug into her shoulders, putting bruises on her for the first time. "You can't. I need you, Emma. I can't get Darren back, but I won't lose you."

"I hate God," she said, dry-eyed and fierce.

So do I, Brian thought as he gathered her close. So do I.

◆ ◆ ◆ ◆

THERE HAD BEEN over a hundred people in and out of the McAvoy house on the night of the murder. Lou's pad was overflowing with names, notes, and impressions. But he was no closer to an answer. Both the window and the door of the boy's room had been found open, though the nanny was adamant that she had closed the window after putting the boy to bed. She also insisted the window had been locked. But there had been no signs of a forced entry.

There had been footprints beneath the window. Size 11, Lou mused. But there had been no impressions in the ground a ladder would have made, and no traces of rope on the windowsill.

The nanny was little help. She'd awakened when a hand had clamped over her mouth. She'd been blindfolded, bound, and gagged. In the two interviews Lou had had with her, she'd changed her estimate of the time she'd been bound from thirty minutes to two hours. She was low on his lists of suspects, but he was waiting for the background check he'd ordered.

It was Beverly McAvoy that Lou had to see now. He'd postponed the questioning as long as possible. Longer, after he'd scanned the police photos of little Darren McAvoy.

"Keep this as brief as possible." The doctor stood with Lou outside the door. "She's been given a mild sedative, but her mind is clear. Maybe too clear."

"I don't want to make this any harder on her than it already is." What could, he wondered as the image of the young boy fixed itself in his mind. "I need to question the girl as well. Is she up to it?"

"She's conscious. I don't know if she'll talk to you. She hasn't spoken more than two words to anyone but her father."

With a nod, Lou stepped into the room. The woman was sitting up in bed. Though her eyes were open, they didn't focus on him. She looked very small and hardly old enough to have had a child, and to have lost one. She wore a pale blue bed jacket, and the hands lying on the white sheets were absolutely still.

Beside her Brian sat in a chair, his unshaven face an unhealthy shade of gray. His eyes looked old, red and puffy from tears and lack of sleep, clouded with grief. When he looked up, Lou saw something else in them. Fury.

"I'm sorry to disturb you."

"The doctor told us you'd be coming." Brian didn't rise or gesture to a chair. He simply continued to stare. "Do you know who did this?"

"Not yet. I'd like to talk with your wife."

"Bev." Brian laid a hand over hers, but there was no response. "This is the policeman who's trying to find . . . to find out what happened. I'm sorry," he said, looking back at Lou. "I don't remember your name."

"Kesselring. Lieutenant Kesselring."

"The lieutenant needs to ask you some questions." She made no move. She barely breathed. "Bev, please."

Perhaps it was the despair in his voice that reached down

deep to where she had tried to hide herself. Her hand moved restlessly in his. For a moment she closed her eyes, held them closed, wishing with all her heart that she was dead. Then she opened them again and looked straight at Lou.

"What do you want to know?"

"Everything you can tell me about that night."

"My son was dead," she said flatly. "What else matters?"

"Something you tell me could help me find who killed your son, Mrs. McAvoy."

"Will that bring Darren back to me?"

"No."

"I don't feel anything anymore." She stared at him with huge, tired eyes. "I don't feel my legs or my arms or my head. When I try to feel it hurts. So it's best not to try, isn't it?"

"Maybe, for a while." He drew up a chair beside the bed. "But if you could tell me what you remember from that night?"

She let her head fall back and stared up at the ceiling. Her monotone description of the party was similar to her husband's, and to those of the others Lou had interviewed. Familiar faces, strange faces, people coming in, going out. Someone on the kitchen phone ordering pizza.

That was a new one, and Lou noted it down.

Talking with Brian, then hearing Emma scream—finding her at the foot of the steps.

"People crowded around," she murmured. "Someone, I don't know who, called an ambulance. We didn't move her—we were afraid to move her. We heard the sirens coming. I wanted to go to the hospital with her, her and Brian, but I needed to check on Darren first, and to wake Alice and let her know what had happened.

"I stopped to get Emma's robe. I don't know why really, I just thought she might need it. I started down the hall. I was annoyed because the lights were out. We always leave the hall light on for Emma. She's afraid of the dark. Not Darren," she said with a half-smile. "He's never been afraid of a thing. We only keep a night-light in his room because it's easier for us if he wakes in the night. He often does still. He likes company." She brought a hand to her face as her voice began to shake. "He doesn't like to be alone."

"I know this is hard, Mrs. McAvoy." But she had been the

first on the scene, had found, and had moved the body. "I need to know what you found when you went into his room."

"I found my baby." She shook off Brian's hand. She couldn't bear to be touched. "He was lying on the floor, by the crib. I thought, I thought, Oh God, he's climbed up and fallen out. He was lying so still on the little blue rug. I couldn't see his face. I picked him up. But he wouldn't wake up. I shook him, and I screamed, but he wouldn't wake up."

"Did you see anyone upstairs, Mrs. McAvoy?"

"No. There was no one upstairs. Just the baby, my baby. They took him away, and they won't let me have him. Brian, for God's sake, why won't you let me have him?"

"Mrs. McAvoy." Lou rose. "I'm going to do everything I can to find out who did this. I promise you that."

"What difference does it make?" She began to cry, huge, silent tears. "What possible difference does it make?"

It made a difference, Lou thought as he stepped into the corridor again. It had to.

◆ ◆ ◆ ◆

EMMA STUDIED LOU with a straightforward intensity that made him feel awkward. It was the first time he could remember a child making him want to check his shirt for stains.

"I've seen policemen on the telly," she said when he introduced himself. "They shoot people."

"Sometimes." He groped for something to say. "Do you like television?"

"Yes. We like *Sesame Street* the best, Darren and I."

"Who do you like best, Big Bird or Kermit?"

She smiled a little. "I like Oscar because he's so rude."

Because of the smile, he took a chance and lowered the bed guard. Emma didn't object when he sat on the edge of the bed. "I haven't seen *Sesame Street* in a little while. Does Oscar still live in a garbage can?"

"Yes. And he yells at everyone."

"I guess yelling can make you feel better sometimes. Do you know why I'm here, Emma?" She said nothing, but gathered an old black stuffed dog to her chest. "I need to talk to you about Darren."

"Da says he's an angel now, in heaven."

"I'm sure he is."

"It's not fair that he went away. He didn't even say good-bye."

"He couldn't."

She knew that because she knew, deep in her heart, what you had to do to become an angel. "Da said that God wanted him, but I think it was a mistake and God should send him back."

Lou brushed a hand over her hair, moved as much by her stubborn logic as he had been by the mother's grief. "It was a mistake, Emma, a terrible one, but God can't send him back."

Her lip poked out, but it was more defiance than a pout. "God can do anything He wants."

Lou stepped uneasily onto shaky ground. "Not always. Sometimes men do things and God doesn't fix it. We have to. I think you might be able to help me find out how this mistake happened. Will you tell me about that night, the night you fell down the steps?"

She shifted her eyes to Charlie and plucked at his fur. "I broke my arm."

"I know. I'm sorry. I have a little boy. He's older than you, almost eleven. He broke his arm trying to roller-skate on the roof."

Impressed, she looked up again, eyes wide. "Really?"

"Yes. He broke his nose, too. He skated right off the roof and landed in the azalea bushes."

"What's his name?"

"Michael."

Emma wanted to meet him and ask him what it had felt like to fly off a rooftop. It sounded very brave. Like something Darren would have wanted to try. Then she began to pluck at Charlie's fur again. "Darren would have been three in February."

"I know." He took her hand. After a moment she curled her fingers around his.

"I loved him best of all," she said simply. "Is he dead?"

"Yes, Emma."

"And he can't come back, even though it was a mistake?"

"No. I'm very sorry."

She had to ask him, ask him what she hadn't dared ask her father. Her father would cry, and might not tell her the truth. This man with his pale eyes and quiet voice wouldn't cry.

"Is it my fault?" Her eyes were desperate as they shifted up to his.

"Why would you think so?"

"I ran away. I didn't take care of him. I promised I always would, but I didn't."

"What did you run away from?"

"Snakes," she said without hesitation, remembering only the nightmare. "There were snakes and things with big teeth."

"Where?"

"Around the bed. They hide in the dark and like to eat bad girls."

"I see." He took out his notepad. "Who told you that?"

"My mam—my mam before Bev. Bev says there aren't any snakes at all, but she just doesn't see them."

"And you saw the snakes the night you fell?"

"They tried to stop me from going to Darren when he cried."

"Darren was crying?"

Pleased that he hadn't corrected her about the snakes, Emma nodded. "I heard him. Sometimes he wakes up at night, but he goes back to sleep again after I talk to him and take him Charlie."

"Who's Charlie?"

"My dog." She held him out for Lou's inspection.

"He's very handsome," Lou said as he patted Charlie's dusty head. "Did you take Charlie to Darren that night?"

"I was going to." Her face clouded as she struggled to remember. "I kept him with me to scare the snakes and the other things away. It was dark in the hall. It's never dark in the hall. They were there."

His fingers tightened on his pencil. "Who was there?"

"The monsters. I could hear them squishing and hissing. Darren was crying so loud. He needed me."

"Did you go into his room, Emma?"

She shook her head. She could see herself, clearly, standing in the shadowed hallway with the sounds of hissing and snapping all around. "At the door, there was light under the door. The monsters had him."

"Did you see the monsters?"

"There were two monsters in Darren's room."

"Did you see their faces?"

"They don't have faces. One was holding him, holding him too tight and making him cry hard. He called for me, but I ran. I ran away and left Darren with the monsters. And they killed him. They killed him because I ran away."

"No." He gathered her close, letting her weep against his chest as he stroked her hair. "No, you ran to get help, didn't you, Emma?"

"I wanted my da to come."

"That was the right thing to do. They weren't monsters, Emma. They were men, bad men. And you couldn't have stopped them."

"I promised I would take care of Darren, that I wouldn't ever let anything happen to him."

"You tried to keep that promise. No one blames you, baby."

But he was wrong, Emma thought. She blamed herself. And always would.

◆ ◆ ◆ ◆

*I*T WAS NEARING midnight when Lou got home. He'd spent hours at his desk going over each note, every scrap of information. He'd been a cop for too long not to know that objectivity was his best tool. But Darren McAvoy's murder had become personal. He couldn't forget the black-and-white photo of the boy, barely out of babyhood. The image had imprinted itself into his brain.

He had an image of the child's bedroom as well. The blue and white walls, the scatter of toys as yet unpacked, the little overalls neatly folded on a rocking chair, the scuffed sneakers beneath them.

And the hypodermic, still full of phenobarbitol, a few feet away from the crib.

They'd never had a chance to use it, Lou thought grimly. They hadn't been able to stick it into a vein and put him soundly to sleep. Had they been going to carry him out the window? Would Brian McAvoy have gotten a call a few hours later demanding money for the boy's safe return?

There would be no call now, no ransom.

Rubbing his gritty eyes, Lou started up the steps. Amateurs, he thought. Bunglers. Murderers. Where the hell were they? Who the hell were they?

*What difference does it make?*

It made a difference, he told himself as his hands clenched into fists. Justice always made a difference.

The door to Michael's room was open. The soft sound of his
son's breathing drew him. He could see in the faint moonlight
the wreckage of toys and clothes strewn over the floor, heaped on
the bed, mounded on the dresser. Usually it would have made
him sigh. Michael's cheerful sloppiness was a mystery to Lou.
Both he and his wife were tidy and organized by nature. Michael
was a tornado, a rushing wind that hopped from spot to spot and
left destruction and chaos behind.

Yes, usually he would have sighed and planned his lecture for
the morning. But tonight, the wild disarray brought tears of
gratitude to his eyes. His boy was safe.

Picking his way through the rubble, he crept toward the bed.
He had to push the traffic jam of Matchbox cars aside to find a
place to sit. Michael slept on his stomach, the right side of his
face squashed into the pillow, his arms flung out and the sheets
in a messy tangle at his feet.

For a moment, then five, then ten, Lou simply sat, studying
the child he and Marge had made. The thick dark hair he'd
inherited from his mother was tousled around his face. His skin
was tanned, but still had the dewy softness of first youth. His
nose was crooked, giving character to what might have been a
face too pretty for a boy. He had a firm, compact little body that
was already beginning to sprout. Bruises and scrapes colored it.

Six years and two miscarriages, Lou thought now. Then finally he and Marge had been able to unite sperm and egg into
strong, vital life. And he was the best and brightest of both of
them.

Lou remembered Brian McAvoy's face. The stunned grief,
the fury, the helplessness. Yes, he understood.

Michael stirred when Lou stroked a hand over his cheek.
"Dad?"

"Yes. I just wanted to say good night. Go back to sleep."

Yawning, Michael shifted and sent cars clattering to the floor.
"I didn't mean to break it," he murmured.

With a half-laugh, Lou pressed his hands to his eyes. He
didn't know what *it* was, and didn't care. "Okay. I love you,
Michael."

But his son was fully back to sleep.

# Chapter Ten

• • • •

IT WAS BRIGHT, almost balmy. The breeze from the Atlantic ruffled the tall green grass. Emma listened to the secret songs it whispered. Over its music was the low, solemn voice of the priest.

He was tall and ruddy-faced with his white, white hair a shocking contrast to his black robes. Though his voice carried a lilt very similar to her father's, Emma didn't understand much of what he was saying. And didn't want to. She preferred listening to the humming grass and the monotonous lowing of the cattle on the hill beyond the gravesite.

Darren was to have his farm at last, in Ireland, though he would never ride a tractor or chase the lazy spotted cows.

It was a lovely place, with the grass so green it looked like a painting. She would remember the emerald grass and the fresh, vital scent of earth newly turned. She would remember the feel of the air against her face, air so moist from the sea it might have been tears.

There was a church nearby, a small stone structure with a white steeple and little windows of stained glass. They had gone inside to pray before the little glossy casket had been carried out. Inside it had smelled strongly, and too sweetly, of flowers and incense. Candles had been burning even though the sun ran through the stained glass in colorful streams.

There had been painted statues of people in robes, and one of a man bleeding on a cross. Brian had told her it was Jesus who was looking after Darren in heaven. Emma didn't think anyone who looked so sad and tired could take care of Darren and make him laugh.

Bev had said nothing at all, only stood, her face pale as glass. Stevie had played the guitar again, as he had at the wedding, but this time he was dressed in black and the tune was sad and quiet.

Emma didn't like it inside the church, and was glad when they stood outside in the sunlight. Johnno and P.M., whose eyes had been red from weeping, had carried the casket, along with four other men who were supposed to be her cousins. She wondered why it had taken so many to carry Darren, who hadn't been heavy at all. But she was afraid to ask.

It helped to look at the cows, and the tall grass and the birds that glided overhead.

Darren would have liked his farm, she thought. But it didn't seem right, it didn't seem fair that he couldn't be standing beside her, ready to race and run and laugh.

He shouldn't be in that box, she thought. He shouldn't be an angel, even if it meant he had wings and music. If she had been strong and brave, if she had kept her promise, he wouldn't be. She should be in the box, she realized as tears began to fall. She had let bad things happen to Darren. She hadn't saved him from the monsters.

Johnno picked her up when she began to cry. He swayed a little, and the movement was comforting. She laid her head on his shoulder and listened to the words he spoke along with the priest.

" 'The Lord is my shepherd, I shall not want . . .' "

But she did want. She wanted Darren. Blinking tears from her eyes, she tried to watch the grass move with the wind. She heard her father's voice, thick with grief.

" ' . . . walk through the valley of the shadow of death I will fear no evil . . .' "

But there was evil, she wanted to shout. There was evil, and it had killed Darren. Evil had no face.

She watched a bird swoop overhead, and followed its path. On the hilltop nearby she saw a man. He stood, overlooking the small grave and the grief, silently taking pictures.

◆ ◆ ◆ ◆

$\mathscr{H}$E WOULD NEVER be the same, Brian thought as he drank steadily, a bottle of Irish whiskey on the table near his elbow.

Nothing would ever be the same. The drink didn't ease the pain as he had hoped it would. It only made it sink its roots deeper.

He couldn't even comfort Bev. God knew he'd tried. He'd wanted to. He'd wanted to comfort her, to be comforted by her. But she was buried so deep inside the pale, silent woman who had stood beside him as their child had been put in the ground that he couldn't reach her.

He needed her, dammit. He needed someone to tell him there were reasons for what had happened, that there was hope, even now, in these the darkest days of his life. That was why he'd brought Darren here, to Ireland, why he'd insisted on the mass and the prayers and the ceremony. You were never more Catholic than you were at times of death, Brian thought. But even the familiar words, and scents, even the hope the priest had handed out as righteously as communion wafers hadn't eased the pain.

He would never see Darren again, never hold him, never watch him grow. All that talk about everlasting life meant nothing when he couldn't take his boy up in his arms.

He wanted to be angry, but he was far too tired for that, or any kind of passion. So if there was no comfort, he thought as he poured another glass, he would learn to live with the grief.

The kitchen smelled of spice cakes and good roasted meat. The scents hung on though his relatives had been gone for several hours. They had come—he wanted to be grateful for that. They had come to stand beside him, to cook the food that was somehow supposed to feed the soul. They had grieved for the loss of the boy most of them had never met.

He had pulled away from his family, Brian admitted. Because he had had his own, had made his own. Now what was left of the family he'd made was sleeping upstairs. Darren was sleeping a few miles away, beneath the shadow of a hill, beside the grandmother he had never known.

Brian drained his glass, and with oblivion on his mind, poured another.

"Son?"

Looking up, Brian saw his father hesitating in the doorway. He wanted to laugh. It was such a complete and ironic role reversal. He could remember, clear as a bell, creeping into the kitchen as a boy, while his father sat at the table getting unsteadily drunk.

"Yeah." Lifting the glass, Brian watched him over the rim.

"You should try for sleep."

He saw his father's eyes dart and linger on the bottle. Without a word, Brian pushed it toward him. He entered then, Liam McAvoy, an old man at fifty. His face was round and ruddy from the cross-stitches of broken capillaries under his skin. He had the blue, dreamy eyes that had been passed on to his son, and the pale blond hair now wiry with gray. He was gaunt, brittle-boned, no longer the big, powerful man he had seemed in Brian's youth. When he reached for the bottle, Brian felt a jolt. His father's hands might have been his own, long-fingered, graceful. Why had he never noticed before?

"It was a fine funeral," Liam said, groping. "Your mother'd be pleased you brought him here to lie with her." He poured, then thirstily downed three fingers.

Outside the soft rain of Ireland began.

They'd never drunk together before, Brian realized. He poured more whiskey into both glasses. Perhaps, at last, they would find some common ground. With a bottle between them.

"Here's a farmer's rain," Liam said, soothed by the sound and the whiskey. "A nice soft soaker."

A farmer's rain. His little boy had dreamed of being a farmer. Had he passed that much of Liam McAvoy into Darren?

"I didn't want him to be alone. I thought he should be back in Ireland, with family."

"It's right. You done right."

Brian lit a cigarette, then pushed the pack toward his father. Had they ever talked before, the two of them? If they had Brian couldn't remember. "It shouldn't have happened."

"There's a lot that happens in this world shouldn't." Liam lit the cigarette, then picked up his glass. "They'll catch the bastards who did this, boy. They'll catch them."

"It's been a week." It already seemed like years. "They've got nothing."

"They'll catch them," Liam insisted. "And the bloody bastards will rot in hell. Then the poor little lad'll rest easy."

He didn't want to think of vengeance now. He didn't want to think of his sweet little boy resting easy in the ground. Time had passed, and was lost. There had to be reasons for it.

"Why didn't you ever come?" Brian leaned forward. "I sent you tickets, for the wedding, when Darren was born, for Emma's birthday, for his. For God's sake, you never saw him until his wake. Why didn't you come?"

"Running a farm's busy work," he said between swallows. Liam was a man filled with regrets so that one easily melded into another. "Can't go larking off anytime you please."

"Not even once." Suddenly, it seemed vital that he have an answer, a true one. "You could have sent Ma. Before she died, you could've let her come."

"A woman's place is with her husband." Liam tilted his glass toward Brian. "You'd do well to remember that, boy."

"You always were a selfish bastard."

Liam's hand, surprisingly strong, clamped down on Brian's. "Mind your tongue."

"I won't run and hide this time, Da." His eyes, his voice were steady. In both was an eagerness. He would have relished a battle, here, now.

Slowly, Liam removed his hand, then picked up his glass. "I won't butt heads with you today. Not the day my grandson's been laid to rest."

"He was never yours. You never even saw him until he was dead," Brian tossed back. "You never bothered, just cashed in the tickets I sent to buy more whiskey."

"And where were you these last years? Where were you when your mother died? Off somewhere playing your bloody music."

"That bloody music put a roof over your head."

"Da." With the stuffed dog clutched in her arms, Emma stood in the doorway, her eyes wide and frightened, her lower lip trembling. She had heard the angry voices, smelled the hot odor of liquor before she stepped into the room.

"Emma." A bit unsteady, Brian walked over to pick her up, careful not to jar her arm with the cast. "What are you doing down here?"

"I had a bad dream." The snakes had come back, and the monsters. She could still hear the echo of Darren's cries.

"Hard to sleep in a strange bed." Liam got to his feet. His hand was awkward, but it was gentle as he patted her head. "Your grandda will fix you some warm milk."

She sniffled as he took out an old, dented pan. "Can I stay with you?" she asked her father.

"Sure." He carried her to a chair and sat with her on his lap.

"I woke up, and I couldn't find you."

"I'm right here, Emma." He stroked her hair, studying his father over her head. "I'll always be here for you."

◆ ◆ ◆

EVEN THERE, LOU thought. Even at such a time. He studied the grainy tabloid pictures of Darren McAvoy's funeral. He'd seen the paper at the checkout of the supermarket when he'd picked up the whole wheat bread Marge had sent him out for. Like anything that had to do with the McAvoys, it had caught his interest, and his sympathy. He'd been more than a little embarrassed to have bought it, in public, from Sally the checker.

In the privacy of his own home, he felt even more like a voyeur. For a few pieces of loose change he, and thousands of others, could witness the intimacy of grief. It was there on all the faces, though they were blurred. He could see the little girl, her arm in a cast and sling.

He wondered how much she had seen, how much she would remember. The doctors he had consulted had all claimed that if she had witnessed anything, she had blocked it. She could remember tomorrow, five years from tomorrow, or never.

### DEVASTATION AT GRAVESITE

There had been other headlines, dozens of others. Lou already had a drawerful.

### DID EMMA MCAVOY WITNESS HER BROTHER'S HORRIBLE DEATH?

### SON'S DEATH ROCKS DEVASTATION

### CHILD MURDERED DURING PARENTS' ORGY

### RITUAL KILLING OF ROCKER'S BABY: ARE MANSON FOLLOWERS RESPONSIBLE?

Garbage, Lou thought. It was all garbage. He wondered if Pete Page managed to shield the McAvoys from the worst of it. Frustrated, he rested his head in his hands and continued to stare at the picture.

He couldn't pull himself away from the case. He was bringing his work home with him now, and bringing it home with a vengeance. Files, photos, notes littered his desk in the corner of Marge's tidy living room. Though he had good men assigned with him, he double-checked all their work. He had personally interviewed everyone on the guest list he'd been given. He'd pored over the forensic reports, then had gone back again and again to comb through Darren's room.

More than two weeks after the murder, and Lou had absolutely nothing.

For amateurs, they certainly covered their tracks, he thought. And they had been amateurs, he was certain. Professionals didn't end up smothering a child that might have been worth a million in ransom, nor would they made such a poor attempt to give the illusion of a break-in.

They had been in the house. They had walked right through the front door. That was something else Lou was sure of. That didn't mean their names were on the list Page had managed to compile. Half of Southern California could have walked into the house that night—and been given a drink or a joint or whatever party drugs had been available.

There hadn't been any fingerprints in the boy's room, not even on the hypodermic needle. There were only fingerprints of the McAvoys and their nanny. It seemed that Beverly McAvoy was an excellent housekeeper. The first floor had shown the disorder expected in the aftermath of a party, but the second floor, the family floor, had been clean and ordered. Marge would have approved, he thought as he imagined the rooms. No fingerprints, no dust, no signs of struggle.

But there had been a struggle, a life-and-death struggle. Sometime during it a hand had clamped over Darren McAvoy's mouth and, perhaps inadvertently, his nose.

That struggle had occurred sometime between the time Emma had heard her brother cry—if indeed she had—and when Beverly McAvoy had gone up to check on her son.

How long had it taken? Five minutes, ten. Certainly no longer. According to the coroner, Darren McAvoy had died between two and two-thirty A.M. The ambulance call for Emma had been logged in at two-seventeen.

It didn't help, Lou thought now. It didn't help to have the times correlated, to have reams of notes and neatly labeled file folders. He needed to find just one thing out of place, one name that didn't fit, one story that didn't jibe.

He needed to find Darren McAvoy's killers. If he didn't, he knew he would forever be haunted by the boy's face, and his young sister's tearful question.

*Was it my fault?*

"Dad?"

Lou jolted, then turned to see his son standing behind him, tossing a football from hand to hand.

"Michael, don't sneak up on me like that."

"I didn't." Michael rolled his eyes when his father turned around again. If he slammed doors and walked through the house like a normal person, he was being too noisy. If he tried to be quiet, he was sneaking. A guy couldn't win.

"Dad," he said again.

"Hmmm?"

"You said you'd pass me a few this afternoon."

"When I'm finished, Michael."

Michael shifted from foot to foot in his scruffy black sneakers. In the past few weeks "When I'm finished" had been his father's standard answer. "When will you be finished?"

"I don't know, but I'll be finished faster if you don't bother me."

Hell, Michael thought, wisely keeping the oath in his mind. Nobody had time for anything anymore. His best friend was at his stupid grandmother's, and his second best friend was sick with the dumb flu or something. What good was a Saturday if you didn't get to fool around?

He tried, really, to take his father's advice. There was the Christmas tree to look at, and all the presents stacked beneath it. Michael picked up one with his name on it, the one wrapped in the paper with goofy elves dancing all over it. He shook it, carefully. The rattle was only slight but brought tremendous satisfaction.

He wanted a remote-controlled plane. It had been first on his Christmas list and written in capital letters, then underlined three times. Just so his mom and dad knew he was serious. He was sure, dead sure, it was inside that box.

He set it down again. It would be days before he could unwrap it, days before he could take it outside and make it do loops and dives.

He needed something to do *now*.

There were baking smells in the kitchen, which pleased him.

But he knew if he wandered in there, his mother would rope him into rolling out cookie dough or decorating gingerbread men. Girl stuff.

How was he ever supposed to play wide receiver for the L.A. Rams if nobody passed him the stupid football, for crying out loud?

And what was so interesting about a bunch of dopey papers and pictures anyway? Wandering back toward the desk, he ran his tongue over the tooth he'd chipped the week before while practicing wheelies on his three-speed. He liked the fact that his dad was a cop, and bragged about it all the time. Of course, when he bragged he had his dad shooting from the hip and locking up crazies like Charlie Manson for life. It would be a sad state of affairs if he had to tell the gang that his father typed out forms and studied files. Might as well be a librarian.

Tucking the football under his arm, he leaned over his father's shoulder. He had an idea that if he made a pest of himself, his father would push the papers aside and come outside. Then his gaze fell on the picture of Darren McAvoy.

"Jeez. Is that a dead kid?"

"Michael!" Lou turned, but the lecture dried on his tongue as he looked into his son's shocked and fascinated eyes. Going with instinct, he put a hand on Michael's shoulder. "Yes."

"Wow. What happened? Did he get sick or something?"

"No." He wondered if he should feel guilty for using the tragedy of one child as a lesson to another. "He was murdered."

"He's just a little kid. People aren't supposed to murder little kids."

"No. But sometimes they do."

Staring at the police photo, Michael faced his own mortality for the first time in his whirlwind eleven years. "Why?"

Lou remembered telling Emma that there were no monsters. The longer he looked at what had been done to Darren, the more certain he was that there were. "I don't know. I'm trying to find out. That's my job, to find out."

Having a cop for a father had never stopped Michael from embracing the television image of justice at work.

"How do you find out?"

"By talking to people, studying the evidence. Thinking a lot."

"Sounds boring." But he couldn't take his eyes off the picture.

"It is, mostly."

Michael was glad he'd decided to be an astronaut. He looked away from the picture and spotted the tabloid his father had just brought home. He had a sharp mind, and put it together quickly. "That's Brian McAvoy's little boy. Somebody tried to kidnap him or something but he died instead. All the kids're talking about it."

"That's right." Lou slipped the picture of Darren back into a folder.

"Wow. Wow! You're working on that case. Did you get to meet Brian McAvoy and everything?"

"I met him."

His father had met Brian McAvoy. Michael could only stare in a kind of dazed awe. "That's boss, really boss. Did you meet the rest of the group? Did you talk to them?"

Lou shook his head as he began to tidy his papers. How simple life was when you were eleven. And how simple it should be, he added as he ruffled Michael's dark, untidy hair. "Yes, I talked to them. They seem very nice."

"Nice?" Michael goggled. "They're the best. The very best. Wait until I tell the guys."

"I don't want you to tell anyone about this."

"Not tell?" Michael pushed a hand through his tousled hair. "How come? The guys'll just about fall over dead. I've got to tell them."

"No. No, you don't. I want you to keep this to yourself, Michael."

"But why?"

"Because some things are personal." He glanced back at the glaring headlines. "Or should be personal. This is one of them. Come on." He took the football, fitted it to his hand. "Let's see if you can catch my bomb."

# Chapter Eleven

♦ ♦ ♦ ♦

*P*.M. WATCHED THE sea roll up on the sand. Even after a month, it still surprised him that this house was his. The Malibu beach house, his Malibu beach house, had everything the real estate broker had promised. High, soaring ceilings, a giant stone fireplace, acres of glass. In the bedroom upstairs where his lover still slept were twin skylights, another fireplace, and a balcony that roped around the second story.

Even Stevie had been impressed when he'd passed through. It had given P.M. a wonderful sense of accomplishment to show off the rooms, the tasteful furniture, the up-to-the-minute stereo unit he'd had built in. But now Stevie was in Paris. Johnno was in New York. Brian was in London. And P.M. felt very much alone.

There was still talk about a tour when the new album was released that spring, but P.M. wasn't sure Brian would be up to it. It was nearly two months since that horrible night, and Brian was still in seclusion. He wondered if Brian knew that "Love Lost" was topping the singles charts and had gone gold. He wondered if it would matter to him.

P.M. knew the police were no closer to finding out who had killed Darren. He made it a point to stay in touch with Kesselring. It was the least he could do for Brian, and for Bev.

He thought of Bev, how pale and stricken she had looked on the day of the funeral. She hadn't spoken a word, not to anyone. He'd wanted so badly to comfort her. He hadn't known how, and the fantasy he'd had about taking her to bed, tenderly loving her until her grief passed, had shocked him so much he'd been unable to do more than pat her cold, rigid hand.

Angie Parks came down the circular stairs in a pink T-shirt that barely covered her hips. She'd taken the time to add a bit of makeup—a little mascara, a touch of lip gloss. She'd brushed out the knots sleep and sex had tied in her long blond hair, then had carefully arranged it to give it a tousled, bedroom look.

The best way to get what you wanted from a man was with sex. And she wanted quite a bit from P.M.

She glanced around the big, glass-walled living room. It was a nice start, she decided. A very nice start. She'd like to keep it as a weekend place once she'd talked P.M. into Beverly Hills. That was where stars lived, and she had every intention of being a star.

P.M. was her stepping-stone. Her romantic liaison with him had already led to a handful of commercials and a nice supporting role in a TV movie. She wanted better things, bigger things, and was willing to keep P.M. happy to get them.

She was grateful to him. Without the interest that had come her way since the press had picked up on their affair, she might have had to take a turn doing some porno flicks. A girl had to pay the rent. Angie flexed her wrist so that the light caught the diamonds and sapphires in the bracelet P.M. had given her. She wouldn't have to worry about rent any longer.

She turned toward the glass doors and saw him standing on the deck. As he stood in the early sunlight she thought he looked almost handsome. And lonely. Even a heart as naturally ambitious as Angie's could feel some pity. He hadn't been the same since the little boy had died. She was sorry about it, really, but the tragedy had made P.M. even more dependent on her. And the press was worth its weight in gold. A smart woman took whatever opportunities came her way and made the most of them.

She ran a hand over her breasts, pleased that they were firm enough to stand without a bra. She walked up behind him, pressed them against his back as she wound her arms around his neck.

"I missed you, honey."

He lifted a hand to hers, embarrassed that his first thought had been of Bev. "I didn't want to wake you up."

"You know I love it when you wake me up." She slipped around him, her arms like long, soft ropes. With a little catchy sigh, she closed her mouth over his. "I hate to see you looking so sad."

"I was just thinking about Bri. I'm worried about him."

"You're a good friend, honey." She played light, quick kisses over his face. "That's one of the things I love most about you."

He drew her closer, as always stunned and delighted to hear her say she loved him. She was so beautiful with her big brown eyes and kewpie-doll mouth. Her breathy voice was like music she played only for him.

She only pressed closer when he ran his hands up her legs to knead the firm flesh of her buttocks. Her body was like a dream, long and lush and tanned as golden as a peach. When she shuddered, he felt like a king.

"I need you, Angie."

"Then take me."

She let her head fall back, looking at him from under carefully darkened lashes. Slowly, keeping her eyes on him, she reached down, and taking the hem of her shirt, pulled it up and over her head. In the sunlight, she stood erotically naked, her breasts rosily tipped and as golden as the rest of her. He kept his senses long enough to pull her inside the doors before he lowered her to the floor.

She let him do whatever he liked, enjoying most of it, adding a few calculated groans and cries when she thought it appropriate. It wasn't that he didn't excite her. He did, in a mild sort of way. She would have preferred it if he'd been a bit more forceful, put a few bruises on her.

But P.M.'s chunky drummer's hands were almost reverent as they skimmed over her. Even when his breath began to chug and the sweat began to roll, he treated her like fine glass, too considerate to put his full weight on her, too polite, even in passion, to ram himself into her and make her cries sincere.

He took her gently, with a steady rhythm that brought her just inches from full satisfaction. He lay on her only a moment, while he collected himself and she studied the glossy wood of the ceiling. Ever mindful of his weight, he rolled aside and cushioned her head with his arm.

"Oh, that was wonderful." She stroked his damp, pale chest. Always practical, she knew she could finish herself off when she went upstairs. "You're the best, honey. The very best."

"I love you, Angie." He let his hand linger in her hair. This was what he wanted, he realized. All that crazed, nameless sex had never been for him. He wanted to know, when he went on the road, that there was someone waiting for him, at home, or in those miserable hotel rooms. He wanted what Brian had.

Not Bev, P.M. assured himself on a painful twinge of disloyalty. But a wife, a family, a home. With Angie, he could have it all.

"Angie. Will you marry me?"

She went very still. It was everything she'd hoped for, and it was happening. She could already see the casting agents scrambling for her—and the huge white house in Beverly Hills. The smile lit her face. She nearly laughed with it. Then, taking a deep breath, she shifted. There were tears in her eyes when she looked down at him.

"Do you mean it? Do you really want me?"

"I'll make you happy, Angie. Look, I know it can't be easy being married to someone who's part of what I'm part of. The tours and the fans and the press. But we can make something for ourselves, just the two of us, that's ours, only ours."

"I love what you are," she told him with complete honesty.

"Then will you? Will you marry me, and start a family?"

"I'll marry you." She threw her arms around him. A family was a different matter altogether, she thought as he lowered her to the floor again. But as the wife of P. M. Ferguson, her career had no place to go but up.

♦ ♦ ♦ ♦

BRIAN DIDN'T KNOW how much more he could take, kicking around the big house day after day, sleeping night after night beside a woman who cringed away from his slightest touch.

He was on the phone nearly every day, hoping Kesselring could give him something, anything. He needed a name, a face that he could vent his helpless fury on.

He had nothing but an empty nursery, and a wife who drifted through the house like the ghost of the woman he loved.

And Emma. Thank God for Emma.

Rubbing his hands over his face, he pushed back from the table where he'd been trying to compose. He knew if it hadn't been for Emma over the past weeks, he'd have gone insane.

She was grieving too, silently, sadly. Often he sat up with her long past her bedtime, telling her stories, singing, or just listening. They could make each other smile, and when they did the pain eased.

He was terrified every moment she was out of the house. Even the bodyguards he'd hired to see her to school and back again didn't take away the gut-knotting fear he felt when she walked out the door.

And how would he feel when it was time for him to walk out the door? No matter how much he missed his son, the day would come when he needed to go back to the stage, back to the studio, back to the music. He could hardly tie a six-year-old girl around his waist and haul her with him.

And there was no leaving her with Bev. Not now, and not, as Brian saw it, in the near future.

"Mr. McAvoy, excuse me."

"Yes, Alice." They had kept her on, though there was no child to nurse. She nursed Bev now, Brian thought and dug a cigarette from the pack he'd tossed on the table.

"Mr. Page is here to see you."

Brian glanced back at the table, the scatter of paper, the jumble of lyrics and half-phrases. "Bring him on in here."

" 'Lo, Bri." With one look Pete took in the evidence of a man struggling to work without much success. Balls of paper, a cigarette smoldering in an overflowing ashtray, the faint scent of liquor, though it was barely noon. "Hope you don't mind me popping 'round. I have some business and I didn't think you'd care to come in to the office."

"No." He reached for the bottle that was never far from his hand. "Have a drink?"

"I'll hold off a bit, thanks." He sat, trying for an easy smile. The mood between them was stiff and uncharacteristically formal. No one seemed to know how to behave around Brian, what questions to ask, what questions to avoid. "How's Bev?" he ventured.

"I don't know." Remembering his cigarette, Brian plucked it out from among the butts. "She won't say very much, won't go out at all." He let out smoke with a long, uneven sigh. When he looked at Pete there was both a plea and defiance in his eyes. The same, Pete thought, as there had been years before when Brian had come to him, asking for management. "Pete, she sits in Darren's room for hours at a time. Even at night, sometimes I'll wake up and find her in there, just sitting in that bloody rocking chair." He took a swallow from his glass, then another, deeper. "I don't know what the hell to do."

"Have you thought of therapy?"

"You mean a psychiatrist?" Brian pushed away from the table. The ash from his cigarette crumbled onto the rug. He was a simple man, from simple people. Problems, private problems, were handled privately. "What good would it do for her to talk about her sex life and how she hated her father or some bloody thing?"

"It's just an idea, Bri." Pete reached out a hand, then dropped it to the arm of his chair. "Something to think about."

"Even if I thought it might help, I don't know if I could get her to agree."

"Maybe she just needs a bit more time. It's only been a couple of months."

"He'd have been three last week. Oh, Jesus."

Saying nothing, Pete rose to pour more whiskey into Brian's glass. He handed it over, then eased Brian into a chair. "Do you hear anything from the police?"

"I talk to Kesselring. They're no closer. That makes it worse somehow. Not knowing who."

Pete sat again. They needed to get past this thing, all of them, and move ahead. "What about Emma?"

"The nightmares have stopped, and the cast comes off in a few weeks. She has school to keep it off her mind, but it's always there. You can see it in her eyes."

"She hasn't remembered any more?"

Brian shook his head. "Christ, Pete, I don't know if she saw anything or just had a bad dream. It's all monsters with Emma. I want it behind her. Somehow we've got to put it behind all of us."

Pete paused a moment, considering. "That's one of the reasons I'm here. I don't want to push you, Bri, but the record company would very much like a tour to commence with the release of the new album. I've put them off, but I wonder if it might not be good for you."

"A tour would mean leaving Bev, and Emma."

"I realize that. Don't give me an answer now. Think about it." He took out a cigarette, lighted it. "We can go through Europe, America, Japan, if you and the lads are willing. The work might be just what you need to help you through."

"And it would sell plenty of records."

Pete gave a thin smile. "There's that. No pushing an album over the top these days without touring. Speaking of records, I signed that new boy on. Robert Blackpool. I think I mentioned him."

"Yes. You said you had high hopes."

"And so I do. You'd like his style, Bri, which is why I want you to let him record 'On the Wing.'"

Simple surprise had Brian pausing before he drank again. "We always record our own music."

"So you have, thus far. But it's good business all around to expand a bit." Pete waited a moment, gauging Brian's mood. Because he sensed it was more responsive than he'd expected, he pressed on. "You pulled that particular piece from the last album, and it suits Blackpool to the ground. It wouldn't hurt to have a new artist record a ditty you and Johnno turned out. In fact in this case it'll only enhance your reputations as songwriters."

"I don't know." He rubbed his hands over his eyes. It didn't seem to matter. "I'll run it by Johnno."

"I already have." Pete smiled. "He's agreeable if you are."

◆ ◆ ◆ ◆

𝓑RIAN FOUND BEV in Darren's room. Though it cost him, he went inside, trying not to look at the empty crib, at the toys neatly stacked on the shelves, at the huge teddy bear he and Bev had bought before Darren had been born.

"Bev." He laid a hand on hers and waited, fruitlessly, for her to look at him.

She was too thin. The bones in her face were too prominent for elegance now. The luster in her eyes, her hair, her skin was gone. He found himself gritting his teeth to keep from grabbing her by the shoulders and shaking her until life bloomed in her again.

"Bev, I was hoping you'd come down and have some tea."

She could smell the liquor. It turned her stomach. How could he sit and drink and scribble his music? She took her hand from his and laid it in her lap. "I don't want any tea."

"I have some news. P.M.'s gotten himself married."

She looked at him then, a flick of a disinterested glance.

"He was hoping we'd come out for a short while. He'd like to show off his house at the beach and his chesty new wife."

"I'll never go back there." There was such quick, angry violence in her voice, he nearly stepped back. But it wasn't emotion that stunned him nearly so much as the look in her eyes when they met his. Loathing.

"What do you want from me?" he demanded. He bent close, gripping both arms of the rocker. "What the hell do you want?"

"Just leave me alone."

"I have left you alone. I've left you alone to sit in here hour after hour. I've left you alone when I've needed so badly just to hold on to you. And at night, I've left you alone when I've waited for you to turn to me. Just once to turn to me. Goddamn you, Bev, he was mine, too."

She said nothing, but the tears began. When he reached for her, she jerked away. "Don't touch me. I can't bear it." When he backed off, she slipped out of the chair to go to the crib.

"You can't bear me to touch you," he began as his fury built. "You can't stand me to look at you, or speak to you. Hour after hour, day after day, you sit in here as if you're the only one who hurts. It's time to stop, Bev."

"It's easy for you, isn't it?" She snatched a blanket from the crib to press it to her breasts. "You can sit and drink and write your music as if nothing happened. It is so bloody easy for you."

"No." Weary, he pressed his fingers to his eyes. "But I can't just stop living. He's gone, and I can't change it."

"No, you can't change it." The helpless grief welled up to rub the wound raw. "You had to have the party that night. All those people in our home. Your family was never enough for you, and now he's gone. You had to have more, more people, more music. Always more. And one of those people you let into our home killed my baby."

He couldn't speak. If she had taken a knife and slashed him from heart to gut there might have been less pain. Certainly less shock. They stood, with the empty crib between them.

"He didn't let the monsters in." Emma stood in the doorway, her books dangling from their strap, her eyes dark against her white skin. "Da didn't let the monsters in." Before Brian could speak, she was rushing down the hall, her sobs trailing behind her.

"Good job," Brian managed to say while his jaw clenched and unclenched. "Since you want to be alone, I'll take Emma and go."

She wanted to call after him, but couldn't. Tired, much too tired, she sank into the rocker again.

♦ ♦ ♦

$\mathscr{I}$T TOOK HIM AN HOUR to calm Emma. When her tears had put her to sleep, he began his calls. His decision made, he ended with Pete.

"We're leaving for New York tomorrow," he said shortly. "Emma and I. We'll hook up with Johnno, take a few days. I need to find her a good school and arrange security. Once she's settled, and safe, we'll go to California and begin rehearsals. Fix up the tour, Pete, and make it a long one." He took a hard pull of whiskey. "We're ready to rock."

# *Chapter Twelve*

♦ ♦ ♦ ♦

$S$HE DOESN'T WANT to go back." Brian watched Emma wander around the rehearsal hall with her new camera. He'd given it to her during their tearful goodbye at Saint Catherine's Academy for Girls in upstate New York.

"She'd barely been there a month before this spring-break thing," Johnno reminded him. But he felt a twinge for the little girl as she snapped a picture of Stevie's Martin on its stand in the corner. "Give her a bit of time to adjust."

"It seems all we do is adjust." It had been eight weeks since he'd walked out on Bev, and he still ached for her. The women he'd taken since were like a drug, the drugs like women. Both only eased the pain for moments at a time.

"You could call her," Johnno suggested, reading his partner's thoughts with the ease of a long relationship.

"No." He'd considered it, more than once. But the papers had been full of their separation, and his appetite since. He doubted if he and Bev would have anything to say to each other that wouldn't make things worse. "My concern now's for Emma. And the tour."

"Both'll be smashing." Johnno glanced over, giving a pointed look toward Angie. "With a few exceptions."

Brian merely shrugged and began to noodle on the piano. "If she clinches that movie deal, she'll be out of our hair."

"Smarmy little bitch. Did you see that rock she had P.M. spring for?" Johnno tilted his head and affected an upper-class accent. "Too, too tacky, dearie."

"Draw the claws. As long as P.M.'s bonkers over her, we're stuck. And we've more to worry about than our little Angie." He watched Stevie come back into the hall.

He was spending more and more time in the bathroom, Brian noted. And it didn't have anything to do with his bladder. Whatever Stevie had jabbed or swallowed or snorted this time had him flying. He stopped by Emma to give her a quick swing, then picked up his guitar. As the amp was off, his frantic riff was soundless.

"Best to wait until he's down to talk to him about it," Johnno suggested. "If you can catch him when he is." He started to add something, then decided that Brian had enough on his mind. It would hardly do any good to tell him what he'd heard before they'd left New York.

Imagine Jane Palmer writing a book. Of course someone else would do the work, like putting sentences together. Still, he imagined Jane would get a princely sum for it. And whatever she said in her little public diary wasn't likely to please Brian. Best to let Pete handle it, he decided, and not hit Brian with what was already going on until after the tour.

Emma paid little attention to the rehearsal when it got back into swing. She'd heard all the songs before, dozens of times. Most of them were from the album her da and the others had made when they'd been in California before. She'd been allowed to go to the studio a few times. Once Bev had brought Darren.

She didn't want to think of Darren because it hurt too much. Then she was struck with a miserable wave of guilt because she tried to block him out.

She missed Charlie, too. She'd left him behind in London in Darren's crib. She hoped Bev would take care of him. And maybe one day, when they went back home, Bev would talk to her again, and laugh, as she once had.

She didn't understand very much about penance, but she thought leaving Charlie behind was only right.

Then there was school. She was certain that having to go to that place, so far away from everyone she loved best, was her punishment for not taking care of Darren as she'd promised.

She remembered being punished before, the slaps and shouts. It seemed easier, she thought now, because once the slaps were over, so was the punishment. There seemed no end to her current banishment.

Da didn't call it a punishment, she mused. He said she was going to a good school where she would learn to be smart. Where she would be safe. There were men there to watch her. Emma hated that. They were big, silent men with bored eyes. Not like Johnno and the others. She wanted to go from city to city with them, even if it meant going on airplanes. She wanted to stay in hotels and bounce on the beds and order tea from room service. But she was going back to school, back to the sisters with the kind eyes and firm hands, back to morning prayers and grammar lessons.

She glanced back as her father peeled into "Soldier Blues." It was another song about the war, its hard-edged lyrics set to a harder-edged beat. She didn't know why it appealed to her. Perhaps it was P.M.'s cymbal-crashing style or Stevie's frantic, blood-pumping guitar. But when Johnno's voice merged with Brian's, she lifted her camera.

She liked to take pictures. It never occurred to her that the camera was too expensive and difficult to master for a child of her age. Just as it had never occurred to her that giving it had been a sop to Brian's guilt for tucking her away in an obscure school.

"Emma."

She turned to study a tall, dark man. He wasn't one of the bodyguards, she realized, but there was something familiar about his face. Then she remembered. She smiled a little because he had been kind when he'd come to see her in the hospital, and he hadn't embarrassed her when she'd cried on his shoulder.

"Do you remember me?" Lou asked her.

"Yes. You're the policeman."

"That's right." He put a hand on the boy beside him, trying to draw his son's attention away from the group rehearsing. "This is Michael. I told you about him."

She brightened even more, but was too shy to ask him about roller-skating off rooftops. "Hello."

"Hi." He gave her a quick glance, a fleeting smile. It was all he could spare before his eyes were riveted to the four men in the center of the hall.

"We need the horns," Brian began when he signaled a halt. "Can't get the full sound without them." His heart stopped when he spotted the man beside Emma, then slowly, thickly began beating again. "Lieutenant."

"Mr. McAvoy." After a quick warning glance at his son, Lou crossed the hall. "I'm sorry to interrupt your rehearsal, but I wanted to speak to you again, and your daughter, if possible."

"Do you—"

"No. I have very little to add to what you already know. But if I could have a few minutes of your time?"

"Sure. You chaps want to go for lunch? I'll catch up with you."

"I could hang around," Johnno offered.

"No." Brian gave his shoulder a quick squeeze. "Thanks."

Emma caught the look in Michael's eyes. She'd seen the same expression in those of the girls at school when they'd discovered who her father was. Her lips curved a little. She liked his face, the slightly crooked nose, the clear gray eyes.

"Would you like to meet them?"

Michael had to wipe his sweaty palms on his jeans. "Yeah. That'd be boss."

"I hope you don't mind," Lou said to Brian as he noted that Emma had spared him from asking. "I brought my son along. Not strictly procedure, but—"

"I understand." Brian took a long, envious look at the boy as Michael beamed up at Johnno. Would Darren have been so bright, so sturdy at eleven? "Why don't I send him an album? The new one won't be released for a couple of weeks yet. He'll be the hit of the schoolyard."

"That's very kind of you."

"It's nothing. I've a strong feeling that you've put more time in on what happened to Darren than you're required to."

"Neither one of us has nine-to-five jobs, Mr. McAvoy."

"Right. I always hated cops." He gave a thin smile. "I guess you do until you really need one. I've hired a private-detective firm, Lieutenant."

"Yes, I know."

It was strange, but Brian felt the easiness of his own laugh. "Yes, I suppose you do. They reported to me that you've covered more ground than five cops might in the last months. That's the only thing they've been able to tell me that you haven't. One would almost think you want them as much as I do."

"He was a beautiful boy, Mr. McAvoy."

"Yes, by Jesus he was." He looked down at the guitar still in his hands. Because he wanted to fling it, he set it with exaggerated care on its stand. "What would you like to talk to me about?"

"Just a few details I'd like to go over again. I know it's repetitious."

"It doesn't matter."

"I'd also like to talk to Emma again."

The easiness passed as quickly as it had come. "She can't tell you anything."

"Maybe I haven't asked the right questions yet."

Brian ran a hand through his hair. He'd had several inches cut off and was still surprised when his hand ran through it and into air. "Darren's gone, and I can't risk Emma's state of mind. She's delicate at the moment. She's only six, and for the second time in her life, she's been uprooted. I'm sure you've read that my wife and I are separated."

"I'm sorry."

"It's hardest on Emma. I don't want her upset again."

"I won't push." He tabled his idea of suggesting hypnosis.

Enjoying her role as hostess, such as it was, Emma brought Michael over to her father. "Da, this is Michael."

"Hello, Michael."

"Hello." Finding his tongue tied in knots, Michael could only grin foolishly.

"Do you like music?"

"Oh yeah. I've got lots of your records." He wanted desperately to ask for an autograph, but was afraid he'd seem like a jerk. "It was great hearing you play, and all. Just about the greatest."

"Thanks."

Emma took a picture. "My da can send you a copy," she said, admiring Michael's chipped front tooth.

♦ ♦ ♦ ♦

WHEN LOU LEFT, leading his reluctant son out of the rehearsal hall, he had the beginnings of a headache and a nasty case of frustration. He'd kept his promise and hadn't pushed Emma. He hadn't been able to. The moment he had mentioned the night her brother had died her eyes had gone blank and her body had stiffened. Instinct told him she had seen or heard something, but her memory of that night was already blurred. It was peopled with monsters and snarling shadows.

He didn't care to admit that breaking the case depended on a terrified six-year-old whose memory of that night, according to the psychologists he'd interviewed, might never return.

There was still the pizza man, Lou thought grimly. It had taken him two days to locate the right shop and the clerk who'd been working the graveyard shift. He'd remembered the order for fifty pizzas, and had considered it a joke. But he'd also remembered the name of the person who'd placed the order.

Tom Fletcher, a session musician who played both alto and tenor sax, had had a yen for pizza that night. It had taken weeks to track him down, and weeks more to put through the paperwork to bring the musician back from his gig in Jamaica.

Lou preferred pinning his hopes there. Whoever had been in Darren's room hadn't come back down the main stairs or climbed out of the window. That left the kitchen stairs where Tom Fletcher had been trying to convince the night clerk to deliver fifty pizzas with everything.

"Hey, Dad, that was the best." Michael dragged his feet on the sidewalk to give himself a few more moments. He pulled open the door of his father's '68 Chevelle, craning his neck to look at the upper windows of the building at his back. "The guys are going to go nuts when I tell them. It's okay to tell them now, right? Everybody knows you've got the case."

"Yeah." Lou pinched the bridge of his nose between his thumb and forefinger. He wasn't sure if the headache had been brought on by tension or the furious pulse of music. "Everybody knows." He'd burrowed his way through a trio of press conferences.

"How come they got all those security guards?" Michael wanted to know.

"What guards?"

"Those." As his father settled into the driver's seat, Michael pointed to the four dark-suited, broad-shouldered men near the entrance of the building.

"How do you know they're guards?"

"Come on." Michael rolled his eyes. "You can always tell cops. Even rent-a-cops."

Lou wasn't sure if he should wince or laugh. He wondered how his captain would feel if he knew the average eleven-year-old could make an undercover cop. "To keep people from hassling them, maybe hurting them. And the little girl," Lou added. "Someone might try to kidnap her."

"Jeez. You mean they've got to have guards all the time?"

"Yes."

"Bummer," Michael murmured sincerely, no longer sure he wanted to pursue the idea of becoming a rock star. "I'd hate to have people watching me all the time. I mean, how could you have any secrets?"

"It's tough."

As his father pulled away from the curb, Michael cast one last look over his shoulder. "Can we go to McDonald's?"

"Yeah. Sure."

"I guess she doesn't get to do that much."

"What?"

"The little kid. Emma. I guess she doesn't get to go to Mc-Donald's."

"No." Lou ruffled his boy's hair. "I guess not."

It took only a few minutes to get Michael settled in with a cheeseburger, fries, and a shake. Lou left his son in the booth to call in. From the phone outside the window he could see Michael dousing more ketchup on the burger. "Kesselring," he said. "I'll be in the station in an hour."

"I got some bad news for you, Lou."

"What else is new?"

"It's Fletcher, your pizza man."

"Didn't he make it into L.A.?"

"Yeah, he made it in. Sent a couple of uniforms to pick him up this morning for questioning. Seems they were about six hours too late. He'd been dead that long."

"Shit."

"Looks like a standard OD. He had the works and some top-grade heroin. We're waiting on the coroner's report."

"That's great. That's fucking great." He slammed a hand against the wall of the booth, hard enough to make a mother hurry her three children by. "Have the lab boys been over his hotel room?"

"Top to bottom."

"Give me the address." He fumbled for his notebook. "I have to drop my kid at home, after that I'll have a look."

Lou noted it down, swore again, and banged the receiver. He opened the door, then to give himself a moment, leaned against it. Through the window he could see his son cheerfully plowing through the cheeseburger.

# Chapter Thirteen

• • • •

Saint Catherine's Academy, 1977

*T*WO MORE WEEKS, Emma thought. Two more long, boring, rotten weeks, and she'd be out for the summer. She'd be able to see her father, and Johnno and the rest. She'd be able to breathe without being told she was breathing for God. She'd be able to think without being warned about impure thoughts.

As far as she could see, the nuns must be full of impure thoughts or else they wouldn't be so sure everyone else had them.

She would be going back to the real world for a few precious weeks. New York. Emma closed her eyes a moment, trying to bring its noise, its smells, its life into her quiet room. With a sigh, she propped her elbows on her desk, slouching in a way that would have made Sister Mary Alice crack her ruler. She didn't bend over the French verbs she was supposed to conjugate, but looked out over the green lawns to the high stone walls that closed the school off from the sinful world.

Not all the sinful world, she thought. She was full of sin, and was grateful her roommate, Marianne Carter, was equally blighted. Her days at Saint Catherine's would have been torture without Marianne.

She grinned as she thought of her funny, freckled, redheaded roomie and best friend. Marianne was sinful, all right, and was even now doing penance for her latest transgression. The caricature Marianne had sketched of Mother Superior was worth a couple of hours scrubbing bathrooms.

If it hadn't been for Marianne, she might have run away. Though where she would have run, she hadn't a clue.

There was really only one place she wanted to go, and that was to her father. And he would have shipped her right back.

It wasn't fair. She was nearly thirteen, nearly a real teenager, and she was stuck in this antiquated school conjugating verbs, reciting catechism, and dissecting frogs. Gross.

It wasn't that she hated the nuns. Well, she admitted, perhaps she did hate Sister Immaculata. The Warden. But who wouldn't hate someone with a pruny mouth, a wart on her nose, and a fondness for giving young girls extra chores for the teeniest infractions?

But Da had only been amused when she'd told him about Sister Immaculata.

She missed him; she missed all of them.

She wanted to go home. But she wasn't sure where home would be. Often she thought about the house in London, the castle where she had been so happy for such a short time. She thought about Bev and hated it that her father never spoke of her. Even though they had never divorced, Emma thought. Some of the girls at school had parents that were divorced, but you weren't supposed to talk about it.

She still thought of Darren, her sweet little brother. Sometimes she could barely remember how he had looked, how he had sounded. But when she dreamed of him, his face, his voice, were as clear as life.

She remembered almost nothing about the night he had died. Nuns tended to drum such pagan nonsense as monsters out of young girls' heads. But again, if she dreamed of that night, as she did when she was ill or upset, she remembered the terror of walking down the dark hall, the sounds all around, the dark monsters holding Darren as he cried and struggled. She remembered falling.

And when she awoke, she would remember nothing at all.

Marianne came through the door in an exaggerated stagger. She held out her hands. "Ruined." She dropped backward onto her bed. "What French count would want to kiss them now?"

"Rough going?" Emma asked, struggling not to grin.

"Five bathrooms. Dis-gus-ting. Ugh. When I get out of this joint, I'm going to have a housekeeper for my housekeeper." She rolled over on her stomach, crossing her ankles in the air. Emma only smiled, enjoying the sound of Marianne's brisk American voice. "I heard Mary Jane Witherspoon talking to Teresa

O'Malley. She's going to do it with her boyfriend when she goes home this summer."

"Who?"

"I dunno. His name's Chuck or Huck or something."

"No, I mean Mary Jane or Teresa?"

"Mary Jane, you dork. She's sixteen and built."

Emma frowned down at her own flat chest. She wondered if she'd have boobs to speak of when she hit sixteen. And if she'd have a boyfriend to do it with.

"What if she gets pregnant like Susan did last spring?"

"Oh, Mary Jane's folks would fix it up. They've got piles of money. Anyway, she's got something. A diaphragm."

"Everyone has a diaphragm."

"Not that kind, dummy. It's birth control."

"Oh." As always, Emma was ready to defer to Marianne's greater knowledge.

"You put it in, you know, inside the sacred vault, with jelly and it kills off the sperm. You can't get knocked up with dead sperm." Marianne rolled over to yawn at the ceiling. "I wonder if Sister Immaculata ever did it."

The thought was enough to bring Emma completely out of the dumps. "I don't think so. I'm pretty sure she bathes in her habit."

"Holy hell, I nearly forgot." Marianne rolled again, and digging into the pocket of her rumpled uniform, pulled out a half-pack of Marlboros. "I struck gold in the second-floor john." She scrambled up to search through her underwear drawer for a pack of matches. "Somebody had them taped to the back of the tank."

"And you took them."

"The Lord helps those who help themselves. I helped myself. Lock the door, Emma."

They shared one, blowing little puffs of smoke out the open window. Neither enjoyed the taste particularly, but gamely dragged on. It was adult and sinful, two things both of them craved.

"Two more weeks," Emma said dreamily.

"You're going to New York. They're sending me to camp again."

"It won't be so bad. Sister Immaculata won't be there."

"That's something." Marianne tried to adopt a sophisticated

pose with the cigarette. "I'm going to try to talk them into letting me stay with my grandmother for a couple of weeks. She's pretty cool."

"I'll take lots of pictures."

Marianne nodded, thinking further ahead. "When we get out of this place, we're going to get an apartment, like in Greenwich Village or L.A. Someplace cool. I'll be an artist and you'll be a photojournalist."

"We'll have parties."

"The biggest. And we'll wear all kinds of gorgeous clothes." She held out the hem of her uniform. "No plaids."

"I'd rather die."

"It's only four more years."

Emma turned to gaze out the window. It was hard to think in terms of years when she wasn't sure how to get through the next two weeks.

◆ ◆ ◆ ◆

*A* CONTINENT AWAY, Michael Kesselring studied himself in cap and gown. He couldn't believe it. It was finally over. High school was behind him and life was just around the next bend. There was college, of course, but that was a summer away.

He was eighteen, old enough to drink, to vote, and thanks to President Carter, had no military draft to interrupt his plans.

Whatever they were, he thought.

He hadn't a clue what he wanted to do with the life that was ahead of him. His part-time job at Buzzard's Tee Shirt Shop was mainly for gas and date money. He had no intention of spending his life screen-printing T-shirts. But just what he would do was still a cloudy mystery.

It was a little scary taking off the cap and gown. Like shedding his youth. He held them both in his hands as he scanned his room. It was cluttered with clothes, mementos, record albums, and since his mother had long since given up on cleaning it herself, his cache of *Playboys*. There were the letters he'd earned in track and baseball. The letters, he remembered, that had convinced Rose Anne Markowitz to climb into the backseat of his secondhand Pinto and do it to the tune of Joe Cocker's *Feeling Alright.*

He'd been blessed with a tough athletic body, long legs, and quick reflexes. Like his father, his mother was fond of saying. He supposed in some way he took after the old man, though their relationship had had its share of battles. Over hair length, wardrobe, politics, curfews. Captain Kesselring was a stickler.

Came from being a cop, Michael supposed. He remembered being careless enough once to bring a single joint into the house. He'd been grounded for a month. And a few lousy speeding tickets had cost him just as dearly.

The law was the law, old Lou was fond of saying, Michael thought now. Thank God he himself had no intention of being a cop.

He took the tassel from the cap before tossing it and the gown onto his unmade bed. Maybe it was sentimental to keep it, but nobody had to know. He routed through his dresser drawers for the old cigar box that held some of his most valued possessions. The love letter Lori Spiker had written him in his junior year—before she'd dumped him for a biker with a Harley and tattoos. The ticket stub from the Rolling Stones' concert he had, after a lot of blood and sweat, convinced his parents to let him attend. The pop top from his first illegal beer. He grinned and, pushing it aside, found the snapshot of himself and Brian McAvoy.

The little girl had kept her word, Michael thought. The picture had arrived in the mail only two weeks after the incredible day his dad had taken him to meet Devastation. The new album had come with it, the hot-off-the-presses copy. He had been the envy of his contemporaries for weeks.

Michael thought back to that day, the almost unendurable excitement he'd felt, the sweaty armpits. He hadn't thought about that day in a long time. Now, perhaps because of his newly acquired adult status, it occurred to him that it had been a terrific thing for his father to do. And uncharacteristic. Not that the old man couldn't come up with terrific things, but he had gone to the rehearsal hall on police business. Captain Lou Kesselring never mixed police business and personal pleasures.

But he had that day, Michael thought.

It was strange, but now that he was remembering it all, he could picture his father dragging home files, night after night. As far as Michael could recollect, his father had never brought home work that way before, or since.

The little boy, Brian McAvoy's little boy, had been murdered. It had been in all the papers, and still cropped up from time to time, perhaps because the police had never solved the case.

His father's case, Michael recalled.

That had been the year Michael had been named MVP on his Little League team. And his father had missed most of the games. And a lot of dinners.

It had been a long time ago, Michael mused, but he wondered if his father ever thought about Brian McAvoy and his dead son. Or the little girl who had taken the picture. Some people said that she'd seen what had happened to her brother and had gone crazy. But she hadn't looked crazy when Michael had met her. He remembered her only vaguely as a slight girl with pale hair and big sad eyes. And a soft, prettily accented voice, he recalled now. A voice a lot like her father's.

Poor kid, he thought as he placed the tassel over the snapshot. He wondered what had ever happened to her.

# Chapter Fourteen
♦ ♦ ♦ ♦

$E$MMA COULDN'T BELIEVE her time was almost up. In less than a week she would head back to New York and Saint Catherine's. True, she missed Marianne. It would take weeks for them to talk through all the things that had happened over the summer. The best summer of her life, even though they'd only spent two weeks of it in New York.

They'd flown to London to film part of a recording session for a new documentary, and had had tea at the Ritz just as she and Bev had so many years before. She'd been able to spend time with Johnno and Stevie and P.M., listening to them play, eating fish and chips in the kitchen while they discussed their next album.

She'd taken rolls of pictures and could hardly wait to store them in her photo album where she could look at them over and over and relive the memories.

Her father had treated her to her first grown-up salon session as an early birthday gift. Now her shoulder-length hair was permed in corkscrew curls that made her feel very grown-up.

And she was starting to develop.

Emma took a quick, surreptitious look down at her bikini top. They weren't much as breasts went, but at least she wouldn't be as easily mistaken for a boy. And she was tanned. Emma hadn't been too certain she would enjoy spending her last weeks in California, but the tan made it worthwhile.

And there was the surfing. She'd had to launch a major campaign before Brian had agreed to let her try her hand at shooting the waves. Emma knew she had Johnno to thank for the bright red board. If he hadn't joked and teased Brian into it, she would still be whiling away her hours on the beach watching everyone else skim the water.

Maybe she couldn't do much more than paddle out and fall in, but at least the process took her farther away from the bodyguards who sweated under nearby beach umbrellas. It was ridiculous, she thought as she carried her board toward the water. No one even knew who she was.

Each year she was sure her father would let them go, and each year they remained with their solemn faces and big shoulders. At least they couldn't follow her out here, she thought as she stretched out on her board and began to paddle through the cool water. Though she knew they watched her through binoculars, she pretended she was alone, or, better, with one of the groups of teenagers who haunted the beaches.

She crested over a wave, enjoying the swells and the way her stomach seemed to dip with the motion. The roar of the sea was in her ears, mixed with the riot of music from dozens of portable radios. She watched a tall boy in navy trunks catch a curl and ride it smoothly to shore—and envied him both his skill and his freedom.

If she couldn't have the second, Emma decided, she would work on developing the first.

She waited with the edgy patience of a surfer watching for the right wave. Sucking in her breath, she brought herself up to a crouch on the board, then stood, and with the faith of the young let the roll take her. She was up for nearly ten seconds before she overbalanced. When she surfaced, she saw the boy in the navy trunks glance her way, tossing his wet, dark hair out of his face with a careless hand. Pride had her struggling back onto the board.

She tried again, and again, each time lasting only seconds before the wave snatched the board from under her feet and sent her flying. Each time she dragged herself back on the board, and with muscles aching, paddled and waited.

She imagined the bodyguards sipping their warming drinks and discussing how clumsy she was. Each failure became a public humiliation and made her only more determined to succeed, just once. Just once to ride the wave all the way to shore.

Her leg muscles trembled as she pushed herself up. She could see the wave curling toward her, the glassy blue-green tunnel, the dancing white froth. She wanted it. Needed it. Just one ride— one success completely and totally her own.

She caught it. Her heart slammed into her throat as she skimmed along the pipe. She could see the beach rushing toward her, the glint of the binocular lens. The drum of water was like music in her head, in her heart. For an instant she tasted it. Freedom.

The tower of water closed in behind her, shoving her off the board, tossing it and her up. One moment she was in the sun, the next she was tumbling in the wall of water. It slammed her, knocking away her breath, sending her wheeling, arms and legs flailing like rubber.

Lungs burning, she struggled to break the surface. She could see it shimmering above her, but the power of the water dragged her deeper, viciously pitching her. She clawed at the water, then was plunged down, gyrating helplessly until the surface was below her and just as out of reach.

As her strength failed she wondered giddily if she should pray. The Act of Contrition floated dreamily through her brain.

*Oh my God, I am heartily sorry for having offended thee.*

As she was sucked back, sucked down, the prayer faded and music seemed to fill her head.

*Come together. Right now. Over me.*

Panic stabbed through her. It was dark. Dark, and the monsters were back. Her efforts to reach the surface were only wild flailings now. She opened her mouth to scream and gagged.

There were hands on her, and in her terror she fought them, beat at them as the water beat at her. It was the monster, the one who had smiled at her, the one who wanted to kill her as it had killed Darren. As an arm hooked around her throat, red balls danced in front of her eyes. They faded to gray as she broke the surface.

"Just relax," someone was telling her. "I'll get you in. Just hang on and relax."

She was choking. Emma started to drag at the arm around her throat before she realized it wasn't cutting off her air. She could see the sun, and when she dragged in a painful breath it was air that burned her throat, not water. She was still alive. The tears started as much in shame as in gratitude.

"You're going to be okay."

She laid a hand on the arm around her. "I wiped out," she managed.

There was a chuckle, quick and a little breathless. "Big time. But, man, you had a hell of a ride first."

Yes, she had, she realized, and concentrated on not humiliating herself further by being sick. Then there was sand, hot and rough on her skin. She let her rescuer lay her down, but the first faces she saw were of her bodyguards. Too weak to speak, she sent them a furious look. It didn't make them back off, but it kept them from coming closer.

"Don't try to stand up for a few minutes."

Emma turned her head, coughed up some seawater. There was music—the Eagles, she thought groggily. "Hotel California." There had been music before, in the dark, but she couldn't remember the words now, or the melody. She coughed again, blinked against the dazzle of sunlight then focused on her savior.

The boy in the navy trunks, she thought and managed a weak smile. Water was dripping from his dark hair. His eyes were dark too, rich deep gray, as clear as lake water.

"Thanks."

"Sure." He settled down beside her, feeling awkward in the role of white knight. The guys would razz him for weeks. But he couldn't bring himself to just leave her there. She was only a kid, after all. A great-looking kid, he thought—then felt still more awkward. He gave her shoulder a brotherly pat and thought she had the biggest, bluest eyes he'd ever seen.

"I guess I lost my board."

He shielded his eyes with the flat of his hand as he looked out to sea. "No. Fred's bringing it in. It's a nice board."

"I know. I've only had it for a couple of weeks."

"Yeah, I've seen you around." He glanced back down at her. She'd risen up on her elbows and her wet curls tumbled down her back. Her voice was pretty, he thought, sort of soothing and musical. "You English or something?"

"Irish. For the most part. We'll be here only a few more days." She sighed as the boy named Fred dragged in her board. "Thanks." Not knowing what else to say, she concentrated on rubbing the wet sand from her knee.

The boy in the navy trunks gave Fred and the others who had gathered around a friendly wave that sent them about their business.

"When my father hears about this, he'll never let me surf again."

"Why does he have to hear about it?"

"He always does." She made a concentrated effort not to look at her bodyguards.

"Everybody wipes out." Beautiful eyes, he thought again, then looked deliberately out to sea. "You were doing pretty good."

"Really." She colored a bit. "You're wonderful. I've watched you."

"Thanks." He grinned and showed a chipped tooth.

Emma stared at him as memory came flooding back. "You're Michael."

"Yeah." His grin widened. "How'd you know?"

"You don't remember me." She pushed herself up to sit. "I met you, well, it was a long time ago. I'm Emma. Emma McAvoy. Your father brought you to the rehearsal hall one afternoon."

"McAvoy?" Michael dragged a hand through his dripping hair. "Brian McAvoy?" As he said the name he saw Emma take a quick look round to see if anyone had heard him. "I remember you. You sent me a picture. I've still got it." His eyes narrowed as he glanced over his shoulder. "So that's what they're doing here," he murmured, studying the guards. "I thought they were narcs or something."

"Bodyguards," she said dully, then shrugged it off. "My father worries."

"Yeah, I bet." He remembered, clearly, the police photograph of a little boy. It left him with nothing else to say.

"I remember your father." She began to draw idle circles in the sand. "He came to the hospital to see me after we lost my brother."

"He's a captain now," Michael said for lack of anything else.

"That's nice." She'd been raised to be polite under any circumstances. "You'll tell him I said hello, won't you?"

"Sure." They ran out of things to say so that the whoosh of the waves filled the gaps. "Ah, listen, do you want a Coke or something?"

She looked up, dazzled to be asked. It was the first time in her life she had had more than a five-minute conversation with a boy. Men, certainly. Her life had been full of men. But being asked to have a Coke with a boy only a few years her senior was a wonderful, and heady, experience. She nearly agreed before she remembered the guards. She couldn't bear them watching.

"Thanks, but I'd better go. Da was going to pick me up in a couple of hours, but I don't think I'm up to any more surfing today. I'll have to call him."

"I could take you." He made a restless movement with his shoulders. It was stupid to feel so tongue-tied with a kid. But he couldn't remember being more nervous since he'd asked Nancy Brimmer to the ninth-grade Valentine's Dance. "Give you a ride home," he continued as Emma stared at him. "If you want."

"You probably have something you want to do."

"No. Not really."

He wanted to meet her father again, Emma decided after one ecstatic moment. A boy like him—why, he must have been at least eighteen—wouldn't be interested in her. But the daughter of Brian McAvoy was different. She drummed up another smile as she got to her feet. He had saved her life. If seeing her father was the only payment she could make, then she would make it.

"I'd like a ride, if it's not too much trouble."

"No big deal." He caught himself before he shifted his feet in the sand. She probably thought he was a jerk.

"I'll just be a minute." She rushed off in the direction of the guards, snatching up her beach wrap and bag on the way. "My friend is giving me a ride home," she said in her most dismissive tone.

"Miss McAvoy." The guard named Masters cleared his throat. "It would be better if you called your father."

"There's no need to bother him."

The second guard, Sweeney, mopped his sweaty forehead. "Your father wouldn't like you taking rides from strangers."

"Michael's not a stranger." The haughty tone made her feel nasty inside, but she would not, could not, be humiliated in front of Michael. "I know him, and so does my father. Michael's father is a captain on the police force here." She pulled the long, rainbow-colored T-shirt over her suit. "You'll be following behind us, so what does it matter?" She turned, and keeping her head up, walked back to where Michael waited with their boards.

"Hold it." Sweeney put a hand on Masters's shoulder. "Let's give the kid a break. She don't get many."

Michael's gas gauge was hovering dangerously close to empty

when he pulled up at the high iron gates in Beverly Hills. He saw the faint surprise on the guard's face before the switch was thrown and the gates swung inward. He was sorry as he drove down the tree-lined drive that he had nothing but scruffy sandals and his old track jersey to wear with his bathing trunks.

The house was all pink stone and white marble, four towering stories of it that took up more than an acre of the trim green lawn. Double arched doors of etched glass stood at the entrance. He wasn't sure if he should be amused or impressed by the peacock that strutted across the grass.

"Nice place."

"It's P.M.'s really. Or P.M.'s wife's." Emma found herself faintly embarrassed by the life-sized marble lions that flanked the entrance. "It used to belong to someone in the cinema—I can never remember who—but Angie did it all over. Anyway, she's in Europe filming so we're staying a few weeks. Have you got time to come in?"

"Ah, yeah, I got time." He frowned down at the sand clinging to his feet. "If you're sure it's okay."

"Of course it is." She stepped out of the car, the same '68 Chevelle that Lou had once driven to the rehearsal hall. She waited for Michael to unstrap her board from the roof, then started up the steps. "I'll have to tell Da what happened. The guards will anyhow. I hope you don't mind if I, well, make it sound minor. You know?"

"Sure." He grinned at her again, making her young heart flutter. "Parents always overreact. I guess they can't help it."

He heard the music the moment she opened the door. A piano, a series of thunderous chords, then an experimental noodling of notes, and the chords again. Emma took her board from him to prop it against the wall.

"They're back here." After a moment's hesitation, she took Michael's hand and led him down the wide white hallway.

He'd never seen a house like it, though he was too embarrassed to say so. Arched doorways opened on room after room where abstract paintings were slashes of frantic color against white walls. Even the floors were white so that Michael was unable to shake the feeling he was walking through some kind of temple.

Then he saw the goddess, the portrait of the goddess above a fireplace of white stone. She was blond and sulky-mouthed, wearing a white sequined dress that skimmed dangerously over the globes of her lush breasts.

"Wow."

"That's Angie," Emma told him. Her nose wrinkled quickly, automatically. "She's married to P.M."

"Yeah." He had the oddest feeling that the portrait's eyes were alive and fixed on him hungrily. "I, ah, saw her last movie." He didn't add that after he had, he'd experienced fascinating and uncomfortably erotic dreams. "Man, she's something."

"Yes, she is." And even at not-quite thirteen, Emma was aware what that something was. She gave Michael's hand an impatient tug, then continued on.

It was the only room Emma felt at ease in—the only room in the mausoleum of a house where she imagined P.M. had been given a chance to express his own taste. There was color here, a mix-match of blues and reds and sunny yellows. Music awards lined the mantel; gold records dotted the walls. There were a couple of thriving plants near the window. A pair of lemon trees that Emma knew P.M. had started from seed.

Her father was seated at a beautiful old baby grand that had been in a movie whose title always escaped Emma. Johnno sat beside him, smoking his habitual French cigarettes. There was a litter of papers on the floor, a big pitcher of lemonade sprinkled with condensation on the coffee table. The glasses, ice melting lazily inside them, were already leaving a duo of rings on the wood.

"We'll keep it moving through the bridge," Brian was saying as he pounded out chords. "Keep it fast, overlap the strings and horns, but keep the guitar the dominant force."

"Fine, but it's still the wrong beat." Johnno brushed Brian's hands aside. His diamonds winked on each pinky as he moved them over the keys.

Brian took out a cigarette, flipping it through his fingers. "I hate you when you're right."

"Da."

He looked up. The smile came first, then faded as he focused on Michael. "Emma. You were supposed to ring if you wanted to come back early."

"I know, but I met Michael." Her lips curved, charmingly, so that her dimple flashed. "I wiped out, and he helped me get my board." Because she wanted to leave it at that, she hurried on. "And I thought you'd like to meet him again."

There was something enormously disturbing about seeing his girl, his little girl, standing with her hand in the hand of a boy who was nearly a man. "Again?"

"Don't you remember? His father brought him to a rehearsal. His father, the policeman."

"Kesselring." The muscles in Brian's stomach clenched. "You're Michael Kesselring?"

"Yes, sir." He wasn't sure if it was proper to extend his hand for a shake with a music giant, so stood, rubbing his palms on his sandy trunks. "I was like eleven when I met you before. It was great."

He was too used to being onstage, under the lights, to let the ache show. He looked at Michael, tall, dark, sturdy, and saw not Lou Kesselring's son, but the potential of his own lost little boy. But he smiled as he stood up from the piano.

"It's nice to see you again. You remember Michael, Johnno?"

"Sure. Ever talk your old man into that electric guitar?"

"Yeah." Michael grinned, flattered to be remembered. "I took lessons awhile, but they gave me up as hopeless. I play the harmonica some, though."

"Why don't you get Michael a Coke, Emma?" Brian dropped to the arm of a chair, gesturing to the couch. The glint of his wedding ring caught a sliver of light. "Have a seat."

"I don't want to interrupt your work."

"We live to be interrupted," Johnno told him, mellowing the sarcasm with a smile. "What'd you think of the song?"

"It was great. Everything you do is great."

Johnno's brow lifted not so much in sarcasm now as amusement. "Here's a smart boy, Bri. Maybe we should keep him."

Michael grinned, unsure if he should be embarrassed. "No, really. I like all your stuff."

"Not into disco?"

"Disco sucks."

"A very smart boy," Johnno decided. "So how'd you come to meet our Emma on the beach?" He continued talking, knowing Brian needed another moment to adjust.

"She had a little trouble with a wave and I helped her out." He breezed over the incident with the skill of a teenager used to outwitting adults. "She's got pretty good form, Mr. McAvoy. Just needs more practice."

Brian managed another smile and toyed with his warm lemonade. "You surf a lot?"

"Every chance I get."

"How's your father?"

"He's cool. He's a captain now."

"I'd heard. You must be out of high school by now."

"Yes, sir. I graduated in June."

"Going on?"

"Well, yeah. I thought I'd give college a shot. My father's counting on it."

Johnno pulled out his cigarettes, carelessly offering one to Michael. He took it, and the first pull of the strong, exotic smoke had his stomach bouncing. "So," Johnno asked, mildly amused, "do you plan to follow in your father's flat feet? Isn't that what they call cops?" he continued. "Flat foots?"

"Oh." Michael tried another small, experimental puff on the Gauloise. "I don't think I'm cut out to be a cop. Dad, he's great at it. Patient, you know. Like with your son's case. He worked on that for years, even after the department closed the files." He caught himself, appalled that he'd brought it up. "He's like, dedicated," he finished weakly.

"Yes, he is." More at ease, Brian smiled the charming, heartwarming smile that made his fans love him. He wished he'd added rum to the lemonade. "You'll give him my best, won't you?"

"Sure." It was with great relief that Michael saw Emma bringing in cold drinks on a tray.

An hour later, Emma walked him back to his car. "I want to thank you for not telling Da how stupid I was today."

"No big deal."

"Yes, it was. He gets . . . upset." She gazed out to the high stone walls that surrounded the estate. Wherever she went there were walls. "I think he'd put me in a bubble if he could."

The urge to touch her hair was so strong, so unexpected, that he'd lifted his hand before he caught himself and brushed it through his own. "It must be tough, with what happened to your brother and everything."

"He's always afraid, afraid someone will try to take me, too."

"Aren't you?"

"No. I don't think so. The guards are always there, so I've never had a chance to be, really."

He hesitated, one hand on the door handle. It wasn't like he was stuck on her or anything, he told himself. She was just a kid. "Maybe I'll see you at the beach tomorrow."

A woman's heart fluttered in her young chest. "Maybe."

"I could give you some pointers on the board—you know, help you with your form."

"That would be great."

He got in, fiddling with the keys before starting the engine. "Thanks for the Coke and everything. It was really far out getting to meet your dad again and all."

"Any time. Goodbye, Michael."

"Yeah. See you." He drove down the tree-lined drive, nearly steering onto the lawn because he was watching her in the rearview mirror.

◆ ◆ ◆

*H*E WENT BACK to the beach every day, but he never saw her there again that summer.

# Chapter Fifteen

♦ ♦ ♦ ♦

*T*HEY HAD AN hour before bed check. An hour before Sister Immaculata shuffled her way down the halls in her black, sensible shoes to poke her disapproving, warty nose in each of the rooms to make sure all music was off and clothes were neatly hung in closets.

They had an hour, and Emma was afraid it was going to be enough time.

"Are they numb yet?"

"I don't think so."

Marianne narrowed her eyes as she tapped her foot along with her latest Billy Joel album. She was convinced he was right. Catholic girls did start much too late.

"Emma, you've had that ice on your ears for twenty minutes. You should have frostbite by now."

Ice was melting cold down her wrists, but she kept it firmly against her ears. "Are you sure you know what you're doing?"

"Of course I do." Marianne's hips swayed in her prim cotton nightgown as she walked to the mirror. There, she admired the little gold balls in her newly pierced ears. "I watched every move my cousin made when she did mine." She switched to an exaggerated German accent. "Und ve have all de instruments. Ice, needle." Gleefully she held it up so it glinted in the lamplight. "The potato we ripped off from the kitchen. Two quick jabs and your dull, dreary ears become sophisticated."

Emma kept her eye on the needle. She was searching for a

way out, ears and pride intact. "I never asked Da if it was all right."

"Jesus, Emma, ear piercing's a personal choice. You've got your period, you've got your boobs—such as they are," she added with a grin. "That makes you a woman."

She wasn't sure she wanted to be a woman if it meant having her best friend stick a needle in her earlobe. "I don't have any earrings."

"I told you, you can borrow some of mine. I've got scads. Come on, let's see that British stiff upper lip."

"Right." Having a deep breath, Emma took the ice from one ear. "Don't screw up."

"Me?" Marianne knelt by the chair to draw a tiny *x* on Emma's earlobe with a purple felt-tip pen. "Listen, just in case I miss and drive this into your brain, can I have your record collection?" Then she giggled, held the potato behind Emma's ear, and plunged.

It was a toss-up as to who was more queasy.

"God." Marianne tucked her head between her knees. "At least my parents don't have to worry about me becoming a drug addict. Shooting up must be disgusting."

Emma slid bonelessly out of the chair. "You didn't say I'd feel it." As her stomach roiled, she concentrated on keeping very still and breathing. "Oh gross. You didn't say I'd hear it."

"I didn't. But then Marcia and I had swiped a bottle of bourbon from Daddy's bar. I guess we weren't feeling or hearing anything." She lifted her head, focused. There was blood, just a drop of it on Emma's earlobe, but it made her think of the slasher movie she and her cousin had seen over the summer.

"We've got to do the other one."

Emma just closed her eyes. "Oh Christ."

"You can't go around with one ear pierced. We've come this far, Emma." Her hands were clammy as she clipped the needle free of the thread and prepared it for round two. "I've got the hard part. Just lie there."

Gritting her teeth, Marianne aimed and fired. Emma only groaned and slid the rest of the way to the floor.

"It's over. Now you have to clean them with peroxide so they don't get infected. And keep your hair over them so none of the sisters notice for a while."

When the door opened, both girls struggled up. But it wasn't

Sister Immaculata. Teresa Louise Alcott, the bright and annoying girl from across the hall, popped in wearing her pink cotton robe and feather mules.

"What's going on?"

"We're having an orgy." Marianne flopped down again. "Don't you ever knock?"

Teresa only grinned. She was one of the feverishly pert girls who volunteered for everything, always completed her assignments, and wept at the Stations of the Cross. Marianne detested her on principle. Being thick-skinned as well as pert, Teresa considered the insults signs of friendship.

"Wow. You're getting your ears pierced." She knelt down to study the strings dangling from Emma's lobes. "Mother Superior'll have a cat."

"Why don't you have a cat, Teresa?" Marianne suggested. "In your own room."

But Teresa only grinned and sat back on her heels. "Did it hurt?"

Emma opened her eyes and wished Teresa to everlasting hell. "No. It felt great. Marianne's going to do my nose next. You can watch."

Teresa ignored the sarcasm and studied her newly manicured fingernails. "I'd love to have mine done. Maybe after Sister Immaculata comes through you could do it."

"I don't know, Teresa." Marianne pushed herself up to change the record to Bruce Springsteen. "I haven't finished my report on *Silas Marner*. I was going to work on it tonight."

"Mine's done." Teresa smiled her pert smile. "If you do my ears, I'll give you my notes."

Marianne moved her shoulders as if debating. "Well, okay then."

"Great. Wow, I almost forgot why I came over." She dug into the deep pocket of her frilly pink robe and pulled out a magazine article. "My sister sent this to me because she knows I go to school with you, Emma. She cut it out of *People*. Have you ever seen that magazine? It's just great. It has pictures of everybody. They have like Robert Redford on the cover and Burt Reynolds. All the hunks."

"I've seen it," Emma said, because she knew it was the only way to shut Teresa up.

"Sure you have, because your dad's been in there lots of

times. Anyway, I knew you'd just be dying to see it, so I brought it over."

Because her stomach had settled, Emma propped herself up, then took the article. The nausea came back with a vengeance.

## ETERNAL TRIANGLE

There was Bev rolling on the floor with another woman. And Da, with a look of stunned fury on his face, reaching down for her. Bev's dress was ripped, and there was a kind of wild anger in her eyes. The same kind, Emma remembered, as had been there the last time she'd seen her.

"I knew you'd want it," Teresa was saying cheerfully. "So I brought it over. That's your mother, isn't it?"

"My mother," Emma murmured, staring at Bev's picture.

"The blond lady in the glittery dress. Wow, I'd just die to have a dress like that. Jane Palmer. She's your mother, right?"

"Jane." She focused on the other woman now. The old fear came back, just as real, just as ripe as it had been ten years before. Just as stunning as it had been when another girl had shown her a smuggled-in copy of *Devastated* with Jane's picture on the back cover.

It was Jane. Bev was fighting with her, and Da was there. What could they have been fighting about? Hope flashed through the fear. Perhaps Da and Bev were together. Perhaps they would all be together again.

She shook her head to clear it and focused on the text.

Those of the British upper crust who paid two hundred pounds a head for salmon mousse and champagne at a charity dinner at the Mayfair in London got more than their money's worth. Beverly Wilson, successful decorator and estranged wife of Brian McAvoy of Devastation, went head to head with Jane Palmer, McAvoy's former lover and author of the best-selling roman à clef, *Devastated.*

What prompted the hair-pulling match is up for speculation, but sources say the old rivalry has never cooled down. Jane Palmer is the mother of McAvoy's daughter, Emma, age thirteen. Emma McAvoy, who inherited her father's poetic looks, attends a private school somewhere in the States.

Beverly Wilson, who has been estranged from McAvoy for several years, was the mother of McAvoy's only son, Darren. The child was tragically murdered seven years ago in a case that still baffles police.

McAvoy did not attend the function with either Miss Palmer or Miss Wilson, but with his current flame, singer Dory Cates. Though McAvoy separated the wrestlers personally, few words were exchanged between Wilson and McAvoy before she left with date P. M. Ferguson, drummer for the veteran rock group. Neither McAvoy nor Wilson were available for comment on the incident, but Palmer claims she will include the scene in her new book.

To borrow McAvoy's own lyrics, it seems "old fires run hot and run long."

There was more, talk about others who had attended and the comments they made about the incident. There was a description of the clothes and a tongue-in-cheek remark about what both Jane and Bev had worn, and torn off each other. But she didn't read any further. Didn't need to.

"It's neat, isn't it, the way they were ripping each other's dresses, right out in public?" Teresa's eyes shone with excitement. "Do you think they were fighting over your father? He's so dreamy, I bet they were. It's just like in the movies."

"Yeah." Since strangling Teresa would only get her suspended, Marianne vetoed it. There were other, subtler ways to deal with idiots. She picked up the needle. She'd pierce Teresa's flappy ears all right. And if she forgot the ice, it was an honest mistake. "You'd better get going, Teresa. Sister Immaculata's going to be coming through any minute."

With a little squeal, Teresa sprang up. She didn't want to spoil her perfect record with a demerit. "Come over at ten, and I'll give you the notes. Then you can do it."

"Fine."

Teresa put her hands on her earlobes. "I can't wait."

"Neither can I." She waited until the door closed. "Little shit," she muttered, then moved over to drape an arm around Emma's shoulders. "You okay?"

"It never goes away." She stared at the picture. It was a good one, she thought dispassionately, well focused, well lit. The faces weren't blurred, the expressions quite clear. It was easy, all too easy to see the hate in her mother's eyes. "Do you think I could be like her?"

"Like who?"

"My mother."

"Come on, Emma. You haven't even seen her since you were a baby."

"There's genes, heredity and all that."

"All that's bull."

"Sometimes I'm mean. Sometimes I want to be mean, the way she was."

"So what?" She rose to take Springsteen off. Sister Immaculata might come along any minute and confiscate it. "Everybody's mean sometimes. That's because our flesh is weak and we're loaded with sin."

"I hate her." It was a relief to say it, a terrible, terrible relief. "I hate her. And I hate Bev for not wanting me, and Da for putting me here. I hate the men who killed Darren. I hate them all. She hates everyone, too. You can see it in her eyes."

"It's okay. Sometimes I hate everyone. And I don't even know your mother."

That made her laugh. She couldn't say why, but it made her laugh. "Neither do I, I guess." She sniffled, sighed. "I hardly remember her."

"There, you see." Satisfied, Marianne plopped down again. "If you don't remember her, you can't be like her."

It sounded logical, and she needed to believe it. "I don't look like her."

Wanting to judge fairly, Marianne took up the article and studied the pictures. "Not a bit. You've got your father's bone structure and coloring. Take it from an artist."

Emma lifted a hand to her tender lobes. "Are you really going to pierce Teresa's ears?"

"You bet—with the dullest needle I can find. Want to do one?"

Emma grinned.

# *Chapter Sixteen*

* * * *

STEVIE HAD NEVER been so scared. There were bars all around and the steady drip, drip, drip, of a faucet somewhere down the hall. Voices were raised occasionally and echoed. There was the shuffling of feet, then the godawful silence.

He needed a fix. His body was trembling, sweating. His stomach was knotted, refusing to let him release the nausea in the scarred porcelain john in the corner. His nose and eyes were running. It was the flu, he told himself. He had the freaking flu and they'd locked him up. He needed a bloody doctor, and they'd shut him up and left him to rot. Sitting on the cot, he brought his knees up to his chest, pushing his back into the wall.

He was Stevie Nimmons. He was the greatest guitarist of his generation. He was somebody. But they had put him in a cage like an animal. They had locked him up and walked away. Didn't they know who he was? What he'd made himself?

He needed a fix. Oh Jesus, just one sweet fix. Then he'd be able to laugh this off.

It was cold. It was so goddamn cold. He yanked the blanket from the cot and huddled under it. And he was thirsty. His mouth was so dry he couldn't even work up enough spit to swallow.

Someone would come, he thought as his eyes began to fill. Someone would come and make it all right again. Someone would fix it. Oh God, he needed a fix. His mother would come and tell him everything had been taken care of.

It hurt. He began to weep against his knees as the pain

wracked through him. Every breath he took seemed to hold tiny slivers of glass. His muscles were on fire, his skin like ice.

Just one. Just one toke, one hit, one line, and he'd be all right again.

Didn't they know who the fuck he was?

"Stevie."

He heard his name. With eyes bleary with tears, he looked toward the cell door. Dragging the back of his hand over his mouth, he struggled to focus. He tried to laugh, but the sound came out in a whooping sob as he struggled up. Pete. Pete could fix it.

He tripped over the blanket, and lay sprawled on the floor a moment as Pete watched him. Stevie's body was stick-thin. His legs angled awkwardly out from it and ended in five-hundred-pound snakeskin boots. His face as he pushed himself up was gray and pasty with lines dug deep and dug hard. The whites of his eyes were streaked fiery red. There was a trickle of blood from his lip where he had hit the floor. And he stank.

"Man, I'm sick." He began to pull himself up, hand over sweaty hand on the bars. "I got the flu."

The junkie flu, Pete thought dispassionately.

"You got to get me out." Stevie wrapped his trembling fingers around the bars. Though his breath was stale, Pete didn't back away. "It's fucking crazy. They came into my house. Into my goddamn house like a bunch of bloody Nazis. They waved some kind of paper in front of my face and started pulling out drawers. Jesus, Pete, they dragged me in here like I was some kind of freaking murderer. They put handcuffs on me." He began to cry again and wiped his nose with the back of his hand. "People were watching when they took me out of my own house with handcuffs on me. They were taking pictures. It ain't fucking right, Pete. It ain't fucking right. You got to get me out."

During the outburst Pete had stayed very still. His voice was low and calm. He'd handled crises before, and knew how to turn them in his favor. "They found heroin, Stevie, and what's politely called drug paraphernalia. They're going to charge you with possession."

"Just get me the fuck out."

"Are you listening to me?" The question whipped out, cool and quiet. "They found enough in your place to put you away."

"It was planted. Somebody set me up. Somebody—"

"Don't bullshit me." His eyes hardened, but whatever disgust he felt he kept carefully inside. "You have two choices. You can go to jail, or you can go into a clinic."

"I've got a right—"

"You've got no rights here. You're messed up, Stevie. If you want me to help you, you're going to do exactly what I tell you."

"Just get me out." Stevie sank to the floor and folded into himself. "Just get me out."

◆ ◆ ◆ ◆

"*H*OW LONG WILL he have to stay in?" Bev poured the chilled Pouilly Fumé into glasses.

"Three months." Johnno watched her, pleased that the old Bev wasn't buried too deeply in the newer, sleeker model. "I'm not sure how Pete pulled it off, nor do I think I want to know, but if Stevie spends his time in the Whitehurst Clinic, he won't stand trial."

"I'm glad. He needs help, not a jail sentence." She settled on the sofa beside him, feeling foolishly nervous. "The news is all over the radio. I was just wondering what to do, what I could do, when you knocked at the door. Perhaps, in a few weeks, I could go to see him."

"I'm not sure he'll be such a pretty sight."

"He'll need his friends," she said, and set her wine down untasted.

"And are you still?"

She looked up. Her face softened before she lifted a hand to his cheek. "You look good, Johnno. I always wondered what you were hiding under that beard."

"The sixties are over. More's the pity. I actually wore a tie last week."

"Please."

"Well, it was white leather, but a tie nonetheless." He leaned over and kissed her. Time, he thought, was only time after all. "I've missed you, Bev."

"The years went by so quickly."

"For some of us. I hear you and P.M. are an item."

She picked up her wine, sipping, stalling. "Did you come to gossip, Johnno?"

"You know how I adore gossip, luv. Shall I pretend I didn't see the pictures of you and P.M.?" The familiar sarcasm was

back, faint, but sharp as a blade. "Of course my favorite is of you
and Jane, right after you bloodied her lip." He grabbed Bev's
hand before she could rise, and kissed it. "My hero."

The laughter bubbled up, and though she took her hand
away, she relaxed again. "I had no intention of fighting with her,
and no regret that I did."

"That's the spirit. You Amazon."

"She made a comment about Darren," Bev murmured.

"I'm sorry." His smile faded. When he took her hand again,
she let hers lie comfortably in it.

"I just saw red. I know that's a cliché, but you do when
you're viciously angry. The next thing I knew I was plowing into
her, for Darren, for myself. And for Emma. A lot of nerve I have
defending Emma after what I did to her."

"Bev."

"No, we won't get into all that," she interrupted. "It's done
now. I imagine Jane will say some filthy things about me in her
next book, and my business will boom as a result." Push it aside,
she told herself, and go on. "P.M. tells me that you're about to
form your own label."

"It should be official in a couple of weeks. Just where is our
boy?"

"He had to fly to California a couple of days ago. The divorce business. Actually, he's expected back anytime now."

"Expected back here?"

She drank again, but met his eyes levelly. "Yes, here. Is that a
problem, Johnno?"

"I don't know. Is it?"

A trace of the old fire came into her eyes—stubborn, defen-
sive. "He's a very sweet man, a kind man."

"I know. I'm rather fond of him myself."

"I know you are." She sighed, and let the fire die. "Don't
let's make it complicated, Johnno. We're just looking for a little
happiness, a little peace of mind."

"That's bullshit. P.M.'s been in love with you for years."

"So what if he is?" she demanded. "Don't I deserve someone
who loves me? Someone who puts me first?"

"Yes. And doesn't he deserve the same?"

She shoved away from the sofa to pace to the window and
back. The rain slicked down the glass like bars. "I'm not going to

hurt him. He needs someone right now. So do I. What's so wrong about that?"

"Brian," he said simply.

"What does he have to do with this? That was over long ago."

He got up slowly. "I won't insult you by calling you a liar, or by calling you a fool. I will say that I care about you, and P.M. And Bri. And I care about the band, what we are, what we've done, what we still can do."

"I'm hardly a Yoko Ono," she said stiffly. "I won't come between your precious band. Have I ever? Could I ever?"

"You never have. Maybe you've never known how easily you could. Brian's never loved anyone like he loved you, Bev. Believe me, I know."

"Don't say that to me."

He started to speak again, but they both heard the door open, and the rush of footsteps down the hallway. "Bev! Bev!" P.M. turned into the room, his coat wet from the rain and flapping open. "Johnno, thank God. I just heard about Stevie on the radio. What the hell's going on?"

"Have a seat, son." Johnno settled back on the sofa himself. "And I'll tell you."

◆ ◆ ◆ ◆

𝓗E LOVED HER so sweetly. He touched her so gently. The candles flickered, flames dancing with the dark as Bev stroked a hand down P.M.'s back. His whispers were soft, the words lovely. It was easy, so easy to give herself to him, to let the strength of his feelings carry her along.

She would never have to ask herself if he needed her, if she would be, could always be, enough for him. With him, she would never have to spend nights wondering, worrying, aching. And she would never, never, feel that thrill of unity, of rightness, of belonging.

She gave him all she could, arching up to him, opening for him, accepting, even welcoming him into her. Her body didn't shudder as his did, her heart didn't threaten to burst through the wall of her chest. But after a good, clean climax came the peace. And she was grateful.

But she should have known such simple things don't last.

The candles still flickered as he drew her close, to hold her warmth to him. He loved the serenity that always cloaked her after sex, the complete and somehow elegant stillness of her body.

Her eyes were half closed, her lips soft and just parted. Her limbs were pliant. If he rested his head, as he often did, on her breast, he would hear the strong, steady beat of her heart.

Sometimes they talked like this—as he had never talked with his wife of seven years. They talked of what had happened to them during the day, or what had happened to the world. Or they lay and listened to the radio that had played during their lovemaking. They would drift to sleep like that, quiet and content. And in the morning he would wake, dazzled and delighted that she was beside him.

He shifted her so that he could brush his hand through her hair. "The divorce is going through."

Roused out of a half-doze, she opened her eyes and watched the pattern of light and shadow on the wall. "I'm glad."

"Are you?"

"Of course. I know how hard it's been on you the last few weeks. You want it behind you."

"I do. I married Angie for the wrong reasons, Bev. I wanted to settle down so badly, to have a wife, a home, a family. Of course that monster in Beverly Hills was never a home, and she always had an excellent excuse for putting off starting a family. Just as well. I was as poor a choice for her as she was for me."

She linked her fingers with his. "You're too hard on yourself."

"No, it's true. I was a career choice for Angie. The pity is, she didn't realize I was fond enough of her once to have helped her there without marriage. But we jumped in and were both too lazy or too cautious to jump out again when it went bad." He studied her fingers, long and slender, tangled with his chunky ones. "Looking back, I can see every mistake so clearly. I won't make them again, Bev—if you give me a chance."

"P.M." She moved then, flustered and frightened. His hands came to her shoulders, surprisingly firm, holding her face-to-face.

"I want you to marry me, Bev, for all the right reasons."

She hesitated, surprising herself. The answer didn't come through her lips as quickly, as surely, as it had jumped into her head. It was her heart that stopped it, she realized. Her heart that wanted to give him what he wanted. She lifted her hands to cover his.

"I can't. I'm so sorry I can't."

He stared at her, watching her eyes, the regret in them—and the trace of pity that made him want to scream. "Because of Brian."

She started to agree, then found that answer unclear as well. "No, because of me." She drew away, and pulling on a robe, got out of bed. "I can't let go, you see. I thought I had, I've wanted to, but I can't." She turned back, her face in shadows, her voice clear and filled with regrets. "Being with you is the best thing to happen to me in a long, long time. It's made me feel happy again. And it's made me see things clearly for the first time in years."

"You're still in love with him."

"Yes. I think I could live with that, I think I could accept that somehow and go on, with you, with someone. But I'm the one who drove him away, you see."

"What are you talking about?"

"Didn't he ever tell you?" She smiled a little as she sat on the edge of the bed. It was easy to talk to him like this, to think of him as friend now, rather than lover. "No, I suppose he wouldn't speak of it. Not even to you. After Darren was killed, I cut Brian out of my life. I punished him, P.M., and Emma. I hurt Brian when he needed me most, blaming him because I was too afraid to blame myself."

"For God's sake, Bev, neither of you was to blame."

"I've never been sure of that. I wouldn't let him grieve with me. And when he was suffering, when we both were suffering, I turned him away. He didn't leave me, P.M. I left him. And poor little Emma. In our way, I suppose we both abandoned her. Seeing you again, being with you, has made me realize just what I did. To all of us. You deserve better than a woman who didn't love enough, and who'll always regret it."

"I could make you happy, Bev."

"Yes, I think you could." She cupped his face in her hands. "But I wouldn't make you happy, not for long. You'd always know I loved him first, and in a way I'll never love anyone else."

Yes, he had known, he had known that and her answer before he had asked the question. It would have helped if he could have hated her for it, and hated Brian. But he loved. "Why don't you go back to him, talk to him?"

"Darren would be almost ten years old now. It's too far to go back, P.M."

◆ ◆ ◆ ◆

*E*MMA HURRIED ACROSS the grounds. If she looked as though she had a purpose, none of the sisters would stop and question her. She had an excuse prepared—a botany report for a science project.

She only wanted to be alone. She was ready to scream and wail with the need to be alone. She didn't even want Marianne's company. Emma was sorry she'd had to lie to her closest friend, and would confess the sin to Father Prelenski in the afternoon. But she needed an hour, an hour alone, to think.

She cast one quick look over her shoulder, then skirted around a row of hedges. Tucking the notebook she carried more securely under her arm, she dove into a small grove of trees.

Since it was Saturday, she was allowed her jeans and sneakers. It was cool enough in the shade of the greening trees to make her glad she'd worn the sweater. Once she was certain she was out of view from any of the windows of the academy, she dropped to the ground. Inside the notebook were more than a dozen clippings, most of which had been passed on to her by Teresa and other equally curious classmates.

The first was of herself, and Michael, from the summer before. She smoothed it carefully, battled embarrassed delight as she studied her face and form, depicted so clearly in newsprint. She looked wet and disheveled, and unfortunately for her ego, didn't fill out the bikini very interestingly.

But Michael looked wonderful.

Michael Kesselring, she thought. Of course the paper hadn't printed his name, hadn't bothered to find it out. It had been her the press had been interested in. But all the girls had squealed over Michael and demanded to know who he was and if Emma had had a summer romance.

It had made her feel very grown-up to talk about him. Of course, she'd embellished the tale more than a little, about how he'd carried her in his arms, given her mouth-to-mouth, pledged his undying love. She didn't think Michael would mind—especially since he'd never know about it.

With a sigh, she replaced the clipping and took out another. It was the one Teresa had brought over the night Emma had had her ears pierced. She couldn't count the number of times she had taken it out, stared at it, studied it, tried to dissect it. Her eyes were constantly drawn to her mother's face, frightened as they searched and searched for some resemblance. But not all heredity could be seen, she knew. She was a very good student, and had taken a special interest in biology when discussions of heredity and genes had come up.

That was her mother, and there was no denying it. She had grown inside that woman, had been born from her. No matter how many years had passed, Emma could still smell the stink of gin, she could still feel the pinches and slaps and hear the curses.

It terrified her—terrified her so that just looking at the picture had her digging bitten-down nails into her palms, had the palms themselves sweating.

On a choked cry, she tore her gaze from Jane's picture and looked at her father's. She prayed every night she was like him— kind, gentle, funny, fair. He had saved her. She had read the story often enough, and even without the printed words, she remembered. The way he had looked when she'd climbed out from under the sink, the kindness in his voice when he had spoken to her. He'd given her a home, and a life without fear. Even though he had sent her away, she would never forget the years he had given her. That he and Bev had given her.

It was hardest to look at Bev somehow. She was so beautiful, so perfect. Emma had never loved another woman more, never needed one more. And to look at her made it impossible not to think of Darren. Darren who had had the same rich dark hair and soft green eyes. Darren whom she had sworn to protect. Darren who had died.

Her fault, Emma thought now. She was never to be forgiven for it. Bev had sent her away. Her father had sent her away. She would never have a family again.

She put it away, and spent some time going through older clippings. Pictures of herself as a child, pictures of Darren, the wide, stark headlines about the murder. These she kept hidden deep in her drawer, knowing if the nuns found them and told her father, he would get that sad, hurt look in his eyes. She didn't want to hurt him, but she couldn't forget.

She read the stories through, though she could have recited

them by heart by this time. Looking, she was always looking for something new, something that would tell her why it had happened, how she might have stopped it.

There was nothing. There never was.

There were new clippings now—pictures and stories about Bev and P.M. Some said Bev would at last get a divorce and marry P.M. Others played up the juicy angle of two men who had been like brothers torn apart by a woman. There was the announcement of Devastation's new label, Prism, and pictures of the party in London on the day it had become official. There was her father with another new woman, and again with Johnno and P.M. and Pete. But not Stevie. With a sigh, Emma took out another clipping.

Stevie was in a clinic where they put drug abusers. They called him an addict. Others called him a criminal. Emma remembered she'd once thought he was an angel. Emma thought he looked tired in the picture, tired and thin and afraid. The papers said it was a tragedy; they said it was an outrage. Some of the girls snickered about it.

But no one would talk to her. When she had questioned her father, he had told her only that Stevie had lost control and was getting help. She wasn't to worry.

But she did worry. They were her family, the only family she had left. She had lost Darren. She had to make sure she didn't lose the rest.

Carefully, in her best penmanship, she began to compose letters.

# *Chapter Seventeen*

♦ ♦ ♦ ♦

$S$TEVIE READ HIS in the sunlight, as he sat on a stone bench in the garden during his morning walk. It was a lovely spot, filled with tea roses and hollyhocks and bird songs. Little brick paths wound through it, under arbors of wisteria and morning glories. Both the staff and the patients at Whitehurst were given free rein there. Until the sturdy stone walls rose up.

He detested the clinic, the doctors, the other patients. He despised the therapy sessions, the scheduling, the determined smiles of the staff. But he did what he was told, and he told them what they wanted to hear.

He was an addict. He wanted help. He would take one day at a time.

He would take their methadone and dream of heroin.

He learned to be calm, and he learned to be cunning. In four weeks and three days, he would walk out a free man. This time he would be more careful. This time he would control the drugs. He would smile at the doctors and reporters, he would lecture on the evils of drugs, and he would lie through his teeth. When he was out, he would live his life as he chose.

No one had the right to tell him he was sick, no one had the right to tell him he needed help. If he wanted to get high, he'd get high. What did they understand about the pressures he lived with day after day? The demands to excel, to be that much better than the rest?

Maybe he'd gone too far before. Maybe. So he'd keep it a

social thing. The frigging doctors swilled their bourbon. He'd do a line if he felt like a line. He'd smoke some hash if he had a yen for it.

And fuck them. Fuck them all.

He tore open the envelope. He was pleased that Emma had written him. He could think of no other female he'd had such pure and honest feelings for. Taking out a cigarette, he leaned back on the bench and drew in the scent of smoke and roses.

*Dear Stevie,*

*I know you're in a kind of hospital and I'm sorry I can't visit you. Da says he and the others have been there, and that you're looking better. I wanted you to know that I was thinking about you. Maybe when you're well we can go on vacation together, all of us, like we did in California last summer. I miss you a lot and I still hate school. But it's only three and a half more years. Remember when I was little and you always asked me who was the best? I'd always say Da and you'd pretend to get mad. Well, I never told you that you play the guitar better. Don't tell Da I said so. Here's a picture of you and me in New York a couple of years ago. Da took it, remember? That's why it's out of focus. I thought you'd like to have it. You can write me back if you feel like it. But if you don't that's okay. I know I'm supposed to have paragraphs and stuff in this letter, but I forgot. I love you, Stevie. Get well soon.*

*Love,*
*Emma*

He let the letter lie on his lap. He sat on the bench and smoked his cigarette. And wept.

♦ ♦ ♦ ♦

*P*.M. OPENED HIS LETTER as he sat in the empty house he'd just bought on the outskirts of London. He was on the floor with the ceilings towering over him, a bottle of ale by his knee and the cool blues of Ray Charles coming from his only piece of furniture, the stereo.

It hadn't been easy to leave Bev, but it had been harder to

stay. She had helped him find the house, as she'd promised. She would decorate it. She would, now and then, make love with him in it. But she would never be his wife.

He blamed Brian for it. No matter what Bev had told him, P.M. eased his pain by placing the blame squarely on Brian. He hadn't been man enough to stay with her through the bad times. He hadn't been man enough to let her go. Right from the beginning Brian had treated Bev badly. Bringing her a child from another woman, asking her to raise it as her own. Leaving her for weeks at a time while he toured. Pushing her, he thought viciously, pushing her into a lifestyle she never wanted. Drugs, groupies, and gossip.

And what would Brian say, what would they all say, if he announced he was leaving the group? That would make them sit up and take notice, P.M. thought as he swallowed some ale. Brian McAvoy could go to hell and take Devastation with him.

More out of habit than curiosity, he opened Emma's letter. She wrote him every couple of months. Cute, chatty letters that he answered with a postcard or a little gift. It wasn't the girl's fault that her father was a bastard, P.M. thought, and began to read.

> *Dear P.M.,*
>
> *I guess I'm supposed to say I'm sorry about your divorce, but I'm not. I didn't like Angie. The sisters say that divorce is a sin, but I think it's a bigger one to pretend you love someone when you don't. I hope you're happy again because when I saw you last summer you were sad.*
>
> *There are lots of things in the paper about you and Bev. Maybe I'm not supposed to talk about something like that, but I can't help it. If you and Bev get married, I won't be mad. She's so beautiful and good you can't help it if you love her. Maybe if she's happy with you, she won't hate me anymore. I know you're not fighting with Da like it says in some of the papers. It would be stupid to blame him for loving Bev if you love her, too.*
>
> *I found this picture I took of you and Da a long time ago. I know you're going to start the new album soon, so*

*you can show it to him. I hope you're happy, because I
love you. Maybe I'll see you in London this summer.*

> *Love,*
> *Emma*

P.M. studied the picture for a long time, then slipped it inside the folded letter, and the letter inside the envelope. Divorcing his wife had been one thing, he realized. Divorcing his family was something else again.

◆ ◆ ◆ ◆

*J*OHNNO SPENT HIS first day back in New York sleeping, and his second composing. He was living alone at the moment, and gratefully so. His last lover had driven him to distraction with obsessive cleanliness. Johnno was fastidious himself, but when it had come to washing all the bottles and cans that had come into the house from the market, even he had been baffled.

He appreciated the silence—after the housekeeper had left. He thought idly about spending the evening out, but decided he was too lazy. It wasn't jet lag as much as it was the strain of the last few weeks. The legalities and hassles of the new label, the difficult visit with Stevie at the clinic, and worse somehow, the time he had spent with Brian, watching his oldest friend snuggle down deeper into a bottle.

Yet the music Brian was writing was better than ever. Stinging, lyrical, sharp-edged, dreamy. He wouldn't speak of his feelings, of his hurt or anger over P.M.'s relationship with Bev. But it was there in his music.

That was enough to keep Pete happy, Johnno thought as he stripped off his shirt. As long as Devastation kept rocking, all was right with the world.

He took out the shrimp salad his housekeeper had made up, uncorked a bottle of wine, and pushed idly through the mail which had accumulated during his absence. When Emma's handwriting caught his eye, he grinned.

*Dear Johnno,*
    *I've snuck away from the nuns for a little while. I
guess I'll do penance for it later, but I felt I might scream
if I didn't have a few minutes alone. Most of the sisters*

*are cranky today. Three seniors were expelled yesterday.
There's a rule about smoking in uniform so Karen Jones,
Mary Alice Plessinger, and Tomisina Gibralti stripped
down to their slips in the locker room and lit up. Most of
the girls think it was cool, but Mother Superior doesn't
have much of a sense of humor.*

With a laugh, Johnno pushed aside the salad, lifted his wine, and settled into the letter.

*I've been thinking a lot lately about Da, and you and
the others. I've seen the stories about Stevie, and I hate
the things everyone's saying about him. Have you seen
him? Is he all right? The picture I have came from the
London Times and makes him look so old and sick. I
don't want to believe that he's a drug addict, but I'm not
a child. Da won't talk to me about it, so I'm asking you.
You always tell me the truth. Some of the girls say that all
rock singers are drug addicts. Some of the girls are
complete asses.*

*Gossip manages to get through the walls here, too. I
have the article and the pictures of Bev and Da and P.M.
from People. Jane was in the picture, too. I don't want to
call her my mother. Please don't tell Da that I wrote you
about it. He gets so upset and it doesn't change anything.
I was upset at first, but I thought about it for a long
time. It's okay if Bev loves P.M., isn't it? It almost makes
it like she's family again.*

*I guess I'm really writing to ask you to look after Da.
I know he pretends he doesn't think about Bev anymore,
that he doesn't love her. But he does. I can tell. When I
get out of school, I'll be able to take care of him myself.
I'm going to have a base in New York with Marianne,
and I can travel all over with him, taking pictures.*

*The one enclosed is a self-portrait. I took it last week.
Note the earrings. Marianne pierced my ears, and I nearly
fainted. I haven't broken the news to Da yet, so keep
mum, will you? Spring break's just nine days off, and that
should be soon enough for him to see the damage himself.*

*Da says we'll spend Easter on Martinique. Please come, Johnno. Please.*

*I love you,
Emma*

And what was he supposed to do about Emma? Johnno wondered. He could show the letter to Brian and say "Look, read this and straighten your ass up. Your daughter needs you." And if he did, neither Brian nor Emma would forgive him.

She was growing up, and growing up fast. Pierced ears, training bras, and philosophy. Brian wouldn't be able to keep her in a bubble much longer.

Well, he would try to be there when the blow came, for both of them. Tilting back his glass, he drained the wine. And it looked as though he'd be spending a few days in Martinique.

◆ ◆ ◆ ◆

$W$ITH THE WHITE sand heating under him, and his rum growing warm, Brian watched his daughter cut through the surf. What was she racing against? he wondered. Why did she always seem to be in a hurry to get from one point to the next? He could have told her that once she reached the finish line the glory was only momentary. But she wouldn't have listened.

A teenager. Sweet Jesus, how had she come to be a teenager? And how had he come to be a thirty-three-year-old icon?

At thirteen it had all seemed very simple to him. His goals had been perfectly defined. To get out of the slums, to play his music, to be someone. He'd accomplished all of that. So where was the thrill? He picked up his glass and drank deeply. Where the hell was the thrill?

He watched Emma dive under a wave, then come up, sleek as an otter, on the other side. He wished she wouldn't swim out so far. It was so much easier to worry when he could see her. The months when she was tucked away in school, he never worried. She was a good student, well mannered, quietly obedient. Then the holidays would come, and she would pop back into his life. That much more grown-up, that much more beautiful. He would see that look in her eyes, that dark, determined look he recognized as his own. It frightened him.

"God, what energy." Johnno dropped down beside him. "She doesn't slow down much, does she?"

"No. We getting old, Johnno?"

"Shit." Johnno adjusted his panama and tried a sip of Brian's rum. "Rock stars don't get old, son. They play Vegas." Grimacing, he screwed the glass back into the sand. "We ain't there yet." He settled back on his elbows. "Of course, we ain't Shaun Cassidy, either."

"Thank Christ."

"Keep that up and you'll never get your picture in *Tiger Beat*." They sat in silence a moment, listening to the whoosh of the waves. Johnno was glad he'd come. The quiet of the private villa and beach was the perfect contrast to the crowded rush of New York, or the rainy spring in London. The villa behind them was three stories, with terraces jutting out over the sea—high walls and hedges on three sides and the white curve of beach on the fourth. The pretty pastel stones glinted in the sunlight, and there was the scent of water and hot flowers everywhere.

Yes, he was glad he'd come, not just because of the sunshine, but because of the time it had given him, the quiet time, with Brian and with Emma. The time he knew would come all too quickly to an end.

"Pete rang up a little while ago."

Brian watched Emma stand in thigh-high water, lift her face to the sun. Her skin had warmed—not tanned, he thought, not browned, but warmed. The color of apricots. He worried about how soon some hungry young boy would want a taste. "And?"

"Things are set for next month. We can start recording."

"And Stevie?"

"They're going to put him on some kind of outpatient program. He's a registered junkie now." Johnno shrugged. "Methadone program. If you can't get drugs from the street, you get them from the government. Anyhow, he'll be ready. Will you?"

Brian picked up his glass, drained it. The rum had been heated by the sun and ran mellow down his throat. "I've been ready."

"Glad to hear it. You don't intend to take a punch at P.M., do you?"

"Give me a break, Johnno."

"I'd rather see you smash his nose than spend the next months freezing him out, or working up to killing him in his sleep."

"I've got no problem with P.M.," Brian said carefully. "It's his life."

"And your wife."

Brian shot Johnno a vicious look, but he managed, barely, to control the ugly words that sprang to mind. "Bev hasn't been my wife for a long time."

Johnno glanced over to be certain Emma was still out of earshot. "That line's all right for anyone else. Not for me, Bri." He put a hand on Brian's wrist, squeezed, then released. "I know it's going to be hard for you. I just want to make sure you're ready."

He lifted his glass, remembered it was empty, and set it down again. Despite the breeze off the water, he was finding the heat oppressive. "You can't go back, Johnno. And you can't stand still. So you keep going forward whether you're ready or not."

"Oh, that was great!" Emma dropped to her knees between her father and Johnno, her hair streaming. "You should come out."

"In the water?" Johnno said, tilting down his blue-lensed sunglasses. "Emma, luv, there are *things* in the water. Slimy things."

Laughing, she leaned over to kiss his cheek, then her father's. She caught the sharp scent of rum and fought to keep her smile in place. "Old people sit on the beach," she said lightly. "Middle-aged people sit on the beach."

"Middle-aged?" Brian caught a hank of her hair and tugged. "Just who're you calling middle-aged?"

"Oh, just people who sit on the beach all morning with umbrellas at their backs." She grinned. "Why don't you two sit right here, rest yourselves. I'll fetch you a cold drink. And I'll get my camera. I can take pictures so you can look back and remember your nice, restful vacation."

"She's got a mouth on her, Bri."

"I've noticed."

"Shall we let her get by with it?"

He glanced at his friend. "Not a chance."

She squealed when they lunged. She could have been quicker, if she'd wanted to, but put up a good wriggling fight as her father grabbed her legs and Johnno hooked his hands under her arms.

"Into the brink, I'd say." Johnno tossed back his head so that his hat landed in the sand. Then keeping pace with Brian raced to the water. Emma held her breath, and took them under with her.

◆ ◆ ◆ ◆

SHE'D NEVER BEEN happier in her life. It had all been perfect, completely, wonderfully perfect. Days in the sun, nights listening to Johnno and her father play. Cheating with Johnno at cards. Walks along the beach with her father. She had rolls of film to develop, pockets of memory to store.

So how could she sleep? Emma wondered. It was her last night on Martinique, her last night with her father. Her last night of freedom. Tomorrow she would be on a plane, headed back to school, where there were rules for everything. What time to get up, what time to sleep, what to wear, what to think.

With a sigh, she shook her head. It would be summer soon, she reminded herself. And she would go to London. She would see Stevie and P.M. then as well. She could watch while they recorded.

She'd get through the next few weeks somehow. She had to. It was so important to Da, she thought, that she get her education, that she be safe and well looked after. Well, the nuns did that, she decided. There was hardly a moment in the day when you weren't looked after.

She could hear the water. Smell it. Going with instinct, she dragged on a pair of shorts. It was late. Even the guards would be asleep. She would go to the beach alone for her last night. Alone. She could sit and watch the water, and no one would watch her.

She hurried out, down the hall of the rented villa, down the stairs. Holding her breath, she slipped out of the tall glass doors and ran.

She gave herself only an hour. When she tiptoed back to the villa, she was soaking wet. It hadn't been enough to watch the water after all. She came in quietly, with the idea to make a dash to her room. When she heard her father's voice, she sunk into the shadows.

"Just keep it down, luv. Everyone's asleep."

There was a feminine giggle, then a whisper, thickly French. "I'm quiet as a mouse."

Brian came into the room with a curvy little brunette wrapped around him. She was wearing a hot-pink sarong and carrying gold high heels. "I'm so glad you came in tonight, *chéri*." She ran her hands up his sides, then hooking them tightly around his neck, brought his mouth to hers.

Embarrassed and confused, Emma shut her eyes. But she could hear the quick, wet moans.

"Mmm. You're in a hurry." The French woman laughed, working her way under Brian's shirt. "I'll give you your money's worth, *chéri*, don't you worry. But you promised me a party first."

"Right." And that would help, he thought. Her hair was dark and sleek, but her eyes were brown instead of green. After a couple of lines it wouldn't matter. Nothing would. He went to a table and, unlocking a drawer, took out a small white vial. "Party time."

The brunette clapped her hands. Hips swinging, she walked to the glass coffee table and knelt.

Appalled, Emma watched her father set up the cocaine. Straws, mirrors, the razor blade. His movements were competent, practiced. His head bent close to the brunette's.

"Ah." The French woman leaned back, eyes brilliant. She dipped a fingertip into the dust on the mirror then rubbed it over her gums. "Delicious."

Brian hooked a finger in her sarong, drew her to him. He felt incredible. Young, powerful, invincible. He was hard and ready and full of needs. He bent her back, intending to take her quickly the first time. After all, he'd paid for all night.

"Da."

His head whipped up. He focused, but it seemed like a dream. His daughter, with shadows at her back, her face pale, her eyes dark and wet, her hair streaming over her shoulders. "Emma?"

"Emma?" The French woman purred the name. "Who is this Emma?" Annoyed that Brian's attention had shifted, she twisted around. There was speculation, then interest. "So, you like children, too. *Ça va.* Come then, pretty one. Join the party."

"Shut up, goddamn you. She's my daughter." He struggled up. "Emma . . . I thought you were in bed."

"Yes." Her voice was flat. "I know."

"You shouldn't be down here." He stepped forward to take her arm. "You're cold. And wet," he said, fighting the sharp-edged buzz of the coke. "Where have you been?"

"I went down to the beach." Avoiding his eyes, she tried to turn toward the stairs.

"Alone? You went down to the beach alone? At night?"

"Yes." She whirled back to him, gritting her teeth at the scent of the French woman's perfume. "I went down to the beach alone. Now I'm going to bed."

"You know better." He took both her arms now, shaking her. "You know you're not to go anywhere without the guards. For Christ's sake you've been swimming. What if you'd had a cramp?"

"Then I'd have drowned."

"Come, *chéri*, let the child go to bed." The brunette prepared another line. "This is a party."

"Shut the fuck up," he shouted at her. She only shrugged and snorted. "Don't you ever do this again," he demanded, turning back to Emma. "Do you understand?"

"Oh yes. I understand." She jerked away from him, eyes dark and dry. "I wish to God I didn't, but I understand."

"We'll talk about this later."

"About my walk on the beach, or about this?" She gestured toward the woman still kneeling at the table.

"This is none of your business."

"No." Her lips curved, but her voice was flat and dull. "No, you're quite right about that. I'll just go to bed then and leave you with your whore and your drugs."

He slapped her. His arm swung up before he knew it would. His hand whipped across her face before he could stop it. He saw the mark of it on her cheek, the red flag of violence he so detested. Stunned, he looked down at his own hand . . . and saw his father's.

"Emma—"

She stepped back in a quick, jerky motion, shaking her head. Rarely had he ever raised his voice to her, and now, the first time she questioned him, the first time she criticized, he struck her. Turning, she bolted up the stairs.

Johnno let her pass. He stood, halfway down, shirtless, cotton sweatpants low on his hips. His hair was disheveled, his eyes tired. "Let me talk to her," he said before Brian could rush by. He took a strong grip on his friend's arm. "She won't hear you now, Bri. Let me hold her hand for a while."

He nodded. His palm stung where it had connected with her face. His baby's face. "Johnno—I'll make it up to her."

"Sure." Johnno squeezed his shoulder, then gestured. "You'd best tidy up your mess down here."

Her eyes were dry. Emma sat, heedless of her wet clothes, on the edge of her bed. But she didn't cry. The world, the beautiful world she had built around her father had crumbled. She was lost again.

She bolted up when the door opened, then sank back to the bed when she saw Johnno. "I'm all right," she told him. "I don't need anyone to kiss it and make it better."

"Okay." He came in nonetheless, and sat beside her. "Want to yell at me awhile?"

"No."

"That's a relief. Why don't you get out of those wet things?" He put his hands over his eyes, then spread his fingers and grinned. "No peeking."

Because it was something to do, she rose and went to her closet for a robe. "You knew, didn't you?"

"That your father liked women? Yes. I guess I first suspected it when we were twelve."

"I'm not joking, Johnno."

So, she wouldn't give him an easy way out. "Okay. Listen, Emmy luv, a man's entitled to sex. It just isn't something he likes to flaunt in front of his daughter."

"He paid her. She was a whore."

"What do you want me to say?" When she stopped in front of him, wearing a white terry-cloth robe, he took her hands. She looked pitifully young now, her hair wet and sleek around her head and shoulders, her eyes dark and disillusioned. "Should I tell you the nuns are right, and it's a sin? They probably are. But this is real life, Emma, and people sin in real life. Brian was lonely."

"Then it's all right to have sex with a stranger if you're lonely."

"This is why God saw to it that I wouldn't be a father," Johnno murmured. He tried again, the best way he knew. With the truth. "Sex is easy, and it's empty, no matter how exciting it is at the moment. Making love with someone is a whole different experience. You'll find that out for yourself. When feelings are involved, I guess you could practically say it's holy."

"I don't understand. I don't think I want to. He went out, found that woman and paid for her. He had cocaine. I saw it. I know Stevie . . . but I never believed Da. I never believed it."

"There are all kinds of loneliness, Emma."

"Do you do it, too?" She set her jaw.

"I have." He hated admitting a weakness to her. Strange, but until that moment when he had to confess his own flaws, he hadn't realized how much he loved her. "I probably haven't missed much. The sixties, Emma. You had to be there." He laughed a little, and drew her down beside him. "I stopped because I didn't like it. I didn't like giving up my control for a quick buzz. That doesn't make me a hero. It's easier for me. I don't have the pressure Brian does. He takes everything to heart, I take everything as it comes. The group's what's important to me, you see. With Bri, it's the world. It always has been."

She could still see him, her father, with his head bent over the line of white powder. "That doesn't make it right."

"No." He leaned his head on hers. "I guess not."

The tears came now, hot and fast. "I didn't want to see him like that. I didn't want to know. I still love him."

"I know. He loves you, too. We all do."

"If I hadn't gone out, if I hadn't wanted to be alone, none of this would have happened."

"You wouldn't have seen it, but it would still have been there." He kissed her hair. "Now you just have to accept that he's not perfect."

"It's not going to be the same, is it, Johnno?" On a sigh, she leaned against him. "It's not going to be quite the same ever again."

# Chapter Eighteen

**• • • •**

New York, 1982

*W*HAT DO YOU think he's going to say?" Marianne hauled her suitcase out of the cab while Emma paid off the driver.

"I imagine he'll say hello."

"Come on, Emma."

Emma pushed back her hair as the late evening wind tugged at it. "He'll ask what the hell we're doing here, and I'll tell him."

"Then he'll call your father and we'll be dragged off to the gallows."

"They don't hang in this state anymore." Emma picked up her own suitcase, then drew a deep breath. New York City. It was good to be back. This time, she intended to stay.

"Gas chamber, firing squad, it's all the same. Your father's going to kill us both."

Emma paused with her hand on the knob of the lobby door. "Want to back out?"

"Not on your life." Marianne grinned, then scooped a hand through her cap of red hair. "Let's do it."

Emma strolled in, pausing on her way across the lobby to smile at the security guard. "Hello, Carl."

"Miss—why, Miss McAvoy." He set down his late-evening pastrami sandwich and beamed at her. "It's been over a year now, hasn't it? You're all grown-up."

"A college woman." She laughed. "This is my friend Miss Carter."

"Nice meeting you, Miss Carter." Carl brushed crumbs from

the sleeve of his uniform. "Does Mr. Donovan know you're coming?"

"Of course." She lied sweetly, with a smile. "Didn't he tell you? Well, that's Johnno. We'll only be staying for a couple of days." She moved to the elevators as she spoke. It would be best if he didn't buzz upstairs and let the cat out of the bag. "I'm going to school here now."

"I thought you were going to some fancy university in London."

"I transferred." She winked at him. "You know my heart's in New York."

As the doors closed in front of them, Marianne rolled her eyes. "Very smooth, McAvoy, very smooth."

"Most of it was true." She laughed, then let out a nervous breath. "I've been eighteen for two months. It's time I tried my independence."

"I've been eighteen for seven months and my father still pitched a fit when I transferred to NYCC. Well, it's done. Tomorrow we're going to start looking for an apartment. Then we're going to live just the way we always planned it."

"Yeah. Well, over the first hurdle." They stepped out of the elevator and walked down the wide, quiet hall to Johnno's condo. "Let me do the talking," Emma warned. At Marianne's bland look, she sighed. "I mean it. The last time you did the talking we ended up polishing pews for three Saturdays running."

"I'm an artist, not a lawyer," she muttered, then put on her best smile when the door opened.

"Johnno!" Emma launched herself into his arms. "Surprise," she said, then kissed him.

"Hold up." He was only half dressed, and groggy with after-dinner wine and sleep. With his hands on her shoulders, he held Emma back. She'd grown tall. In the last eighteen months she'd sprung up like a willow, slim, graceful, with hints of elegance. Her pale blond hair was scooped back with combs, so that it fell full and straight to brush her shoulders. She wore snug faded jeans with a skinny ribbed shirt tucked into them. Wide gold hoops swung at her ears. "For Christ's sake, you look like an off-duty model." He shifted his gaze to Marianne. "And here's my favorite redhead. What have you done to your hair?" He rubbed a hand over Marianne's short spiked do.

"It's what's happening now," she told him, then leaned her cheek in for a kiss. "Did we get you up?"

"Yes. I suppose I should let you in before I ask what the hell you're doing here." He glanced down. "With suitcases."

"Oh, Johnno, it's so good to be here. The minute I got in the cab at the airport, I felt at home." She dropped her suitcase, then took a quick spin around the room. She plopped onto the couch, rubbed a hand over the oyster-colored cushions, then popped up again. "How are you?"

"Uh-uh." He knew her well enough to recognize the restless energy as nerves. "I'll ask the questions. Drink?"

"Yes, please."

He walked over to a circular glass bar and rooted out two soft drinks. "Is there a school holiday I don't know about?"

"Liberation Day. Marianne and I have both transferred to NYCC."

"Have you now?" He poured Diet Pepsi into two glasses. "Strange Brian didn't mention it."

"He doesn't know." Emma took the two glasses and passed one to Marianne along with a warning look. "Before you say anything, I'd like you to listen."

In response, he gave her ear a quick tug. "How did you slip by Sweeney and the other one?"

"A brown wig, horn-rimmed glasses, and a limp."

"Very clever." Johnno took her glass and sipped, not certain he was comfortable in the role of avuncular confidant. "Do you have any idea how worried Brian's going to be?"

There was a flash of regret in her eyes, then it hardened into determination. "I intend to call him, and explain everything. My mind's made up, Johnno. Nothing you or he or anyone says can change it."

"I haven't tried to change it yet." He frowned at Marianne. "You're awfully quiet."

"I've been warned. I've already been through all this with my parents," she added quickly. "They don't particularly like it, but we're set. Emma and I are both eighteen now. We know what we want."

He felt suddenly, uncomfortably old. "And being eighteen means you can do as you please?"

"We're not kids anymore," Marianne began before Emma put a hand over her mouth.

"Sit down, Marianne, and be quiet."

Emma took her glass back from Johnno. "I know how much I owe my father, and you. Since I was three years old, I've done everything he's asked of me. Not just out of gratitude, Johnno, you know that, but because I love him more than anyone in the world. I can't go on being a child for him, being content in whatever safe little box he's picked out for me. You wanted something, and so did he. You went for it. Well, I want something, too."

She walked over to her suitcase, popped it, then took out a portfolio. The nerves had faded. The energy hadn't. "These are my pictures. I'm going to try my hand at making a living from them, and I'm going to go to school here, to learn how. I'm going to share an apartment with Marianne. I'm going to make friends, and go out to clubs and walk in the park. I'm going to be a part of the world for a change instead of standing right on the edge looking in. Please understand."

"How unhappy were you?"

She smiled a little. "I couldn't begin to explain."

"Maybe you should have."

"I tried." She turned away a moment. "He didn't understand. He couldn't. I only wanted to be with him, with you. Because that wasn't possible I tried to be what he wanted. That night in Martinique." She paused, choosing her words carefully. Even Marianne didn't know what she had seen. "Things changed for me, and for Da. I finished out what I'd started, Johnno. I owed him that—so much more than that. But this is for me."

"I'll talk to him for you."

"Thank you."

"Don't thank me yet. He's liable to take one leap over the Atlantic and lop off my head." Idly, he opened the portfolio. "You always were clever," he murmured. "Both of you." He nodded to a sketch of Devastation that hung on the east wall. "Told you I was going to frame it."

With a cry of pleasure Marianne leaped up. She had drawn it on the evening of their graduation celebration. The house Brian had rented on Long Island had been full of people. Never one to be shy, Marianne had ordered all four men to pose. "I didn't think you meant it. Thanks."

"I suppose you're going to make your way drawing pictures while Emma snaps them."

"That's right. It'll be a bit hard to be starving artists with the inheritance my grandmother left me, but we're going to give it a shot."

"Speaking of starving, have you eaten?"

"I had a hot dog at the airport while I was waiting for Emma's flight to get in." Marianne grinned. "It wasn't enough."

"I suppose we should eat then, before I call Brian." Johnno came from around the bar. "It may be our last meal."

"Hey, Johnno. Couldn't you sleep?" Both girls turned at the sound of another male voice. They watched the man, the truly gorgeous man, come down the curving stairs in nothing but a pair of jogging shorts. "I wondered where you'd gone off to. Oh." He paused, combed his fingers through dark, tousled hair, and smiled at the girls. "Hello. I didn't know we had company."

"Luke Caruthers, Emma McAvoy and Marianne Carter." Johnno stuck his hands in the pockets of his sweats. "Luke writes for *New York* magazine." He hesitated, then shrugged. "He lives here."

"Oh," was all Emma could think of to say. She'd seen enough of intimacy, envied it enough, to recognize it. "Hello."

"So you're Emma. I've heard so much about you." He smiled, holding out his hand. "Somehow I expected a little girl."

"Not anymore," she managed.

"And you're the artist." He offered his dazzling smile to Marianne. "Nice work."

"Thanks." She tilted her head, smiled back, and hoped she looked sophisticated.

"I was just offering the ladies a meal. They've been traveling."

"A midnight snack sounds good to me. But let me whip it up. Johnno's cooking is poison."

Marianne stood a moment, torn between fascination and middle-class shock. "I'll—ah—I'll give you a hand." She cast a quick look at Emma and fled behind Luke to the kitchen.

"I guess we came at a bad time," Emma began. "I didn't realize you had a . . . roommate." Blowing out a breath, she sat on the arm of a chair. "I had no idea, Johnno. I really had no idea."

"Rock and roll's best-kept secret," he said lightly, but his hands were clenched in his pockets. "So would you like me to help you make an excuse, and reservations at the Waldorf?"

Her cheeks heated as she looked down at her hands. "No, of course not. Does Da know—of course he does," she said quickly. "Stupid question. I don't know what to say. He, ah, Luke's very attractive."

A trace of amusement lit Johnno's eyes. "Yes, I think so."

Her blush deepened, but she managed to look at him again. "You're making fun of me now."

"No, luv." His voice was soft. "Never you."

She studied him, carefully, trying to see if he looked different somehow—if she could find something odd or wrong with the face she knew so well. There was nothing, only Johnno. Her lips curved a little. "Well, I guess my plans do have to change."

He felt the twist—harder, sharper than the fists of the boys from his youth. "I'm sorry, Emma."

"Not half as sorry as I am," she told him. "I have to give up my fantasy about seducing you." For the first time in her life she saw his face go totally blank.

"I beg your pardon?"

"Well, I always thought, when I grew up, when you saw me as a woman." She stood up, spreading her arms out, then down her sides. "I'd come to visit you here, fix you a meal by candle-light, put on the music, then seduce you." She pulled a chain from under her blouse. On it hung a little plastic ring with a gaudy red stone. "I always thought you'd be my first."

Speechless, he stared at the ring, then looked up and into her eyes. There was love there, the kind that lasted lifetimes. And there was understanding without blame. Stepping forward, he took her hands. His voice was thick when he found it. "Very rarely have I regretted being gay." He brought her hands to his lips to kiss them. "This is one of those very rare times."

"I love you, Johnno."

He held her against him. "I love you, Emma. God knows why, since you're such an ugly bitch." When she laughed, he drew her back for a kiss. "Come on then, not only is Luke good to look at, but he's a hell of a cook."

◆ ◆ ◆ ◆

EMMA AWOKE EARLY and followed the scent of coffee and the muted sounds of the television to the kitchen. It wasn't jet lag she felt now, but the restless disorientation of waking up in a strange bed after only snatches of sleep. There was an awkward moment as she stood in the kitchen doorway watching Luke butter toast across from the television set where David Hartman interviewed Harrison Ford.

She'd almost been able to relax around Luke the night before as they'd all eaten soup and hot sandwiches in the kitchen.

He was well mannered, witty, intelligent, and mouthwateringly attractive. And gay. So was Johnno, Emma reminded herself and tried a smile.

"Good morning."

Luke turned. He looked different this morning with his hair styled, his face shaven. He wore gray pleated slacks and a trim blue shirt set off with a thin tie of a darker shade. He looked alert and hiply professional. The upwardly mobile young executive, she thought, and such a complete contrast to Johnno.

"Hi. Didn't think you'd surface till this afternoon. Coffee?"

"Thanks. I couldn't sleep. Marianne and I are going apartment hunting this afternoon. And I guess I'm worried about how my father reacted when Johnno called him."

"Johnno's very persuasive." He slid the coffee in front of her. "Why don't I put you out of your misery? Toast?"

"No." She pressed a hand to her stomach. "Do you know what happened?"

"They argued, a lot." Luke checked his watch, then sat beside her. "Johnno called him a few names I'm not sure he'd like me to repeat to you."

She dropped her head into her cupped hands. "Terrific."

"He also vowed, and I think a blood oath was mentioned, to keep an eye on you."

"Bless him."

"In the end, and it was a long time coming, Brian agreed to your attending college here, but—" he added before Emma could leap up and dance. "You have to keep the guards."

"Dammit, I will not have those two hulking bastards dogging my every move. I might as well be back in Saint Catherine's. When is he going to realize that there isn't a kidnapper behind every bush? People don't even know who I am, and they don't care."

"He cares." He put a hand over hers. "Emma, sometimes we have to take what we can get. I know."

"I only want to live a normal life," she began.

"Most of us want that." He smiled again when she looked up and flushed. "Look, we both care about Johnno, so I figure that makes us friends. Right?"

"All right."

"Then this is my first friendly advice. Think of it this way. You want to be in New York, right?"

"Yes."

"You want to go to NYCC."

"Yes."

"You want your own place."

She blew out a frustrated breath. "Yes."

"Well, you've got it."

"You're right," she said after a moment. "You're absolutely right. And I can ditch the guards when I want to."

"I didn't hear that." He checked his watch again. "Listen, I've got to run. Tell Johnno I'll pick up Chinese." He grabbed a briefcase, then stopped. "I forgot. Are these yours?" He pointed to the portfolio open on the kitchen counter.

"Yes."

"Good work. Mind if I take them with me, show them around?"

"You don't have to do that. Just because I'm friends with Johnno doesn't mean—"

"Hold on. Look, I happened to see them sitting out in the other room. I took a closer look and liked what I saw. Johnno didn't ask me to pump up your ego. He wouldn't."

She rubbed her palms on her thighs. "Do you really like them?"

"Yes. I know some people. I could get you some input if you want."

"I would, very much. I know I have a lot to learn—that's why I'm here. I've entered some competitions and shows, but . . ." She trailed off, knowing she was babbling. "Thanks. I appreciate it."

"Sure. See you later." He tucked the portfolio under his arm and headed out.

She sat alone, taking very careful breaths. She was on her way, Emma thought. Finally, she was on her way.

# Chapter Nineteen

♦ ♦ ♦ ♦

$\mathcal{I}$T'S OURS."

Emma and Marianne stood, their arms tossed around each other's shoulders, looking out the windows of their newly purchased loft in SoHo. Emma's voice was both dazed and exhilarated as she made the statement.

"I still can't believe it," Marianne murmured.

"Believe it. It's ours—twenty-foot ceilings, bad plumbing, and interest rates from hell." On a quick laugh, Emma did three spins. "We're property owners, Marianne. You, me, and Chase Manhattan."

"We bought it." Marianne sat down on the scarred wide-planked floor. The rattle and hum of downtown traffic echoed up from three stories below. Something crashed outside, and even through the closed windows they heard the shouts and swearing. It was like music.

The loft was a huge square of space, banked by a band of windows in the front and a towering panel of glass on the right.

A sound investment, Marianne's father had grudgingly called it.

Complete insanity, had been Johnno's verdict.

Investment or insanity, it was theirs. Still dressed in the tidy suits they'd worn to the settlement, they each studied their new home, the fruit of weeks of search, endless calls to realtors, and numerous bank interviews. It might have been a huge, empty space with spotted ceilings and grimy glass, but for them, it was the dream they had shared throughout childhood.

Then they studied each other, their faces mirrors of giddy terror. It was the laughter that broke the last strain. It bubbled up from Emma first, then echoed off the high plaster walls. Grabbing each other, they did an impromptu polka up and down the length of their new home.

"Ours," Emma panted out when they teetered to a stop.

"Ours." They shook hands formally, then laughed again.

"Okay, co-owner," Marianne began. "Let's make some decisions."

They sat on the floor with Marianne's sketches, warming Pepsis, and an overflowing tin ashtray between them. They needed a wall here, the staircase there. Studio space above, darkroom space below.

They arranged, rearranged, constructed, destructed. At length Marianne waved her cigarette. "This is it. Perfect."

"It's inspired." Emma took the cigarette out of self-defense and rewarded herself with a puff. "You're a genius."

"Yes, I am." She shook her spiky hair as she leaned back on her elbows. "You helped."

"Right. We're both geniuses. A space for everything and everything in its space. I can't wait until we—oh, shit."

"Shit? What do you mean, shit?"

"There's no bathroom. We forgot the bathroom."

After a brief study, Marianne shrugged. "Screw the bathroom. We'll use the Y."

Emma simply put a hand on Marianne's face and shoved.

◆ ◆ ◆ ◆

PERCHED ON A stepladder, Marianne painted full-length portraits of herself and Emma between two windows. Emma had taken on the more pedestrian chore of marketing and was storing food inside their reconditioned Frigidaire.

"That's our buzzer," Marianne called out over the boom of the radio.

"I know." Emma balanced two grapefruits, a six-pack of Pepsi, and a jar of strawberry preserves. When the buzzer sounded again, she dumped all of them on a shelf. Beside the elevator, which opened up into their living area, she pushed the intercom. "Yes?"

"McAvoy and Carter?"

"That's right."

"Delivery from Beds, Beds, Beds."

Emma released the entrance door, let out a war whoop.

"What?" Marianne demanded, sitting back far enough to frown at her work.

"Beds!" Emma shouted. "We've got beds."

"Don't joke about something like that, Emma. Not while I'm painting, or I'll give you a wart."

"I'm not joking. They're on their way up."

Marianne paused, dripping brush in hand. "Real beds?"

"Mattresses, Marianne." Emma leaned a hand on the ladder. "Box springs."

"Jesus." Marianne shut her eyes, then gave a dramatic shudder. "I think I had an orgasm."

At the elevator's ding, Emma was across the room like a shot. When the doors opened, all she could see was a queen-sized mattress covered in plastic. "Where do you want it?" was the muffled question.

"Oh. You can take that one right up those stairs in the far corner." The man with "Buddy" stitched across his cap rolled his eyes, hefted the mattress over his head, and started for the stairs. "We could only fit one at a time in the elevator. My partner's waiting downstairs."

"Oh, right." She pushed the release button again. "Real beds," she said as Marianne joined her.

"Please, not while we have company. Damn, there's the phone. I'll get it."

The elevator dinged. Emma directed the second man—Riko according to his cap—then smiled at Buddy as he went out to get box springs. When the elevator opened, she grinned at the box springs that filled the car. "One goes up, one goes down. Want a cold drink?"

Brian eased his way from behind the springs. "Yeah."

"Da!"

"Mr. McAvoy," Marianne shouted over the radio. She stopped in midstream, wiped her painty hands on her overalls. "Hi."

"You want to move?" Buddy complained, then maneuvered the box springs toward the stairs.

"Da," Emma managed again. "We didn't know you were here."

"Obviously. Christ, Emma, anyone could ride up in that elevator. Do you always leave the entrance unlatched?"

"They're delivering. Beds." She gestured as Riko struggled in with his load. She drummed up a smile and kissed her father. "I thought you were in London."

"I was. I decided it was time I got a look at where my daughter was living." He stepped farther into the room to take a long, frowning study. Drop cloths covered most of the floor. The packing crate from the stove served as both a table and a stool and was now covered with old newspapers, a lamp, a half-filled glass, and a paint can. The radio sat on a windowsill, blasting away as Casey Kasem ran down the top forty. The stepladder, the card table, and a single folding chair composed the rest of the furniture.

"Jesus," was all Brian could think of to say.

"We're a construction zone," Emma told him with forced cheerfulness. "It doesn't look like it, but we're nearly done. The carpenters just have a bit of finish work here and there and mister—I mean the tile man is coming Monday to finish the bath."

"It looks like a warehouse."

"Actually, it was a factory," Marianne chimed in. "We've sectioned it off here and there with glass brick. That was Emma's idea. It's great, isn't it?" She pointed to the waist-high wall that separated the living area from the kitchen. "We got some terrific old appliances," she continued, and taking his arm, gave him the tour.

"Emma's bedroom's going to be here. The glass makes it private, but still lets in the light. I'm upstairs—a sort of combination studio and bedroom. Emma's darkroom's already set up through there, and come Monday the bath should be not only functional but attractive."

He hated the fact that he could see the potential. Hated it because it made Emma seem less like his little girl than a woman, and a stranger.

"Have you decided to do without furniture?"

"We wanted to wait until it was finished." Emma knew her voice was stiff, but couldn't prevent it. "We aren't in any hurry."

"Wanna sign here?" Buddy pushed a clipboard under her nose. "You're all set." He blew his nose into a red bandana, then eyed Brian. "Hey. Hey, aren't you—well, sure you are. I'll be damned. McAvoy. You're Brian McAvoy. Hey, Riko, this here's Brian McAvoy. Devastation."

"No shit?"

Automatically Brian's lips curved into a charming smile. "Nice to meet you."

"This is great, just great," Buddy went on. "My wife's never going to believe it. We had our first date at your concert here in '75. Can I get your autograph?"

"Sure."

"Jesus, she's never going to believe this." While he searched in his pockets for a snatch of paper, Emma picked up a notepad and handed it to her father.

"What's your wife's name?" Brian asked Buddy.

"It's Doreen. Man, she's going to drop dead."

"I hope not." Still smiling, Brian handed over the autograph.

It took another ten minutes, and an autograph for Riko, before they were alone again. Taking her cue, Marianne disappeared up the curving wrought-iron stairs.

"Got a beer?" Brian asked.

"No. Just some soft drinks."

With a restless move of his shoulders, Brian wandered to the front windows. She was so exposed here. Couldn't she see it? The big windows, the city itself. The fact that he'd bought the first-floor unit and installed Sweeny and another man inside didn't seem to matter now that he was here to gauge the situation himself. She was vulnerable. Every time she walked out on the street.

"I was hoping you'd choose something uptown, with security."

"Like the Dakota?" she said, then cursed herself. "I'm sorry, Da. I know Lennon was a friend."

"Yes, he was." He turned back. "What happened to him should make you understand how I feel. He was shot down on the street—not for robbery, not for passion. Just because of who and what he was. You're mine, Emma. That makes you every bit as vulnerable."

"What about you?" she countered. "Every time you step out onstage, you're exposed. It only takes one sick person among the thousands with the price of a ticket. Do you think that never goes through my mind?"

He shook his head. "No, I didn't think it went through your mind. You never said."

"Would it have made a difference?"

He was silent as he sat on the windowsill and took out a cigarette. "No. You can't stop being what you are, Emma, even if you'd like to. But I've lost one child." He struck a match, watched it flare. "I couldn't survive losing another."

"I don't want to talk about Darren." The old grief welled up, thickening her voice.

"We're talking about you."

"All right then. I can't live for you anymore, or I'll hate you. I gave you Saint Catherine's, Da, and a year at a college I detested. I have to start living for myself. That's what I'm doing here."

He drew in smoke and wished for a drink. "I almost think I'd rather you hated me. You're all I've got."

"That's not true." She went to him then. Resentments and disillusionments were crowded aside by love. "I've never been all, and I never will be." She took his hand as she sat beside him. He was beautiful to look at. Even without a daughter's prejudiced eye. The years, the strains, the life, hadn't scarred him. Not on the outside. Perhaps he was a bit too thin, but time hadn't lined his poetic face or grayed his pale blond hair. What magic was it, she wondered, that had caused her to grow up while he hadn't grown older? She kept her hand over his and chose her words carefully.

"But the trouble is, for most of my life, you're all I've had." Her fingers tightened on his. "And just about all I've needed. I need more now, Da. All I want is a chance to find it."

He glanced around the room. "Here?"

"To start."

It was impossible to argue with something he understood so perfectly. "Let me put in a security system."

"Da—"

"Emma," he interrupted, squeezing her hand. "I need my sleep."

She laughed a little and relaxed. "All right. I'll look at it as a housewarming present." She kissed him. "Want to stay for dinner?"

He took another look around. It reminded him of his first place, though that had only been a fraction of this space. Still it brought back the memories, lugging in old furniture, slopping paint on stained walls. Making love with Bev on the floor.

"No." Suddenly he didn't want to be there, to feel the youth and the hope and the innocence. "Why don't I take you and Marianne out?"

Marianne leaned dangerously over the stair rail. "Where?"

Brian grinned up at her. "Your choice."

♦ ♦ ♦ ♦

ONCE HE WAS forced to accept Emma's decision, Brian played the indulgent father. He bought her a Warhol lithograph, an exquisite Tiffany lamp with signs of the Zodiac, and an Aubusson rug in shades of powder blue and pink. For the week he stayed in town, he dropped in daily with a new present. She couldn't stop him, and after seeing the pleasure it gave him, stopped trying.

They gave their first party on the night before he left for London. Packing crates stood on the priceless rug. The Tiffany graced the card table. There was food both in plastic bowls and in the fragile Limoges Marianne's mother had shipped to them. The radio had been replaced, thanks to Johnno, by a wall-trembling stereo unit.

A handful of college students mingled with musicians and Broadway stars. Dress ranged from denim to silks and sequins. There were arguments and laughter, all drowned out by the music blasting against the windows.

It made Emma nostalgic for the parties she remembered from her youth, the people sprawled on the floor, on pillows, the bright and beautiful discussing their art. She sipped mineral water and, as she had always done, watched.

"An interesting soirée," Johnno stated, swinging an arm around her shoulders. "Got any beer left?"

"Let's see."

She steered him into the kitchen. There wasn't much left in the fridge but a bottle of jug wine and part of a six-pack of Beck's. Emma opened a bottle and handed it to him.

"Just like old times," she said.

"More or less." He sniffed the glass in her hand. "What a good girl you are."

"I'm not much of a drinker."

"That doesn't require an apology. Bri's enjoying himself."

He nodded over the wall to where Brian was sitting on the floor and, like a traveling minstrel, plucking an acoustic guitar.

When she looked at him, strumming, singing for himself as much as for the group surrounding him, the love poured through her. "He enjoys playing like this as much as in any stadium or studio."

"More," Johnno said before he tipped back the beer. "Though I don't think he knows it."

"I think he's feeling better about all of this now." She glanced around at the mix of people crowded into her home. Her Home. "After all, he'd had a security system put in that would make the queen's guards at Buckingham Palace look like pikers."

"Annoying?"

"No. No, really it's not. Of course, I don't remember the code numbers most of the time." She sipped, content to stand in the kitchen a half-wall away from the crowd and the laughter. "Did Luke tell you that he sent my portfolio over to Timothy Runyun?"

"He mentioned it." Johnno cocked his head. "Problem?"

"I don't know. He's offered me a part-time job, as an assistant."

He took a little tug on the hair she'd pulled back in a ponytail. "There are pitiful few who start at the top, Emmy luv."

"It's not that. It's not that at all. Runyun is one of the top ten photographers in the country. Starting out with him as a janitor would be a dream come true."

"So?"

She turned away from the party to look at him, to watch his eyes. "So why did he offer me a job, Johnno? Because of my pictures, or because of you and my father?"

"Maybe you should ask Runyun."

"I intend to." She set her glass down, then picked it up again. "I know that *American Photographer* printed my shot because Luke suggested it."

"Do you?" Johnno said mildly. "I suppose the shot wasn't worthy of that honor?"

"It was a damn good shot, but—"

Johnno leaned back against the refrigerator and drank. "Lighten up, Emma. You can't go through life second-guessing everything that happens to you, good or bad."

"It's not that I'm ungrateful to Luke. He's been great, right from the start. But this isn't like giving Marianne and me cooking lessons."

"Nothing could be," Johnno said dryly.

"I want this job with Runyun to be mine." She swung back her hair. Thin gold columns danced at her ears. "You have your music, Johnno. I feel the same way about my photography."

"Are you good?"

Her chin came up. "I'm very good."

"Well, then." He considered the subject closed and glanced back at the party. "Quite a group."

She started to continue, then dragging a hand through her hair, let it go. "I'm sorry P.M. and Stevie aren't here."

"Maybe next time. Still, we have some old faces among the new. I see you dug up Blackpool."

"Actually, Da ran into him yesterday. He's doing Madison Square Garden next weekend. There isn't a ticket left in the city. Are you going to catch it?"

"I wouldn't dream of it." He cocked a brow. "I'm hardly a fan."

"But he's recorded three McAvoy/Donovan songs."

"That's business," Johnno said, and dismissed it.

"Why don't you like him?"

Johnno shrugged and drank again. "I've never been sure. Something about that smug smile."

Turning, Emma reached in the cupboard for more chips. "I suppose he's entitled to be smug. Four gold albums, a couple of Grammys, and a stunning wife."

"Stunning estranged wife, I'm told. He's certainly coming on to our favorite redhead."

"Marianne?" Tossing the bags of chips aside, Emma shifted, scanned, then spotted her roommate cuddled on the shadowy window seat with Blackpool. She felt a surge of emotion that was tangled jealousy and alarm. "Let me have a cigarette," she murmured as she struggled to shrug it off.

"She's a big girl, Emma."

"Of course she is." She drew in the strong French smoke and winced. "He's old enough to . . ." She trailed off, remembering that Johnno was four or five years Blackpool's senior.

"Atta girl," he said with a chuckle. "Bite your tongue."

But she didn't smile. "It's just that she's been so sheltered."

"Of course, Mother Superior."

"Cram it, Johnno." She picked up her drink again, and kept her eye on Blackpool. The name suited him, she thought. He had dark, lush hair and favored black clothes. Leathers, suedes, silks. He had one of those moody, sensual faces. Heathcliff, as Emma had always imagined him. And she'd always thought Brontë's character more self-destructive than heroic. Beside him, Marianne looked like a bright, slender candle ready to be lit.

"I'm only saying that she's spent most of her life in that damn school."

"In the bed next to yours," Johnno pointed out.

She wasn't in the mood to laugh. "All right, that's true. But I also had all that time with all of you, seeing things, being a part of things. Marianne went from school, to camp, to her father's estate. I know she puts on a front, but she's very naïve."

"I'd give odds on our favorite redhead. Blackpool's slick, dear, but he's not a monster."

"Of course not." But she was going to keep her eye on Marianne nonetheless. She lifted the cigarette again, then froze.

Someone had put on a new album. The Beatles. *Abbey Road.* The first cut on the A side.

"Emma." Alarmed, Johnno gripped her wrist. Her pulse was scrambling, her skin was ice. "What the hell? Emma, look here."

*"He say one and one and one is three."*

"Switch the record," she whispered.

"What?"

"Switch the record." She could feel the breath backing up in her lungs. Clogging there. "Johnno, please. Turn it off."

"All right. Stay here."

He skimmed his way through the crowd, moving quickly, smoothly enough to prevent himself from being detained.

Emma gripped the edge of the wall until her fingers went numb. She wasn't seeing the party any longer, the pretty people mixing together, laughing over plastic glasses of white wine or chilled bottles of imported beer. She could only see the shadows of a hallway, hear the hissing and snapping of monsters. And her little brother's cries.

"Emma." It was Brian now, standing in the tiny kitchen alcove, Johnno at his side. "What is it, baby? Are you sick?"

"No." It was Da, she thought. Da would make it all go away. "No, it's Darren. I heard Darren crying."

"Oh Christ." He took her shoulders and shook. "Emma, look at me."

"What?" Her head snapped up. The glaze seemed to melt away from her eyes into tears. "I'm sorry. I'm so sorry. I ran away."

"It's all right." He gathered her close. His eyes, anguished, met Johnno's over her head. "We should get her out of here."

"In her bedroom," Johnno suggested, then casually began to clear a path. He slid the frosted-glass doors closed behind them, muffling the sounds of the party.

"Let's lie down, Emma." Brian kept his voice soothing as he set her on the bed. "I'll stay right here."

"I'm okay." Her worlds had separated again. She didn't know whether to feel grief or embarrassment. "I don't know what set that off. Something just clicked and I was six years old again. I'm sorry, Da."

"Ssh." He pressed his lips to her temple. "It doesn't matter."

"It was the music," Johnno said, then settled beside her. "The music upset you."

"Yes." She moistened her dry lips. "Yes, it was the music. It was playing that night. When I woke up and heard Darren. It was playing when I started down the hall. I'd forgotten. I've never been able to listen to that cut, but I didn't know why. Tonight, I guess with the party, it all rushed back."

"Why don't I start clearing people out?"

"No." She took Johnno's hand before he could rise. "I don't want to spoil it for Marianne. I'm all right now, really. It was so strange. Almost as if I were there again. I wonder if I'd gotten to the door, if I'd have seen—"

"No." Brian's hand clamped down on hers. "It's over and done with. Behind us. I don't want you to think about it, Emma."

She was too weary to argue. "I think I'll just rest awhile. No one's going to miss me."

"I'll stay with you," Brian told her.

"No. I'm fine now. I'm just going to sleep. Christmas is only a few weeks away. I'll come to London, like I promised. We'll have a whole week."

"I'll stay until you sleep," Brian insisted.

◆ ◆ ◆ ◆

HE WAS GONE when she woke from the nightmare. It had been so real, so horribly clear. Just as the reality had been over twelve years before. Her skin was clammy with sweat as she reached for the light. She needed the light. There was so much that could hide in the dark.

It was quiet now. Five A.M. and calm, quiet. The party was over and she was alone, behind the glass walls of her room. Painfully, like an old woman, she rose out of bed to strip off her clothes and pull on a robe. She slid the door back, hit another light.

The room was a jumble. There were scents—beer going stale, smoke trapped near the ceiling, the lingering breath of perfumes and sweat. She glanced up the stairs to where Marianne slept. She didn't want to disturb her by tidying up now, though her ingrained neatness rubbed at her. She would wait until sunrise.

There was something else she had to do, and she wanted to do it quickly before cowardice could take over. Sitting by the phone, she dialed information.

"Yes. I'd like the numbers for American, TWA, and Pan Am."

# Chapter Twenty
• • • •

SHE WASN'T GOING to feel guilty. In fact, at the moment, Emma didn't want to feel much of anything. She knew if her father discovered she'd flown to California, without her guards, he'd be furious. She could only hope he didn't find out. With luck, she would have her two days in California, catch the red-eye Sunday night and be in New York again, attending class, Monday morning, with no one but Marianne the wiser.

Bless Marianne, Emma thought as the plane touched down. She hadn't asked any questions once she had seen that the answers would be painful. Instead, she had roused herself barely past dawn, tossed on a blond wig, sunglasses, and Emma's overcoat and had cabbed it to early mass at Saint Pat's. With the guards trailing behind her.

That had given Emma enough time to dash to the airport and catch her plane to the Coast. As far as Sweeney and his partner would be concerned, Emma McAvoy would be spending a quiet weekend at home. Marianne would have to do some fast talking if Brian or Johnno called, but then Marianne was nothing if not a fast talker.

In any case, Emma decided while she deplaned, the die was cast. She was here, and she would do what she had come to do.

She had to see the house again. It had been sold all those years ago, so it was doubtful she could wangle her way inside. But she had to see it.

"The Beverly Wilshire," she told the cab driver.

Exhausted, she let her head fall back, let her eyes close behind her dark glasses. It was too warm for her winter coat now, but she couldn't find the energy to shrug out of it. She needed to rent a car, she realized, and let out an annoyed breath. She should have taken care of that already. With a shake of her head, she promised herself she would arrange it through the concierge as soon as she had unpacked the few things she'd tossed into her bag.

There were ghosts here, she thought. Along Hollywood Boulevard, in Beverly Hills, on the beaches at Malibu and throughout the hills looking over the L.A. basin. Ghosts of herself as a young girl on her first trip to America, of her young, heroic father hoisting her on his shoulders in Disneyland. Of Bev, smiling, a hand laid protectively over the child she carried in her womb. And always of Darren as he giggled and ran his tractor over the turkey rug.

"Miss?"

Emma blinked and focused on the uniformed doorman who stood waiting to help her from the cab.

"Checking in?"

"Yes, thank you." Mechanically, she paid off the driver, walked into the lobby to registration. She took her key, forgetting for the moment that this was the first time she had stayed alone.

In her room she opened the discreet Gucci carry-on, by habit neatly folding her lingerie, hanging her clothes, setting out her toiletries. Once done, she picked up the phone.

"This is Miss McAvoy in 312. I'd like to arrange for a rental car. Two days. Yes, as soon as possible. That'll be fine. I'll be down."

There was something else that had to be done, though she was afraid. Picking up the phone book, she opened it, skimmed through to the Ks. Kesselring, L.

Emma noted down the address in her neat hand. He was still here.

◆ ◆ ◆ ◆

"ARE YOU GOING to eat all morning, Michael, or are you going to cut the lawn?"

Michael grinned at his father and shoveled in more pancakes. "It's a big lawn. I need my strength. Right, Mom?"

"The boy doesn't eat right since he moved out." Pleased to

have both men at her table, Marge filled the coffee cups. "You're skin and bones, Michael. I've got the best part of a nice ham I cooked earlier in the week. You take it home with you."

"Don't give this deadbeat my ham," Lou objected.

Michael lifted a brow, then doused the remaining pancakes with Aunt Jemima. "Who you calling a deadbeat?"

"You lost the bet, but I don't see my grass getting mowed."

"I'll get to it," Michael grumbled and snatched another sausage. "I think that game was fixed."

"The Orioles won, fair and square. And they won over a month ago. Pay up."

Michael gestured with the sausage. It was a conversation they'd had every weekend since the World Series, and one they would undoubtedly continue to have until the first of the year when the bet would be paid in full.

"As a police captain you should be aware that gambling's illegal."

"As a rookie, assigned to my precinct, you should have better sense than to make a sucker bet. Mower's in the shed."

"I know where it is." He rose, swung an arm over his mother's shoulder. "How do you live with this guy?"

"It isn't easy." Marge smiled and patted Michael's cheek. "Be sure to be careful with that weed whacker around the rose-bushes, dear."

She watched him go out, slamming the screen door as he had always done. For a moment she wished he could be ten again, but that feeling passed quickly, leaving a quiet pride. "We did a good job, Lou."

"Yeah." He took both his and Michael's dishes to the sink. He'd aged well, putting on less than ten pounds over the last twenty years. His hair was fully gray now, but he'd kept most of it. Though he occasionally realized he was uncomfortably close to sixty, he felt better than he had in his life. Due, he thought as he put his arm around Marge, to his wife's diligent watch on things like cholesterol and sugar.

As for herself, Marge had settled contentedly into middle age. She was as trim as she'd been the day they'd been married. Nothing kept her from her twice-weekly aerobic classes. Her hair was colored a flattering ash-brown.

Five years before, she'd gotten what Lou had thought was a bee in her bonnet about starting her own business. He'd considered himself indulgent when he'd stood back and let his "little woman" open a small bookstore. He'd been kind and considerate, like an adult patting a child on the head. Then she had astonished him by showing a keen and often ruthless head for business. Her little shop had expanded. Now she had three doing brisk business in Hollywood, Bel Air, and Beverly Hills.

Life was full of surprises, he thought as he heard the mower gun. His wife, who had seemed content for years dusting furniture and baking pies was a businesswoman with her own accountant. His son, who had breezed carelessly through college, then had spent nearly eighteen months drifting, had enrolled in the police academy, without saying a word. As for himself, Lou was giving serious thought to something that had always seemed years off. Retirement.

It was a good life, Lou thought, drawing in scents of sausage and roses. On impulse, he spun his wife around and planted a long hard kiss on her mouth.

"The kid's going to be busy for at least an hour," he murmured as he cupped her breasts. "Let's go upstairs."

Marge tilted her head back, then grinned.

Michael turned the mower, enjoying the physical release and the light sweat that was working over his skin. Not that he liked losing the bet, he thought. He hated to lose anything.

But he missed a lawn, the look of it, the smell of it. His apartment suited him with its postage-stamp pool and noisy neighbors. But the suburbs, he mused, with their big, leafy trees and tidy yards, their backyard barbecues and station wagons, were home. You always felt like a kid again there. Saturday-morning bike rides. Ricky Jones down the street trying out his skateboard. Pretty girls walking by in thin cotton dresses while you traded baseball cards on the curb and pretended not to notice.

The old neighborhood hadn't changed much since his youth. It was still a place where paperboys rode bikes on delivery and tossed today's news into bushes. Neighbors still competed with each other over the best lawn, the best garden. They borrowed tools and forgot to return them.

Being there gave him a sense of continuity. Something he hadn't known he wanted until he'd moved away from it.

A movement caught his eye, and he glanced up in time to see the shade of his parents' bedroom window go down. He stopped, openmouthed, the grip of the mower vibrating under his hands. He might not have had his gold shield, but it didn't take a detective to figure out what was going on behind the shade. At nine o'clock in the morning. He continued to stare a moment, unsure if he should be amused, embarrassed, or delighted. He decided it was best not to think about it at all. There was something spooky about imagining your parents having sex.

He steered the mower one-handed, unbuttoning his shirt as he went. Christmas lights might have been strung along the eaves of the houses, but it would be eighty degrees before noon. Michael sent a casual wave to Mrs. Baxter who had come out to weed her gladiolas. She merely frowned at him, so he went back to singing along with the Bruce Springsteen number that played through his headphone. He'd sent a long fly ball through Mrs. Baxter's picture window more than ten years before, and she had yet to forgive him.

He had the backyard trimmed, and half of the front when he began to wonder why his father had never invested in a riding mower. A trim Mercedes convertible pulled up at the curb. Michael wouldn't have given it more than a glance, except there was a blonde behind the wheel. He had a weakness for blondes. She merely sat, dark glasses hiding her eyes, as a minute stretched into five.

At length she slowly got out of the car. She was as trim and sleek as the Mercedes, long, elegant legs beneath a thin cotton skirt. He noticed her hands as well, delicate, tea-serving hands that clutched tight on a gray leather purse.

Beautiful, nervous, and from out of town, Michael deduced. Rich, too, he thought. Both her bag and her shoes were leather and expensive. And there was the dull glint of real gold at her wrist and ears. There was the way she moved that whispered of wealth and privilege. Her hands might have given away her nerves, but her movements were smooth as a dancer's.

She didn't hesitate on the walk. Obviously she had made up her mind in the car to approach him. He caught her scent, light, quietly seductive, over the fragrance of fresh-cut grass.

When she smiled, his heart nearly stopped. Shutting off the motor with one hand and dragging off his headphones with the other, he stared at her. In the sudden quiet Springsteen and the E Street Band could be heard jamming metallically.

"Hello. I'm sorry to interrupt your work."

His mouth went dry. It was foolish. It was ridiculous. But he couldn't stop it. That voice—it had played through his head for years. Sneaking up on him in sleep, in front of the television, in conversations with other women. When he saw her bite her lip, he snapped himself together. Taking off his sunglasses, he smiled at her.

"Hi, Emma. Catch any good waves lately?"

Her lips parted in surprise, then recognition and pleasure curved them. "Michael." She wanted to throw her arms around him. The idea made color flutter in her cheeks, but she only held out a hand for his. "It's so good to see you again."

His hand was hard against hers, hard and damp. He released hers almost immediately to wipe his palm against his worn jeans. "You—never made it back to the beach."

"No." She continued to smile, but the dimple faded away from the corner of her mouth. "I never learned to surf. I didn't know if you'd still be living at home."

"Actually, I'm not. I lost a bet with my old man, so he gets free gardening service for a few weeks." He didn't have a clue what to say to her. She looked so beautiful, so fragile somehow, standing on the freshly shorn grass in her expensive Italian pumps, her pale hair stirring slightly in the light breeze. "How've you been?" he managed at last.

"Fine. And you?"

"All right. I've seen your picture now and again. Once you were in one of those ski places."

"Saint Moritz."

"I guess." Her eyes were the same, he thought. Big, blue, and haunted. Looking into them made his stomach dance. "Are you —visiting around here?"

"No. Well, yes. Actually—"

"Michael." He turned at his mother's voice. She stood in the doorway, neat as a pin. "Aren't you going to ask your friend in for a cold drink?"

"Sure. Got a few minutes?" he asked Emma.

"Yes. I was hoping to speak to your father."

He felt his hopes deflate like a used party balloon. Where had he gotten the idea that she had come to see him? "Dad's inside." He managed to smile. "Gloating."

Emma followed him to the door Marge had left open. She

had a death grip on her purse now, and no amount of mental effort could relax her fingers.

They had their tree up. Emma glimpsed it, standing full of tinsel and shiny balls near the front window. There were presents under it, neatly wrapped and bowed, and sprigs of pine here and there that scented the house.

The furniture was old, not shabby but established. A family had shared these pieces, she thought. Had shared them so long, they hardly saw them now, but settled into the couch or a chair comfortably day after day, evening after evening. Curtains were pulled back to let in the light. A trio of African violets bloomed lavishly on a stand by the east window.

She had taken off her sunglasses and was folding and unfolding the earpieces as she studied the room.

"Want to sit down?"

"Yes, thank you. I won't stay long. I know I'm disrupting your weekend."

"Yeah, I've been looking forward to cutting the grass all week." He grinned, relaxed again, and gestured to a chair. "I'll get my father."

Before he could, Marge walked in carrying a tray crowded with a pitcher of fresh iced tea and glasses and a plate of her homemade sugar cookies. "Here we are. Michael, button your shirt," she said casually, then set the tray on the coffee table. "It's nice to have one of Michael's friends drop by."

"Emma, this is my mother. Mom, Emma McAvoy."

Recognition came swiftly. Marge worked hard to keep both sympathy and fascination out of her eyes. "Oh yes, of course." She poured the tea. "I still have the clipping from the paper—where you and Michael met on the beach."

"Mom—"

"A mother's allowed," she said mildly. "It's nice to meet you at last, Emma."

"Thank you. I'm sorry to just drop in this way."

"Nonsense. Michael's friends are always welcome here."

"Emma came to see Dad."

"Oh." The frown in her eyes came and went quickly. "Well, he's out in the back making sure Michael didn't run down any of his rosebushes. I'll get him."

"One rosebush—when I was twelve," Michael said as he

snatched up a cookie. "And I'll never be trusted again. Try a cookie, Mom makes the best on the block."

She took one out of politeness, terrified to put anything in her stomach. "You have a lovely home."

He remembered his brief tour through the Beverly Hills mansion where she'd spent that summer. "I've always liked it." He leaned over, laid a hand on hers. "What's wrong, Emma?"

She couldn't have said why that quiet question, that gentle hand almost snapped the last of her control. It would be so easy to lean on him, to pour out her heart and be comforted. But that would just be running again. "I'm not really sure."

She rose when Lou came in. Her smile was hesitant, vulnerable, and for Michael, devastatingly appealing. "Captain."

"Emma." Obviously pleased, he crossed to her to take both of her hands. "All grown-up."

She nearly broke down then, almost laid her head on his chest and wept as she once had so long ago. Instead she gripped his hands tightly, searching his face. "You've hardly changed at all."

"That's exactly the kind of flattery a man needs from a beautiful woman."

She smiled, easily this time. "No, really. I'm studying to be a photographer so I try to observe and remember faces. It's kind of you to see me again."

"Don't be silly. Sit, sit." He spied the iced tea and chose a glass, wanting to give her time to be comfortable. "Is your father in town?"

"No." She ran her fingers up and down her own glass, but didn't drink. "He's in London—or on his way. I'm living in New York now, going to college there."

"I haven't been to New York for years." He settled back in a striped wing chair that suited him so perfectly Emma imagined he rarely sat elsewhere in that room. "Photography, you say. I remember, last time I saw you, you had a camera."

"I still have it. Da often says he created a monster when he gave me that Nikon."

"How is Brian?"

"He's fine." Though she was far from sure of that. "Busy." Of that she was sure. Then she took a deep breath and plunged into the truth. "He doesn't know I'm here. I don't want him to."

"Why?"

She lifted her hand, then helplessly let it fall again. "He'd only be upset, and miserably unhappy if he knew I'd come to see you, to talk about Darren."

"Michael, will you give me a hand with something?" Marge started to rise, but Emma shook her head.

"No, please. There's no need for you to go. It's certainly not private. I suppose it never has been." Agitated, she set down her glass. "It's only that I wondered if there was something, something you might know, something the press didn't get their hands on, and that I was considered too young to be told at the time. I've been able to put it aside, for long stretches of time anyway. But it never really goes away. And last night I remembered . . ."

"What?" Lou leaned forward.

"Just a song," she murmured. "A song that was playing that night. I remembered hearing it coming from downstairs as I walked toward Darren's room. It was all so clear, for a moment, so clear. The song, the lyrics, Darren crying. But I can't get to the door, you see. In my head, when I try to remember, I can only see myself standing in the hall."

"Maybe that's all you did." Lou frowned into his glass. Like Emma, he'd been able to put the case aside for long stretches. But it always came back. He knew the face of that little boy would always haunt him. "Emma, we were never sure you went into the room, or saw anything. At the time, you thought you did, but you were very confused. It was just as likely that you heard something that frightened you, ran to the stairs to call your father, and fell. You were only six, and afraid of the dark."

Was, and am, she thought. "I've never been able to sort it out, you see. And I hate not knowing, not being sure I couldn't have stopped it. Saved him."

"I can put your mind at rest there." He put the glass aside. He wanted her to see him as a cop now, an official. "There were two men in your brother's room that night. The nanny claimed that she heard two people whispering as she was being bound. The forensic evidence corroborated it. The syringe found on the floor of your brother's room contained a sedative, a child's dose. From what we were able to piece together, the time that elapsed between the nanny being bound and your fall was less than twenty minutes. It was a bungled attempt, Emma, with tragic results, but it was well thought out. Something happened to confuse their plans, to confuse them. We may never know what it was. But if you had gone into that room, had tried to fight them off yourself, you wouldn't have been able to save Darren, and in all likelihood would have been killed as well."

She hoped he was right. She prayed he was right. But it did little to soothe her. When she left an hour later she promised herself she would try to believe it.

"You have wonderful parents," she told Michael as he walked her to her car.

"Yeah. I've almost broken them in." He put his hand on the door handle. There was no way he was going to let her walk out of his life so quickly again. He remembered how she had looked on the beach that day—had it been five years before? She'd looked sad—sad and beautiful. Something about her had struck a chord in him then. She struck the same one now.

"Are you staying in town long?"

She gazed down the street. Such a pretty neighborhood. She could hear children playing a few doors down, and the low hum of another mower trimming green suburban grass. She wondered, wistfully, what it might be like to live in such a place. "I leave tomorrow."

He wanted to swear. "Quick trip."

"I have classes Monday." She looked up, feeling as awkward as he. He was more attractive than she remembered—the chipped tooth, the slightly crooked nose. "I wish I had more time."

"What are you doing now?"

"I—I was going to go for a drive. Up in the hills."

He understood, and wasn't sure he cared for the idea. "Want some company?"

She started to refuse, politely, as she'd been taught. "Yes, very much," she heard herself say.

"Give me a minute." He was off, before she could change her mind. The screen slammed behind him as he went into the house, then slammed again when he came out. He grinned at her as he settled in the passenger seat. "You saved me from another hour's mowing. Dad'll never be able to let it sit like that until I get back. Too organized."

"Glad I could help."

She drove aimlessly for a while, content to let the wind move through her hair, listen to the music on the radio, pass idle conversation. When she heard her father's voice come clear and strong through the speakers, her lips curved.

"Does it ever feel weird?"

"Hearing him?" Her smile widened. "No, not really. I knew his voice before I knew him. It's hard to think of Da without thinking of his music. It must be the same for you. I mean he's your father, but he's a cop. I'm sure it's natural for you to think of him wearing a gun or a badge or whatever."

"Whatever. Still, it was pretty strange when I first started working for him."

"Working for him?"

"Yeah. I caved in." He sent her a breezy grin. "As Johnno once said, I'm following in the old man's flat feet."

# Chapter Twenty-one
• • • •

$\mathcal{Y}$OU'RE A COP?" Emma braked at a stop sign and took the opportunity to turn and study him.

"What my father's fond of calling a rookie." He grinned again. "What? Have I grown a snout?"

"No." She sat a moment, then drove on. It was silly, she supposed, to have her idea of police focused by her impression of Lou, and at the other end of the spectrum, shows like *Starsky and Hutch.* "It's just odd thinking of you that way."

"Well, that's something. I never figured you thought of me at all."

She laughed. "Of course I did. When our picture hit the paper, I was the most popular girl at school for weeks. Of course, I exaggerated the whole business for my own benefit."

"So did I." He tossed his arm over the seat to play with the ends of her hair. "I got a date with Sue Ellen Cody on the strength of that clipping alone."

"Really?" She shot him a quick, slanted look.

"It was my fifteen minutes of fame. I kept hoping you'd come back."

"Sweeney spilled it to Da." She shrugged. "And that was the end of that. Do you like being a cop?"

"Yeah. Right up to the time I walked into the academy I was sure I'd hate it. But there you go. Some things are just meant, and no matter how many times you walk away, you end up where you belonged all along. You take this road here if you want to go up to the house."

She stopped again, staring straight ahead. "How do you know?"

"My father used to drive up there. I'd go with him sometimes. He'd just sit and look. I thought you might like to know that he's never forgotten what happened, and he's never really accepted that he couldn't find them."

"I think I knew," she said slowly. "That's why I wanted to see him, talk with him again." She let out a sigh. "You knew what I intended when I said I was going for a drive."

"I had a pretty good idea."

"Why did you come?"

"I didn't want you to go alone."

She stiffened. It was only a barely perceptible movement, but he sensed her shoulders straightening, her chin firming. "I'm not fragile, Michael."

"Okay. I wanted to be with you."

She turned. His eyes were kind, like his father's, but in them she could still see the boy who had driven her home from the beach. Degree by degree her body relaxed. "Thanks."

She turned the car and followed his directions. The roads didn't seem familiar. She'd thought they would. It occurred to her, and made her feel foolish, that she would never have found the house on her own. They didn't talk now, except for Michael's occasional "turn right," "bear left," but listened to the soft, soothing sounds of Crosby, Stills, and Nash through the car speakers.

He didn't have to tell her to stop. She recognized the house. It was like a picture, developed and stored in her mind. It was very much the same as it had been, secluded by trees, hedges, the winter bloomers of the hills. It was rustic, as only the wealthy could afford. Redwood and sheets of glass, terraced lawn falling into woods and stream.

She saw, as Michael did, the sign speared into the ground that proclaimed the house up for sale.

"We could call it fate," he said, and touched her arm. "Do you want to go in?"

Her hands were linked hard in her lap. She could see her window, her bedroom window where she had once stood with Darren and gleefully watched a fox dart through the trees.

"I can't."

"Okay. We can sit as long as you like."

She could see herself, wading in the stream, Bev laughing as Darren splashed madly in his bare feet and rolled-up overalls. She remembered a picnic the four of them had shared, a blanket spread under a tree, her father quietly strumming his guitar, Bev reading a book while Darren dozed in her lap.

She'd forgotten that day. How could she have forgotten it? It had been such a beautiful day, such a perfect day. The grass had been cool, the sun warm and lazily yellow where it pushed through the leaves, the shade soft and gray where it hadn't. She could hear her father's voice, and the words he'd been singing.

*Never too late to look for love / Never too soon to find it.*

They had been happy, Emma thought. They had been a family. Then, the next day they had given a party and everything had changed.

"Yes," she said abruptly. "I want to go in."

"Okay. Look, it might be better if they didn't know who you are, about the connection, I mean."

She nodded, and drove through the open gates.

Michael closed a hand over hers as they stood in front of the door. Hers was like ice, but steady. He put on his best smile as the door opened. "Hi. We were driving by and saw your sign. We've been house hunting for weeks. We've got an appointment to see another place in about an hour, but we just couldn't resist this. It isn't sold yet, is it?"

The woman, fortyish, dressed in countrywear of Bass loafers and Calvin Kleins, took a long, cautious look. She took in Michael's work shirt, worn Levi's, and scuffed high tops. But she was also sharp enough to note Emma's discreetly expensive pumps and the casual Ralph Lauren skirt and blouse. As well as the Mercedes convertible parked in the drive. She smiled. The house had been on the market for five months without a firm offer.

"Well, actually we do have a prospective buyer, but the contract won't be signed until Monday." Her gaze swooped down to the small but elegant diamond and sapphire ring on Emma's hand. "I suppose it wouldn't hurt to show you through."

She opened the door further, lifting a brow as Emma hesitated before stepping inside. "I'm Gloria Steinbrenner."

"Nice to meet you." Michael extended a hand and took hers. "Michael Kesselring. This is Emma."

Ms. Steinbrenner gave them both a dazzling smile. The hell

with the real estate broker, she thought. She'd opened the door to her own hot prospect, and intended to make the most of it.

"The place is in beautiful condition. I adore it." She detested every board and brick. "It's breaking my heart to sell, but—to be frank—my husband and I are divorcing, so we're liquidating."

"Oh." Michael put what he hoped was an appropriately sympathetic, but interested, look on his face. "I'm sorry."

"No need." She waved a hand. "Are you from the area?"

"No, actually, we're . . . from the Valley," he said, inspired. "We're just dying to get out, crowds, smog. Isn't that right, Emma?"

"Yes." She forced a smile. "It's a beautiful house."

"Thank you. The living area, as you can see, is magnificent. High ceilings, genuine oak beams, lots of glass and open space. It's a working fireplace, of course."

Of course, Emma thought. Hadn't she sat in front of it? The furniture was new, and she hated it on sight. Pretentious modern sculptures and glossy enameled tables. Where were all the cushions, the funny baskets filled with balls of yarn and ribbon that Bev had arranged?

"The dining area's through here, but this spot in front of the terrace windows is just perfect for cozy little suppers."

No, that wasn't right, she thought as she mechanically followed. Bev had put plants in front of those windows. A jungle of plants in old pottery bowls and urns. Stevie and Johnno had brought her a tree once, grunting and panting as they'd hauled it in. They'd done it as a joke, but Bev had left it there, and bought a silly plaster robin to sit on one of the branches.

"Emma?"

"What?" She jolted, dragging herself back. "I'm sorry."

"Oh, that's quite all right." The woman was delighted that Emma seemed to be mesmerized. "I was just asking if you cooked?"

"No, not very well."

"The kitchen is up-to-the-minute. I had it remodeled just two years ago." She pushed open the swinging doors and gestured. "All built-ins. Microwave, Jenn-Air range, a convection oven, naturally. Acres of counter space. A pantry, of course."

Emma stared at the streamlined, soulless kitchen. It was all white and stainless steel. Gone were the copper pots Bev had kept shiny and hung from hooks. There were no more little pots of herbs on the windowsill. No high chair for Darren, no clutter of cookbooks or colorful apothecary jars.

The woman droned on, obviously considering the kitchen her *pièce de résistance*, while Emma stood, grieving.

When the phone rang, she closed a slick white cabinet door. "Excuse me, just a moment."

"Are you all right?" Michael murmured.

"Yes." She wanted to be. "I'd like to go upstairs."

"Listen, Jack." Ms. Steinbrenner's voice had lost its cooing flow. "I'm not interested in your complaints or your lawyer's threats. Got it?"

Michael cleared his throat. "Excuse me." He offered the woman an easy smile. "Would it be all right if we wandered through?"

She waved them away and snarled into the phone. "Listen, asshole."

"Sounds like she'll be tied up awhile," he said lightly. "You sure you want to go up?"

No, she wasn't sure. She was anything but sure. "I can't come this far and not finish."

"Right." Whatever her claims against fragility, he put an arm around her shoulders as they started up.

The doors were open—the bedroom door where her father and Bev had once slept. Where Emma had sometimes heard them laughing late at night. Alice's room, which had always been so bland and neat, had become a sitting room with walls of books and a console television. Her room. She stopped, gazing in.

The dolls were gone, the Mickey Mouse night-light, the frilly pinks and whites that Bev had indulged her in. No little girl had slept there, dreamt there, in a very long time. It was obviously a guest room now. Silk flowers, a Hollywood bed plumped with vivid cushions, reading material carefully arranged. Roman shades had replaced the priscillas she remembered, and wall-to-wall carpeting the pretty, frivolous shag rug.

"This was my room," she said dully. "There was wallpaper with little roses and violets, frilly pink curtains at the windows and a big white quilt for the bed. I had dolls on the shelves, and music boxes. I guess it was the kind of room all little girls want, at least for a while. Bev understood that. I don't know why I thought it would be the same."

He remembered a quote he'd read in college, one that had stuck. " 'All things change; nothing perishes.' " He shrugged self-consciously. He wasn't the type of man who quoted. "It is the same, in your head. That's what counts."

She said nothing, but turned and looked down the hall to Darren's room. The door was open too, as it should have been that night.

"I was in bed," she said flatly. "Something woke me up. The music. I thought it was the music. I couldn't really hear it, but I could feel it. The bass vibrating. I tried to guess what the song was, and what people were doing. I couldn't wait until I was old enough to stay up for the parties. I heard something. Something," she murmured, rubbing an annoyed hand on the headache that was building behind her temple. "I don't know what. But I—footsteps," she remembered abruptly, and her heart began to thud against her ribs. "I heard someone coming down the hall. I wanted it to be Da or Bev. I wanted them to talk to me for a while. Maybe I could con them into letting me go downstairs. But it wasn't Da or Bev."

"Easy." He could see the sweat beading on her brow, and rubbed her hand between both of his. "Just take it slow."

"Darren was crying. I heard him crying. I know it. It wasn't a dream. I heard him crying. I got up. Alice had told me not to take Charlie in, but Darren liked to sleep with Charlie, and he was crying. I was going to take Charlie into Darren and talk to him for a while until he slept again. But the hall was dark."

She looked around now, with the sunlight creeping into it from the bedroom windows. "It was dark, but it wasn't supposed to be. They always left a light on for me. I'm so afraid of the dark. There are things in the dark."

"Things?" he repeated, his brows drawing together.

"I didn't want to go out in the hall, in the dark. But he kept crying. I could hear the music now, as I stepped into the hall, into the dark. It was loud, and I was frightened."

She started to walk then, dreamlike, toward the door. "I could hear them, hissing in the corners, scraping along the walls, swishing on the rugs."

"Hear what?" he said quietly. "What did you hear?"

"The monsters." She turned and looked at him. "I heard the monsters. And . . . I don't remember. I don't remember if I went to the door. It was closed, I know it was closed, but I don't know if I opened it."

She stood on the threshold. For an instant she saw the room as she remembered it—cluttered with Darren's toys, painted in bright, primary colors. His crib, his rocker, his shiny new tricycle. Then the picture dissolved into what was there.

An oak desk and leather chair. Framed pictures, glass shelves crowded with bric-a-brac.

An office. They had turned her brother's room into an office.

"I ran," she said at length. "I don't remember anything except running, and falling."

"You said you'd gone to the door. You told my father, when he saw you in the hospital right after it happened, that you'd opened the door."

"It was like a dream. And now, I don't really remember at all. It all faded away."

"Maybe it was supposed to."

"He was beautiful." It hurt too much to face the room. "He was absolutely beautiful. I loved him more than anything or anyone. Everyone did." Tears were blurring her vision. "I need to get out of here."

"Come on." He led her down the hall, down the stairs where she had tumbled that night years before. He sent a quick, apologetic glance to Gloria Steinbrenner as she hurried in from the kitchen. "I'm sorry, my wife's not feeling well."

"Oh." Annoyance and disappointment came first. Then hope. "Make sure she gets some rest. As you can see, this house was just made for children. You wouldn't want to raise a baby in the Valley."

"No." He didn't bother to correct her, and steered Emma out. "We'll be in touch," he called, and took the driver's seat himself. If he hadn't been concerned with Emma's pale face, and the prospect of driving a thirty-thousand-dollar car, he would have noticed the dark blue sedan that trailed after them.

"I'm sorry," she murmured after they started down the winding roads.

"Don't be stupid."

"No, I am. I didn't handle that well."

"You did fine." He reached over to give her hand an awkward pat. "Look, I've never lost anybody close to me, but you only have to be human to imagine what it would be like. Don't beat yourself up, Emma."

"Put it behind me?" She drummed up a weak smile. "I hope I can. I thought if I could stand there, right there, and think about what had happened, it would all come back to me. Since it didn't . . ." She shrugged, then pushed her sunglasses back on. "You've been a good friend."

"That's me," he muttered. "Always a pal. Hungry?"

She started to shake her head, then stopped. "Yes," she realized. "I'm starved."

"I can spring for a burger. I think," he added, struggling to remember just what was in his wallet.

"I'd love a burger. And since you've been a pal, my treat."

He pulled into a McDonald's, and since he discovered the contents of his wallet included three singles and the phone number of a redhead he barely remembered, he put aside what he told himself was dumb macho pride. Emma didn't argue with his suggestion that they make it to go, or with his casual assumption that he would continue in the driver's seat.

"Thought we'd take it to the beach."

"I'd like that." She shut her eyes again and leaned back. She was glad she'd come. Glad she had climbed those stairs. Glad she was here, with the warm wind in her hair and Michael beside her. "It was sleeting in New York when I left."

"There are colleges in sunny California, too."

She smiled, enjoying the breeze on her face. "I like New York," she said absently. "I always have. My roommate and I bought a loft. It's nearly livable now."

"Roommate?"

"Yes. Marianne and I went to Saint Catherine's together." Since her eyes were still closed, she didn't notice his look of pleased relief. "We always swore we'd live in New York one day. Now we do. She's taking art classes."

He decided he was kindly disposed toward Marianne. "She any good?"

"Yes, very. One day galleries are going to be cutting their throats to get her paintings. She used to do the most incredible caricatures of the nuns." She glanced over, noting his frown.

"What is it?"

"Probably just rookie-cop instincts on overtime. See that sedan, just behind us?"

She glanced over her shoulder. "Yes. So?"

"It's been behind us since we picked up the burgers." He switched lanes. The sedan followed suit. "I'd say he was tailing us, if he wasn't so stupid about it."

She let out a long, tired sigh. "It's probably Sweeney."

"Sweeney?"

"Bodyguard. He always finds me. Sometimes I think Da planted a homing device under my skin."

"Yeah, it could be. I guess it makes sense." But he didn't care to be shadowed, so amaturely shadowed, on what he considered his first date with a longtime crush. "I could lose him."

Emma tilted down her glasses. Behind them her eyes glinted with the first real laughter he'd seen in her. "Really?"

"I could give it my best shot. This little baby's bound to leave him in the dust."

"Do it," she said, and grinned.

Delighted, Michael punched the gas, cut off a station wagon, and peeled up to eighty. "We used to race on the freeway—in my callow and misspent youth." He swerved again, dodging between a pickup and a BMW, then with a twist of the wrist shot in front of a Caddy and let the Mercedes cruise at ninety.

"You're good." Laughing, Emma twisted in her seat and peered at the traffic. "I can't see him."

"He's back there, trying to get around the Caddy. I pissed the Caddy off so he's hogging the road. Hang on." He swerved, spun, and jockeyed, then raced off an exit. One illegal U-turn, and the Mercedes's powerful engine, and he was back on the freeway, heading in the opposite direction. They whizzed by the sedan, slowed to a decorous speed and sailed calmly down another ramp.

"Really good at it," Emma said again. "Did they teach you that at the police academy?"

"Some skills you're born with." He stopped, then stroked the steering wheel. "What a honey."

Emma leaned over and kissed his cheek. "Thanks. Again." Before he could respond, she had snatched up the bag of burgers and was racing toward the sand.

"I love this!" Still laughing, she spun in a circle. "I really love the water, the smell of it, the sound of it. If they could just plop an ocean down next to Broadway I'd be in heaven."

He wanted to take hold of her then, to grab her in mid-spin

and find out if she tasted nearly as good as she looked. Then she dropped down on the sand and dug into the bag.

"These smell great, too." She held one up before she realized he was staring at her. "What is it?"

"Nothing." But his mouth was dry again. "I was, ah, remembering that I once wondered whether you ever got to go to McDonald's. The first time I met you, at the rehearsal? Dad took me for a burger after and I wondered, with all the guards, if you ever got to go."

"No, not really, but Da or Johnno or someone would sometimes bring takeout. Don't feel sorry for me." She groped in the bag again. "Not today."

"Okay. Hand over the fries."

They ate hungrily, leaving not even a crumb for the gulls. The breeze was up, carrying a mist of the sea. There were other people, a few families, young girls showing off tans and slender figures, the inevitable radios pumping out music, but for Emma it was one of the most peaceful and secluded interludes of her life.

"I could get used to this." She sighed, stretched her arms up. "Sitting on the beach, listening to the water." She shook her head so that her hair rained like gold dust down her back. "I wish I had more time."

"So do I." He had to touch her. He couldn't remember not wanting to. When he stroked a finger down her cheek, she turned her head and smiled. What she saw in his eyes had her heart pounding in her throat, had her lips parting, not so much in surprise as in question.

She didn't resist as he touched his mouth to hers. On a quiet moan she shifted toward him, inviting something she didn't completely understand. A gentle nip of his teeth had her lips heating. When he entered her mouth, she heard the low sound of pleasure in his throat, felt his hands tense on her arms.

Without hesitation, she pressed her body to his and absorbed the sensation.

Would he have believed that it was the first time she'd been kissed, like this? The first time she felt like this? Warm, liquid, achingly sweet desire swam into her. Had she been waiting for this? Even as she wondered, her lashes lowered to help her seal the memory.

"You do," he murmured, and kissed her again, gently, because it seemed the right way.

"Do what?"

"Taste as good as you look. I've wondered for a long time."

She had to swallow, had to draw back. There were feelings growing inside her she didn't know what to do with. They were too big, and came too fast. "It's the salt." Confused, she rose and stepped closer to the sea.

It was easy for a man to mistake confusion for casualness. He sat where he was, giving himself time. He had no casual feelings for her. Stupid as it might have sounded, he was in love. She was beautiful, elegant, and certainly accustomed to being wanted by men. Rich and important men. And he was a rookie cop from a middle-class family. He let out a long breath, rose, and tried to be as offhand as she.

"It's getting late."

"Yes." Was she crazy? Emma wondered. She wanted to cry and laugh and dance and mourn all at once. She wanted to turn to him, but tomorrow she would be three thousand miles away. He was only being kind. She was the poor little rich girl, a title she detested, and he—he was doing something with his life.

"I should be getting back." She turned, smiled. "I'm really glad you went with me today, that we had some time."

"I'll be around." He took her hand—a friendly gesture, he told himself. The hell with friendly. "I want to see you again, Emma. I need to."

"I don't know—"

"You can give me a call when you come back."

The way he was looking at her had her skin going hot then cold. "I will. I'd like to—I don't know when I'll make it out here again."

"I thought you might be coming out for the movie."

"Movie?"

They had started walking to the car, but now he stopped. "Yeah. They're going to start filming in a couple weeks in London, I think, then here. They're putting on extra security. The movie," he continued when she just looked blank. "*Devastated*, you know, based on your mother's book. Angie's starring in it. Angie Parks." He could see by her face that he'd made a very large and a very stupid mistake. "I'm sorry, Emma, I thought you knew."

"No," she said, suddenly tired beyond belief. "I didn't."

♦ ♦ ♦ ♦

*H*E SNATCHED THE phone up before it had completed its first ring. He'd been waiting, and sweating, for hours. "Yes?"

"I found her." The voice, and he knew that voice very well, trembled.

"And?"

"She went to see the cop, Kesselring. She was with him for over an hour. Then she went to the house, she went to the goddamn house where it happened. We've got to do something, and do it fast. I told you then, and I'm telling you now, I won't take the fall for this."

"Pull yourself together." The tone was brisk, but his hand shook slightly as he reached for a cigarette. "She went to the house. She went inside?"

"The fucking place is for sale. She and the guy she was with strolled right in."

"What guy? Who was she with?"

"Some guy. The cop's son, I think."

"All right." He noted it down on the pad beside the phone. "Where did they go when they left the house?"

"They went to a goddamn hamburger joint."

The tip of the pencil snapped off. "I beg your pardon?"

"I said they went for burgers, then joyriding on the freeway. I lost them. I know where she's staying tonight. I can get somebody to take care of it, quick, easy."

"Don't be an idiot. There's no need."

"I told you she saw the cop, she went to the house."

"Yes, I understood you." His hand was rock-steady again. He poured a drink, but not for his nerves. For his pleasure. "Think, for Christ's sake. If she had remembered something, anything, would she have calmly ridden off to buy a hamburger?"

"I don't think—"

"That's your problem, and has been from the beginning. She didn't remember then, she doesn't remember now. Perhaps this impulsive little trip of hers was a last-ditch effort to bring it all back, or more likely, it was just a sentimental journey. There's no need to do Emma any harm, any harm at all."

"And if she does remember?"

"It's unlikely. Listen to me now, and listen carefully. The first time was an accident, a tragic and unforeseen accident. One that you committed."

"It was your idea, the whole thing was your idea."

"Exactly, since of the two of us I'm the only one who's capable of an original thought. But it was an accident. I have no intention of committing premeditated murder." He thought of a session musician who'd wanted pizza, but didn't remember his name. "Unless it's unavoidable. Understood?"

"You're a cold sonofabitch."

"Yes." He smiled. "I'd advise you to remember that."

# Chapter Twenty-two

♦ ♦ ♦ ♦

$\mathcal{I}$T WAS SNOWING in London, wet, thick flakes that slid down collars and melted cold on the skin. It was pretty, postcard snow, unless one was fighting the clogged traffic along King's Road.

Emma preferred to walk. She imagined Sweeney was annoyed with her choice, but she couldn't worry about him now. She had the address on a slip of paper in the pocket of her thick, quilted coat. But she didn't need that for a reminder. She'd memorized it.

It was odd to be in Chelsea, as an adult, free to walk where she chose. She didn't remember it. Indeed, she felt a tourist in London, and Chelsea, the grand stage for punks and Sloane Rangers, was as foreign to her as a Venetian canal.

The streets were dotted with boutiques and antique shops where last-minute shoppers hurried in their fashionable coats and boots to search out that perfect gift among the horde of offerings. Young girls laughing, their pearls and sweatshirts tucked under their jackets. Young boys trying to look tough and bored and worldly.

Despite the snow, there had been a flower seller in Sloane Square. Even in December spring could be bought for a reasonable price. She'd been tempted by the color and the scent, but had walked on without digging in her purse for pounds and shillings. How odd it would have been to have walked up to the door, and offered a bouquet to her mother.

Her mother. She could neither deny nor accept Jane Palmer

as her mother. Even the name seemed distant to her—like something she had read in a book. But the face lingered, the face that came in odd, sporadic flashes in dreams, the face that flushed dark with annoyance before a slap or a shove was administered. The face from articles in *People* and the *Enquirer* and the *Post*.

A face from the past, Emma thought. And what did the past have to do with today?

Then why had she come? The question drummed in her head as she walked along the narrow, well-kept street. To resolve something that should have been resolved years before.

Emma wondered if Jane thought it a fine joke to have moved into the posh and prosperous area where Oscar Wilde, Whistler, and Turner had lived. Writers and artists had always flocked to Chelsea. And musicians, Emma mused. Mick Jagger had a home here. Or he'd had one. It hardly mattered to Emma whether he and the Stones were still in residence. There was only one person she'd come to see.

Perhaps it was the contrasts that appealed to Jane. Chelsea was punk, and domestic. It was relaxed and frenetic. And it cost the earth to live in one of the stylish homes. Or perhaps Jane's reason had something to do with the fact that Bev had established herself in the same district.

That too hardly mattered.

She stopped, clenching and unclenching her hand on the strap of her bag while the snow drifted and clung to her hair and shoulders. The house was a long way from the tiny walk-up flat where she had lived with Jane. It pretended to be old, but the fussy copy of a Victorian row house missed the mark by inches. Someone had decided to add cupolas and tall, narrow windows. It might have been charming, in its way, but curtains were drawn tight and the walk had yet to be shoveled or swept. No one had bothered to hang a wreath or a string of lights.

It made her think wistfully of the Kesselring home. There had been no seasonal snow in California, but the house had offered the warmth and cheer that meant Christmas. Then again, Emma thought, she wasn't coming home for Christmas. She wasn't coming home at all.

Taking a deep breath, Emma pushed through the gate and waded through the snow to the front door. There was a knocker against the ornately carved wood. She stared at it, half expecting the brass lion's head to dissolve and re-form into the battered countenance of Jacob Marley. Perhaps it was the season, or the ghosts of her childhood that made her fanciful.

With hands icy inside her fur-lined gloves, she lifted it, just an old brass lion's head, and let it fall against the wood.

When there was no response, she knocked again, hoping there was no one to hear. If no one answered, could she tell herself she'd done her best to erase Jane and the need to see her from her mind and her heart? She desperately wanted to run away, from the house that pretended to be something it wasn't, from the brass lion's head, from the woman who never seemed to be completely out of her life. As she stood, ready to turn away in relief, the door swung open.

She couldn't speak, could only stare at the woman in the red silk robe that dipped carelessly over one shoulder, strained over hips that had spread beyond lush. Her hair was a blond tangle around a wide, doughy face. A stranger's face. It was the eyes Emma recognized and remembered. The narrowed, angry eyes, reddened now from drink or drugs or lack of sleep.

"Well?" In deference to the cold air, Jane hitched the robe up. There was the glitter of diamonds on her fingers, and to Emma's horror, the stink of stale gin. "Look, lovey, I got better things to do on a Saturday afternoon than stand in the doorway."

"Who the hell is it?" The annoyed male roar came from the second floor. Jane cast a bored glance over her shoulder.

"Hang on, will you?" she shouted back. "Well?" She turned back to Emma. "You can see I'm busy."

Go, she thought frantically. Just turn around and walk away. "I'd like to speak with you." Emma heard her own voice, but it sounded like a stranger's. "I'm Emma."

Jane didn't move, but her eyes changed, narrowing further, struggling to focus. She saw a young woman, tall, slender, with a pale, delicate face and flowing blond hair. She saw Brian—then her daughter. For an instant she felt something almost like regret. Then her lips curved.

"Well, well, well. Little Emma come home to her mam. Want to talk to me?" She gave a quick, high laugh that caused Emma to jolt and brace for a slap. But Jane merely stepped back from the doorway. "Come right on in, dear. We'll have ourselves a chat."

Jane was already calculating as she led the way down the hall into a cluttered parlor made dim by the thick curtains. There was a scent there—old liquor, stale smoke that wasn't tobacco. It seemed they hadn't come so far from the old flat after all.

Her annual check from Brian would soon stop, and no amount of threatening or wheedling would pry another pence from him. But there was the girl. Her own little Emma. A woman had to think ahead, Jane decided. When she had expensive tastes, and an expensive habit.

"How about a drink? To celebrate our reunion."

"No, thank you."

With a shrug, Jane poured a glass for herself. When she turned back, the red silk shifted over her plump hips. "To family ties?" she offered, raising her glass. Then she laughed when Emma looked down at her hands. "Imagine finding you at my door after all these years." She drank deeply, then topped off the glass before sitting on a sofa of purple velvet. "Sit down, Emma luv, and tell me all about yourself."

"There's nothing to tell." Stiffly, Emma sat on the edge of a chair. "I'm only in London for the holidays."

"Holidays? Ah, Christmas." She grinned, tapping a chipped nail against the glass. "Did you bring your mam a present?"

Emma shook her head. She felt like a child again. Terrified and lonely.

"The least you could have done after all these years was bring your mother a little gift." With a wave of her hand, Jane settled back. "Never mind. You never were a considerate child. All grown-up now, aren't you?" She eyed the quiet diamond studs in Emma's ears. "And done well for yourself, too. Fancy schools, fancy clothes."

"I'm in college now," Emma said helplessly. "I have a job."

"A job? What the hell do you want with a job? Your old man's got nothing but money."

"I like it." She hated the fact that she couldn't control the stutter. "I want to work."

"You never was a bright kid." Frowning, Jane tossed back more gin. "When I think of all the years I scrimped and saved and did without to put dresses on your back and food in your belly. Never a bit of gratitude from you." She reached for the gin bottle and slopped more into her glass. "Just sniveling and crying, then going off with your father without a backward glance.

Been living high, haven't you, my girl? Daddy's little princess. Not a thought for me in all these years."

"I've thought of you," Emma murmured.

Jane tapped her fingers against the glass again. She wanted to get her stash, take a quick fix, but was afraid if she left the room Emma would disappear and her chance would be lost. "He poisoned you against me." Self-pitying tears began to fall. "He wanted you all to himself when I was the one who went through the misery of childbirth, the misery of raising a kid on my own. I could've gotten rid of you, you know. Even then it was simple enough if you knew the right people."

Emma lifted her eyes then. Dark and intense, they fixed on her mother's face. "Why didn't you?"

Jane gripped her hands on the glass. They were beginning to shake. She hadn't had a hit in hours and gin was a poor substitute. But she was shrewd, too shrewd to admit that she'd been more frightened at the prospect of a back-alley abortion than of childbirth in a clean hospital ward.

"I loved him." And because she believed it, it sounded true. "I always loved him. We grew up together, you know. And he loved me, was devoted to me. If it hadn't been for his music, his stinking career, we would have been together. But he tossed me aside like it was nothing. He never cared about anyone or anything but his music. Do you think he cared about you?" She rose, lumbering a bit under the gin. "He never gave a damn. It was just his image. Wouldn't want the bloody public to think Brian McAvoy was the kind of man to abandon his own child."

The old doubts, the old fears sprang up so quickly, she had to force the words out. "He loves me. He's done everything for me."

"He loves Brian." Jane braced her hands on the arms of Emma's chair and leaned close. There was a glitter in her eyes. Pure pleasure. She could do very little to hurt Brian now—God knew she'd tried whatever had come to mind to cause him pain. But she could hurt Emma, and that was the next-best thing.

"He would've walked right out on the pair of us if it hadn't been for the scandal. That's just what he started to do until I threatened to go to the papers."

She didn't mention the threat to kill herself, and Emma. In truth it had been so unimportant, she'd forgotten it.

"He knew, and that worthless piss of a manager knew, what

would have happened if the press had started whining about rock's hottest flame leaving his bastard child in the slums. He knew, so he took you and he paid me a handsome sum to keep out of your life."

She felt sick, sick from the words, sick from the smell that struck out at her when Jane spoke them. "He paid you?"

"I earned it." Jane took Emma's chin in her fingers and squeezed. "I earned every pound and more. He bought you, and his peace of mind. The price was cheap enough for him, but he never got it, did he? Never could buy that peace of mind."

"Let go of me." Emma gripped Jane's wrist and shoved it away. "Don't touch me again."

"You're as much mine as his."

"No." She pushed herself out of the chair, praying her legs would hold her. "No, you sold me, and any claims to motherhood you might have had. He may have bought me, Jane, but he doesn't own me, either." She fought back the tears. She wouldn't cry here, not in front of this woman. "I came here today to ask you to stop the movie, the one they're making from your book. I'd hoped that you might have some feelings for me, enough that you'd respect my wishes in this one thing. But I've wasted my time."

From up the the stairs Jane's current lover began to bellow curses.

"I'm still your mother!" Jane shouted. "You can't change that."

"No, I can't. I just have to learn to live with it." She turned, walking quickly to the door.

"You want me to stop the movie?" Jane snatched at Emma's arm. "How badly do you want it stopped?"

Deadly calm, Emma turned back. She took one long last look. "Do you think I'd pay you? You've miscalculated this time, Jane. You'll never get a penny out of me."

"Bitch." Jane's hand cracked across her cheek. Emma didn't bother to dodge it. She simply opened the door, and walked away.

◆ ◆ ◆ ◆

SHE WANDERED FOR a long time, dodging shoppers and dog walkers, ignoring the laughter, the gunning motors, and the frantic Christmas cheer around her. The tears never fell. It amazed her how easily they were controlled now. Perhaps the cold helped, or the noise. It made it so easy not to think at all. So when she found herself standing in front of Bev's door, she wasn't completely aware of having walked there, or having intended to.

She knocked quickly. It wasn't the time to think. It wasn't the time to feel. It was, she told herself, the time to tie up all the loose ends and get on with her life.

The door opened. Warm air and Christmas carols. The scent of pine and welcome. With the snow swirling at her back, Emma stared down at Alice. How odd it was, she thought, to look down at her old nanny. Time had made her taller, and Alice older. She saw recognition flicker in Alice's eyes, and the nanny's lips quiver.

"Hello, Alice." Her own lips were stiff as she forced them into a smile. "It's nice to see you again."

Alice stood where she was as tears began to spurt out of her eyes.

"Alice, don't forget to give Terry that package if he makes it by." Bev came hurrying down the hall, a dark mink over her arm. "I'll be home by—" She stopped, the little black bag she held slipping out of her nerveless hands. "Emma," she whispered.

They stood four feet apart with the weeping Alice between them. Bev felt the pleasure first, the need to rush forward and grab Emma close. Then she felt the shame.

"I should have called," Emma began. "I was in town, so I thought I'd—"

"I'm so glad you did." Recovered, Bev smiled and stepped forward. "Alice." Her voice was gentle as she placed a hand on the woman's shoulder. "We'll need some tea."

"You're on your way out," Emma said quickly. "I don't want to disrupt your plans."

"It doesn't matter. Alice," she repeated. The woman nodded and hurried down the hall. "You're so grown-up," Bev murmured. She gripped her hands together to keep herself from reaching out to touch. "It's hard to believe—but you must be freezing." Steadying, she took Emma's gloved hand in hers. "Come in, please."

"You have plans."

"A client's party. It's not important. I'd really like you to stay." Her fingers tightened on Emma's while her eyes searched almost hungrily over the girl's face. "Please."

"Of course. For a few minutes."

"I'll take your coat."

They settled, like two polite strangers, in Bev's bright, spacious parlor.

"This is beautiful." Emma pasted on a practiced smile. "I'd heard you were making a splash with decorating. I can see why."

"Thank you." Oh God, what should she say? What should she not say?

"My roommate and I bought a loft in New York. We're still having it done." She cleared her throat, glancing toward the fire smoldering in the stone hearth. "I had no idea it was so complicated. You always made it look so easy."

"New York," Bev said, folding and unfolding her hands in her lap. "You're living there now?"

"Yes. I'm going to NYCC. Photography."

"Oh. Do you like it?"

"Very much."

"Will you be in London long?"

"Until just after the first."

The next pause was long and awkward. Both women glanced over in relief as Alice wheeled in the tea caddy. "Thank you, Alice. I'll pour the tea." Bev put a hand over Alice's briefly, and squeezed.

"She stayed with you," Emma commented when they were alone again.

"Yes. Or I suppose it's more that we stayed with each other." It helped to have the tea, the pot, the cups, the pretty little biscuits arranged on a Sèvres platter. She had no thirst, no appetite, but the mechanics, the simple, civilized mechanics of serving the tea relaxed her. "Do you still take too much cream and sugar in your tea?"

"No, I've been Americanized." There were fresh flowers in a blue vase. Tulips. Emma wondered if Bev had bought them from the flower seller in the square, or if she'd forced them herself. "Now it's just too much sugar."

"Brian and I were always afraid you'd be fat and toothless with your penchant for sweets," Bev began, then winced and struggled to find an easy topic of conversation. "So, tell me about your photography. What sort of pictures do you like to take?"

"I prefer shots of people. Character portraits, I suppose, more than abstracts or still lifes. I'm hoping to make a career of it."

"That's wonderful. I'd love to see some of your work." She cut herself off again. "Perhaps the next time I'm in New York."

Emma studied the Christmas tree in front of the window. It was covered with hundreds of tiny handpainted ornaments and lacy white bows. She hadn't bought a present for Bev, no shiny wrapped box that could sit under the tree. But perhaps there was something she could give.

"Why don't you ask how he is, Bev?" Emma said gently. "It would be easier for both of us."

Bev shifted her gaze to meet Emma's eyes. Those beautiful dark blue eyes so like her father's. "How is he?"

"I wish I knew. His music's going better than ever. The last concert tour . . . well, you probably know about all of that."

"Yes."

"He's scoring a film and talking about doing a conceptual album. Then the videos. You could almost believe music videos were made with Da in mind. Everything comes across, just as it does in concert." She paused, then blundered on. "He's drinking too much."

"I've heard that, too," Bev said quietly. "P.M.'s worried about him. But they—for the last few years their relationship's been strained."

"I want to talk him into a clinic." Emma gave a quick, restless shrug. "But he won't listen. He can see it in Stevie—but then it's so hard to miss there. It's difficult to reason with him about it because it hasn't affected his work, his creativity, or even his health to this point. But—"

"You're worried."

"Yes. Yes, I am."

Bev's smile was softer, easier, a ghost of the one Emma remembered. "Is that why you came?"

"Partly, I suppose. There seem to be a lot of parts to why I came."

"Emma, I swear to you, if I thought I could help, if I thought there was anything I could do, anything at all, I would."

"Why?"

She picked up her cup to give herself time to choose her words. "Brian and I shared a great deal. No matter how long it's been, no matter how much hurt, you don't forget all those feelings."

"Do you hate him?"

"No. No, of course I don't."

"And me?"

"Oh, Emma."

With a quick shake of her head, Emma rose. "I didn't mean to ask you that. I didn't mean to bring all of this back. It's just that all at once I've felt . . . unfinished somehow. I don't know what I thought I would accomplish today." She stared down at the fire that crackled sedately in the hearth. "I went to see Jane."

Bev's cup clattered against her saucer before she managed to still her hands. "Oh."

With a laugh, Emma dragged at her hair. "Yes. 'Oh.' I felt that I had to, that seeing her would help clear up my feelings. And foolishly, that I might influence her to put a stop to the film they're making from her book." She turned back. "You can't know what it's like to look at her, to see her for what she is and know she's my mother."

"I don't know what to say to you, Emma, but the truth." She studied Emma a moment. Perhaps there was something she could do, some small thing to redeem the mistake she had made all those years ago. She set down her cup, folded her hands. When she spoke, her voice was very calm and very sure.

"You're nothing like her. Nothing. You were nothing like her when you came to us, nothing like her now."

"She sold me to Da."

"Oh God." Bev pressed both hands to her face, then let them drop. "It wasn't like that, Emma."

"He gave her money. She took it. I was like some piece of merchandise they passed between them, and foisted off on you."

"No!" She sprang up, clattering china. "That's a cruel thing to say, and a stupid one. Yes, he paid her. He'd have paid her whatever it took to keep you safe."

"She said he did it to preserve his image."

"She's a liar." She walked over, took both of Emma's hands. "You listen to me. I remember the day he brought you home, the way you looked. The way he looked. He was nervous, maybe even frightened, but he was determined to do what was right for you. Not because of some bloody public image, but because you were his."

"And every time he looked at me, every time you looked, you must have seen her."

"Not Brian. Never Brian." She sighed, and putting an arm around Emma's shoulders, lowered to the sofa. "Maybe I did at first. I was young. Christ, the same age you are now. We were wildly in love, planning to be married. I was pregnant with Darren. And then suddenly there you were—a part of Brian I'd had nothing to do with. I was terrified of you. Maybe I even resented you. The truth was, I didn't want to feel anything for you. Oh maybe a little pity." When Emma pulled away, Bev took her by the shoulders. "I didn't want to love you, Emma. Then suddenly, I just did. I didn't plan it, I didn't stop one day and tell myself that you deserved a chance. I just fell in love with you."

Emma broke down then, dropping her head onto Bev's shoulder and weeping, weeping brokenly, shamelessly, as the fire crackled and Bev stroked her hair.

"I'm so sorry, luv. So sorry I haven't been there for you. Now you've grown up, and I've missed my chance."

"I thought you hated me—because of Darren."

"No, oh no."

"You blamed me—"

"No." Bev drew back, stunned. "Good God, Emma. You were a child. I blamed Brian, and I was wrong. I blamed myself, and I pray I was wrong. But whatever unforgivable things I did, or thought, I never blamed you."

"I heard him crying—"

"Ssh." She gripped Emma's hands, bringing them up to her cheek. She'd had no idea Emma had suffered this way. If she had . . . Bev closed her eyes for a moment. If she had, she hoped she would have been strong enough to have put her own pain aside for the child's sake. "Listen to me. It was the most horrible thing that's ever happened in my life, the most destructive, the most painful. I lashed out at the people I should have been holding close. The first few years after Darren's death, I was . . . I hardly knew what or where I was. In and out of therapy, contemplating suicide, wishing I could find the courage to end it. There was something about him, Emma, something special, something almost magical. Sometimes I couldn't believe he'd come from me. And when he was gone, like that, so quickly, so cruelly, so needlessly, it was as if someone had taken out my heart. There was nothing I could do. I had lost my child. And then, in my grief, I turned away from my other child. And I lost her."

"I loved him, too. So much."

"I know." She smiled, gently. "Oh, I know."

"And you. I've missed you."

"I never thought I would see you again. Or that you'd be able to forgive me."

It amazed her. Forgiveness? For years Emma had thought she was the one who would never be forgiven. Now, with a few words, the rawness she had carried with her all day eased, and she was able to smile.

"When I was little, I used to think you were the most beautiful woman in the world." Emma leaned forward, rested her cheek against Bev's. "I still do. Would you mind if I called you Mum again?"

Emma felt the shaky sigh as Bev gripped her tightly. "Wait here a minute. I have something for you."

Alone, Emma groped in her bag for a tissue. Resting against the cushions, she dried her eyes. Her mother had always been, and would always be, Bev. Perhaps at last this was one quest she could put behind her.

"I've saved him for you," Bev said as she came back into the room. "Or maybe I saved him for myself. He helped me through some very lonely nights."

With a cry of pleasure, Emma sprang up. "Charlie!"

# Chapter Twenty-three

• • • •

$\mathcal{T}$WENTY-TWO ORCHESTRA PLAYERS, including violins, cellos, flutes, bassoons, and a harpist, crowded into the recording studio. A couple of assistants had taken considerable time and trouble to decorate. There were shiny red balls hanging from the ceiling, boughs of pine draped on the walls, and an aluminum tree, just tacky enough to be amusing, revolving on a stand in the corner.

Johnno had mixed together what he grandly termed a wassail. After he'd drunk two cups and survived, others were lured into sampling. No one was drunk, yet, but there was plenty of cheer being passed about.

They'd been working on a single song for over four hours, and Brian was nearly satisfied with the cut. Through his headphones, he listened to the last take. It still amazed him that a song, once only a vague melody in his mind, could take on such a clear and powerful life of its own. There were still times when he listened to what he had helped create that he felt an echo of the thrill he'd experienced in writing his first song.

He could see Pete standing in the engineering booth, annoyed and impatient as always with Brian's nit-picking perfectionism. Brian didn't give him a second thought, and let the music wash over him.

Johnno was playing poker with one of the flutists and the stunning, slender-fingered harpist. Johnno had unearthed a green visor from somewhere and livened up the game with straightforward cheating and wild betting.

P.M. was reading what appeared to be a paperback mystery. A lurid one if one could tell a book by its cover. He seemed to prefer his own company and a couple of grisly murders at the moment.

Stevie was in the bathroom again. His last attempt at coming clean had lasted less than a week after he'd checked himself out of the newest clinic.

They were satisfied, Brian thought, and more than ready to call it a day. He listened to the final sustained note.

"I want to do the vocals again."

Johnno pulled in the pot. Who said you couldn't draw to an inside straight? He sent the harpist a lusty wink. With a laugh, she handed over a five-pound note.

"How did you know he'd want another take?"

"I know my boy," Johnno told her. He rose and lifted a fist toward the engineering booth. Like Brian he noted Pete's irritated scowl and ignored it. "Once more into the breech."

"You can't want another one, son." Stevie lurched into the studio. He was flying high now, pumped full of top-grade cocaine with a heroin chaser. "Don't you know what day it is? It's Christmas fucking Eve."

"Not for a couple of hours yet." Brian buried his irritation. Sad as it was, they'd get a good twenty minutes out of Stevie before he crashed. "Let's get it done so you can go home and hang up your stocking."

"Well, look who's here," Stevie announced as Emma slipped into the studio. "It's our little girl." He swung an arm around her shoulder. "Okay, Emma luv, who's the best?"

She managed to smile and kiss his thin, bony cheek. "Da."

"Nothing but coal in your stocking, pet."

"I thought you'd still be here." Because Stevie's arm was still around her, she walked with him to the mike. She could feel him vibrate like a tightly strung wire. "Is it all right if I listen for a while?"

"Tickets are five pence and two." Noting her distress, Johnno gently disengaged Stevie. "But seeing it's Christmas, we'll forget the shillings."

"We won't be much longer," Brian stated.

"He said the same thing two hours ago." Johnno gave her a quick, reassuring squeeze. "The man's a maniac. We're turning him in right after the audition."

Brian put out his cigarette then cleared his throat with plain water. "Just the vocals on 'Lost the Sun.' "

"The twentieth take of the vocals," P.M. put in. He was pleased when Emma brushed her lips over his cheek.

"Sorry to take you away from your dip into literature," Brian snapped.

Automatically, Emma shifted to stand between them as she shrugged out of her coat. " 'Lost the Sun'?" she repeated. "I'm in luck then, that's my favorite of this lot."

"Good. You can sing backup."

She laughed at Johnno, then started to take her seat.

"No, wait." Brian grabbed her arm, grinning. "That's it. That's what we need." He was already signaling for another set of headphones. "You come in on the second verse."

"Da, I couldn't."

"Of course you could. You know the lyrics, the melody."

"Yes, but—"

"It's perfect. I don't know why I didn't think of it before. This song needs a feminine touch. Keep it light, just a little sad."

"No use arguing," Johnno said as he fit the headphones over her ears. "He's on a roll."

Emma let out a sigh. It wouldn't hurt to humor him. "What's my percentage? Do I get a mention in the liner notes? What about artistic control?"

Brian twisted her nose, hard.

It was enough to see him happy, she thought. There was nothing like a new idea to send her father off. He was calling out instructions, deferring to Johnno now and again, keeping what seemed like an eagle eye on Stevie, and subtly staying aloof from P.M.

She heard the music in her head, the sad and moody strings and flutes. It was a full, almost classical sound. Like rain, she realized—not a storm, but a gray, unrelenting rain.

Her father's voice flowed into her ears, clear and somehow sweet despite the melancholy lyrics.

"I looked for your face / I called your name / You were the light / But shadows covered me / I lost the sun."

She listened, struck as she had always been by the close, almost eerie harmony he achieved with Johnno. Her father's voice soared up, hanging on notes, caressing them. The sad, hopeless lyrics went straight to her heart.

Why it's Bev, she realized all at once. He was singing about Bev. To Bev. Emma's eyes widened as her gaze fixed on Brian. Why hadn't she seen it before? Why hadn't she understood?

He was still in love. Not resentful or angry, but miserably in love.

She didn't think, but only felt, as she did what he had asked and added her voice to his.

She didn't realize that Johnno had backed off, leaving her and her father alone. It wasn't a planned gesture when she reached out to take his hand. She wasn't aware that tears had spilled over to cling to her lashes. Her voice melded with his as her heart did.

"My life is shadows without you / Without you / Dreaming of the light I wake to darkness / I lost the sun."

As the music swelled and faded, she lifted his hand to her cheek. "I love you, Da."

He brushed his lips over hers, fighting the need to let his own tears go. "Let's hear the playback," he called out.

It was nearly one before the session musicians began to file out. The best part of another hour passed before Brian was satisfied with the overdubbing. Emma watched her father pour a tumbler full of Chivas Regal and drink it like water over a technical discussion with an engineer. She didn't want to be upset by it, not now, not when she was beginning to understand some of his pain. But neither could she sit calmly and watch while he doused that pain with whiskey.

She wandered out, then detoured to the bathroom to freshen her makeup. There had been some talk about winding down at a local club. Tired or not, she was going to go along, and keep an eye on her father.

When she opened the door, she could only stand in speechless shock. The pristine white tiles were streaked with blood. The smell of it, cold and metallic, mixed with the raw stink of vomit, had her throat slamming shut so that she reached up with her hand, pressing and squeezing to clear it. She backstepped quickly, nearly tripping before she managed to turn and race back into the studio.

"Da!"

He was finishing up his drink with one hand while struggling into his coat. The flush of success was on his face, but the laughter at something Johnno had said died when he saw Emma.

"What is it? What's wrong?"

"In the loo. Quick." She grabbed his hand to drag him with her. "It's all over the walls. I don't—I can't go in."

She stood back, gripping Johnno's arm as Brian pushed open the door.

"Goddammit." After one quick glance, he slammed the door again. "Get somebody to clean this up," he snapped to Pete. Taking Emma's arm, he started to haul her back into the studio.

"Clean it up?" She pulled away from him. "Da, for God's sake, there's blood all over the walls. Someone's been hurt. We have to—"

"Get your coat, and let's go."

"Go? We have to call the police, or a doctor, or—"

"Ease down, Emma," Pete murmured. "There's no need to call the police."

"No need?" She spun on him, then her father. "We have to call them."

"We're not calling anyone, and you're to forget it."

"But—"

"It's Stevie." Furious, Brian took her by the shoulders, and turned her to where Stevie had nodded out in a corner. "He's using heavy again. You can't jam a needle into any available vein and not lose some blood."

"My God." A horrible afterimage of the red-streaked walls flashed into her mind. "He's doing that to himself? He's killing himself."

"Very likely."

"Why aren't you doing something about it?"

"What the hell am I supposed to do?" Snatching up her coat, he dragged it over her arms. "It's his life."

"That's a despicable thing to say," she whispered.

Stepping in as peacemaker, Pete touched her shoulder. "You can't blame Brian, Emma. He's tried, I promise you. We've all tried. As soon as the album is finished, we'll convince him to go into detox again."

"As soon as the album's finished," she repeated. "The bloody album." Revolted, she swung back to her father. "He's your friend."

"Yes, he's my friend." He didn't bother to tell her of the times he'd begged Stevie to get help, of the times he'd covered up the problem by disposing of needles and mopping up blood. "You don't understand, Emma."

"No, I don't." After one last look, she turned away. "I'm going home."

"Emma—" Torn, he turned back to stare helplessly at Stevie.

"Go on along," P.M. told him and half lifted Stevie to his feet. "I'll get him to bed."

"Right." Brian caught up with Emma outside. The snow had stopped, and the moon had come out to shine blue light. Automatically he clamped his coat together to shut out the keen wind. "Emma." He laid a hand on her shoulder. It was enough to stop her, but she didn't turn. "I don't blame you for being upset. I know it's a shock to see something like that, to know that someone you care about is into that sort of thing."

"Yes." She took a deep breath before she turned to face him. Her eyes were very clear. "Yes, it is."

"I don't use needles, Emma. I never have."

There was a quick wave of relief, but she shook it away. "And everything else is all right?"

He dragged a frustrated hand through his hair. "I'm not saying it's right or wrong. I'm just saying it's reality."

"Not my kind of reality."

"I know, and I'm glad of it." He cupped her face in his hand. "Emma, if I could, I'd shield you from everything that hurts or upsets you."

"I don't want to be shielded. I don't need to be." They both turned as P.M. and Johnno carried Stevie out to a waiting car. "Is that the kind of life you want? Is that what you've worked for, what you've dreamed of?"

She made him ashamed by asking. Made him furious because he wasn't sure of the answer. "I can't explain it, Emma. But I know you don't get everything you want, and you sure as hell don't get everything you dream of."

She turned away again, but didn't leave. Gently he pressed a kiss to her hair. They didn't speak as they walked to the car. Like a shadow, Sweeney fell in behind them.

◆ ◆ ◆ ◆

LIVING NEAR HOLLYWOOD all his life hadn't spoiled the fantasy and glamour for Michael. He appreciated star-watching as much as the next guy. Nor did he mind spending a few days in February working crowd control and security for the filming of *Devastated*. It had been a disappointment that Angie Parks hadn't been involved in the early location shots. Still he enjoyed watching the twin girls who were playing Emma.

Casting had done a remarkable job of finding a pair of kids who resembled Emma. Of course, Emma had been prettier, he thought. Was prettier. Her eyes were bluer, bigger. And her mouth . . . It didn't do him a hell of a lot of good to think about her mouth.

It was a better idea to concentrate on his job—which was not, as some of the vets had sneeringly called it, pansy duty. Fans turned out day after day. The hard-core Devastation fans weren't pleased with Jane Palmer's book, or the fact that it was to be a movie. Some carried banners or placards, others just booed. There were a few, wearing leather and sporting mohawks and dog collars, who looked as though they would have enjoyed knocking heads with the cops.

Added to them were clutches of young girls who shrieked and giggled every time Matt Holden came in view. The young actor who played Brian McAvoy was the current teen dream. Michael had had his ankle kicked, his shoulder bruised, and his uniform wept on by adoring fans.

Glamour, my ass, he thought as he stood on the studio lot. The sun was high and hazy. The air-quality index was in the disgusting range, even for L.A., Michael thought. The producers had decided it would make good press to invite some of the fans to observe a few days' shooting, play extras, fill in the background. Security had enough trouble keeping the mobs back behind a police line. Now, with people free to mill around what stood in for a London cross street, every muscle had to stay on alert.

Then there she was. Angie Parks. The lusty, busty movie queen who redefined the term hot sex. The press had already fallen gleefully on the irony of P.M. Ferguson's ex-wife playing the role of Brian McAvoy's ex-lover.

Men broke into sweats as she walked by in her snug skirt and cotton blouse. Her hair was brushed smooth, puffed at the crown, tipped up at the ends in the fashion of the early sixties. She smiled at the fans—a friendly gesture, but more aloof than a wave. After a huddle with her director and her co-star, they were set for the first run-through.

It was simple enough. Jane and Brian were walking down the dingy street, arms tight around each other's waist. There was a sense of romance as well as intimacy. As the morning wore on, they repeated that stroll for different camera angles, for close-ups when Jane's face was tipped adoringly toward her lover's.

It wasn't until the lunch break that Michael noticed Angie staring at him. Abruptly his collar seemed too tight and his brow, under the shade of his cap, pearled with sweat.

He watched her murmur something to one of the assistants that hovered, then stroll off on the arm of her director.

They ran the dialogue later in the day. The same walk, the same movements. For the life of him Michael couldn't remember what was being said. Something about undying love, promises of devotion, plans for the future. He only knew that between every take, Angie sent him one long, level look. Each time she did, his stomach muscles jolted.

She was coming on to him, Michael thought with a dull, throbbing excitement that bordered on raw fear. And she wasn't being subtle about it. Despite his fascination with her, he hadn't missed the envious glances and rude remarks of the other officers on security duty.

Still, it was a shock when the scene was wrapped and she signaled him by crooking one long finger. "My trailer's over there."

"I beg your pardon?"

"My trailer?" She smiled, the slow, seductive smile he'd seen a half-dozen times on the screen. Her mouth was painted a bright pink for the scene. Watching him, she flicked out her tongue and ran it over her top lip. "I have to change and get out of makeup. You can wait outside."

"But—"

"You're taking me home," she said and began to walk.

"Miss Parks. I'm, ah, on duty."

"Yes. You're assigned to me now." She smiled again, enjoying that particular phrase. "I've been getting some threatening letters —about this role. I feel so much safer having a strong man around." She paused, flashing that smile as she signed a few autographs. "The producers arranged it with your superiors this afternoon." She slanted a look at him under her lashes, then strolled off to her trailer where she was immediately surrounded by a bevy of assistants.

Michael stood where he was.

"Kesselring."

Michael blinked, then focused on the wide, red face of Sergeant Cohen. "Sergeant?"

"You're to escort Miss Parks home. Until your orders change, you're to pick her up every morning, drive her to the studio, then accompany her back to her residence." Cohen didn't like the arrangement. It was obvious from the way he bit off the words. Michael thought if the man hadn't been in uniform, he would have spat on the street.

"Yes, sir."

"I expect you to conduct yourself in an appropriate manner."

"Yes, sir." Michael was careful to keep the grin off his face until Cohen turned away.

She came out of the trailer thirty minutes later wearing a loose red jumpsuit cinched at the waist with a studded leather belt. Her scent flowed with her—a hot, heady fragrance designed to make a man's mouth water. Her hair was attractively tousled, her eyes hidden behind oversized sunglasses. She tipped them down to take another long look at Michael, then waited beside the patrol car until he opened the door for her.

She gave him the address, then closed her eyes and remained chillingly silent along the drive. Long before they had reached the gates to her estate, Michael had decided he'd mistaken her intentions. He felt both relieved and foolish. Hadn't he heard that she was having a screaming affair with her co-star? Of course, a lot of that gossip was just speculation and publicity, but it certainly made more sense for her to be attracted to an up-and-comer like Matt Holden than a lowly uniformed cop.

She signaled the guard at the gate so that the ornately worked wrought-iron swung majestically open. Michael remembered driving to the house before, Emma beside him in the old Chevelle, their surfboards strapped to the roof. It made him smile a little. And regret. She wasn't going to be a part of his life except in his own fantasies.

Conscious of his duty, he got out, rounded the hood, and opened the passenger door.

"Come in, Officer."

"Ma'am, I—"

"Come in," she repeated, then moved up the steps in her patented style.

She left the door wide for him to close, then walked through the foyer without a backward glance. Angie didn't doubt he would follow. Men always followed. After tossing her sunglasses aside she turned into what she liked to call the drawing room. She opened a Louis Quinze cabinet and removed two glasses.

"Scotch or bourbon?" She knew he was in the doorway, hesitating.

"I'm on duty," he murmured. His eyes were drawn, and she had known they would be, to the full-length portrait over the fireplace. He'd seen it before, standing in the same spot, with Emma beside him.

"Of course. It's comforting to know you take your duty seriously." She turned to the bar, chose a soft drink, and poured it into a glass. "You do take your duty seriously, don't you?"

"Yes."

Smiling, Angie held the glass up. "You're allowed a Coke, right? I'd like to talk with you for a few minutes. Get to know you." She took a sip from her own drink, her eyes steady over the rim. "Since you're going to be taking care of me for a while. Come on." She ran her tongue over her top lip. Angie considered each word, each move another strand in the web she enjoyed weaving. There was nothing more satisfying than catching a man in the soft, sticky web of sex. "I won't bite."

She waited until he'd accepted the glass before she spread herself on the sofa. It couldn't be called sitting. She arched her back into the corner plumped with cushions, stretched her arm lazily over the back. The silk of her jumpsuit rustled quietly as she crossed her legs.

"Sit down." She sipped her drink again. Beneath the practiced seductive smile an excitement was building. He was so young, and lean. His body would be hard as rock. And he'd be eager. Once she eased him over his initial shyness—that itself an attraction—he'd be beautiful. She decided he was just into his middle twenties, and able to fuck for hours. Angie wagged her fingers at the neighboring cushion. "Tell me about yourself."

He sat, because he felt like an idiot standing in the middle of the room with a glass of Coke in his hand. He wasn't stupid. His initial impression of her intentions had been right on the mark. The problem was, he wasn't sure what he wanted to do about it.

"Second-generation cop," he began. "Native Californian." He drank, telling himself he was relaxed. For Christ's sake, he was twenty-four. If the amazing Ms. Parks wanted to flirt, he could oblige her. "And a fan." He smiled. Angie nearly purred.

"Really?"

"I've seen all your movies." Once again, his gaze was drawn to the portrait.

"Do you like it?"

"Yeah. It's stunning."

Her movements slow and fluid, she reached over to pluck a cigarette from a Lalique holder. She held it up, watching him until he remembered himself and reached for the matching table lighter. "Help yourself," she told him, indicating the cigarettes.

He was already planning on what he would tell the guys in the locker room. They'd drool with envy at the thought of him sitting on Angie Parks's sofa. "I've seen it before."

"What's that?"

"The portrait." He drew smoke in and nearly relaxed. "It's funny when you think of it. I was here, seven or eight years ago, I guess. With Emma."

Angie's gaze sharpened. "McAvoy?"

"Yeah. I ran into her on the beach one summer. We'd met a few years before that. I gave her a lift home. Well, here. I think you were in Europe filming."

"Mmmm." She considered the idea a moment, then smiled. It made it all the more interesting somehow. Here she was on the verge of seducing one of little Emma McAvoy's friends—and playing Emma's mama in what was sure to be the hottest movie of the year. And it would be all the more interesting to think of herself as Jane while they made love. "Small world." She set her glass aside to lean forward and toy with the buttons of his shirt. "Do you see much of Emma?"

"No. Well, actually I saw her last month when she was in town."

"Isn't that sweet." The first button popped open. "Are you two . . . involved?"

"No. That is . . . No. Miss Parks."

"Angie." She blew a light stream of smoke in his face, then crushed out her cigarette. "And what is your name, darling?"

"Michael. Michael Kesselring. I don't—"

Her movements stopped. "Kesselring? Any relation to the investigating officer on the McAvoy murder?"

"He's my father. Miss—"

She laughed then, long and loud and delighted. "Better and better. Let's call it fate, Michael." Her hand slid up his thigh. "Relax."

He wasn't stupid. And he wasn't dead. When she closed her hands over him, the pleasure speared through him like a heated blade. And so did the guilt. It was ridiculous, he told himself. She was gorgeous, dangerous—every man's darkest fantasy. He'd had his share of women, starting with Caroline Fitzgerald on the night before his seventeenth birthday. They'd lost their virginity together, sweatily and clumsily. He'd learned a lot since good old Caroline.

Angie slipped the cigarette from his fingers, leaving it to smolder in the ashtray as he hardened against her palm. He was going to be sweet, she thought. So very sweet. And the irony— the irony was beautiful.

"I've never had a cop," she murmured as she nipped at his lip. "You'll be the first."

He felt the breath back up in his lungs, thick and hot. He shook his head to clear it. He had one flash, achingly lucid, of sitting with Emma on the winter beach. Then Angie stood up. With a flick of her hands, she unsnapped her belt. She had only to shrug her shoulders to have the red silk slithering to the floor. Beneath it her body was white and lush and naked. She ran her hands over it, lingering, caressing as adoringly as a lover. Before he could find the strength to stand, she was straddling him. On a groan of pleasure, she pressed his mouth against one perfect, polished breast.

"Do things to me," she murmured. "Do anything you like."

# *Chapter Twenty-four*

· · · ·

$\mathcal{T}$HE SUPERMARKET TABLOIDS had a field day.

### ANGIE PARKS'S ROOKIE LOVER

### *The Inside Story*

### TRIANGLE OF PASSION AND MURDER IN HOLLYWOOD

They leaped on the connection with the McAvoys and played it like a brass band. In New York, Emma tried to ignore the gossip and prayed it wasn't based in fact.

It was none of her business, she reassured herself as she spent hours in her darkroom. Michael was no more than a friend—an acquaintance, really. They had no actual ties, and certainly no relationship. Except for the kiss they had shared.

She was romanticizing. One kiss meant nothing. She hadn't let it, couldn't let it. Even if she had felt—she wasn't sure what she had felt. It hardly mattered. If Michael had indeed been drawn into Angie's web, she could only feel sorry for him. The idea of feeling betrayed was ludicrous.

They each had their own life. He on one coast, she on the other. And she was at last, at long last, doing something with hers.

She was working for Runyun. She might be a lowly assistant, but she was Runyun's lowly assistant. In the past ten weeks, she'd learned more from him than she had learned in years of classes, stacks of books. Working by the glow of her red light, she gently moved a print in the developing fixer. She was getting better. And she intended to be better yet.

One day, she thought, she would give Runyun a run for his money.

Professionally, she was going exactly where she wanted to go. Personally . . . her life was in upheaval.

Her mother. How could she explain what it felt like to know that the woman she had faced in the dim room in London had given birth to her? Would she ever be able to separate and understand her feelings? And her fears? No matter what reassurances Bev had given her, she'd never be able to shake the greatest fear of all. Could she be like Jane? Deep down, were there seeds that would sprout one day, changing her from what she wanted to be into what she had been born to be?

A drunk. A cheap, bitter drunk.

How could she escape a fate that rushed at her from all sides? Her mother, her grandfather. Her father. No matter how she blinded herself to it, she had to accept that the man she loved most was as much a slave to drink as the woman she wanted to hate.

It terrified her.

She didn't want to believe it. She was afraid not to.

No good. It did no good to dwell on it, she told herself and hung the rinsed print to dry. Emma studied it, critically, before moving back to her enlarger.

Since she was sick of worrying about herself, she decided to worry about Marianne. Emma knew her friend had taken to cutting classes, meeting Robert Blackpool for lunch or drinks in whatever spot was currently trendy. From there they would often crawl the clubs—Elaine's, Studio 54, Danceteria—where Blackpool could be seen.

There were nights Marianne came in at dawn, shadow-eyed and bubbling with stories. Worse were the nights Blackpool stayed in the apartment, in Marianne's studio. In Marianne's bed.

With all her heart she wanted to wish for Marianne's happiness. Marianne was happy. She was wildly in love for the first time with a man who by all appearances adored her. She was living the exciting, glittery, and decadent life they had both pined for while trapped within Saint Catherine's prim walls.

It annoyed Emma to find herself jealous and critical. She

resented not having Marianne to talk to, and called herself petty. It irritated her to see the glow of lovemaking on Marianne's face. And she called herself spiteful.

But with all that aside, Emma couldn't make herself comfortable with Marianne's romance. He was a gorgeous, exciting, and talented man. There was no denying that, especially as she studied the drying prints. She had agreed, with Marianne's urging, to photograph Blackpool. He had been a perfect gentleman, Emma remembered. At ease, amusing, flattering—in the platonic manner suited to her roommate's lover.

Lover. With a wistful little sigh, Emma frowned at the prints. Perhaps that was the crux of it. She and Marianne had shared everything—every thought, every deed, every dream, for over ten years. This was something they couldn't share, and Marianne's bubbling happiness was a rub—a constant reminder of something Emma had never experienced.

That was something to be ashamed of, she thought. She could justify her feelings day in and day out. Blackpool was too smooth, he was too experienced, he was too fond of clubs and women. His eyes were too dark when they rested on her—and too cocky when they rested on Marianne. But the truth was, she was desperately envious of Marianne.

It didn't matter that she didn't like him, Emma told herself. It didn't matter that Johnno didn't like him and continually made snide comments about Blackpool's penchant for leather pants and silver chains. What mattered was that Marianne was in love.

She switched on the light, arching her back. Spending the best part of the day developing had given her a ravenous appetite. She hoped Runyun and the contact she'd made at *Rolling Stone* would approve of the shots she'd taken of Devastation in the recording studio.

She was scrounging in the refrigerator for something more interesting than molding bologna when she heard the elevator open. "I hope you bought supplies," she called out. "We're getting down to science projects in here."

"Sorry."

Emma whipped around at Blackpool's voice. "I thought you were Marianne."

"No. She gave me a key." He smiled easily, holding it up

before tucking it into his jeans. "I'd have stopped by the deli if I'd known I'd find a hungry woman."

"Marianne's at class." Emma checked her watch. "She should be back soon."

"I've got time." He swung into the kitchen to peer over her shoulder. Emma shifted away automatically. "Pathetic," he decided, but helped himself to the imported beer Marianne kept stocked for him. There was a brass opener screwed into the wall. He popped the top, then studied her.

She'd scooped her hair on top of her head to keep it out of the way while she worked. At his scrutiny, she became aware that her jeans were too tight and her T-shirt too big. She dragged at it as it slipped off one shoulder.

"I'm sorry I can't offer you anything else."

He merely lifted a brow, smiled, then drank. "Don't worry about it. Just think of me as one of the family."

She didn't care to be backed into the tiny kitchen with him. When she started through the doorway he shifted just enough to have their bodies brush. It was deliberately suggestive, and shocking because he'd been nothing but the polite friend of a friend to that point. When she jerked away, he laughed.

"Do I make you nervous, Emma?"

"No." It was a lie, and not a very good one. She had tried not to think of him as a man, not the way a woman thought of a man. But his thighs had been long and hard when hers had knocked against them. "Are you and Marianne going out?"

"That's the plan." He had a habit of running his tongue over the top of his teeth before he smiled, like a man about to enjoy a long, succulent meal. "Want to join us?"

"I don't think so." On the one occasion Marianne had talked her into going with them, Emma had found herself dragged from club to club, dodging paparazzi.

"You don't get out enough, sweetheart."

She jerked her head back when he reached out to toy with her hair. "I've got work to do."

"Speaking of which, did you ever print those shots you took of me?"

"Yes. They're drying."

"Mind if I have a look?"

With a restless move of her shoulders, she started toward her darkroom. She wasn't afraid of him, she assured herself. If he was testing the waters to see if she wanted to make it a threesome, she would set him straight quickly enough.

"I think you'll be pleased," she began.

"Ah, but I have very high standards, Emmy luv."

She stiffened at the sound of the pet name, but continued on. "I tried for moody, with a touch of arrogant."

His breath was warm on the back of her neck. "Sexy?"

Her shiver was quick and uncontrollable. "Some women think arrogant is sexy."

"And you?"

"No." She gestured toward the prints that hung drying. "If there's one that suits you, I can blow it up."

He was distracted enough by his own image to abandon the flirtation. They'd held the shoot informally, right in the loft. He'd gone along with the idea because Marianne had been so set on it, and because he'd wanted a chance to ply a little of his charm on Emma. He preferred younger women—fresh off the farm, so to speak—particularly after the ugly breakup with his wife. She'd been thirty, sharp as a scalpel, and prone to bitchiness whenever she'd suspected him, rightly enough, of being unfaithful.

He enjoyed Marianne's quick enthusiasm, dry wit, and her uninhibited responses in bed. But Emma, young, quiet Emma, was a different matter. He'd wondered what it would be like to peel away that cool reserve. Certain that he could. It would make her father crazy—a fact that added to the intrigue. Blackpool had entertained more than one fantasy about luring both women into bed. Two slick, lithe bodies, two agile young students. His suspicion that Emma was as virginal as Marianne had been only heightened the appeal.

But he put that thought aside a moment and studied the shadowy black-and-white prints.

"Marianne said you were good, but I thought that was because you're her friend."

"No." Even in the small room, Emma managed to keep at arm's length. "I am good."

He laughed at that, a low rumble that rushed along her skin. When she felt her muscles tighten, she shifted farther away. Dammit, he was sexy. But beneath the primitive appeal was something that repelled her.

"So you are, sweet thing." When he turned she caught the

light scent he carried with him—leather from his jacket, sweat, and the faint whisper of beer. "So, still waters run deep."

"I know my work."

"It's more than work." Casually he braced a hand against the wall and effectively trapped her. There was an element of danger here he couldn't resist. "Photography's an art, isn't it? An artist is born with things other people lack." He reached out and plucked a pin from her hair. She stood still, as jumpy and dazed as a rabbit caught in the beams of a truck. "I know. Artists recognize each other." Slowly, he drew out another pin. "Do you recognize me, Emma?"

She couldn't speak or move. For an instant she couldn't even think. As she started to shake her head, he swooped, dragging his hand through her hair, scattering pins, crushing his warm and ready mouth on hers.

She didn't struggle, not at first, and would always hate herself for that stunned moment of torrid pleasure. He invaded, delighted most of all by her perfect innocence. His tongue stabbed through her parted lips. As she moaned, the beginnings of a protest, his hands raced up and under her shirt and caught her breasts, squeezing and releasing, squeezing and releasing, while she fought to catch her breath.

"No. Don't."

He only laughed again. Her trembles had ignited what had only been a passing interest into real fire. He ground himself against her until her reluctant passion turned to real fear.

"Let go of me."

She fought him now, nails scraping down the leather of his jacket, body bucking. When he slammed her back against the wall, bottles clattered from the shelf. Now there was terror, like an animal inside her, clawing until she couldn't find the courage to scream. His hands were on her zipper, dragging at her jeans. She didn't know she was weeping, or that it excited him.

He released her to tug at his own jeans. Freed, she looked wildly for a means of escape. With terror still pumping through her, she snatched up a pair of scissors and gripped them in both hands.

"Stay away from me." Her voice was low and raw, as shaky as the hands that held the scissors.

"What's this?" He was clever enough to know that the wild look in her eyes meant she would strike first and be sorry for it later. He'd been right about the virginal part, he thought while his breath heaved. And he wanted to be the one to relieve her of the obstacle. "Defending your honor? You were ready to cast it aside a minute ago."

She only shook her head, jabbing with the blades as he took a cautious step forward. "Get out. I want you to get out. Don't come near me again, or Marianne. When I tell her—"

"You won't tell her a thing." Through his fury, he smiled. "If you do, you'll only lose a friend. She's in love with me, and she'll believe exactly what I tell her. Imagine, coming on to your best friend's lover."

"You're a bastard, and a liar."

"Quite true, Emmy luv. But then you're a frigid tease." Calmer, he picked up his discarded beer and swigged. "And here I was, trying to do you a favor. You've got problems, sweetheart, big ones, but nothing a good fuck wouldn't cure." Still smiling, he rubbed himself. "And believe me, I'm a very good fuck. Just ask your best friend."

"Get out."

"But you wouldn't know about that, would you? Sweet little Catholic girl, all hung up in sins and those sweaty dreams you have when you listen to me upstairs with Marianne. Your kind likes it to be rape, so they can pretend they're innocent all the time they're screaming for more."

Setting her teeth, Emma looked deliberately down to where he continued to caress himself. "If I use these," she said quietly, "I'm going straight for your balls."

She had the satisfaction of seeing him pale at that, from rage and, she was sure, from fear. He stepped back, and the sneer that had women screaming for him sent sweat dripping down her back.

"Bitch."

"Better a bitch than a eunuch," she said calmly enough, though she was afraid the scissors would slip any moment from her nerveless fingers.

They both heard the elevator open. They both braced.

"Emma!" Marianne's cheerful voice sang through the loft. "Emma, are you home?"

Blackpool sent Emma a quick cocky look. "Right here, lover. Emma's been showing me the prints."

"Oh, she's finished them."

He turned and strolled out, leaving Emma to stay or to follow. "I've been waiting for you," she heard him say in a voice like cool silk.

"I didn't know you'd be here." The breathlessness in Marianne's answer told Emma she was being kissed. Prying one hand from the scissors, she rubbed it hard against her mouth. "Let's have a look at the prints."

"Why look at pictures when you've got the real thing?"

"Robert—" Marianne's protest ended on a muffled groan. "But Emma's—"

"Don't worry about her. She's busy. I've been waiting to get my hands on you all day."

Emma stood where she was as their murmurs and whispers trailed up the stairs. Very quietly, she closed the door to the darkroom. She didn't want to hear. She didn't want to imagine. Her legs nearly gave out before she made it to her stool. Once there, she let the scissors drop with a ringing clatter to the floor, then curled her legs up and hugged them to her chest.

He had touched her, she thought in disgust. He had touched her, and God help her, for a moment she'd wanted him to go on touching her. She'd wanted him to take the choice out of her hands, just as he'd accused her of. She hated him for that. And she hated herself.

The phone beside her rang three times before she drummed up the energy to answer. "Yes."

"Emma—Emma is that you?"

"Yes."

There was a crackle on the line, a hesitation. "It's Michael. Michael Kesselring."

She stared dully at the prints drying above her work table. "Yes, Michael."

"I . . . are you all right? Is something wrong?"

She found she wanted to laugh then, long and loud. "No, why should anything be wrong?"

"Well, you sound . . . I guess you've read some of the tabloids."

"I've seen them."

He let out a long breath. The speech he'd prepared so carefully had vanished from his mind. "I wanted to call and explain—"

"Why? It's none of my business what you do, or whom you

do it with." The anger she hadn't been able to feel through fear came bubbling to the surface. "I can't think of any reason I should care who you're screwing. Can you?"

"Yes. No, dammit. Emma, I didn't want you to get the wrong idea."

She was trembling now, but mistook grief and nerves for rage. "Are you going to tell me you haven't slept with her?"

"No, I'm not going to tell you that."

"Then we really have nothing more to discuss."

"Emma. Shit, I don't know how all of this got so out of hand. I want to talk to you about it, but I can't do it over the frigging phone. I can try to trade some duty, fly out for a couple of days."

"I won't see you."

"For Christ's sake, Emma."

"I won't. There's no reason to, Michael. As I said, you're free to be with whomever you choose, and my blessing if you want it. I'm going to put all of that part of my life behind me. All of it. So seeing you again wouldn't suit my plans. Do you understand?"

"Yes." There was a long, long pause. "Yes, I guess I do. Good luck, Emma."

"Thank you, Michael. Goodbye."

She was crying again, but didn't bother to brush the tears away. Reaction, she told herself. Reaction was setting in from that horrible scene with Blackpool. She wished Michael well, she really did. Damn him and all men.

She locked her door, turned the radio up loud, sat on the floor and wept.

# *Chapter Twenty-five*
#### ♦ ♦ ♦ ♦

New York, 1986

THE LOFT LOOKED as though it had been struck by a hurricane. But then, Emma supposed, Marianne had always been a strong wind. There was a scatter of papers and magazines, three empty handbags, two of which were Chinese red, a single slingback pump of the same bold color, and a pile of records that were spread out on the floor like a deck of cards. Choosing one, Emma set it on the turntable and was met with a blast of Aretha Franklin.

She smiled, remembering that Marianne had played it the night before while she'd finished her furious packing. It was hard to believe that both Emma and the loft would have to do without Marianne for the better part of a year.

Emma picked up a purple silk blouse and a red Converse hightop. Two more items that had somehow escaped Marianne's maniacal search for the essentials. The chance to study for a year in Paris, at the Ecole des Beaux Arts, was an opportunity Marianne hadn't been able to turn down. Emma was thrilled for her —but it was hard, very hard, to stand in the middle of the loft alone.

She remained for a moment, listening. Over the sound of Aretha was the rumble of traffic from the street below. Through the open windows she could hear the high, strong soprano of a neighboring opera student practicing an aria from *The Marriage of Figaro*. Maybe it was ridiculous to consider herself alone in New York, but that was precisely what she was.

Not for long, she reminded herself and set the blouse and

shoe on the bottom step. She had her own packing to do. In two days she would be in London. She was going to tour with Devastation again, but this time, she had a title. Official photographer. It was a title she'd earned, Emma thought as she hauled the first suitcase onto her bed. She'd been given her shot when her father had asked her to photograph the group for the album cover. The *Lost the Sun* cover, Emma remembered. The stark black-and-white portrait had earned enough acclaim that even Pete had stopped mumbling about nepotism. And he hadn't said a word when she'd been asked to shoot the cover for their current album.

It gave her a good deal of satisfaction that it had been he, as the group's manager, who had called to invite her on the tour. Salary and expenses included. Runyun had muttered, but only briefly. Something about the commercialization of art.

London, Dublin, Paris—a quick visit with Marianne—Rome, Barcelona, Berlin. Not to mention all the cities in between. The European tour was slated to take ten weeks. When it was done, she would do something she'd been promising herself for almost two years. She would open her own studio.

Unable to find her black cashmere suit, Emma headed out and up the stairs, pausing to pick up the blouse and shoe. There was a fascinating mix of scents. Turpentine and Opium. Marianne had left her studio exactly as she preferred it. In chaos. Brushes and pallet knives and broken pieces of charcoal were stuffed into everything from mayonnaise jars to a Dresden vase. Canvases were stacked drunkenly against the walls. Three paint smocks, their bright colors splattered with even brighter paint, were tossed over tables and chairs.

An easel still stood by the window, along with a cup of something Emma wasn't sure she wanted to investigate. With a shake of her head Emma moved over to the bedroom area. It was hardly more than an alcove. As the years had passed, Marianne's art had taken over. The big bed with its ornate rattan headboard was squeezed between two tables. A lamp with a shade fashioned like a lady's straw bonnet sat on one, and half a dozen candles of various lengths stood on the other.

The bed was unmade. Marianne had refused to make her bed on principle since they'd left Saint Catherine's. In the closet Emma found three items, all hers. The black cashmere suit hung between a red leather skirt she'd forgotten she owned, and an "I Love New York" sweatshirt torn at the sleeve.

Emma gathered them up, then sat on Marianne's rumpled sheets.

Good God, she was going to miss her. They had shared everything—jokes, crises, arguments, tears. There were no secrets between them. Except one, Emma remembered. Even now it made her shudder.

She'd never told Marianne about Blackpool. She'd never told anyone. She had meant to, especially the night Marianne had come home drunk with the certainty that he was going to ask her to marry him.

"Look, he gave this to me." Marianne had showed off the diamond heart that hung on a gold chain around her neck. "He said he didn't want me to forget him while he was in Los Angeles working on his new album." She had all but cartwheeled around the loft.

"It's beautiful," Emma had forced herself to say. "When does he leave?"

"Tonight. I took him to the airport."

The relief had come in waves.

"I sat in the parking lot and cried like a baby for a half hour after his plane took off. Stupid. He'll be back." She had whirled then to throw her arms around Emma. "Emma, he's going to ask me to marry him. I know it."

"Marry him?" Relief had skidded into panic. She had remembered the feel of his hands on her, bruising her breasts. "But, Marianne, he's—how—"

"It was the way he said goodbye, the way he looked at me when he gave me the necklace. Christ, Emma, it took everything not to beg him to take me with him. But I want him to send for me. I know he will. I know he will."

Of course, he hadn't.

Marianne had sat by the phone every night, had rushed home from classes day after day to check for messages. There hadn't been a word from him.

Three weeks later, the first inkling of why had come in via the airwaves. There had been Blackpool, in his trademark black leather, escorting a young, sultry brunette backup singer to some Hollywood bash. The first clips ran on television. Then the tabloids dug in.

Marianne's first reaction had been to laugh it off. Her next had been to try to reach him. He had never returned her calls. *People* ran a feature on him and his hot new love. Marianne was told that Mr. Blackpool was vacationing in Crete. He'd taken the brunette with him.

Emma rose and walked to the studio window. Before or since she'd never seen Marianne so devastated. It had been a relief, a great one, when Marianne had finally broken out of her weepy depression, had cursed Blackpool with an expertise that had warmed Emma's heart. Then, ceremonially, she had tossed the diamond heart out of the window. Emma had always hoped some sharp-eyed bag lady had happened across it.

She'd gotten over it, Emma mused. She'd bounced back into her work with a crack that she'd owed Blackpool. No artist could be worth her salt if she hadn't suffered.

Emma could only wish she herself had been able to forget it as easily. She would remember, always, everything he'd said to her, every name he'd called her. Her only revenge had been to burn his prints and negatives.

That was the past, she thought briskly and rose. Her problem was she remembered things too clearly. It was both a blessing and a curse that she could see things that had happened a year before, twenty years before, as easily as she could see her own face in the mirror.

Except for one night in her life, she thought. And that only came in misty dreams.

With her recovered clothes over her arm, she started downstairs. The buzzer sounded, making her frown. Everyone knew Marianne was gone, and that she herself was practically out the door.

The intercom squawked a bit when she pushed the button. "Yes?"

"Emma? It's Luke."

"Luke?" Delighted, she released the outside door. "Come on up."

She dashed to the bedroom to toss the clothes on her bed, then raced back in time to greet him when the elevator doors opened.

"Hello." She hugged him, tight, a little surprised that he hesitated before he returned the embrace. "I had no idea you were in town."

She pulled back to study him, and had to force her smile in place. He looked dreadful, pale, shadow-eyed, too thin. The last time she'd seen him he'd been on his way to Miami. A new job, a new life.

"I got in a couple days ago." His lips curved, but there was no answering smile in his eyes. "Prettier than ever, Emma."

"Thanks." Because his hand seemed so cold in hers, she chafed it automatically. "Come in, sit. I'll get you a drink. We might have some wine."

"Got any bourbon?"

Her brows lifted. In all the years she'd known him, he'd never indulged in anything stronger than Chardonnay. "I don't know. I'll check."

She waited until he'd lowered himself onto the sprawling L-shaped sectional before she darted into the kitchen.

Miami didn't agree with him, she thought, pulling open cupboards and searching through their meager liquor supply. Or perhaps it was the breakup with Johnno that didn't agree with him. He looked dead on his feet. Haggard. Like some survivor of a catastrophe. The Luke she remembered, the Luke she had kissed goodbye eighteen months before, had been a gorgeous, muscular, sleek specimen of humanity.

"Cognac," she called out. Someone had given them a bottle of Courvoisier for Christmas.

"Fine. Thanks."

There wasn't a brandy snifter in the house, so she chose a wine glass, then poured a glass of Perrier for herself.

His smile seemed easier when she sat on the ottoman across from him. "I've always liked this place." He pointed to the mural Marianne had painted on the plaster. "Where is she?"

"In Paris." She glanced at her watch. "Or nearly. She's going to spend a year studying there."

He shifted his gaze to the photographs that lined a nearby wall. "I saw your photo study of Baryshnikov."

"The greatest thrill of my life. I was stunned when Runyun let me have the assignment."

"And the album cover." He drank, and felt every drop of the brandy slide down his throat.

"Wait until you see the new one." She kept her voice light and easy, but there was concern in her eyes as they skimmed over

Luke. "It should hit the stands by the end of the week. Of course, the music's not bad, either."

Emma saw his fingers whiten on the stem of the glass. "How is Johnno?"

"He's fine. I think they've talked him into doing a cameo on *Miami Vice* . . . I'm sure he'll get in touch if he comes down your way."

"Yeah." He drank again. "He's not in town."

"No, he's in London." The opera singer began soaring over scales. "They're prepping for the tour. I'm going along. In fact, I'm flying out day after tomorrow."

"You're going to see him?"

"Yes, in a couple of days. There's an enormous amount of work to be done before we start. Luke, what is it?"

He shook his head. Carefully, he set the cognac aside, then reached inside his jacket. Taking out a plain white envelope, he handed it to Emma. "Would you give this to him for me?"

"Of course."

"As soon as you see him."

"Yes, if you like." She started to set it on the table, but caught the look in his eye. "I'll just put it in my suitcase." She left him sitting there, looking dully out of the windows. He was standing when she returned, holding the empty wine glass in both hands. She started to speak, then he swayed. The glass shattered on the floor before she caught him. She had braced for his weight. The brittle fragility of his body shocked her more than the pallor.

"Sit. Come on, sit down. You're ill." She knelt on the cushion beside him, stroking his hair as he wearily closed his eyes. "I think you've got a fever. Let me take you to a doctor."

"No." He let his head fall back. His eyes were bright with fury when they met hers. "I've been to a doctor. A whole fucking fleet of doctors."

"You need to eat," she said firmly. "You look as though you haven't eaten in a week. Let me fix—"

"Emma." He caught her hand. She knew. He could see by her face that she already knew, but refused to believe. He'd spent quite a while refusing to believe himself. "I'm dying." It sounded easy, almost peaceful. "It's AIDS."

"No." Her fingers bit into his. "Oh God, no."

"I've been sick for weeks. Months really," he admitted on a

sigh. "I thought it was a cold, the flu, vitamin deficiency. I didn't want to face going to the doctor. Then, well, I had to. I didn't accept the first diagnosis, or the second, or the third." He laughed, letting his eyes close again. "There are some things you can't run away from."

"There are treatments." Frantic, she pressed his hand to her cheek and rocked. "I've read about treatments, drugs."

"I'm pumped full of drugs. Some days I feel pretty good."

"There are clinics."

"I'm not spending whatever time I've got in a clinic. I sold my house so I've got some money. I'm going to rent a suite at the Plaza. See plays, go to movies, museums, the ballet. All the things I haven't had time to do in the last few years." He smiled again, touching a finger to her cheek. "Sorry about the glass."

"Don't worry about it."

"It looked like Waterford," he murmured. "You've always had class, Emma. Don't cry." His voice tightened as he turned away from the tears in her eyes.

"I'll clean up the glass."

"Don't." He took her hand again. He so badly needed someone to hold his hand. "Just sit for a minute."

"All right. Luke, you can't give up. Every day they're, oh, I know it sounds trite," she said desperately, "but every day they're coming closer. There's so much research being done, and the media is making the public more aware." She brought his hand back to her cheek. "They're bound to find a cure. They have to."

He said nothing. She wanted a solace he couldn't give. How could he explain how he had felt when the results had come in? Would she understand, could she, that fear and anger were only two components? There had been humiliation too, and despair. When pneumonia had set in weeks before, the ambulance attendants wouldn't touch him. He'd been isolated from human contact, from compassion, from hope.

She was the first one to touch him, to weep for him. And he couldn't explain.

"When you see Johnno, don't tell him how I looked."

"I won't."

That seemed to comfort him. His hand relaxed again. "Remember when I tried to teach you to cook?"

"I remember that you said I was hopeless, but that Marianne took ineptitude to new heights."

"You finally caught on to the spaghetti."

"I still make it once a week whether I want it or not."

He was crying, slow, silent tears that slipped between his closed lashes.

"Why don't you put off the Plaza awhile and stay here?" When he shook his head, she went on. "Tonight then. Just for tonight. It's so lonely without Marianne, and I'll show you the improvements I've made in your spaghetti sauce."

She sat with him, holding on, when he buried his face in his hands and wept.

♦ ♦ ♦ ♦

*I*T WAS RAINING when she touched down at Heathrow. A soft spring rain that made her think of daffodils. With her camera case slung over her arm, she walked through the gate. Johnno met her and gave her a smacking kiss. Then kept his arm around her to steer her through the terminal. "Pete's having your luggage sent over." He turned her away from baggage claim and toward the exit doors.

"Remind me to kiss his feet."

When he opened the door of a limo, Emma lifted her brow.

"I hate airport traffic," Johnno claimed. When he'd settled in, he poured two glasses of Pepsi and offered her a bag of chips. "Besides, this way we can eat. How'd you handle the flight?"

"With Dramamine and prayer." She dove into the chips. Eating on a plane was a luxury her stomach couldn't afford. "Don't worry. I stocked up on both for the tour."

"Glad to have you aboard."

She stalled, asking questions, keeping it light. He said nothing when she reached up and closed the privacy glass between the backseat and the driver.

"I appreciate your coming to pick me up."

"I figured you had a reason."

"Yes. Can I have a cigarette?"

He took two out, lighted them both. "Serious?"

"Very." She took two long pulls on the Gauloise. "Luke came to see me a couple of days ago."

"He's in New York?"

"Yes . . . We had dinner."

"That's nice. So how is he?"

Keeping her eyes lowered, Emma took the envelope out of her purse. "He wanted me to give you this."

She turned to study the dreamy rain while he opened the envelope. He read in silence. There was only the quiet hum of the motor, the gentle lap of rain, the muted music of a Chopin prelude from the speakers. She waited, a minute, then five, before she looked at Johnno again.

He was staring straight ahead, his eyes blank. The letter lay in his lap where he had dropped it. When he turned to look at her, her heart wrenched.

"You know?"

"Yes, he told me." Not knowing what else to do, she took Johnno's hand in both of hers. "I'm sorry, Johnno. So sorry."

"He's worried about me." Johnno's voice was dull as he stared back down at the letter. "He wants to make sure I go in for tests. And he—he wanted to reassure me that he'd keep quiet about our relationship. Jesus." His head fell back on a hollow laugh. "Jesus Christ. He's dying and he wants me to know my reputation's safe."

"It matters to him."

His throat was raw. There were tears in it, he realized and took another rough drag on his cigarette. "He was important to me, dammit. Now he's dying, and what am I supposed to say? Thanks, old man. Damn sporting of you to take my secret to the grave."

"Don't, Johnno. It's important to him to do this his way. He's—Luke's trying to tie up his loose ends. He needs to tie up his loose ends."

"Oh fuck. Oh bloody fucking hell." The grief and the fury raged inside him. There was nothing he could vent it on. It did no more good for him to curse the disease than it had done for him to curse fate for making him what he was. He took out another cigarette, fingers shaking as he fought with the lighter. "I arranged for some very discreet, very expensive testing about six months ago. I'm clean." He dragged in smoke while he crumpled the letter in his fist. "No nasty problems with my immune system. Nope. No problem here."

Because she understood, her voice was brisk. "It's incredibly stupid to feel guilty because you're well."

"Where's the justice, Emma?" He smoothed out the letter,

then carefully folded it and slipped it into his pocket. "Where's the frigging justice?"

"I don't know." She laid her head on his shoulder. "When Darren was murdered I was too young to ask myself that question. But I've asked it, Johnno, hundreds of times since. Why is it the people we love die, and we don't? The nuns say it's God's will."

"It's not enough."

"No, it's not enough." She searched her conscience. She supposed she'd known all along that she would tell him. "Luke's in New York. He's staying at the Plaza for a few weeks. He didn't want me to tell you."

He tightened his arm around her. "Thanks."

When the limo pulled up in front of Brian's London home, Johnno kissed her. "Tell Brian . . . tell him the truth. I'll be back in a couple of days."

"All right." She watched the limo disappear in the misty rain.

# *Chapter Twenty-six*

◆ ◆ ◆ ◆

$\mathcal{E}$MMA SWITCHED TO a wide-angle lens and crouched at the foot of the stage in the London Palladium. There was no denying that Devastation was as dynamic in rehearsals as they were in concert. She was delighted with the shots she'd taken so far, and was already readjusting her schedule to work in dark-room time.

But now she was shooting the empty stage, the instruments, amps, and cables left behind while the group took an hour's break. There were electric keyboards, horns, even a grand piano. What interested her now, what she wanted to immortalize in her way, were the underpinnings of music-making.

The scarred and sacred Martin made her think of the man who played it. Stevie was as battle-worn and as brilliant as the instrument he had favored for almost twenty years. Its strap, a bold, eye-popping mix of colors, had been her last Christmas gift to him.

There was Johnno's Fender bass, painted a slick turquoise. On its stand next to the Martin, it looked frivolous and funky. Like the man, it was a competent, clever instrument under a coat of fancy varnish.

P.M.'s drum set had the band's logo splashed across the front. From one angle it looked so ordinary. Then, on closer inspection, you could see the complicated arrangement of bass and snare and cymbals. The cautious addition of three sets of drumsticks, the gleam of chrome trim that P.M. still insisted on polishing himself.

Then there was her father's custom-made Gibson. The absolutely plain, working man's guitar with its simple black strap. Not a frill, not a flash. But the wood gleamed, pale gold. And when the strings were plucked it had a tone that brought tears to your eyes.

Lowering her camera, Emma stroked a gentle hand down the neck. She snatched it back quickly when she heard the music. For an instant, she'd thought her touch had brought the guitar to life. Feeling foolish, she glanced stage left. There was music, and it did indeed sound like magic.

Quietly, she crossed the stage, and followed it.

She saw him sitting cross-legged on the floor outside a dressing room. The music echoed, haunted the hallway. His long elegant fingers caressed the strings, slid over them like a lover while he sang softly, for himself.

"While you slept I lay awake / Moonlight streamed across your face, played in your angel hair / While I watched you sighed my name and wishes did I make / That I could creep into your dreams, stay forever with you there."

His voice was warm and soft. As he bent over his guitar, his dark blond hair dipped to hide most of his face. She didn't speak, afraid to disturb him, but she crouched and lifted her camera. When he glanced up at the click of the shutter, she lowered it.

"I'm sorry. I didn't mean to interrupt."

His eyes were gold, like his hair. They met hers, and held. His face suited his voice. It was poetically pale, smooth, the gold eyes longly lashed. His full, sculpted lips curved, shyly, she thought.

"No man's going to think of you as an interruption." He continued to strum the guitar as he studied her. An absent caress. He'd seen her before, of course, but this was the first chance he'd had for a good, close look. She'd pulled her hair back into a careless ponytail, leaving her face unframed so that the delicate features stood on their own. "Hi. I'm Drew Latimer."

"Hello—oh, of course, I should have recognized you." And would have, Emma realized, if she hadn't been so dazed and breathless. She stood to move over and offer a hand. "Lead singer for Birdcage Walk. I like your music."

"Thanks." He took her hand, kept it until she knelt beside him. "Are pictures a hobby or a profession?"

"Both." Her pulse began to scramble as he continued to stare at her. "I hope you don't mind that I took yours. I heard you playing and wandered back."

"I'm glad you did." More than he wanted to say. "Why don't you have dinner with me tonight and take a few hundred more?"

She laughed. "Even I don't take that many while I'm eating."

"Then leave the camera behind."

She waited until she was sure she wouldn't stutter. "I have work."

"Breakfast then? Lunch? A candy bar."

With a chuckle she rose. "I happen to know you've got time for little but a candy bar. You're opening for Devastation tomorrow night."

He didn't release her hand, had no intention of allowing her to slip quietly away. "How about I get you into the show and you have a drink with me after?"

"I'm already coming to the show."

"Okay, who do I have to kill?" He held the guitar in one hand, and her fingers in the other. His denim shirt was nearly unbuttoned and revealed pale, smooth skin. In one lithe move he was standing beside her. "You're not going to walk away from me on the eve of my big break, are you? I need moral support."

"You'll do fine."

He tightened his grip when she started to draw away. "My God, no matter how trite it sounds, it's the truth. You're the most beautiful woman I've ever seen."

Flattered and flustered, she tugged on her hand. "You need to get out more."

His smile was slow, devastating. "Okay. Where do you want to go?"

She tugged again, torn between panic and laughter. She could hear voices and movement from the stage where the musicians were wandering back. "I really have to get back."

"At least tell me your name." He ran a thumb over her knuckles until her knees turned to water. "A man's entitled to know who broke his heart."

"I'm Emma. Emma McAvoy."

"Oh Christ." He winced as he dropped her hand. "I'm sorry, I had no idea. Jesus, I feel like a complete jerk."

"Why?"

After dragging his fingers through his hair, he let them fall. "Brian McAvoy's daughter, and here I am making a fumbling pass."

"I didn't think it was fumbling," she murmured, then cleared her throat when his eyes met hers again. "I do have to get back. It was . . . nice meeting you."

"Emma." He paused, enjoying the way she hesitated and turned back. "Maybe sometime over the next ten weeks, you can find time for that candy bar."

"All right." She let out a long breath as she walked back to the stage.

He sent her a Milky Way tied with a pink ribbon, and her first love letter. Emma stood in the doorway long after the messenger had left, staring down at the note.

> *Emma,*
>   *I'll do better when we get to Paris. But for now, this is just a reminder of our first meeting. When I play "In Your Dreams" tonight, I'll be thinking of you.*
>
> *Drew*

She looked down at the candy bar. If it had been a basket of diamonds, she would have been no more enchanted. With no one to see her, she spun a trio of pirouettes in the wide foyer, then, on impulse, grabbed her jacket and raced from the house.

Alice answered the door again, but this time she didn't cry. Her lips curved, just slightly, as she looked at Emma. "You came back."

"Yes. Hello, Alice." She could hardly keep her feet from dancing. She leaned over and surprised her old nanny by kissing her cheek. "I came back. I was hoping to see Bev. Is she home?"

"She's upstairs, in the office she keeps here. I'll tell her."

"Thank you." She not only wanted to dance, she wanted to sing. Never in her life had she felt like this. Giddy, nervous, and absolutely beautiful. If this was infatuation, she had waited much too long to experience it. There was a bouquet of daffodils and hyacinths in a vase by the door. Bending over them, she knew she'd never smelled anything sweeter.

"Emma." With a pencil tucked behind her ear and big black-framed glasses perched on her nose, Bev hurried down the stairs.

"I'm so glad to see you." She wrapped her arms around Emma and hugged. "I know you mentioned when I saw you in New York last winter that you'd be coming over, but I didn't think you'd have time to visit."

"I have all the time in the world." With a laugh, Emma hugged her again. "Oh, Mum, isn't it a beautiful day?"

"I haven't had a chance to so much as sniff the air, but I'll take your word for it." Bev held her at arm's length, her eyes narrowed behind her reading glasses. "You look as though you've lapped up the cream and the saucer as well. What is it?"

"Do I?" Emma pressed her hands to her cheeks. "Do I really?" Laughing again, she tucked an arm through Bev's. "Oh, I had to talk to someone. I couldn't stand it. Da's off somewhere meeting with Pete and the new road manager. He wouldn't have done me any good anyway."

"No?" Bev slipped her glasses off, setting them on a table as they walked toward the parlor. "What couldn't he have helped you with?"

"I met someone yesterday."

"Someone?" Bev gestured to a chair, then sat on the arm of it herself as Emma continued to move around the room. "A male someone, I take it."

"A wonderful male someone. Oh, I know I sound like an idiot—the type of idiot I've always promised myself I'd never be, but he's absolutely gorgeous, and sweet and funny."

"Does this gorgeous, sweet, and funny man have a name?"

"Drew, Drew Latimer."

"Birdcage Walk."

With a chuckle, Emma gave Bev a hug before she began her nervous pacing again. "You keep up."

"Of course." She frowned a moment, then called herself a prissy fool for worrying about Emma having a romance with a musician. Pot calling the kettle, she reminded herself and smiled. "So is he as wonderful to look at in person as he is in pictures?"

"Better." She remembered the way he had smiled at her, the way his eyes had warmed. "We just sort of ran into each other backstage. He was sitting there on the floor, playing the guitar and singing, like Da does sometimes. Then we were talking, and he was flirting with me. I suppose I babbled a bit." She shrugged. Babbling or not, she wanted to remember every word of the meeting. "The best part, the very best part is, he didn't know me." She swirled back to grab Bev's hands. "He didn't have any idea who I was."

"Does that make a difference?"

"Yes. Oh yes. He was attracted to me, you see. Me, not Brian McAvoy's daughter." She did sit then, for an instant, then was up again. "It seems everyone I've dated has wanted to know about Da, or what it's like to be Brian McAvoy's daughter. But he asked me to dinner before he knew. It didn't make a difference to him. Then when I told him, he was, well, embarrassed. There was something so charming about the way he reacted."

"Did you go out with him?"

"No. I was too flustered, and maybe a little afraid to say yes. Then today, he sent me a note. And—oh, Mum, I'm dying to see him again. I wish you'd come tonight so you could just be there."

"You know I can't, Emma."

"I know, I know." She let out a long breath. "You see, I've never felt this way before. Sort of . . ."

"Light-headed, short of breath."

"Yes." Emma laughed. "Yes, exactly."

She had felt the same way once. Only once. "You have plenty of time to get to know him. Go slow."

"I've always gone slow," she muttered. "Did you go slow with Da?"

It hurt. More than fifteen years had passed, and it still hurt. "No. I wouldn't listen to anyone."

"You listened to yourself. Mum—"

"Let's not talk about Brian."

"All right. Just one thing more. Da goes to Ireland—to Darren—twice every year. Once on Darren's birthday, and once on . . . once in December. I thought you should know."

"Thank you." She gave Emma's hand a squeeze. "You didn't come here to talk about sad things."

"No. No, I didn't." Emma knelt, rested her hands on Bev's thigh. "I came to ask you something vitally important. I need something absolutely wonderful to wear tonight. Go shopping with me and help me find it."

With a delighted laugh, Bev sprang up. "I'll get a jacket."

◆ ◆ ◆ ◆

*E*MMA HAD NEARLY convinced herself she'd been foolish to worry about her attire. She was there to photograph, not to flirt with the lead singer of the opening act. There was so much to do, equipment and lighting to check, stagehands and smoke machines to dodge, that she soon forgot it had taken her over an hour to dress.

The audience was already filing in, though there were more than thirty minutes to the opening. There were stands of merchandise to be plucked through. Sweatshirts, T-shirts, posters, key chains. In the eighties rock and roll was no longer just music for young, rebellious kids. It was big business, umbrellaed by conglomerates.

Anonymous enough in her black jumpsuit, she prowled the stands, snapping pictures of fans as they forked over pound after pound for memorabilia of the big concert. She heard her father discussed, dissected, and cooed over. It made her smile and remember the day so long ago when she had stood in line for the elevator to the top of the Empire State Building. She hadn't been quite three then, and now, nineteen years later, Brian McAvoy was still making giddy teenagers' hearts throb.

She switched cameras, wanting color now to show the screaming streaks of red, blue, green, of the shirts with their boldly emblazoned lettering.

## DEVASTATION 1986

The fans themselves were a rainbow. Spiked hair, razor cuts, flowing manes. The style now was no style at all. Dress ranged from torn jeans to three-piece suits. A good number of the people jostling for space were her father's age and older. Doctors, dentists, executives who had grown up on rock and roll and shared the legacy with their children. There were schoolchildren, toddlers carried on shoulders, women wearing pearls with their daughters clutching newly purchased screen-printed T-shirts. And, like an echo of the sixties, there was the faint but unmistakable aroma of pot to mix with the fragrance of Chanel or Brut.

She wandered away, moving slowly through the crowd. The pass clamped to the second button of her jumpsuit had security giving her the nod to go backstage.

If it was a madhouse out front, it was only madder back here. A faulty amp, another coil of cable, a frantic roadie rushing in and out, desperate to fix the last of the inevitable glitches. She took her shots, then leaving the technicians and grips to do their job, she headed toward the dressing rooms to do hers.

She wanted pictures, like the ones she remembered so well in her mind. Da and the others sprawled around a dressing room, chain-smoking, joking, popping gumdrops or sugared almonds. She was just beginning to smile at the thought when she all but ran into Drew. It was almost as if he'd been waiting for her.

"Hello again."

"Hi." She smiled, nervously adjusting the strap of her camera. "I wanted to thank you for the present."

"I thought of roses, but it was too late." He stood back. "You look incredible."

"Thanks." Struggling to steady her breath, she took her own survey. He was dressed for the stage in snug white leather studded with silver. Boots of the same style and color came halfway to his knees. With his hair tousled and the half-smile on his face, he made Emma think of a smartly dressed cowboy.

"So do you," she managed when she realized how long she'd been staring. "Look incredible."

"We want to make a splash." He rubbed his palms on the thigh of his pants. "All of us are half sick with nerves. Don—the bass player—he's all the way sick. Got his head in the john next door."

"Da always says you perform better when you're nervous."

"Then we ought to be a hell of a smash." Tentatively, he took her hand. "Listen, have you thought about maybe going out after, having a drink?"

She had thought of nothing else. "Actually, I—"

"I'm pushing." Drew let out a long breath. "I can't help it. As soon as I saw you—it was like, wow, there she is." He dragged a hand through his carefully mussed and moussed hair. "I'm not doing this very well."

"Aren't you?" She wondered that he couldn't hear her heart thudding against her ribs.

"No." He took her hand. "Let me put it this way. Emma, save my life. Spend an hour with me."

Her lip curved slowly until the dimple winked at the corner of her mouth. "I'd love to."

◆ ◆ ◆

SHE HARDLY HEARD the cheers. Her brain barely registered the music. When it was over, and her father, dripping sweat, came off the stage for the last time, she knew that if a fraction of the dozens of pictures she'd taken turned out to be worth anything, it would be a miracle.

"Christ, I'm starving." Mopping his face and hair, he headed for the dressing room, cheers and screams still ringing in his ears. "What do you say, Emma? Let's drag the rest of these rock relics out for a pizza."

"Oh, well, I'd love to but—" She hesitated, not sure why she felt uncomfortable. "I've got some things to do." Quickly, she reached up to kiss him. "You were wonderful."

"What did you expect?" Johnno asked as he elbowed his way down the crowded hall. He dropped his voice to a creaky whisper. "We're legends."

His red face streaming, P.M. stopped beside them. "That Lady Annabelle—with the hair." He held his hands out to the side of his own head to demonstrate.

"The one in the red suede and diamonds?" Emma offered.

"I suppose. She wangled a spot backstage." P.M. swiped a hand over his brow. Though his voice was aggrieved, laughter sparkled in his eyes. "When I went by, she—she—" He cleared his throat, shaking his head as if he could hardly go on. "She tried to molest me."

"Good God, call the law." Johnno swung a comforting arm around his shoulder. "Women like that should be locked up. I know you must feel used and dirty, dearie, but don't you worry. Come tell Uncle Johnno all about it." He started to lead P.M. off. "Just what did she touch, and how? Don't be afraid to be specific."

Chuckling, Brian watched them go. "P.M. always attracts the blatant sort. Hard to figure."

There was affection in his tone. Emma caught it, wondering if her father knew he'd forgiven his old friend. Then she saw the smile fade. Stevie stood a few feet away, resting a shoulder against the wall. His face was pale, both it and his hair running with sweat. Emma thought he looked ten years older than his contemporaries.

"Come on, son." In a casual move, Brian slipped an arm around his waist, steadying, taking the weight. "What we need's a shower and some red meat."

"Da, can I help?"

With a brisk shake of his head, Brian turned toward Stevie's dressing room. This wasn't something he would turn over to his daughter or anyone else. "No, I'll take care of it."

"I'll—see you at home," she murmured, but he had already closed the door. Feeling a little lost, she went to find Drew.

♦ ♦ ♦ ♦

SHE EXPECTED HIM to pick a loud, crowded club with hot rock music—Tramp or Taboo. Instead, she found herself sitting in the dim corner booth of a smoky jazz club in Soho. There was a trio spotlighted in dreamy blue on the stage, a pianist, a bass player, and a vocalist. They kept the music low and moody, like the lighting.

"I hope you don't mind coming here."

"No." Deliberately, Emma unlaced her hands and relaxed her shoulders. She was grateful for the low lighting so that Drew couldn't see her nerves—or Sweeney, smoking lazily a few tables over. "I've never been here before. I like it."

"Well, it can't be what you're used to, but most of the other places, it's hard to talk or to be alone. I wanted to do both with you."

Her fingers knotted together again. "I didn't have a chance to tell you how good you were tonight. You'll be looking for your own opening act soon."

"Thanks. That means a lot." He laid a hand on hers, gently stroking his thumb over her knuckles. "We were a little stiff on the opening set, but we'll loosen up."

"How long have you been playing?"

"Since I was ten. I guess I can thank your father."

"Oh? Why?"

"I had a cousin, he did some road work for Devastation when I was a kid and snuck me into a concert. Brian McAvoy. He just blew me away. As soon as I could save up, I bought a secondhand guitar." He grinned. Her hand was firmly lodged in his now. "The rest is history."

"I've never heard that story."

"I guess I've never told anyone else." He shrugged restlessly. "It's a little embarrassing."

"No." Enchanted, she moved closer to him. "It's touching.

That's just the kind of story that endears someone like you to
fans."

He looked at her, his eyes dark gold in the dim light. "I'm
not thinking about fans right now. Emma—"

"Would you like a drink?"

Emma tore her gaze away from Drew's to blink at the cocktail waitress. "Oh, a mineral water."

Drew's brow lifted, but he didn't comment. "Guinness." He
continued to look at Emma, continued to toy with her fingers.
"You must have heard your fill about musicians," he murmured.
"I'd rather hear about you."

"There's not that much to tell."

"I think you're wrong. I want to know everything there is to
know about Emma McAvoy." He lifted her hand to his lips.
"Everything."

She spent the evening in a haze, with the sultry music the
perfect backdrop. He seemed to hang on her every word. And
touching, always touching her—his hand on hers, or brushing
through her hair, skimming along her arm. They never moved
from their shadowy corner, never glanced at the other couples
huddled at tables.

They left the club to walk along the Thames in the breezy
moonlight. It was late, much too late, but it didn't seem to
matter what time it was. She could smell the river, and the cool
spring flowers. Emma thought of gallant knights when Drew
stripped off his jacket and spread it over her shoulders.

"Are you cold?"

"No." She drew in a deep breath and shook her head. "It
feels wonderful. I never remember, until I come back, how much
I love London."

"I've lived here all my life." Walking slowly, he watched the
starlight play on the dark surface of the river. He wanted to see
other rivers, other cities, and knew his time was coming. "Have
you ever thought of moving back here, to live?"

"No, I haven't. Not really."

"Maybe you will." He stopped her, gentle hands on her
shoulders. "I keep wondering if you're real. Every time I look at
you, it's as if you're something I dreamed up." His fingers tensed
as he pulled her closer. The quick, unexpected strength, the sudden intensity of his eyes, his voice, made her mouth go dry. "I
don't want you to vanish."

"I'm not going anywhere," she murmured.

Her heart scrambled as he lowered his head toward hers. She felt the warmth of his mouth, light, and so tender. He drew away, an inch only, then slowly, watching her eyes, pressed his mouth to hers again.

Sweet, so sweet, she thought. So kind. Accepting, she skimmed her hands up his back and let him lead her. With a master's touch he stroked his lips over her face, then brought them back to hers for one long, last caress.

"I'd better get you home." His voice was thick, unsteady. "Emma." As if he couldn't keep from touching her, he ran his hands up and down her arms. "I want to see you again, like this. Is that all right?"

She laid her head on his shoulder. "That's absolutely all right."

# Chapter Twenty-seven

♦ ♦ ♦ ♦

SHE SPENT ALL her free time with Drew over the next weeks. Midnight suppers for two, long walks in the starlight, a stolen hour in the afternoon. There was something more exciting, more intimate, more desperate about the hours they spent together, because they were so few.

In Paris she introduced him to Marianne. They met at a little café on Boulevard St.-Germain where both tourists and locals would sit over red wine or *café au lait* and watch the world strut by.

Marianne looked more like a native in her lacy white tights and slim short skirt. Gone was the spiky hairdo. The bright red hair was worn sleek and short, and very French. But her voice was pure American as she squealed Emma's name and jumped up to embrace her.

"You're here, I can't believe you're here. It seems like years. Let me look at you. Christ, you're beautiful. I hate you."

With a laugh, Emma swung her hair behind her shoulders. "You look precisely the way a French art student should look. *Très chic et sensuel.*"

"Over here that's as important as eating. You must be Drew." Marianne kept an arm around Emma's waist and extended her hand to him.

"It's nice to meet you. Emma's told me all about you."

"Uh-oh. Well, sit down anyway. You know, Picasso used to drink here. I come all the time, and try a different table. I know if I ever find his chair I'll go into a trance." She picked up her glass. "Would you like wine?" she asked Drew. At his nod she signaled the waiter. *"Un vin rouge et un café, s'il vous plaît."* She sent a wink to Emma. "Who'd have thought Sister Magdelina's boring French lessons would have come in handy?"

"Your accent's still a C minus."

"I know. I'm working on it. So how's the tour?"

"Devastation's never been better." Emma smiled at Drew. "And their opening act's creating quite a sensation."

He laid a hand over hers. "The response has been great." He shifted his gaze from Marianne to Emma. "Everything's been great."

Marianne sipped her wine, measuring him. If she had been into religious art, she would have painted him as John the Apostle. He had that dreamy, dedicated look. Or skipping a few centuries, Hamlet. The young prince shadowed by tragedy. She smiled as the waiter served the fresh drinks. Then again, she could have dipped back only a few years and used him as a model for the young Brian McAvoy. She wondered if Emma saw the resemblance.

"Where to from here?" she asked.

"Nice." Drew stretched out his legs. "But I'm not in any hurry to leave Paris." He glanced toward the street where cars and bicycles whizzed by with careless disregard for life and limb. "What's it like to live here?"

"Noisy. Exciting." She laughed. "Wonderful. I have this little apartment right over a bakery. There is nothing, believe me nothing, that smells like a French bakery first thing in the morning."

They spent an hour loitering over their drinks before Drew leaned over to kiss Emma. "Look, I've got to get to rehearsal and I know you want to talk. I'll see you tonight. You too, Marianne."

"I'm looking forward to it." She, along with half the women around the café, watched him walk away. "I believe he's the most beautiful man I've ever seen."

"He is, isn't he?" She leaned over to grip Marianne's hands. "You do like him, don't you?"

"What's not to like? He's gorgeous, talented, smart, funny." She grinned. "Maybe he'll dump you for me."

"I'd really hate to have to murder my best friend, but . . ."

"I figure I'm safe. He doesn't look at anyone but you. Why, I don't know; just because you've got those incredible cheekbones and big blue eyes, a yard of blond hair and no hips. Some guys have no taste." She leaned back. "You look ridiculously happy."

"I am." She took a deep breath, drawing in the scents of wine and flowers. Of Paris. "I think I'm in love with him."

"No kidding? I'd never have guessed." With a laugh she patted Emma's cheeks. "Pal, it's all over your face. If I were to paint you right now, I'd call it *Infatuated*. What does your dad think of him?"

Emma picked up her cold coffee and sipped. "He has a lot of respect for Drew's talent both as a musician and as a songwriter."

"I meant what does he think of Drew as the man his daughter's in love with."

"I don't know. We haven't talked about it."

Marianne's brows disappeared under her sharply cut bangs. "You mean you haven't told him that you're involved?"

"No."

"Why?"

"I don't know exactly." Emma shoved the coffee aside. "I guess I just want to keep it to myself. I want it to belong to me for a while. He still thinks of me as a child."

"All fathers think of their daughters that way. Mine calls me twice a week to make sure I haven't succumbed to some lecherous French *comte*. I only wish." When Emma didn't smile, she tilted her head. "You think he'll disapprove?"

"I don't know." Restless, she moved her shoulders.

"Emma, if it's serious between you and Drew, he's going to find out sooner or later."

"I know. I'm just hoping it'll be later."

◆ ◆ ◆ ◆

𝒥T WASN'T MUCH later.

Emma enjoyed the morning sun on the terrace of her room in Rome. Though it was late for breakfast, she was still in her robe, her coffee growing cold, as she checked over her current batch of prints. In the back of her mind she was assessing them not only for Pete but for her own idea for a book.

Smiling, she took out her favorite of Drew. She'd taken it in the leafy shade of the Bois de Boulogne. Only moments after she'd taken the picture, he'd kissed her. And told her he loved her.

He loved her. Closing her eyes, she reached her arms up to the sky. She had hoped, and she had wished, but she'd had no idea how happy she could be until he'd said the words. Now that he had, she could begin to dream what it would be like to be with him always, to make love with him, to be married to him, to make a home and raise a family.

She hadn't realized how badly she wanted that. A man who loved her, a home of her own, children. They could be happy, so happy. Who understood the life and problems of a musician more than a woman who had been raised by one? She could comfort and support him in his work. And he would do the same for her.

After the tour, she thought. After the tour they could begin to make plans.

The knock on the door broke into her thoughts. She hoped it would be Drew, come to share breakfast with her as he had once or twice. Her smile of welcome faltered only slightly when she saw her father.

"Da. I'm surprised to see you out of your room before noon."

"Maybe I'm too predictable." With a newspaper folded in his hand, he stepped into the room. He glanced first at the bed, then at his daughter. "Are you alone?"

"Yes." She studied him with a puzzled frown. "Why? Is something wrong?"

"You tell me." He slapped the paper into her hand. She had to unfold it, then turn it right side up. But the picture was clear enough. The picture of her and Drew. It wasn't necessary to read Italian to get the drift. They were locked in each other's arms, her face tilted up to his, her eyes slumberous and dreamy as a woman's became when she'd been kissed by her lover.

She couldn't tell where it had been taken. It didn't matter where. What mattered was that someone had intruded on a very private moment, then had splashed that intimacy in newsprint.

Emma tossed the paper across the room, then stalked to the balcony. She needed air. "Damn them," she muttered, knocking her fist lightly against the rail. "Why can't they leave us alone?"

"How long have you been seeing him, Emma?"

She looked over her shoulder. The wind blew strands of pale hair over her eyes. "Since the start of the tour."

Brian jammed his hands into his pockets. "For weeks, then. For weeks, and you didn't bother to tell me."

She tossed her head back as she turned. "I'm over twenty-one, Da. I don't have to ask my father's permission to go on a date."

"You were hiding it from me. Dammit—come inside." He bit the order off. "The bloody press has their telescopic lenses trained on this place."

"What difference does it make?" she demanded, holding her ground. "Everything we do ends up as public fodder eventually. That's part of the price." She gestured to the piles of prints on the table. "Hell, I do it myself."

"It's not the same, and you know it." He stopped himself, dragging a furious hand through his hair. "It hardly matters at this point. I want to know what's going on between you and Drew."

"You mean am I sleeping with him? No, not yet." She braced her hands on the rail. "But it's none of your business, Da. Just as you told me, years ago, that your sex life was none of mine."

"I'm your father, dammit." He heard himself. He was her father. Somehow he'd become the father of a grown woman. And he didn't have a clue what to do about it. He waited until he was sure his voice would be calm. "Emma, I love you, and I worry about you."

"There's no need to worry. I know what I'm doing. I'm in love with Drew, and he's in love with me."

Now he couldn't speak. In defense, he picked up her cold coffee and downed it. A dove flew by the terrace, soft gray wings flapping. "You've only known him for a few weeks, that means you don't know enough about him."

"He plays a guitar for a living," she pointed out. "You'd sound ridiculous criticizing that."

"The last thing I want for you is to see you involved with someone in the business. For Christ's sake, Emma, you know what it can do to people. The demands, the pressures, the egos. I don't know any more about this kid than that he's ambitious and talented."

"I know all I need to know."

"Listen to yourself. You sound like some bubble-brain. Like it or not, you're not in a position to trust a man just because he has a pretty face and says he loves you. You've got too much money, and too much power."

"Power?"

"There's no one who knows me who would doubt I'd do anything for you. Anything you'd ask me."

It took her a minute, but the words slowly sank in. Angry tears blurred her vision as she stepped toward him. "So that's it? You think Drew is interested in me because I have money, because he thinks I could sway you to help him in his career? It's impossible, isn't it, that he or any man might be attracted to me, might fall in love with me? Just me."

"Of course not, but—"

"No, that's just what you think. After all, how could anyone look at me and not see you?" She spun around, pressed her palms against the rail. The sun glinted off a lens in the garden below. She didn't give a damn. Let them take their pictures.

"Oh, it's happened before. Yes, it has. Emma, how about dinner Friday—and by the way, can you get my cousin tickets and a backstage pass to your father's concert in Chicago?"

"Emma, I'm sorry." He reached out, but she jerked away.

"What for? You really can't help it, can you? And I learned to live with that, even to be amused by it. But this, this time I've found someone who cares about me, who's interested in my feelings and my thoughts. Who hasn't asked me for anything but to be with him, and you want to spoil it."

"I don't want to spoil it. I don't want to see you hurt."

"You've already hurt me." Her eyes were dry when she looked at him. "Leave me alone, Da. And leave Drew alone. If you interfere with this, I'll never forgive you. I swear it."

"I'm not going to interfere. I only want to help you. I don't want to see you make a mistake."

"It'll be my mistake. You've made your own, God knows. For years I've watched you do whatever you wanted, with whomever you wanted. You ran away from your happiness, Da. I won't run away from mine."

"You know how to twist the knife," he said quietly. "I hadn't realized." He walked out of the sunlight and left her alone.

◆ ◆ ◆ ◆

DREW SLIPPED AN arm over Emma's shoulders. They were standing on another terrace, in another city. The old-world graciousness of the Ritz Madrid was lost on Emma. She could hear the tinkle of the fountains, smell the lush garden below, but she might have been anywhere. Still, she found Drew's arm comforting and rubbed her cheek against it.

"I hate to see you sad, Emma."

"I'm not. Maybe a little tired, but not sad."

"You've been upset for weeks, ever since you and Brian argued. Over me." He removed his arm and moved aside. "The last thing I wanted to do was cause you trouble."

"It has nothing to do with you." He turned, and in the moonlight his eyes gleamed dark. "It doesn't really. He would have had the same reaction no matter whom I was seeing. Da's always been overprotective. A lot of it comes . . . because of what happened to my brother."

He kissed her, gently, on the temple. "I know it must have been rough for you, and for him, but it happened a long time ago."

"Some things you don't ever forget." She shivered, suddenly cold in the warm summer night. "It's because I understand how he feels that it's so difficult for me. He's done everything for me, not just materially, but in every way."

"He adores you. You can see it every time he looks at you." Smiling again, he brushed a hand over her cheek. "I know just how he feels."

"I love him, too. Still, I know that I can't go on living my life to please him. I've known that for a long time."

"He doesn't trust me." His lighter flared, followed by the sharp sting of tobacco. "I don't blame him. From where he stands I'm on the first rung of the ladder, still fighting my way up."

"You don't need me to reach the top."

He blew out a stream of smoke. "Still, I see where he's coming from. It's easy since we're both crazy about you."

She moved to him then to press a kiss against his shoulder. "He'll come around, Drew. He's just not ready to admit that I'm grown-up. And in love."

"If anyone can soften him up, it's you." He flicked his cigarette away, then turned her into his arms. "I'm glad you didn't want to go out tonight."

"I'm not big on clubs and parties."

"Just an old-fashioned girl, aren't you?" His lips were curved as they touched hers.

"Do you mind?"

"Spending the evening alone with you?" His hands moved up and down her rib cage as he toyed with her mouth. "Do I look crazy?"

"You look wonderful." Her breath caught as he skimmed his fingers over her breasts. She was small and firm. He felt himself harden as she trembled against him.

"Sweet," he murmured. "Always so sweet." His mouth grew hungrier on hers, more demanding, less patient as he circled her off the balcony and toward the bed. "The tour's nearly over."

"Yes." She let her head fall back when his lips raced down her throat.

"Will you come back to London when it's done, Emma?"

She shuddered again. It was the first hint he'd given her that he meant what they had to last. "Yes. I'll come to London."

"We'll have nights like this." He lowered her to the bed, keeping his voice soothing, his hands easy, not wanting to break the mood. "Night after night together." Smoothly, his clever hands tugged her blouse from the waistband of her slacks. "I'll be able to show you, over and over, how I feel about you. How much I want you. Let me show you, Emma."

"Drew." She moaned his name as his mouth roamed lower, as his tongue stroked over and under the slope of her breast. The pleasure and the passion streaked into her. This time, she told herself as his long, callused fingers glided over her skin. This time.

She could feel the tension in his shoulders where her own hands gripped. He had strong shoulders, strong arms for such a slim, delicate-looking man. She loved feeling the bunch and flow of his muscles.

Then his hand roamed down to the waist of her slacks. Those clever fingers fumbled impatiently with hooks.

"No." She hated herself as the word burst out, but she couldn't stop it. When he continued to tug, his mouth coming back to close over hers, she struggled. "No, Drew, please." She was on the verge of tears when she managed to pull away. "I'm sorry," she began. "I'm so sorry. I'm just not ready."

He didn't speak. She couldn't see his face. In the dark, she huddled on the bed until her system leveled.

"I know I'm not being fair." Annoyed with herself, she dashed a tear from her cheek. "I don't know whether the nuns did a better job than they could ever imagine or if it's because of Da, but I need more time. You've every right to be angry, but I just can't do this. Not yet."

"You don't want me?" His voice was quiet and oddly flat.

"You know I do." She groped for his hand and tried to soothe his rigid fingers in hers. "I guess I'm a little frightened, and a little unsure." Ashamed, she brought his hand to her lips. "I don't want to lose you, Drew. Please, give me a little more time."

Her sigh shuddered out when she felt his hand relax in hers. "You couldn't lose me, Emma. Take all the time you need. I can wait." He brought her close, stroking with one hand. The other curled into a tight fist in the dark.

# Chapter Twenty-eight

• • • •

$\mathcal{J}$T FELT ODD spending the summer in London again. During her childhood at least a few weeks of Emma's vacation had been spent there each year. But it was different now. She was no longer a child. She was no longer staying in her father's home. And she was in love.

She knew Drew was hurt that she had refused to move in with him. It wasn't morals—or perhaps only a small part of it was morals. She wanted the romance to go on a little longer— those lush bouquets he sent to her, the funny notes that arrived in the mail or were slipped under the door. She wanted time to enjoy it—the thrill of falling in love. The terror of being in love. The glassy-eyed, light-headed exhilaration that every woman has the right to experience at least once.

And most of all, she wanted time to be sure she had at last stepped out from her father's shadow.

She didn't love Brian any less. Emma doubted she could. But she'd discovered that she wanted more than her photographs to stand on their own. Then there was Bev.

For most of her life Emma had been cheated out of a mother. In the weeks as summer drifted into fall, she made up for a longing of a lifetime by moving into one of Bev's guest rooms.

If Drew was impatient with her, she had to put him off. She needed this time with Bev, not to feel like a child again, but to reforge a bond. How could her new relationship work if she left older ones unresolved?

She had her work. The city where her father had spent his childhood caught her imagination. Emma could spend hours scouring the streets and parks, finding subjects. An old woman who came day after day to feed pigeons in Green Park. The ultratrendy set who walked Labradors or pushed prams along King's Road. The tough-faced punks who haunted the clubs.

So she stayed on, a month, then two months longer. She celebrated with Drew when Birdcage Walk's album settled into *Billboard*'s number twelve slot. She watched in amusement as Lady Annabelle ruthlessly pursued a baffled P.M. She cut asters and mums from Bev's garden. And at last, she took a step forward and submitted prints and a book proposal to a publisher.

"I'm meeting Drew at seven," Emma called out as she tugged on a short suede jacket. "We're going to dinner and a film."

"Have fun." Bev gathered up an armful of samples. "Where are you off to now?"

"Stevie's."

"I thought he was under the weather."

"Apparently he's on the mend." She took time for a quick glimpse in the hallway mirror. The deep, bold blue of the suede picked up the color of her eyes. "I have the last lot of prints from the tour. Da's meeting me there so we can all argue about which ones are best."

"I've got a meeting with Lady Annabelle." Bev rolled her eyes. Behind Emma, she glanced in the mirror, pausing to tighten her left earring. "I'm not sure if she wants me to decorate her parlor, or just pump me for information about how P.M. is in bed."

Emma tucked her portfolio under her arm. "You don't think she already knows?"

Bev considered, then grinned. "I'll certainly find out soon enough." She gave Emma a quick kiss on the cheek, then dashed.

Moments later, Emma popped into her Aston Martin. She tried to imagine sweet, self-effacing P.M. with the brash, over-dressed Lady Annabelle. She couldn't. Then again, she'd never been able to see him with Angie Parks.

She fought the traffic in grim, British style. She was glad that Drew and his band had signed with Pete Page. If anyone could help push Birdcage Walk to the top, it was Pete. Look what he'd done for Blackpool, she thought with a sneer. The man was making a bloody fortune doing commercials. She was well aware how furious Pete had been when Brian had refused to endorse products or lend his music to television ads—tossing away worldwide exposure and millions of pounds. But she was proud of him. Leave it to Blackpool, she thought nastily, then pulled into Stevie's estate.

She'd been pleased when he'd bought the old Victorian home and rolling grounds. He'd even taken up gardening and had appeared on Bev's doorstep with book after book on roses, soil, and rock gardens. It was no longer a secret that his health was poor, but Pete, being Pete, had managed to keep the cause of it out of the press.

Emma had been afraid the tour would exhaust Stevie, but he'd made it through. Now he was writing again, and gearing up to join Brian at some of the benefits her father could never say no to.

Emma thought Brian was truly in his element now. Rock had embraced causes to its gritty bosom. In Europe and America, musicians were organizing to do something new with their talents. Benefits to aid causes from drought-ridden Ethiopia to the struggling farmers in America were as much a part of the eighties scene as political rallies and love-ins had been in the sixties. The glory, and arguably self-indulgent days, of Woodstock were over. Rockers had taken up the cause of humanity and were clasping it to their sweaty bosoms. She was proud to be a part of it, to record the changes, and her view of them.

At the end of the walk a barrel of violas drooped in the full sun. With a shake of her head, Emma shifted them under the slanted shade of the eaves. Apparently, Stevie hadn't read his garden books carefully enough.

She pressed the doorbell. Since her father's car was nowhere in sight, she hoped Stevie might feel up to taking her for a tour of his gardens.

The housekeeper opened the door and eyed Emma with both impatience and distrust.

"Good morning, Mrs. Freemont."

Mrs. Freemont's dusty brown hair was secured in a no-nonsense bun. She might have been anywhere from forty to sixty and kept her sturdy, bullet-shaped body primly attired in good black wool. She had done day work for Stevie for over five years, mopped up his blood and vomit, carted out his empty bottles, and looked the other way when her housekeeping duties brought her in contact with suspicious-looking vials.

Some might have been duped into believing she was devoted to her employer. The staunch Mrs. Freemont was only devoted to the hefty salary Stevie paid her in return for minding her own business.

She sniffed as she opened the door for Emma. "He's around somewhere. Probably bed. I ain't got to the upstairs yet."

Old bat, Emma thought, but smiled politely. "That's all right. He's expecting me."

"None of my concern," Mrs. Freemont said righteously and went off to attack some defenseless table with her dustcloth.

"Don't worry about a thing," Emma said to the empty hall. "I'll just find my own way up."

She started up the old oak stairs, unbuttoning her jacket as she went. "Stevie! Make yourself decent. I haven't all day."

It was a huge barn of a house, which was one of the reasons it appealed to Emma. The paneling along the wide second-floor corridor was mahogany; the gleaming brass fixtures and glass globes bolted to it had once burned gas. It made her think of the old Ingrid Bergman movie in which Boyer, playing against type, had plotted to drive his innocent wife mad. The comparison might have been apt, but for the fact that Stevie had amused himself by hanging Warhol and Dalí lithographs between the lights.

She could hear the music, and with a sigh, Emma knocked, shook her stinging knuckles, and knocked again.

"Come on, Stevie. Rise and shine."

When he didn't answer, she sent up one quick but fervent prayer that he was alone, then pushed open the door.

"Stevie?"

The room was empty—the shades drawn and the air stale. She frowned at the rumpled bed, and at the half bottle of Jack Daniel's on the eighteenth-century table beside it. Swearing, she marched over and lifted it, but she was too late to save the glossy old cherry from the white ring. Still, she set the bottle on a crumpled copy of *Billboard* before she put her hands on her hips.

All the progress he'd made, she thought, and now he'd pumped whiskey into his belly. Why couldn't he understand that he'd already damaged himself so badly that the booze was just as much a killer to him as the drugs.

So he'd gotten drunk last night, she thought as she sent the shades flapping up and pushed windows open. Then he'd probably crawled off to be sick. Asleep on the bathroom floor, she decided. And if he'd caught his death of cold, it would be well deserved. She'd be damned if she'd feel sorry for him.

She pushed open the adjoining door.

Blood. And sickness. And urine. The stench had her stumbling back, gagging. She felt the bile rush up her throat, stared at the red and gray spots that danced in front of her eyes. She fell against the stereo, sending the needle raking across the vinyl. The sudden silence hit her like a slap. On a cry of alarm, she rushed forward to bend over the body sprawled on the floor.

He was naked, and so cold. Terrified, she heaved until she turned him onto his back. She saw the syringe, and the revolver.

"No. Oh God, no." Panicked, she searched for a wound, then for a pulse. She found the first, but it was only the tragic marks of the needle. The sob burst out of her when she found the second, faint and delicate, at his throat.

"Stevie, oh God, Stevie, what have you done?"

She raced to the doorway, to the top of the stairs. "Call an ambulance!" she screamed. "Call a bloody ambulance, and hurry!"

As she ran back, she tore the quilt from the bed to cover him. His face was the color of paste made from water and ashes. The sight of it, of his skin still smeared with blood from the needle, terrified her more than his deathlike stillness. On his forehead, just above his eyebrows, was a nasty gash. Snatching a washcloth, she pressed it against the wound.

When he was covered, she began to slap her open palm over his face.

"Wake up, goddamn you, Stevie. Wake up. I'm not going to let you die this way." She shook him, slapped him, then broke down and wept against his chest. Her stomach pitched and she bit down furiously on nausea. "Please, please, please," she repeated, like a chant. She remembered how Darren had been found, lying alone, a syringe on the turkey rug. "No. No. You're not going to die on me." She stroked his hair, then pressed her fingers against his throat again. This time there was nothing.

"Bastard!" She shouted at him, then tossed the quilt aside

and began pumping on his frail chest. "You're not going to do this to me, to Da, to all of us." She pulled his mouth open to breathe into it, then shifted back to push with the heels of her hands. "You hear me? Stevie," she panted. "You come back."

She pushed the air from her lungs to his, pumped the thin and frail area between his breasts. Threatening, pleading, cursing, she fought to pull him back. The tile bit into her knees, but she didn't notice. So intent was she on his face, on praying for one flicker of life, that she forgot where she was. Memories scrambled through her head—of Stevie in white, singing in the garden. Of him standing onstage, colored lights and smoke, dragging feverish music from a six-string guitar. Board games in front of the fire. An arm around her shoulders, and a teasing question.

*Who's the best, Emmy luv?*

Only one clear thought ran over and over in her mind. She would not lose someone else she loved this way, this useless way.

The sweat was rolling off her when she heard the footsteps running up the stairs.

"In here. Hurry. Oh God, Da!"

"Oh sweet Jesus." He was down beside her in an instant.

"I found him—he was alive. Then he stopped breathing." The muscles in her arms screamed as she continued to pump. "The ambulance. Did she call the ambulance?"

"She called Pete. Got us on his car phone."

"Goddammit. I told her to call an ambulance. He needs an ambulance." Her head flashed up, her eyes met Pete's. "Damn you, can't you see he's going to die if he doesn't get help? Call."

He nodded. He had no intention of calling an ambulance. A public ambulance. But instead, walked quickly to phone a discreet and very private clinic.

"Stop, Emma. Stop, he's breathing."

"I can't—"

Brian took her arms, felt the muscles tremble. "You've done it, baby. He's breathing."

Dazed, she stared down at the shallow but steady rise and fall of Stevie's chest.

◆ ◆ ◆ ◆

SOMETIMES HE SCREAMED. Sometimes he cried. While Stevie's body detoxed, new pains snuck in. Little imps of torment, pulsing in the abscesses along his arms, in the tender flesh he'd abused—between his toes, in his groin. They capered along his skin, first hot, then cold. He could see them, sometimes he could actually see them, with their tiny red eyes and hungry mouths, tap-dancing over his body before they plunged their teeth into him.

Hysteria would follow, with a manic strength that forced the staff to restrain him to the bed. Then he would become quiet, descend into an almost trancelike state where he would stare for hours on end at a single spot on the wall.

When he lapsed into those long silences, he would remember drifting, peacefully, painlessly. Then Emma's voice, angry, hurt, frightened, demanding that he come back. And he had. Then there had been pain again, and no peace at all.

He begged whoever was in the room with him to let him go, to score for him. He promised outrageous amounts of money then swore viciously when his demands went unanswered. He didn't want to come back to the world of the living. When he refused to eat, they fed him through a tube.

They used an antihypertensive medication to trick his brain into believing he wasn't going cold turkey. With that they mixed naltrexone, a nonaddicting opiate antagonist to make his body believe he wasn't getting high. Stevie craved the seductive hazy escape of heroin and the quick buzz of cocaine.

He was rarely alone, but detested and feared even a ten-minute span of solitude. In those moments, it would be only him and the machines that hummed and grumbled in response to his vital signs.

After two weeks he quieted. But he also became sly. He would wait them out—the tight-lipped bastards that had put him here. He would eat his fruit and vegetables, he would smile and answer all their questions. He would lie to the pretty, cool-eyed psychiatrist. Then he would get out.

He dreamed of scoring again, of filling his veins with that glorious combination of Chinese white and top-grade snow. All that beautiful white powder. He fantasized about it—huge, mountainous piles of beautiful white powder heaped on silver platters. He would scoop it up with both hands, fill himself with it.

He dreamed of killing them, the doctors, the nurses. He dreamed of killing himself. Then he would weep again.

They said he'd damaged his heart, and his liver. They said he was anemic and were ruthlessly dealing with that, and his cross-addiction to heroin and coke. No one called him a junkie. They said he had an addictive personality.

It had been hard not to laugh at that. So he had an addictive personality. No shit, Sherlock. All he wanted was for them to leave him and his personality alone. He was the best fucking guitarist in the world, and had been for twenty years. He was forty-five and twenty-year-old girls still wanted the honor of a few hours in his bed. He was rich, filthy rich. He had a Lamborghini, a Rolls. He bought motorcycles like potato chips. He had a twenty-acre estate in London, a villa in Paris, and a hilltop hideaway in San Francisco. He'd like to see any of the smart-mouthed nurses or holier-than-thou doctors top that.

Had they ever stood onstage and had ten thousand people scream for them? No. But he had. They were jealous, all of them jealous. That's why they kept him here, away from his fans, away from his music, away from his drugs.

Wallowing in self-pity, he stared at the room. The walls were papered in a soft blue and gray floral. A thick gray carpet covered the floor, and the windows faced south. The matching drapes tried to disguise the fact that the windows were barred. There was a color-coordinated sitting area across the room, two cushioned sofas, and a spoon-back chair. Festive fall flowers sat in a wicker basket on the coffee table. A tasteful reproduction of a nineteenth-century wardrobe held a television, VCR, and stereo system. An entertainment center, Stevie thought bitterly. He wasn't entertained.

Why had they left him alone so long? Why was he alone?

He felt his breath back up, then release slowly as the door opened.

Visit after visit, Brian tried not to be shocked by his friend's appearance. He didn't want to dwell on the limp, graying hair, the lines sunk deep around Stevie's eyes and mouth. He didn't want to look at the thin, brittle body—a body that had shrunken with misuse as a man's shrinks with age.

Most of all, he didn't want to look at Stevie and see his own future. A rich, pampered, and helpless old man.

"How's it going?"

Because he was grateful for the company, Stevie's smile was genuine. "Oh, it's a barrel of laughs in here. You ought to join me."

The idea sent a slice of fear up Brian's spine. "Then you'd have competition for all these long-legged nurses." He offered a five-pound box of Godiva, a fix for the junkie's notorious sweet tooth. "You're looking almost human, son."

"Yeah. I think Dr. Matthews's real name is Frankenstein. So what's going on in the real world?"

They talked uneasily, and much too politely, while Stevie worked his way steadily through the chocolate-coated creams and nuts in the box.

"Pete hasn't been by in a while," Stevie said at length.

"He's pretty tied up." There was no use mentioning that Pete had his hands full dealing with the press, and the promoters. Devastation's American leg of the tour had been canceled.

"You mean he's pissed."

"Some." Brian smiled and wished desperately for a cigarette. And a drink. "When has that ever bothered you?"

"It doesn't." But it did. Every slight hurt like a seeping wound. "I don't know what he's being so tight-assed about. He got out the press release. Viral pneumonia complicated by exhaustion, right?"

"It seemed the best way," Brian began.

"Sure, sure, no problem. No fucking problem. Wouldn't want the public to know old Stevie mixed one speedball too many and thought about blowing his brains out."

"Come on, Stevie."

"Hey, it's cool." He blinked back tears of self-pity. "Only it burns me, Bri, really burns me. He doesn't want to come see the junkie. He doled out the smack when he was afraid I couldn't perform without it, but now he doesn't want to see me."

"You never told me Pete scored drugs for you."

Stevie dropped his eyes. That had been a little secret. There was always one more little secret. "Now and then, when things got tight and my sources dried up. The show must go on, right? The fucking show always goes on. So he'd score a little H for me, all very disapproving, then when the show was over, he'd put me back in one of these places."

"None of us knew it was going to get this bad."

"No, none of us knew." He began to drum his fingers on the top of the candy box. "Remember Woodstock, Bri? Christ, what a time. You and me sitting in the woods, dropping acid, tripping out, listening to the music. Jesus, what music. How'd we get here?"

"I wish I knew." Brian dug his hands out of his pockets, then pushed them in again. "Look, Stevie, you're going to pull out of this. Hell, you're right in fashion now. Everybody's drying out, cleaning out." He worked up another smile. "It's the eighties thing to do."

"That's me, always on the cutting edge." He grabbed Brian's hand. "Listen, it's hard, you know. Man, it's really hard."

"I know."

"Man, you can't know 'cause you're not here." He swallowed the anger and resentment. He couldn't afford to show either now. "Maybe I'll do it this time, Bri, but I need help."

"That's why you're here."

"Okay, okay, so I'm here." Goddammit, he was sick of platitudes and good wishes. "But it's not enough. I need something, Bri, just a taste of something. You could slip in a couple grams of coke—just to get me through."

It wasn't the first time he'd asked. With a sinking heart, Brian knew it wouldn't be the last. "I can't do it, Stevie."

"Christ, Bri, just a couple grams. Nothing major. All they give me in here's Tinkertoy drugs. It's like going cold turkey with aspirin."

Brian pulled his hand away and turned around. He couldn't bear to look at those dark, haunted eyes. Pleading eyes. "I'm not going to score coke for you, Stevie. The doctors say it'd be like putting a gun to your head."

"I already tried that." Fighting tears, Stevie pressed both hands to his face. "All right, no coke. You could get me something else. Some Dolophine. It's a good drug, Bri. If it was good enough for the Nazis, it's good enough for me." He began to whine, staring at Brian's back. "It's just a substitute, man. You've done it for me before so what's the big fucking deal? It'll keep me straight."

Brian sighed. When he turned, opening his mouth to refuse yet again, he saw Emma in the doorway. She stood like a statue, her lush hair caught back in a braid, baggy blue pants hitched with white suspenders lying on a crimson shirt. There were big gold hoops at her ears, and she carried a game of Scrabble. Brian thought she looked sixteen, until he saw her eyes.

They were cold. A woman's cold, accusing eyes.

"Am I interrupting?"

"No." Brian stuck his hands in his pockets. "I've got to get on."

"I'd like to talk with you." She didn't look at him as she spoke, but moved to the opposite side of Stevie's bed. "Maybe you could wait outside for me. I won't be long. The doctor said Stevie needed rest."

"All right." It was ridiculous, Brian thought, but he felt like a child about to be scolded. "I'll see you in a day or two, Stevie."

"Right." He said nothing else, but his eyes begged as Brian left the room.

"I bought you this." Emma laid the board game over Stevie's bony knees. "I figured you could practice up so you could try to beat me."

"I always beat you."

"When I was a kid, and because you cheated." She lowered the bedguard to sit beside him. "I'm not a kid anymore."

He couldn't keep his hands still. His fingers played a nervous tattoo on the box. "I guess not."

"So you want some drugs." She said it so matter-of-factly, it took a moment for it to register. His fingers picked up the rhythm against the box as he looked at her.

"What was the name of it again? I'll write it down. I imagine I can get my hands on some in a few hours."

"No."

"You said you wanted it. What was the name?" She'd taken out a pad and held a pencil poised over it.

There was hope, and a desperate greed, before shame flushed his skin. For a moment, he looked almost healthy. "I don't want you involved."

She laughed at that, a low, amused sound that made the sweat break out on the back of his neck. "Don't be soft, Stevie. I've been involved since I was three. Do you really believe I had no idea what went on at the parties, on the tours? Give me some credit."

He had believed it, because he'd needed to. She was, and had always been, the quiet light of innocence in all the noise and madness. "I—I'm tired, Emma."

"Tired? Need a lift? A little buzz to take the edge off reality? Give me the name, Stevie. After all, I saved your life. It seems only just that I should help you lose it."

"I didn't ask you to save my life, goddamn you." He lifted a hand as if to push her away, then let it fall limply on the sheet. "Why didn't you leave me the hell alone, Emma? Why didn't you just leave me alone?"

"My mistake," she said briskly. "But we can do our best to fix it right up." She leaned closer, bringing him a whiff of soft scent as her voice and eyes hardened. "I'll get the fucking drug for you, Stevie. I'll get it. I'll feed it to you. I'll push the needle in whatever vein you might have left. Hell, maybe I'll even try it myself."

"No!"

"Why not?" She lifted a brow as if amused. "You said it was a good drug. Isn't that what you said to Da? It's a good drug. If it's good enough for you, it's good enough for me."

"No. Goddammit. Look what I've done to myself." He held out his scarred and scabbed arms.

"I see what you've done to yourself." She threw the pad and pencil across the room. "I see exactly what you've done to yourself. You're weak and pitiful and sad."

"Miss!" A nurse came through the door. "You'll have to—"

"Get out of here." Emma whirled on her, fists clenched, eyes blazing. "Get the hell out. I'm not finished yet."

She left. The hurried sound of her retreating feet echoed.

"Leave me alone," Stevie murmured. The tears were spilling out of his eyes, seeping through the fingers he pressed to his face.

"Oh, I'll leave you alone, all right. When I'm done. I found you lying on the floor, in your own blood and vomit, beside the gun and the needle. Couldn't you make up your mind which way you wanted to kill yourself, Stevie? It was just too damn bad, wasn't it, that I didn't want you to die. I pumped life back into you, right there on the floor. I cried because I was afraid I wouldn't be quick enough or good enough or smart enough to save you. But you were breathing when they took you away, and I thought it mattered."

"What do you want!" he shouted. "What the hell do you want?"

"I want you to think—think about someone else for a change. How do you think I would have felt if I'd found you dead? Or Da—what would it have been like for him? You have everything, but you're so hell-bent to self-destruct you could have twice as much and it wouldn't matter."

"I can't help it."

"Oh, that's a poor excuse, poor and pitiful and sad and completely suitable to what you've made yourself." She was near tears now herself, but she fought them back, letting the bubbling anger pour out instead. "I've loved you ever since I can remember. I've watched you play and year after year been astonished by what you're capable of creating. Now you're going to sit there and tell me that you just can't help killing yourself. That's fine then, but don't expect the people who love you to stand and watch."

She started out, only to be stopped in the doorway by a petite brunette. "Miss McAvoy? I'm Dr. Haynes, Mr. Nimmons's psychiatrist."

Emma's body braced, like a boxer readying for a new match. "I'm on my way out, Doctor."

"Yes, I can see that." The woman smiled and offered a hand. "Nice show, dear. I recommend a brisk walk, then a hot bath." She moved by Emma to go to Stevie's bed. "Ah, Scrabble. One of my favorites. Care for a game, Mr. Nimmons?"

Emma heard the tiles hit the wall, but kept on walking.

She found Brian outside, leaning against the hood of his newest Jaguar. When he spotted her, he took one last drag on his cigarette, then flicked the butt away.

"I thought you might stay a bit longer."

"No, I said all I had to say." As she spoke, she fastened the bottom snap on her dark blue bomber's jacket, then pulled up the zipper. "I wanted to ask you if I'd heard correctly. Did you buy drugs for Stevie?"

"Not the way you mean it. I'm not a dealer, Emma."

"Word games then," she agreed with a nod. "Did you provide him with drugs?"

"I provided him with an opiate substitute—to help get him through the tour and keep him from going out to some alley and trying to score heroin."

"To get him through the tour," she repeated. "I thought Pete was bad, lying to the press, helping Stevie lie to himself."

"Pete's not at fault here."

"Yes he is. You're all at fault here."

"Are we supposed to take out an ad in *Billboard* saying that Stevie's a junkie?"

"It would be better than this. How is Stevie ever supposed to face up to this if he can't admit what he is? And how is he supposed to stop being what he is if his friends, his very dear friends, keep handing him drugs so he can get through one more show, one more city."

"It isn't like that—"

"Isn't it? Or are you deluding yourself into thinking you're doing it out of friendship?"

Too weary for anger, he leaned against the car again. The breeze that ruffled his hair was brisk with autumn and smelled of rain. Peace, he thought as he studied his daughter's furious face. He only wanted peace.

"You don't know anything about it, Emma. And I don't appreciate being lectured by my own daughter."

"I won't lecture you." She turned and walked to her own car. With her hand on the door, she looked back at him. "You know, I never told you, but I went to see Jane a couple of years ago. She's pathetic, wrapped up in her own needs and her own ego. Until now, I hadn't realized how much you're like her."

She slammed the door, gunned the motor. If there was pain on his face, she didn't look back to see it.

# Chapter Twenty-nine

•♦♦♦

$E$MMA MARRIED DREW in a quiet civil ceremony. There were no guests, no advance press. She had told no one, not even Marianne. After all, she was over twenty-one and needed no one's permission or approval.

It wasn't the wedding she had dreamed of. No misty tulle and glowing white silk. No flowers except the single pink rose Drew had given her. No music, and no tears.

She told herself it didn't matter. She was doing exactly what she wanted. It was selfish, perhaps, but she felt justified in committing one purely selfish act. How could she have told Marianne or Bev without telling her father? She hadn't wanted him there, standing beside her, giving her away.

She would give herself away.

She'd done her best to cheer the dull, mechanical ceremony by wearing a fussy silk dress, shades deeper than the rose she carried. Lacy at the bodice and at the drifting, tea-length hem.

She thought of her father's wedding. The first wedding she had ever seen. Bev looking gloriously happy. Brian smiling. Stevie, all in white, singing like an angel. The memory brought tears to her eyes, but she held them back as Drew took her hand.

He was smiling at her. Smiling as he slipped the simple diamond band on her finger. His hand was so warm and steady. His voice was clear and lovely as he promised to love, honor, and cherish. She so desperately wanted to be cherished. When he kissed her, she believed it.

Then they were man and wife. She was no longer Emma

McAvoy, but Emma McAvoy Latimer. A new person. And, in vowing her love and her life to Drew, she was beginning a new life.

It didn't matter that he had to race off directly after the ceremony to the recording studio. She understood the demands and the need for premium session time better than anyone. It had been her idea to be married quickly, quietly, and in the middle of the making of his new album. It gave her time to prepare the hotel suite where they would spend their wedding night. She wanted it to be perfect.

There were flowers now, banks of hothouse roses, orchids, narcissus. For her own pleasure, she arranged them personally, setting tubs and vases throughout the rooms, down to a basket of flowering hibiscus she set in the bath.

A dozen candles waited to be lit, all white and scented with jasmine. Champagne chilled in a crystal bucket. The radio was on low, to enhance the mood.

She indulged in a long bath, fragrant with oils. She creamed and powdered her body, and enjoying the female ritual, dabbed more scent at every pulse point. Like the room, like the night, she wanted her body to be perfect for him. She brushed her hair until her arm went numb. Then slowly, drawing out the pleasure of it, dressed in the white silk and lace peignoir.

When she studied her reflection in the cheval mirror she knew she looked like a bride. Closing her eyes, she felt like a bride. Her wedding night. The most beautiful night of her life. Now she would know what it was like. Drew would come in. He would look at her, those tawny eyes going dark. He would be gentle, sweet, patient. She could almost feel his long, clever fingers skimming over her skin. He would tell her how much he loved her, how much he wanted her. Then he would carry her into the bedroom, and show her.

Patiently. Tenderly. Passionately.

By ten o'clock she was anxious. By eleven, uneasy. By midnight, she was frantic. Her calls to the studio only told her that he had left hours before.

She imagined a terrible accident. He would have been in a hurry to get back to her, as anxious as she to begin their life together in the big soft bed. He might have been careless, and his car . . . They wouldn't know where to reach her—the doctors, the police. Even now Drew could be lying in some hospital bed, bleeding, calling for her.

She was working her way down the lists of hospitals when she heard the key in the lock. Before he could open the door, she was there, swinging it open and falling into his arms.

"Oh, Drew, I was terrified."

"Easy, easy does it." He gave her buttocks a quick squeeze. "Anxious, are we?"

Drunk. Part of her mind tried to deny it, but it was there in the slurred words, the sway of his body, the smell. She stepped back to stare at him. "You've been drinking."

"Just a little celebration with the lads. Not every day a man gets married, is it?"

"But you . . . You said you'd be here by ten."

"Christ, Emma, you're not going to start nagging me already?"

"No, but—I was worried, Drew."

"Well, I'm here now, aren't I?" He struggled out of his jacket and let it fall to the floor. It wasn't often he got drunk, but tonight it had been so easy to let one drink follow another. Tonight, he'd climbed one more rung to the top. "And look at you. The perfect picture of the blushing bride. Beautiful, beautiful Emma, all in white."

She did blush. There was desire in his eyes now. The kind she'd seen before, the kind she'd imagined seeing in them tonight. "I wanted to look beautiful for you." She went easily into his arms, lifted her mouth to his in innocent trust.

He hurt her. His mouth was fierce and hot. He nipped hard at her bottom lip as he pushed himself against her. "Drew." She tried to struggle back, alarmed by the memory flash of Blackpool in her darkroom. "Drew, please."

"Don't play that game with me tonight." He caught her hair in his hand and dragged her head back. "You've made me wait long enough, Emma. No excuses tonight."

"I'm not. I just—Drew, can't we—"

"You're my wife now. We do it my way."

He pulled her to the floor, ignoring her pleas and struggles. His hands were rough, tearing the filmy lace as he bared her breasts to suckle and squeeze. The speed and urgency frightened her. It wasn't right, she thought frantically. It wasn't right lying on the floor, the lights glaring, her gown in tatters.

His fingers dug into her hips as his mouth clamped down on hers. Choking on the smell of whiskey, she tried to say his name. When she began to fight in earnest, he locked her hands in one of his, and took her virginity in one hard swift thrust.

She cried out both in shock and pain. Then he was plunging and pumping into her, panting, groaning. She was weeping when he collapsed, when he rolled aside and fell instantly to sleep.

◆ ◆ ◆ ◆

HE WAS FULL of contrition and shame and tenderness in the morning. With shadowed eyes and trembling voice he cursed himself and begged her forgiveness. He'd been drunk, a poor excuse, but his only reason for behaving like a monster. When he held her, gently stroking her hair and murmuring promises, she believed him. It was as though another man had come to her on her wedding night to show her how cruel and heartless sex could be. Her husband showed her only sweetness. When her first day as a new bride ended, she lay in his arms, content, dreaming only rosy dreams of the future.

◆ ◆ ◆ ◆

MICHAEL STAGGERED INTO the kitchen. He'd meant to get to the dishes. In fact, his intentions had been so firm, he was shocked to find the sink full and the counter cluttered. He gave them a bleary, accusing stare. He'd been working double shifts all week and wondered why things like dishes couldn't just take care of themselves.

In the spirit of self-sacrifice, he decided to deal with them before he settled in with breakfast and the morning paper. He began to stack plates, bowls, cups, forks. Dragging over a five-gallon Rubbermaid kitchen can, he shoved the whole business inside. They were all paper and plastic, a system that appalled his mother, but which suited Michael just fine. Although his modest kitchen boasted a Whirlpool dishwasher, he'd never owned a plate that required its services.

Satisfied, he poked through the cupboards, knocking over a bottle of El Paso salsa and a jar of Skippy peanut butter. Shoving them aside, he grabbed the box of shredded wheat. He shook some into a Chinet bowl, then lifted the coffeepot and poured the steaming brew over the cereal.

He'd discovered this delicacy purely by accident on another groggy morning. He'd nearly eaten his way through his breakfast when he'd realized the coffee was on the cereal and the milk in the Styrofoam cup. Since then, Michael had dispensed with the milk altogether. Before he could sit and enjoy, he was interrupted by a banging on the back screen door.

At first glance it appeared to be a five-foot gray mat. But mats didn't have wagging tails or lolling pink tongues. Michael pushed open the screen and was greeted exuberantly by the scruffy, oversized dog.

"Don't try to make up." Michael shoved the huge paws off his bare chest. The paws hit the floor, but most of the mud on them remained on Michael.

Conroy, pedigree unknown, sat on the linoleum and grinned. He smelled almost as bad as a dog could possibly smell, but was apparently unoffended by his own aroma. His hair was matted and full of burrs. Michael found it hard to believe that he'd picked Conroy out of a litter of cute, gamboling pups less than two years before. As an adult, Conroy had turned out ugly —not homely but down-to-the-ground ugly. This little trick of nature didn't bother the dog, either.

Conroy continued to grin as he lifted a paw in what both he and Michael knew had nothing to do with subservience.

"I'm not going to shake that paw. I don't know where it's been. You went back to that slut again, didn't you?"

Conroy slid his eyes to the left. If he could have whistled between his teeth, he would have.

"Don't try to deny it. You've spent all weekend rolling in the dirt and slobbering over that half-breed beagle tramp. Never a thought to the consequences or my feelings." Turning away, Michael rooted in the refrigerator. "If you knock her up again, you're on your own. If I've told you once, I've told you a thousand times. Safe sex. It's the eighties, bucko."

He tossed over a slice of bologna, which Conroy caught nimbly and swallowed in one gulp. Softening, Michael tossed him two more before he settled down with his coffee-soaked shredded wheat.

He liked his life. Moving to the burbs had been the right decision for him. It had exactly what he wanted: A nice patch of lawn he could grumble about mowing, a few leafy trees, and what remained of the previous owner's flower bed.

He'd given gardening a shot, but when he'd proven inept, had abandoned it. That suited Conroy as well. No one got antsy when he dug up the snapdragons.

He'd bought the small brick rancher on impulse, right after the end of his brief and ill-advised affair with Angie Parks. He'd learned something from her, other than kinky sex. And that was that Michael Kesselring was and always would be middle class.

It had been strange to watch her on the screen after he'd been replaced with a twenty-year-old hockey player. It had given him an eerie, almost creepy feeling to see her depiction of Jane Palmer, and to realize that she'd played that part with him all during the three frenzied months they'd been lovers.

He'd gone alone to the theater. A kind of test to make certain he'd gotten rid of any residual, and unhealthy, attraction for her. When she'd bared those beautiful breasts, he'd felt nothing but discomfort. Though it had been by proxy, he knew he had been to bed with Emma's mother.

And he had wondered, sitting under the dark cloak of the theater, if Emma would see the movie.

But he didn't like to think of Emma.

There had been other women. No one serious, but other women. He had his work. It no longer amazed him that he had both a talent and an affection for law enforcement. Perhaps he didn't have his father's patience and skill with paperwork, but he thought well on his feet, accepted the long, often monotonous hours of legwork and stakeouts, and had a healthy enough respect for his life not to be trigger-happy.

"I got shot at yesterday," he said conversationally to Conroy. The dog began, disinterestedly, to scratch for fleas. "If that pervert had gotten lucky, you'd be out in the cold, pal. Don't delude yourself into thinking that slut would take you in."

Conroy glanced over, burped, and went back to his fleas.

"One trip to the vet," Michael muttered as he spooned up cereal. "Just one trip and a couple of snips, and your letching days are over." Pleased that he'd had the last word, Michael opened the paper.

There was the usual business about the Middle East, the latest in terrorism. Some routine bitching about the economy. Beneath the fold in section B was an article about the capture and arrest of one Nick Axelrod, a small-time second-story man who had hopped himself up on PCP and axed his lover.

"Here's the guy," Michael said, holding out the paper for Conroy's perusal. "Found him in an apartment downtown, shooting up the walls and screaming for Jesus. See, here's my name. Detective Michael Kettlerung. Yeah, I know, I know, but it's supposed to be my name. If you're not interested in current events, why don't you do something useful, like getting my cigarettes. Go on, fetch."

Moaning, Conroy started off. He tried a limp, but Michael had gone back to the paper and wasn't paying attention. Scratching his bare chest, Michael turned to the Entertainment section.

His fingers curled in, fisted, and held against his heart as he stared at the picture.

It was Emma. She looked—God, he thought, she looked outrageous. That shy little smile, those huge, quiet eyes. She was wearing some skimpy strapless dress, and her hair was down, raining over her shoulders in thick, wild waves.

There was an arm over her shoulders as well, and the arm was attached to a man. Michael tore his eyes from Emma's face long enough to stare at the man.

Drew Latimer. His brain connected face and name. He was smiling, too. Positively fucking beaming, Michael thought. He shifted back to Emma, studying every inch, every angle of her face for a long time. Conroy came in and dumped a slobbery pack of Winstons on his lap. But he didn't move.

Very slowly, as if it were a foreign language, he read the headline.

### ROCK PRINCESS EMMA MCAVOY
### MARRIES HER PRINCE

In a secret ceremony two days ago, Emma McAvoy, daughter of Devastation's Brian McAvoy and author Jane Palmer, married Drew Latimer, twenty-six, lead singer and guitarist for the rising rock group, Birdcage Walk. The newlyweds met on Devastation's recent European tour.

Michael didn't read any more. Couldn't. "Jesus, Emma." He closed his eyes and let the paper fall back to the table. "Oh, Jesus."

◆ ◆ ◆ ◆

EMMA WAS THRILLED to be back in New York. She could hardly wait to show off the city to Drew, and to spend their first Christmas together in the loft.

It hadn't mattered to her that their plane had been late, or that a fine icy sleet had been falling. They would have four weeks for the honeymoon that had been delayed by the completion of Drew's new album. She wanted to spend that time in New York, in her home, as she made the transition from bride to wife.

She had the limo driver take them through midtown so she could show Drew the lights, the people, the majestic tree in Rockefeller Center, the carnival of Times Square.

It delighted her to arrive at the loft knowing she was alone. Finally alone, with no Sweeney in residence downstairs.

"It feels like years since I've been here." She knew Marianne's father had complained bitterly over their refusal to sublet, but she was glad, so glad to know that no one had lived there in her absence.

"Well?" She combed her fingers through her damp hair. "What do you think?"

"It's quite a space." He skimmed over the plaster walls, the bare floors, the kitschy china owl Emma had discovered in a neighborhood thrift shop. "A bit . . . spartan."

"Wait until I start decorating for Christmas. Marianne and I collected some truly awful decorations." She fumbled in her bag for a tip when the driver deposited their luggage with a discreet cough. "Thank you."

He pocketed the twenty. "Thank you, ma'am. Merry Christmas."

"Merry Christmas." She tossed off her coat and raced to the windows. "Drew, come look at the view. It's better from Marianne's studio, but I get dizzy."

"Very nice." He saw a dirty street and a maddening crush of traffic. "Emma, I wonder why you never moved into something more upscale."

"I never wanted to."

"Well, this is certainly charming, and I'm sure it was fine for two college girls. But we'll have to do some rethinking." When she turned, he reached out to brush a hand over her hair. "After all, we don't want to share our living quarters with Marianne, however delightful she is."

"I hadn't thought . . . She won't be back for a couple of months yet."

"You'd better start thinking." He took the sting out of the words by kissing her brow. Pretty face and slow wits, he thought, and patted her cheek. "From what I've heard it takes a great deal of time, money, and energy to find a place in New York. Since you want to divide our time between here and London, we'll need the right kind of accommodations. Jesus Christ, it's cold in here."

"I had the agent keep the heat back while we were gone." She hurried over to turn it up.

"Always practical, aren't you, love?" There was a sneer in his voice, but he was smiling when he turned back to her. "I'm sure we'll enjoy ourselves here for a couple of weeks. After all, a honeymoon, even a delayed one, doesn't require much more than a bed." He laughed when she blushed, then walked over to sweep her up in a long, lusty kiss. "We do have a bed, don't we, Emma?"

"Yes." She held him close. "Right through there. It needs fresh linens."

"We'll worry about the linens later." He pulled her through the doorway, tugging at her sweater.

She knew it would be quick, not fierce and painful as it had been on her wedding night, but speedy and soon over. She didn't know how to ask for more. Though she felt, somewhere in her heart, that there should be more than the rapid groping in the dark. The mattress was cold on her back. But his body, as it entered hers long before she was ready, was hot. She wrapped her arms around him, clinging to the warmth and waiting for the starburst she had only read about.

She shivered when he was done. From the cold, she told herself. Moments later, Drew echoed her thoughts.

"Christ Almighty, it's like an ice box in here."

"It won't take much longer to heat up. I've got some blankets in the chest."

She reached for her sweater, but he closed a hand over hers. "I like looking at your body, Emma. Such a sweet little body, just this side of ripe. There's no need to be shy in front of me anymore, is there?"

"No." Awkward, she rose to lift the top of the chest. He fumbled in the pocket of the jacket that was tangled on the floor and found his cigarettes.

"I don't suppose there's any food in this place, or a bottle of something to ward off pneumonia."

"There's some cognac in the kitchen." She remembered the bottle she'd opened for Luke. Luke, who was back in Miami, fighting to hang on to life. She laid the pile of sheets and blankets on the foot of the bed. Already she'd shared nearly all her secrets with Drew—except about Johnno, and Luke.

"I didn't even think about food." She saw him frown as he brought the cigarette to his lips. "Why don't I run around the corner to the market? Pick up some things. You can have some cognac and a hot bath. I'll fix us some dinner."

"Fine." It didn't occur to him to offer to go with her. "Pick me up some cigs too, will you?"

"Sure." He didn't stop her when she reached for her sweater again. "It won't take me long."

He got up when she left, tugging on his jeans more for comfort than modesty. He poured the cognac first, and though he was annoyed there wasn't a proper glass for it, he approved the brand.

It amazed him that she'd expected him to applaud the silly barn of a room. A downtown loft, he thought and drank more cognac. He had no intention of living downtown. He'd been waiting to move up all of his life. It was laughable to think that now that he was on his way he would settle for anything less than the best.

He'd grown up in worse, certainly. Sipping, he studied the mural of Emma on the plaster wall and thought of where he'd come from, and where he was going. He couldn't claim a life in the slums, digging in poverty. But he'd been only shades above it.

A rented house, a muddy yard, mended jeans. He detested coming from the working class, and the father who had kept them there because he'd never had an ounce of ambition. Stoop-shouldered old man, he thought. No spine or balls. Why else would his wife have walked out on him and her three children?

So she'd wanted something better than just eking out a living, Drew mused. How could he blame her? He detested her.

He was going his own way, and that way was straight to the

top. Lifting the glass, he toasted Emma's portrait. If his eager and naïve little wife could give him a couple of boosts, they'd all live happy.

But he would run the show.

He'd indulge her for a week or two here. And then they'd move uptown. One of those big glitzy and expensive flats off Central Park. That would do for a beginning. He didn't mind living part of the year in New York. In fact, he thought New York would suit him just fine. Especially with the contacts Emma had there.

Crossing to the stereo, he flipped through albums until he found one that suited him. *Complete Devastation*. It seemed only right, Drew mused, that he give a nod to the old man. After all, if it hadn't been for the tour, he wouldn't have been able to lure Emma backstage, pour on the charm. Imagine her being stupid enough to believe he hadn't known who she was, or what she could do for him.

With a shake of his head, he put the record on, and let the music rock the room.

No, he wouldn't find it difficult to indulge her. Even though she was lousy in bed—a severe disappointment—she was overeager to please. He'd played her as cleverly as he played his six-string, from the moment he'd set eyes on her. He intended for his ingenuity to pay off. In spades.

Before long, she would have mended fences with her father. The old man had taken their marriage well enough, and had been generous in his wedding gift of fifty thousand pounds. Made out in Emma's name, but already deposited in a joint account.

There was still restraint between father and daughter. That would ease up soon enough. Drew was sure of it. Being Brian McAvoy's favored son-in-law was bound to have its rewards. In the meantime, he had a very, very rich wife. A rich naïve wife.

With a laugh, he strolled over to the window. What better mate for an ambitious man? He only had to control his temper and impatience, keep her happy, and then everything he wanted would fall in his lap.

# Chapter Thirty

♦ ♦ ♦ ♦

THEY MOVED INTO an elegant two-story condo on the Upper West Side. Because it seemed so important to Drew, she tried to ignore the fact that they were living on the eleventh floor. She only really got dizzy when she stood at the window and looked straight down. The phobia was an annoyance to her. She had stood at the top of the Empire State Building and felt exhilarated. Yet if she stood at a fourth-floor window, her head spun and her stomach heaved.

Drew was right, she thought, when he told her she'd have to learn to live with it.

In any case, Emma liked the high, coffered ceilings in the master bedroom, the ornate Deco balustrade that ran along the curving stairs, the niches cut into the walls, and the maroon and white checkerboard tiles in the foyer.

Emma called on Bev to decorate it, hoping her touch, and a few weeks of her company, would make the move from the loft less painful. Emma had to admit the condo was lovely, with its aerielike view of Central Park and its wide, winding staircase. She satisfied her yen for antiques and oddities by furnishing it with a mix of prissy Queen Anne and funky pop art.

She liked its lofty windows, the little glassed-in balcony where she could pot herbs, and the fact that it was only a brisk walk to Johnno's.

She saw him almost every day. He went along with her on her hunts through antique stores, something that bored Drew. It was habitual for Johnno to drop by once or twice a week for dinner, or to join them on an evening out. If she couldn't have her father's approval, it soothed to have Johnno's, to hear him talking music with Drew. Emma was pleased when he and Drew began to write a song together.

She threw herself into domesticity, making a home for herself, for Drew, and for the children she couldn't seem to conceive.

It had surprised and pleased Emma that Drew wanted to start a family right away. Whatever else they disagreed on, whatever differences she had discovered in their tastes and viewpoints, in this they shared the same dream.

She imagined what it would be like to carry a child, to feel Drew's child growing inside of her. Often she daydreamed about how she and Drew would push a pram through the park. Would they wear those smug smiles she noticed on new parents?

As the months passed, she told herself to be patient, that the time would come. It was stress, it was trying too hard. Once she had learned to relax during lovemaking, it would happen.

As spring breezed in, she took dozens of pictures of pregnant women, of babies and toddlers in the park. She watched them enjoying the fine warming afternoons. And envied.

Plans to open her own studio and work on her book were postponed, but she continued to sell her pictures. She was content to pour herself into a new domestic life, to spend her free hours expanding her portfolio. She began to collect cookbooks, and to watch cooking shows on public television. It flattered her when Drew praised her attempts to re-create a meal. Since he became easily bored with her photography, she stopped showing him her prints or discussing her works in progress.

He seemed more content to see her as a housewife. In the first year of their marriage, she was more than happy to oblige him.

Deliberately, she kept busy, trying to mask her disappointment when her body informed her, with regularity, that she wasn't pregnant. Trying not to feel the guilt when Drew sulked each time she failed.

It was Runyun who shook her out of her complacent routine.

◆ ◆ ◆

WITH A BOTTLE of champagne in one hand and a clutch of tulips in the other, Emma burst into the apartment. "Drew? Drew, are you home?"

Setting the bottle down, she switched on the radio.

"Jesus, would you shut that thing off?" Drew appeared at the top of the stairs. He wore only a pair of sweats. Never at his best in the morning, his hair was tumbled, his eyes bleary, his face scruffy with a night's growth of beard. "You know I worked late last night. I don't think it's too much to ask for a little quiet in the morning."

"I'm sorry." Quickly, she pushed the off switch and lowered her voice. A few months of marriage had taught her that Drew's temper was a lit fuse before coffee. "I didn't realize you were still in bed. I thought you were out."

"Some people don't have to get up at dawn to be productive."

She gripped the flowers a little tighter. She didn't want to spoil the moment with an argument. "Shall I fix you some coffee?"

"You might as well. There'll be no getting any sleep here."

Emma took the flowers and wine into the kitchen. It was a narrow room made spacious by the glassed-in breakfast nook. She had chosen blues and white—gleaming navy countertop, white appliances, pale blue and white tiles for the floor. There was an old kitchen hutch in the corner she'd painted white herself. It displayed a collection of cobalt glass.

Emma added fresh water to the trio of cacti she'd started in blue bowls, then began fixing breakfast. They had help three days a week, but she enjoyed cooking a few meals as much as she enjoyed developing a good print. She set Drew's favorite sausage on to grill before she ground beans for coffee.

When he entered a few moments later, still bare-chested and unshaven, the scents were enough to mellow his mood. Besides, he liked seeing her at the stove, cooking for him. It reminded him that no matter who she was, no matter how fat her bank account, she belonged to him.

He strolled over to kiss the side of her throat. "Morning." Her answering smile faded as he slid his hands up to rub her breasts.

"It'll be ready in a minute."

"Good. I'm starved." He gave her nipples a quick, ungentle pinch.

She hated when he did that, but said nothing as she moved over to pour his coffee. When she'd told him she didn't care to be pinched, he'd only begun to do it more often. Just teasing her, he claimed.

*You're too sensitive, Emma. You have no sense of humor.*

"I have news." She handed him the cup. "Oh Drew, it's wonderful news."

His eyes sharpened. Was she pregnant? He badly wanted to present Brian with a grandchild. "You've been to the doctor?"

"No—oh, no, I'm not pregnant, Drew. I'm sorry." She felt the familiar sense of guilt and inadequacy. Disappointment marred his face before he went to sit at the table.

"It's just going to take a little more time," she murmured and cracked two eggs into the pan. "I'm keeping my temperature chart carefully."

"Sure." He took out a cigarette, lit it, and studied her through the smoke. "You're doing your best."

She opened her mouth. Closed it. It wasn't the time to remind him that it took two people to make a baby. The last time they had discussed it, he had smashed a lamp then had stormed out to leave her frazzled and guilty until morning.

"I went to see Runyun. You know, I told you I was going?"

"Hmmm? Oh, right. The snotty old boy of the shutterbugs."

"He's not snotty." It didn't do any good to get her back up over the term "shutterbug." "Cranky," she said with a smile. "Often obnoxious, but not snotty." She carried his plate to the table. She'd forgotten her own coffee, but sat, almost ready to burst. "He's arranging for me to have a showing. My own showing."

"Showing?" Drew said over a bite of sausage. "What the hell are you talking about?"

"For my work, Drew. I told you I thought he was going to offer me a job again, but it wasn't that at all."

"You don't need a job in any case. I told you how I feel about your working with some grabby old fart."

"No, but—well, it doesn't matter now. He thinks I'm good. It was hard for him to admit, but he really thinks I'm good. He's going to sponsor a show."

"You mean one of those precious little gatherings where people wander around staring at pictures and saying things like 'What depth, what vision'?"

She stiffened. Slowly, she rose to unwrap the tulips until her temper cooled. He didn't mean to hurt her, she assured herself. "It's an important step in my career. I've wanted this since I was a child. I'd think you'd understand."

Behind her back he rolled his eyes. He supposed he'd have to pet and soothe now. "Of course I do. Good for you, luv. When's the big day?"

"In September. He wants to give me plenty of time to get my best work together."

"I hope you're going to include a few shots of me."

She made herself smile as she set the tulips in a slant of sunlight on the table. "Of course. You're my favorite subject."

♦ ♦ ♦ ♦

SHE WAS CERTAIN he wasn't trying to make things difficult, but Drew's demands on her time made it next to impossible for Emma to get any work done. It was time they took advantage of New York, he said, and insisted on haunting the clubs. He needed a break, so they flew off for a week in the Virgin Islands. It was natural for him to make friends among the young and rich of New York. The apartment was almost never empty now. If they weren't entertaining, there was a party somewhere else. As one of the bright new couples, they were hounded by the paparazzi. The opening of a new Broadway play, an evening at a new night spot, a concert in Central Park. Everything they did was recorded. Their names and faces adorned papers at every supermarket checkout. They were on the cover of *Rolling Stone,* and *People* and *Newsweek*. Barbara Walters wanted an interview.

Each time she became frantic under the pressure, Emma reminded herself this was precisely the kind of life she'd dreamed of while trapped in Saint Catherine's. But the reality of it was much more wearing, and much more boring, than she would have believed.

Everyone said the first year of marriage was the hardest, she continually reminded herself. It took effort, it took patience. If marriage, and life in general, was more difficult and less exciting than she'd imagined, it only meant that she wasn't trying hard enough.

"Come on, luv, it's a party." Drew swung her around. Her

mineral water sloshed over her glass as he caught her close to dance. "Loosen up, Emma."

"I'm tired, Drew."

"You're always tired."

His fingers dug into her back when she tried to draw away. She'd been up three nights running working in her darkroom. Her showing was only six weeks away, and she was nervous as a cat. And angry, she admitted. Angry because her husband showed no interest in her work. Angry because he'd announced two hours before that he'd invited a few friends over.

A hundred and fifty people crowded the rooms. The music blasted. Over the past month there had been more and more of these little get-togethers. Her liquor bill had soared to five hundred dollars a week. She didn't resent the money. No, it wasn't the money. It wasn't even the time, not when it involved friends. But friends had swelled to hangers-on, groupies. Last week, the apartment had been a wreck after everyone had cleared out. The sofa had been stained with brandy. Someone had put out a cigarette on her Oriental rug. But worse than that, worse than the broken Baccarat vase or the missing Limoges candy dish, were the drugs.

She'd found a group, people she'd never met, cheerfully snorting coke in the guest room she hoped would soon be a nursery.

Drew had promised it would never happen again.

"You're just pissed because Marianne didn't come."

Hadn't been invited, Emma corrected silently. "It's not that at all."

"Since she got back in town you've been spending more time with her over at that loft than here, with me."

"Drew, I haven't even seen her for nearly two weeks. Between my work and our social life I haven't had time."

"You've always got time to bitch, though."

She jerked back. Furious, she shoved his hand aside before he could grab her again. "I'm going up to bed."

She pushed her way through the crowd, ignoring the calls and laughter. He caught her on the stairs. The bite of his fingers told her he was every bit as angry as she.

"Let go of me," she said under her breath. "I don't think you want a fight here, in front of your friends."

"Then we'll take it upstairs." He squeezed until she yelped, then dragged her the rest of the way.

She was prepared for an argument. Indeed, she relished the thought of a good screaming match. When she walked into the bedroom, she snapped.

They were using her antique mirror to cut the coke. Four of them bent over her vanity table, giggling and snorting in the white powder. The old perfume bottles she'd collected had been pushed aside. One lay shattered on the floor.

"Get out."

Four heads popped up, and she was eyed with owlish grins.

"I said out. Get the hell out of my room, get the hell out of my house."

Before Drew could stop her, she had grabbed the closest person, a man about twice her weight, and had dragged him up.

"Hey, look, we'll share."

"Get out," she repeated, shoving him toward the door.

They moved quickly enough then, filing out. One of the women stopped long enough to pat Drew's cheek. Emma slammed the door behind them and rounded on her husband.

"I've had enough. I've had all I'm going to take, Drew. I want those people out of here, and I won't have them coming back."

"Won't you?" he said quietly.

"Doesn't it matter to you? Doesn't it matter at all? This is our bedroom. Christ, Drew, look at my things. They've been in my closet." Enraged, she picked up a heap of silk and linen. "God knows what they've stolen or broken this time, but that's not the worst. I don't even know those people and they're in my bedroom doing drugs. I won't have drugs in my house."

She saw him swing back, but the movement didn't register. The back of his hand connected hard enough with her face to send her sprawling. She tasted blood. Dazed, she lifted a hand to her split lip.

"Your house?" He dragged her to her feet. Her shirt tore as he heaved her away. She landed hard against the bedside table. Her beloved Tiffany lamp crashed to the floor. "Spoiled little bitch. It's your house?"

Too stunned to fight back, she cringed when he advanced on her. The roar of the music drowned out her scream as he picked her up again and threw her on the bed.

"Our house. You bloody well remember that. It's as much mine as yours. It's *all* as much mine as yours. Don't you ever think you can tell me what to do. Do you think you can humiliate me that way and get away with it?"

"I wasn't—" She broke off, drawing her shoulders up as he lifted his hand.

"That's better. I'll let you know when I want to hear you whine. Always get your way, don't you, Emma? Well, we won't let tonight be any exception. You want to sit up here all alone. That's fine." He picked up the phone and ripped it out of the wall. "You just sit up here." He threw the phone up against the wall before he strode out, slamming and locking the door behind him.

She sat curled on the bed, breathing hard, too numb to ache from the cuts and bruises. It was a nightmare, she thought. She'd had other nightmares. Painfully, she remembered the slaps and shouts she'd lived with for the first three years of her life.

*Spoiled little bitch.*

Was that Jane's voice, or Drew's?

Shivering, she reached out. The little black dog from her childhood sat on the pillow. Curling her arm around him, she cried herself to sleep.

◆ ◆ ◆ ◆

*W*HEN HE UNLOCKED the door the next morning, she was asleep. Standing in the doorway, Drew studied her dispassionately. The side of her face was swollen. He'd have to make sure she didn't go out in public for a couple of days.

Stupid to have lost his temper, he thought, rubbing his palms on his thighs. Satisfying, but stupid. But then, she was always pushing him. He was doing his best, wasn't he? And it wasn't easy. A man might as well take a dead fish to bed as sleep with her. And she was always talking about her goddamn show, sneaking off for hours in the darkroom instead of taking care of him.

It was his work, his needs, that came first. It was time she understood that.

A wife was supposed to take care of her husband. That's why he'd married her. She was supposed to take care of him, to help him get where he wanted to go.

Maybe knocking her around had been a good thing. She'd sure as hell think twice before defying him again.

But, now that he'd shown her who was running things, he could afford to be generous. Sweet little Emma, he thought. It only took a little effort to manage her.

"Emma." Carefully, avoiding the shards of the broken lamp, Drew crossed to the bed. He watched her eyes open. Saw the fear. "Oh, baby, I'm so sorry." She winced when he stroked her hair. "I don't know what happened. I just lost it. I deserve to be locked up."

She didn't speak. Like an echo, her mother's thick apologies came back to her.

"You have to forgive me, Emma. I love you so much. It was just the way you were screaming at me, blaming me. It wasn't my fault." He took her rigid fingers and pressed them to his lips. "I know those scum had no right to be in here, in our room. But it wasn't my fault. I tossed them out myself," he improvised. "It was just a rage," he continued. "When I saw them in here, I was so furious. Then you turned on me."

She began to cry again, slow, silent tears that squeezed between her tightly shut lashes.

"I'll never hurt you again, Emma. I swear it. I'll go away if you want. You can divorce me. God knows what I'd do without you, but I won't ask you to let me stay. It's just—Christ, it's just that everything's piling up. The album isn't selling as well as we expected. The Grammy passed right over us. And . . . I think about us having a baby all the time."

He began to weep then, holding his head in his hands. Tentatively, she reached out to touch his arm. He nearly laughed, then gripped her fingers in his, falling on his knees beside the bed. "Please, Emma. I know the fact that you were hounding me, that you turned on me, is no excuse for what I did. Forgive me. Give me another chance. I'll do anything to make it up to you."

"We'll work it out," she murmured.

With his face pressed against the coverlet, he smiled.

# Chapter Thirty-one

· · · ·

$\mathcal{T}$HE PARTIES STOPPED. Oh, there were a few gatherings now and again with people Emma was comfortable with. But there were no more throngs of strangers in her home. Drew was attentive and sweet, the way she remembered him from their courtship. She convinced herself that the rage and the violence had been one isolated incident.

She had pushed him. He reminded her of that often enough to make her believe it. She had blamed him for something that wasn't his doing. She had turned on him, viciously, instead of supporting and believing in him.

And if he lost his temper occasionally, if she saw a flare of violence in his eyes, watched his fists clench or his mouth tighten, he could always give solid, even logical reasons why she had set him off.

Bruises healed. Pain faded. He made an effort to take an interest in her photography, though he pointed out in dozens of subtle ways that her hobby, as he called it, took time away from their marriage and her support of him and his career.

It was a nice print, he might say, if one cared to look at old ladies feeding pigeons. So why had it taken her so many hours away from him to come up with a few black-and-white snaps of people loitering in the park?

He supposed he could eat a cold sandwich, even though he'd been composing for six hours. Apparently it was up to him to drag the laundry to the cleaners, despite the fact that he'd been tied up in a meeting all afternoon.

She wasn't to worry a bit. If her work was so bloody important, he could entertain himself for another evening.

Whatever criticisms he handed out were tempered with compliments. She looked so inviting standing in front of the stove making a meal. It made him feel good to come home and find her waiting for him.

Perhaps he was too forceful about how she should dress, what clothes she bought, how she styled her hair. After all, her image, as his wife, was as important as his own.

He was particularly concerned about what she should wear to the showing. But as he said, he only wanted her to look her best. And, as he told her, she had a rather drab taste in clothes.

It was true that she preferred the column of black silk and hammered-gold jacket to the short, snug concoction of feathers and sequins he'd chosen. But, as he said, she was an artist now and should look the part. Because it touched her that he'd called her an artist, she wore it to please him. He gave her a pair of chunky gold earrings set with multicolored stones. If they were a bit gaudy, it hardly mattered. He had fastened them on her himself.

When they pulled up in front of the small, uptown gallery, her stomach began doing calisthenics. Drew patted her hand.

"Come on, Emma, it's not as though you're going onstage in front of ten thousand screaming fans. It's just a little picture show." With a laugh, he helped her out of the limo. "Loosen up. People are going to buy Brian McAvoy's little girl's snapshots whether they like them or not."

She stopped on the curb, incredibly hurt. "Drew, that's not what I need to hear right now. I want to do this on my own."

"Never satisfied." He snatched her arm hard enough to make her wince. "Here I am, trying to be a good sport about all this, trying to support you in what you're hell-bent on doing no matter what the inconvenience to me, and you bite my head off."

"I didn't mean to—"

"You never do. Since you want to be on your own so badly, perhaps you'd like to go on in alone."

"No, of course I don't." Nerves and frustration intensified the pounding behind her eyes. She could never seem to find the right thing to say, she thought. And tonight of all nights she didn't want to alienate him. "I'm sorry, Drew. I didn't mean to snap at you. I'm just nervous."

"All right then." Satisfied with the apology, he patted her hand and drew her inside.

They had come late—as Runyun had ordered. He'd wanted the crowd there, and already intrigued, when his star arrived. He had his eagle eye on the door, and pounced the moment Emma walked through.

He was a small, bulky man who invariably wore a black turtleneck and black jeans. Emma had once thought he was affecting an artistic image, but the simple fact was he was vain and thought black made him look slimmer. He had a big, bald head, made more prominent by the high necklines, and thick black brows flecked with gray over his surprisingly pale green eyes.

His nose was hooked, his mouth thin. He compensated by sporting a Clark Gable moustache. It did nothing to improve his looks, which had always been poor at best. Yet his three wives hadn't left him because he was ugly, but because he paid more attention to his art than his marriages.

He greeted Emma not with a smile or a kiss but with a scowl. "Good God, you look like a starlet out to lay a director. Never mind," he added before Emma could speak. "Just mingle for a bit." Emma looked at the crowd, the glitter of jewels and silk, the gleam of leather, with a kind of dull horror.

"You're not going to disgrace me by fainting," Runyun said. No one could have called it a question.

"No." She drew a deep breath. "No, I won't."

"Good." He had yet to speak to or acknowledge Drew, whom he had detested on sight. "The press is here. They've already eaten half the canapés. I believe your father's been cornered by someone."

"Da? He's here."

"Over there." Runyun gestured vaguely. "Now mingle, and look confident."

"I didn't think he'd come," Emma murmured to Drew.

"Of course he came." Drew had counted on it. He put an affectionate arm around her shoulders. "He loves you, Emma. He'd never miss an important night like this. Let's find him."

"I don't—"

The affectionate arm squeezed, startling a gasp out of her. "Emma, he's your father. Don't be snotty."

She moved through the crowd beside him, smiling automatically, stopping now and then to chat. It helped a great deal to hear Drew brag about her. His approval, which had been so long in coming, brought a glow inside her. She'd been stupid, she thought now, to think he resented her work. Accepting his kiss of congratulations, she vowed to spend more time with him, give more time to his needs.

She'd always wanted to be needed. Smiling at Drew as he enthusiastically discussed her prints with other guests, she was content that she was.

At his insistence, she accepted a glass of champagne, but barely touched it as they worked the room.

She saw Brian, surrounded by people, in front of a portrait of himself and Johnno. Her face hurt from keeping the smile in place as she crossed to him. "Da."

"Emma." He hesitated, then reached out for her hand. She looked so . . . remote, he thought.

"It was nice of you to come."

"I'm proud of you." His fingers tightened on hers as if he were searching for the connection he felt was lost. "Very, very proud."

She started to speak, then there was a volley of flashes from the surrounding cameras. Was that another flash, she wondered, a flash of annoyance on his face before the easy smile settled in?

"Brian, how does it feel to have your daughter taking the spotlight?"

He didn't glance up at the reporter, but continued to look at Emma. "I couldn't be more pleased." Making the effort, he offered his hand to Drew. "Drew."

"Brian. She's great, isn't she?" He pressed a gentle kiss to her temple. "I don't know who's been more nervous about tonight, Emma or myself. I hope you'll stick around for a few days, come by and see our place. Have dinner."

It infuriated Brian that the invitation had come from Drew and not his own daughter. "I'm afraid I leave for L.A. in the morning."

"Emma."

She turned, and her strained smile vanished in surprise. "Stevie." On a laugh, she threw her arms around him. "I'm so glad to see you." Moving back to arm's length, she studied him. "You look good." And it was true. He would never be the smoothly handsome man she had known in childhood, but he had put on weight, and the heavy shadows no longer haunted his eyes. "I didn't know you'd . . . no one told me . . ." That he was out, she thought.

Understanding, he grinned. "Time off for good behavior," he told her, then gathered her close for another hug. "I even brought my own doctor." He released Emma to put a hand on the shoulder of the woman beside him. After a moment's confusion, Emma recognized the petite brunette as Stevie's psychiatrist.

"Hello again."

"Hello." Katherine Haynes smiled. "And congratulations."

"Thank you."

"I was your first sale," Katherine went on. "The portrait of Stevie and his guitar. It looked as though he were making love to it. I couldn't resist."

"She'll analyze it for hours." He caught the scent of Scotch and had to check an old and deep craving. "P.M.'s around, you know." Stevie leaned close and lowered his voice to a wicked whisper. "He brought Lady Annabelle."

"No, really?"

"I think they're engaged. But he's being coy about it." With a wink, he took Katherine's arm and wandered off.

Emma was laughing as she slipped her arm through Drew's. "I think I'll take a look for P.M." She cast a questioning glance at her father.

What could he say? She'd greeted Stevie with more affection and comfort than she had greeted him. He wanted to have it out with her, but now was hardly the time or place. "Go ahead. I'll see you before I go."

"Yes, go ahead, Emma." Drew kissed her cheek. "I'll just hang around with your da. That way we can both brag about you. Incredible, isn't she?" Drew began as Emma turned away.

She very nearly felt incredible. She'd never expected so many people, or much interest in her work. There was a little voice that asked her if she really thought they'd come to see her work, or her father and his mates. She did her best to ignore it.

She did see P.M. It was obvious he was no longer running away from Lady Annabelle. In fact, he seemed to be having the time of his life. She was dressed in emerald-green leather and snakeskin boots dyed canary-yellow. Her frizzy red hair shot out like shock waves. And after a ten-minute conversation, Emma realized the woman was completely and totally in love.

It was nice, Emma decided. P.M. deserved that kind of devotion. That kind of, well, fun.

People came and went, but more came to linger. Runyun was very cleverly playing a Devastation retrospective through the speakers. She saw, with some astonishment, the discreet blue sticker beneath more than a dozen of her prints. Sold, she thought.

Trapped in a corner by a pretentious little man who wanted to discuss form and texture, she spotted Marianne. "Excuse me," she began. But before she could make her escape, her old roommate was bearing down on her.

"Here's the star of the evening." She gave Emma a big, whopping kiss. "You," she said and pulled Emma toward her and into a cloud of Chanel, "have done it. A long way from Saint Catherine's, pal."

"Yeah." Emma squeezed her eyes tight. It had taken only that to make it all seem real at last.

"Look who I found."

"Bev!" Emma moved out of Marianne's arms, and into Bev's. "I didn't think you'd be able to make it."

"I wouldn't have missed it for anything."

"We walked in together and I recognized her," Marianne explained. "We've been having a marvelous time complimenting you while we shoved through the crowd. This is wild." She snatched one of the few remaining canapés from the table. "You know that shot of me in the loft, wearing a paint smock and rugby socks? Some gorgeous man just bought it. I'm going to go see if he'd like a chance at the real thing."

"It's no trouble seeing why you love her," Bev commented as Marianne maneuvered through the groups of people. "So, how does it feel?"

"Incredible. Terrifying." She pressed a hand to her jumpy stomach, but it wasn't nerves as much as excitement now. "I've been trying to get back to the ladies' room for an hour to have a good cry. I'm so glad you're here." Then she saw Brian, standing a few feet away. "Da's here. Will you speak to him?"

Bev had to turn her head only inches to see him. She twisted her evening bag over and over in her hand. After all these years, she thought, it was still there. Everything she'd felt was still there.

"Of course." She said it lightly. It was safe here, in a crowd. On Emma's night. At least they could share their pleasure for Emma.

He walked toward them. Could it be as difficult for him, Bev wondered, as it was for her? Would his palms be wet with nerves? Would his heart be trembling?

He didn't touch her. Didn't dare. But he struggled to find a voice as casual as his smile. "It's good to see you."

"And you." She fought to relax her death grip on her bag.

"You look . . ." Beautiful, wonderful. "Well."

"Thank you. I am. This is all marvelous for Emma, isn't it?" She glanced over, but Emma had slipped away. Walls of people had closed in around them. "You must be very proud of her."

"Yes." He took a long swallow of the whiskey he held. "Can I get you a drink?"

So polite, Bev thought. So bloody civil. "No, thanks. I'm going to wander around a bit and look. I may just buy something myself." But first she was going to find that ladies' room and have a cry of her own. "It was nice seeing you again, Bri."

"Bev—" It was foolish to think that she could still care for him. "Goodbye."

Emma watched them from across the room and wanted to scream at both of them. Couldn't they see? It wasn't just her imagination, or wishful thinking. She was much too good at studying people, and seeing what they felt. In the eyes, in a gesture, in the set of the body. They were still in love. And still afraid. She drew a deep breath and started toward her father. Perhaps if she talked to him . . .

"Emmy luv." Johnno caught her around the waist. "I'm about to make my escape."

"You can't go yet." She straightened his lapels. He was into retro clothing these days, and they were almost as wide as the palm of her hand. "Bev's here."

"Is she? Well, I'll have to go see if she's ready to run away with me yet. But in the meantime, I've run into someone from your past."

"My past." She laughed. "I don't have a past."

"Ah, but you do. A sultry summer day on the beach. A hunk

in blue trunks." Like a magician pulling a rabbit out of a hat, he swept his arm aside.

"Michael?"

How odd to see him there, she thought, looking handsome and uncomfortable in a suit and tie. His dark hair was thick, and still unstyled. His face had fined down, was lean and bony with the slightly crooked nose an appealing flaw. He had his hands in his pockets, and looked as though he'd rather be anywhere else on earth.

"I—ah—was in town, so—"

She was laughing when she threw her arms around him. He thought his heart stopped. He knew his brain did. Slowly, carefully, he pulled his hands free and pressed them lightly to her back. She felt as he'd remembered, as he'd always imagined she would feel. Slender and firm and fragile.

"This is wonderful. I can't believe you're really here." Everything rushed through her so quickly. An afternoon on the beach. Two afternoons. What she'd felt as a child, then as a woman, slammed into her so fast, so unexpectedly, that she held him close, and held him too long. Her eyes were damp when she drew back. "It's been a long time."

"Yeah. About four years, give or take." He could have given her years, months, and days. "You look great."

"So do you. I've never seen you dressed up before."

"Well—"

"Are you in New York on business?"

"Yeah." It was a bald lie, but he was less concerned with veracity than with looking like a fool. "I read about your show." That was the truth. Only he'd read about it at his breakfast table in California. Then he'd taken three days' personal leave.

"So what do you think?"

"About what?"

"The show." She took his hand and began to walk.

"It's great. Really. I don't know anything about photography, but I like your stuff. In fact—"

"In fact?" she prompted.

"I didn't know you could do something like this. Like this one." He stopped in front of a print. It was of two men, woolen caps over their ears, ragged coats pulled tight. One of them was lying on a sheet of cardboard, apparently asleep. The other looked directly into the camera, his eyes surly and tired. "It's very powerful and very disturbing."

"Not all of New York is Madison Avenue."

"It takes a lot of talent, and sensitivity, to be able to show all the sides equally."

She looked at him with some surprise. That was exactly what she had tried to do, with her studies of the city, of Devastation, of people. "You certainly say the right things for someone who doesn't know much about photography. When are you going back?"

"In the morning, first thing."

"Oh." She walked with him again, surprised at the depth of her disappointment. "I was hoping you'd be able to stay for a few days."

"I wasn't even sure you'd talk to me."

"That was a long time ago, Michael. And I wasn't reacting so much to what was going on with you as to something that had just happened to me. It's not important now." She smiled and kissed his cheek. "Forgive me?"

"That was my question."

Still smiling, she touched a hand to his face.

"Emma."

She jolted when Drew spoke from behind her. Guilt. It spread through her sharply, as if he had found her and Michael in bed rather than in a room crowded with people. "Oh, Drew, you gave me a start. This is Michael Kesselring, an old friend of mine. Michael, Drew, my husband."

Drew hooked one arm firmly around Emma's waist. He didn't offer Michael a hand, but a brisk nod. "There are people who want to meet you, Emma. You've been ignoring your duties."

"My fault," Michael said quickly, concerned with how quickly the glow fled from Emma's eyes. "We haven't seen each other in a while. Congratulations, Emma."

"Thank you. Give my best to your parents."

"I will." It was jealousy, he told himself, plain and simple jealousy that made him want to grab her away from her husband.

"Michael," she said as Drew began to pull her aside. "Keep in touch."

"Sure." He grabbed a glass off a passing tray as he watched

them move away. If it was only jealousy, he wondered why every instinct had him itching to bash Drew Latimer's pretty face in.

Because he's got her, Michael told himself ruthlessly. And you don't.

◆ ◆ ◆ ◆

$\mathcal{D}$REW WASN'T DRUNK. He'd nursed two glasses of champagne during the long, and excruciatingly boring evening. He wanted to be clearheaded and in control. He prided himself that kissing up to Brian McAvoy would reap rewards. Any fool could have seen that Drew Latimer was devoted to and besotted with his wife. He should have won a fucking Oscar for the performance.

And all the while he'd been playing the doting husband, she'd been flaunting her success, her snotty boarding-school education, and her society friends.

He'd wanted to slap her around right there in front of all the cameras. Then the world would have seen who was really on top.

But her daddy wouldn't have liked it. Not him, or any of the producers, promoters, and buttoned-down executives who fawned over the great Brian McAvoy. They'd be fawning over Drew Latimer before long, he promised himself. Then she'd pay.

He'd almost decided to let her have her glory. Then she'd had the nerve to hang all over that "friend." She needed to be taught a lesson for that. And he was just the man to do it.

He was silent on the ride home. It didn't seem to bother Emma. She was half asleep beside him. Pretending to be asleep, Drew decided. She'd probably already made plans to meet that creep Kesselring.

He imagined them together—in some fancy hotel suite, groping around in bed. It almost made him laugh. Kesselring would be in for a disappointment when he discovered pretty little Emma was a dud between the sheets. But Kesselring wasn't going to have the chance to find out. No one cheated on Drew Latimer. He was going to drive that point home very shortly.

She was half dreaming when the limo stopped. With a sigh, she settled her head on Drew's shoulder as he led her into the lobby.

"I feel as though I've been up all night." On a sleepy laugh, she snuggled against him. "And the whole night seems like a dream. I don't think I can manage to wait up for the reviews."

It was as though she were floating, Emma thought. And it felt wonderful. She slipped out of her wrap the moment they were in the door. "I think I'll—"

He hit her. A resounding blow that sent her tumbling down the two tiled stairs into the living room. Moaning, she touched a hand to the side of her face. "Drew?"

"Bitch. You sneaky, conniving bitch."

Dazed, she watched him advance on her. Instinct had her trying to slide away. "Drew, don't. Please. What did I do?"

He yanked her up by the hair, slapping her again before she could scream. "You know what you did. You whore." When he punched a fist into her breast, she sank bonelessly to the floor. "All night, all fucking night I had to stand around, smiling, pretending to care about your stupid pictures. Do you think anybody came to see them?" He hauled her up by the shoulders, leaving reddening trails where his fingers bit in. "Do you think anybody cares about you? They came to see Brian McAvoy's little girl. They came to see Drew Latimer's wife. You're nothing." He tossed her down.

"Oh God, please, don't hit me again. Please."

"Don't tell me what to do." To emphasize his point, he kicked her, missing her ribs but connecting hard against her hip. "You think you're so smart, so special. I'm the one they want to see. And I'm the one who runs things around here. You remember that."

"Yes." She tried to curl up, praying he would leave her there until the pain went away. "Yes, I remember."

"Did Michael come to see you?" He grabbed her hair again, dragging her over onto her back.

"Michael?" Dazed, she shook her head. The pain rolled inside it. "No. No."

"Don't lie to me." He struck her over and over, open-palmed, the back of the hand, until she didn't feel anything. "You had it all planned, didn't you? 'Oh, I'm so tired, Drew. I'm going right to sleep.' Then you were going to sneak out and sleep with him. Weren't you?"

She shook her head, but he hit her again.

"Admit it, you wanted to fuck him. Admit it."

"Yes."

"That's why you wore this dress, you wanted to show off your legs and those useless little tits of yours."

Dimly, she remembered that Drew had chosen the dress. Hadn't he chosen it? She couldn't be sure.

"And you had your hands all over him. Letting him paw you right there in front of everybody. You wanted him, didn't you?"

She nodded. She had hugged Michael. And for a moment, when he'd been warm and solid against her, she had felt something. She couldn't remember what. She couldn't remember anything.

"You're not going to see him again, are you?"

"No."

"Not ever."

"No, I won't see him."

"And you won't wear this whore's dress again." He hooked a hand in the bodice and ripped it down the center. "You deserve to be punished, Emma, don't you?"

"Yes." Her mind was floating in and out. She'd spilled her mam's perfume. She wasn't supposed to touch Mam's things. She was a bad, nasty girl and needed to be punished.

"It's for your own good."

She didn't scream again until he pushed her onto her stomach and began to beat her with his belt. She had stopped screaming long before he finished.

# Chapter Thirty-two

♦ ♦ ♦ ♦

HE DIDN'T APOLOGIZE this time. There was no need to. It took her ten days in bed to recover, and all the while he told her she had brought it on herself. There was a part of her mind that knew he was wrong, knew he was crazy. But he was persistent, and in an odd way loving, as he explained, over and over, that he was only acting in her best interest.

She'd only been thinking of herself, hadn't she, when she'd spent all those weeks preparing for her show? She'd sent her husband to bed alone, night after night, then had flouted her marriage in public by flirting with another man.

She'd pushed him to it. She'd deserved it. She'd brought it on herself.

Though the phone rang constantly for several days following the showing, she didn't answer any of her calls. At first her mouth was too swollen and sore to allow her to speak. Drew brought her ice packs and fed her soup. He gave her pills that took the edge off the worst of the pain and helped her sleep through it.

Then he told her that people were only calling her to get to him. They needed to be alone, to work out their marriage, to make a baby.

She wanted a family, didn't she? She wanted to be happy and be taken care of? If she hadn't put so much time and effort into her work, she would be pregnant by now. Isn't that what she wanted?

And when he asked her, drilling her with the questions one

after another as she lay recovering, she agreed. But agreement was never enough.

She awoke alone to dark and music. A dream, she told herself, gripping the sheets, fighting to wake. But even when her eyes were open, she could hear it, those odd words sung by a man who was dead. Her fingers shook as she groped for the switch on the lamp at the bedside. She turned and turned and turned it, but the light didn't shine, didn't fill the room and chase the shadows.

As the music grew louder, she put her hands over her ears. But she could still hear it, throbbing, pulsing until her screams drowned it out.

"There, Emma. There now." Drew was beside her, stroking her hair. "Another nightmare? You should have outgrown them by now, shouldn't you?"

"The music." She could only gasp and cling. He was her lifeline, the only solid line that could pull her out of the sea of fear and madness. "It wasn't a dream, I heard it. The song—I told you—the song that was playing when Darren was killed."

"There isn't any music." Quietly, he set the remote for the stereo aside. It was a good lesson, he thought, as she trembled against him. A good way to keep her dependent and manageable.

"I heard it." She was sobbing now between chattering teeth. "And the light, the lights won't go on."

"You're too old to be afraid of the dark," he said gently. Reaching down, he plugged in the lamp and turned the switch. "Better?"

She nodded, her face buried against his shoulder. "Thank you." Gratitude rushed through and overwhelmed her. With the light she went limp in his arms. "Don't leave me alone, Drew. Please, don't leave me alone."

"I told you I'd take care of you." He smiled and continued to stroke her hair. "I won't leave you alone, Emma. You don't have to worry about that."

By Christmas, she thought she was happy again. Drew took all the details of day-to-day living out of her hands. He chose her clothes, monitored her calls, took away all the business of handling her money.

All she had to do was tend the house, and him. Decisions were no longer there to trouble her, to make her anxious. Her darkroom equipment and camera were shut away. They no longer held any interest for her. When she thought of her work, it brought on depression.

He bought her a diamond pendant in the shape of a huge teardrop for Christmas. She didn't know why it made her want to cry.

She had a battery of fertility tests. When her most intimate troubles were leaked to the press, she suffered her humiliations in silence, then stopped reading the papers altogether. It hardly mattered to Emma what went on in the outside world. Her world consisted of the seven rooms overlooking Central Park.

When the doctors confirmed that there was no physical reason for her not to conceive, she hesitantly suggested that Drew have some tests of his own.

He knocked her unconscious and locked her in the bedroom for two days.

The nightmares continued, once, sometimes twice a week. Sometimes he would be there to soothe and stroke until she calmed again. Other times he would call her a fool, complain that she was disturbing his sleep, and leave her to tremble in the dark.

When he was careless enough to leave the remote by the bedside and the *Abbey Road* album on the stereo, she was too tired to care.

Dimly, almost dispassionately, she began to realize what he was doing to her. What he was making of her. The whirlwind ten weeks of the tour, and the man she had fallen in love with, were like a fantasy she'd created. There was no portion of him left in the man who kept her a virtual prisoner in the apartment.

She thought of running away. He rarely left her alone for more than a few hours, and was always with her when she went out. But sometimes, when she lay in bed in the middle of the night, she thought of escape. She would call Marianne, or Bev, or her father. They would help her.

Then the shame would take over, blistered by the doubts he'd so deeply embedded in her mind.

He didn't use the belt on her again until the night of the American Music Awards when he and his group were passed over for record of the year.

She didn't resist. She didn't object. As he pounded her with his fists, she crawled inside herself, as she had once crawled under the kitchen sink. And disappeared.

In his rage, he made a drastic error in judgment. He told her why he had married her.

"What the hell good are you?" As she lay on the floor, fighting to hide from the pain, he rushed around the room, smashing whatever came to hand. "Do you think I wanted to get stuck with a spoiled, stupid, sexless bitch?"

He vented his frustration at having to sit, smiling, while someone else mounted the stage and accepted the award, his award, by hurling a Waterford cracker barrel. The exquisite glass shattered, raining down like ice.

"Have you done one thing, one bloody thing to help me? Everything I've done for you, making you feel important, making you believe that I wanted you. Putting romance into your dull, prim little life."

Tired of breaking glass, he swooped down to pull her up by what was left of her dress. "Did you really believe that I didn't know who you were that first day?" He shook her, but she remained limp, hardly focusing on his face. She was beyond fear now. Beyond hope. She watched his eyes, tawny and dark, narrow into slits. And there was hate in them.

"You were such a fool, Emma, stuttering and blushing. I nearly laughed out loud. Then I married you, for Christ's sake. And all I expected was that you'd help me move up. But have you once asked your father to push a few buttons for me? No."

She didn't answer. Silence was the only weapon she had left.

Disgusted, he dropped her to the floor again. Though her vision was blurred, she watched him pace through the chaos of the room she'd tried to make a home.

"You'd better start thinking. You'd better start to figure out a way to make all this time I've spent on you pay off."

Emma let her eyes close again. She didn't weep. It was too late for weeping. But she did begin to plan.

Her first real hope of escape came when she heard that Luke had died.

"He was my friend, Drew."

"He was a fucking queer." He was trying out chords on the grand piano he had bought with his wife's money.

"He was a friend," she repeated, struggling to keep her voice from trembling. "I have to go to the funeral."

"You don't have to go anywhere." He glanced up, smiled at

her. "You belong right here with me, not at some fag's death march."

She hated him then. It amazed her that she could feel it. It had been so long since she'd felt anything. Strange, that a tragedy would make her finally accept what a waste her marriage was. She would divorce him. She opened her mouth, then saw his long, slim fingers run over the keys. Slim they were, but strong as steel. She'd begged for a divorce once before, and he'd nearly choked her.

It would do no good to make him angry. But she did have a weapon.

"Drew, it's public knowledge that he was my friend. He was a friend of Johnno's and Da's and everyone. If I don't go, the press is going to start by saying that I ignored him because he died of AIDS. It won't look good for you, especially now that you're doing that benefit with Da."

He pounded on the chords. If the bitch didn't stop nagging, he was going to have to shut her up. "I don't give a flying fuck what the press says. I'm not going to a funeral for a freak."

She held on to her temper. It was vital. She kept her voice soft and soothing. "I understand how you feel, Drew. A man like you, so virile." She almost choked on the word. "But the benefit is going to be televised here, and in Europe. It's the biggest thing since Live Aid. The money's going to research a cure for exactly what Luke died of." She paused, letting it sink in. "I can go with Johnno. Representing you," she said quickly.

He looked up from the keys again, his eyes flat. Her heart began to pound. It was a look she knew, and feared. "Anxious to get away, are you, dear?"

"No." She forced herself to move to him, to touch a hand to his hair. "I'd much rather you go with me." She gritted her teeth. "We could go on down to the Keys afterward."

"Dammit, Emma, you know I'm working. Typical of you to think only of yourself."

"Of course. I'm sorry." She backed off in a submission that was only partly an act. "It's just that I'd love it if we could get away for a few days. Just the two of us. I'll call Johnno and tell him I can't make it."

Drew considered a moment. The benefit was the break he needed. He intended to dump Birdcage Walk and strike out solo.

He was the star, after all, and the rest of the group was holding him back.

He needed big exposure, and lots of interested press. If a funeral could help him along, that was fine. In any case, he wanted nothing more than to get rid of Emma for a day or two.

"I think you should go."

Her heart nearly stopped. Be careful, she warned herself. Don't make a mistake. "Then you'll come?"

"No. But I think you can manage one day on your own. Especially if Johnno takes care of you. Make sure to weep copiously and say all the right things about the tragedy of AIDS."

◆ ◆ ◆ ◆

SHE WORE A simple black suit. Since Drew watched her every move, she couldn't take anything else. She'd hardly need fancy duds for a spot of mourning, would she? he asked. She was allowed a pair of black pumps and an oversized purse that would double as a carry-on. He even checked through her cosmetics bag while she sat on the bed.

Since he'd locked her passport up, and taken her credit cards away—you really are careless about such matters, Emma—she was totally dependent upon him. He made her flight arrangements. A round-trip. He'd given her fourteen hours of freedom. Her flight left LaGuardia at nine-fifteen, and she was due back at ten twenty-five the same evening. He'd generously allotted her forty dollars in cash. She'd stolen fifteen more, feeling like a thief, from the housekeeping money. She'd tucked it in her shoe. Now and again she wiggled her toes, felt it, and was struck with excitement and shame.

She was lying to him.

*Don't ever lie to me, Emma. I'll always find out the truth and punish you.*

She was never coming back.

*Don't ever try to leave me, Emma. I'll find you. I'll always find you and you'll be sorry.*

She was running away.

*You'll never run fast enough to get away from me, Emma. You belong to me. You need me to take care of you because you make so many stupid mistakes.*

"Emma. Dammit, Emma, pay attention."

She jerked when he tugged hard on her hair. "I'm sorry." Her fingers gripped together, twisting, wringing.

"You're such a damn fool. God knows where you'd be without me."

"I was . . . thinking about Luke."

"Well, save the long face until you're gone. It makes me sick. Johnno's going to be here any minute to get you." He leaned close so that his face was all she could see. "What are you going to tell him if he asks how things are?"

"That they're fine. They're wonderful. You're sorry you can't come, but you felt since you didn't know Luke, you'd be intruding." She recited the instructions he gave her like a parrot. "I've got to come back straight from the service because you've got a touch of the flu and I want to take care of you."

"Just like a devoted wife."

"Yes. A devoted wife."

"Good." It was disgusting really, how cowed she was. She hadn't even uttered a peep when he'd knocked her around the night before. He'd wanted her to leave with his dominance fresh in her mind. Of course, he'd been careful not to hit her in the face, or anywhere it might show. He intended to give her a proper beating when she got back. Just to remind her that a woman's place was in the home.

His mother's place had been in the home, Drew thought viciously. But she'd left soon enough, like the whore she was, leaving him with his wreck of a father. If the stupid old man had given her a few licks now and again, she wouldn't have taken off.

He smiled at Emma. No, like Emma his mother would have sat with her hands folded in her lap and done just what she was told. All a woman needed was a man to set the rules, and enforce them.

"Maybe it's not such a good idea for you to go."

He enjoyed seeing her eyes widen. It was a great game to dangle the funeral in front of her nose like a carrot on a stick.

Her hands sprang wet with sweat, but she fought to keep them steady in her lap. "I won't go if you don't want me to, Drew."

He stroked her face then, gently, so that she could almost remember what it had been like in the beginning. It made it worse somehow, to remember. "No, you go ahead, Emma. You look so good in black. You're sure that bitch Marianne isn't going?"

"No. Johnno said she couldn't make it."

Another lie, and one she prayed Johnno wouldn't reveal. Drew had done all he could to separate her from Marianne. And done it well enough, Emma thought wearily, that her old friend no longer called or bothered to drop by.

"That's fine, then. If I found out she was going, you'd have to skip this little jaunt. She's a bad influence on you, Emma. She's a slut. Only pretended to be your friend so that she could get closer to your father. And then to me. I told you that she came on to me. Remember?"

"Yes."

"Ah, that's Johnno. Come on now, put on that sad sweet smile we all know and love." Her lips curved automatically. "That's a good girl. Now don't forget to mention the benefit to any reporters," he instructed as they walked downstairs. "Make sure you tell them how committed I am to raising money to research a cure for this horrible disease."

"I will, Drew. I won't forget." She was terrified her knees would buckle. Maybe it was best if she didn't go. Drew had told her again and again how helpless she was without him. "Drew, I—" But he was opening the door, and Johnno was standing there.

"Hello, baby." He put his arms around her, as much to comfort as for comfort. "I'm so glad you're going."

"Yes." She looked dully over his shoulder at Drew's face. "I want to go."

She fought demons during the flight. He was going to come after her. He had found out she'd taken the fifteen dollars and would come to punish her. He'd read her mind. He knew she wasn't going back.

So great was her fear that she clung to Johnno's arm as they deplaned and searched the crowd at the gate for Drew. She was sweating by the time they reached the limo, and shaking, and struggling just to breathe.

"Emma, are you sick?"

"No." She moistened her dry lips. There was a man by the curb, lean, blond. What was left of her color drained. But he turned and it wasn't Drew. "I'm just upset. Can I—can I have a cigarette?"

Drew wouldn't let her smoke. He'd dislocated her finger the last time he'd caught her. But he wasn't here now, she reminded herself as she pulled on the cigarette. She was alone in the limo with Johnno.

"Maybe you shouldn't have come. I had no idea it would upset you this badly." He was dealing with his own grief, great, stunning waves of it, and could only wrap an arm around her shoulders.

"I'll be all right," she told him. Then repeated the words over and over in her head like a prayer.

She hardly noticed the service—what words were said, what tears were shed in the warm, moist heat of noontime. In her heart she hoped Luke would forgive her for caring so little that he was being mourned. She felt dead herself, emotionally dead.

As people walked away from the quiet gravesite, away from the white and pink marble stones and lush flowers, she wondered if she would have the strength to follow through.

"Johnno." Marianne stopped him, a gentle hand on his arm. Then instead of condolences, she kissed him. "I wish he could have taught me to cook," she said, and made Johnno smile.

"You were his only complete failure." He turned to Emma. "The driver will take you back to the airport. I need to go over to Luke's apartment. Take care of a few things." He ran a finger down her cheek. "You'll be all right?"

"Yes."

"I didn't expect to see you here." Though she hated herself, Marianne couldn't make her tone friendly.

"I . . . wanted to come."

"Really?" Marianne opened her purse and tossed a balled-up tissue inside. Her anger with Emma was like that, she thought. Balled up and frayed. "I didn't think you had time for old friends anymore."

"Marianne—" She couldn't break down right here. There were still reporters close enough, watching her, snapping pictures. Drew was going to see the pictures, of her and Marianne together. Then he would know she lied. She cast desperate looks over her shoulder. "Can I . . . I need . . ."

"Are you all right?" Marianne tipped down her sunglasses and studied Emma's face. "Christ, you look terrible."

"I'd like to talk with you, if you have a few minutes."

"I've always had a few minutes," Marianne retorted. She dug

in her purse for a cigarette. "I thought you were going straight back."

"No." She took a deep breath, and stepped over the line. "I'm not going back at all."

Through the haze of smoke, Marianne's eyes narrowed. "What?"

"I'm not going back," Emma repeated, and was terrified when her voice began to hitch. "Can we go somewhere. Please. I have to go somewhere."

"Sure." Marianne stuck a hand under Emma's elbow. "We'll take your limo. We'll go anywhere you like."

It took only a short time to reach Marianne's hotel, which, when Emma began to shake, was the best place Marianne could think of to take her. They went straight up to the suite, a beautiful pastel set of rooms overlooking the crowded white sand and blue water. Marianne had already made the space hers by tossing articles of clothing over every available chair. She scooped up the sweatshirt and slacks she had traveled in, gestured for Emma to sit, then went to the phone.

"I want a bottle of Grand Marnier, two cheeseburgers, medium, a basket of fries, and a liter of Pepsi in a bucket of ice. I got twenty bucks for the guy who gets up here in fifteen minutes." Satisfied, she swept her running shoes off another chair and sat. "Okay, Emma, what the hell's going on?"

"I've left Drew."

Not quite ready to forgive, she stretched out her legs. "Yes, I think I picked up on that, but why? I thought you were deliriously happy."

"Yes, I'm very happy. He's wonderful. He takes such good care . . ." She heard her own voice and trailed off with a kind of panicked disgust. "Oh God, sometimes I actually believe it."

"Believe what?"

"What he's trained me to say. Marianne, I don't know who else I can talk to. And I think if I don't say it right here and right now I never will. I wanted to tell Johnno. I started to, but I just couldn't."

"All right." Because Emma looked much too pale, Marianne rose and opened the balcony doors. Sea air fluttered in. "Take your time. Is it another woman?" Marianne said nothing, just watched as Emma began to rock back and forth and laugh.

"Oh Christ, sweet Christ." Before she could stop, the laughter had turned to sobs, great wrenching sobs. Moving quickly, Marianne knelt beside her to take her hands.

"Easy, Emma. You're going to make yourself sick. Hey, hey. We all know most men are bastards. If Drew's been unfaithful, you just kick him out."

"It's not another woman," Emma managed.

"Another man?"

She struggled, sucking in the tears. Afraid if she let them fall too freely she'd never be able to stop. "No. I have no idea if Drew's been unfaithful, and I don't care."

"If it's not another woman, what did you fight about?"

"We didn't fight," Emma said wearily. "I didn't fight." She hadn't known it would be so hard to say, so hard to admit. The words were like a fist lodged in her throat, heated with shame. Taking deep breaths, she wiped her eyes with the back of her hands. "Sitting here, I can almost believe I imagined it all, that it wasn't as bad as I thought while it all happened. He could be so sweet, Marianne, so considerate. I remember how he'd bring me a rose in the morning sometimes. How he'd sing—when it was just the two of us—how he'd sing as though I were the only woman in the world. He said he loved me, that all he wanted was to make me happy, to take care of me. And then I would do something—I hardly know what—but something, and then he would . . . He beats me."

"What?" If Emma had said that Drew sprouted wings and flew off the terrace every afternoon, it would have been easier to believe. "He hits you?"

The disbelief didn't register; she was too deep inside herself. "Sometimes I can't even walk for days after. It's been worse lately." She stared at a pretty pastel print on the wall. "I think he might want to kill me."

"Back up, Emma. Emma, look at me." When she caught her friend's face in her hands, Marianne spoke slowly. "Are you telling me that Drew physically abuses you?"

"Yes."

Slowly, carefully, Marianne let out a breath. Watching Emma's face, trying to make sense of it all, she sat back on her heels. "Does he get drunk, do drugs?"

"No. I've only seen him drunk once—on our wedding night. He doesn't do drugs at all. He likes to be in control. Drew has to be in control. I always seem to do something, something stupid to set him off."

"Stop it." Enraged, Marianne sprang up. Her eyes were flooded as she paced the room. "You've never done a stupid thing in your life. How long has this been going on, Emma?"

"The first time was a couple of months after we moved uptown. It wasn't so bad, he only hit me once that time. And he was so sorry after. He cried."

"My heart breaks for him," Marianne muttered. She stalked to the door to admit room service. "Here, don't worry about setting it up." She signed the check, handed over the twenty, and got rid of him. First things first, she decided, and ignoring the food, poured the Grand Marnier.

"Drink," Marianne ordered. "I know you hate the stuff, but we both need it."

Emma took two small sips and let the warmth course through her. "I don't know what to do. I don't seem to be able to think for myself anymore."

"I'll think for you for a couple of minutes. I vote we castrate the sonofabitch."

"I can't go back. Marianne, I think I'd do something, something really horrible if I went back."

"You seem to be thinking just fine. Can you eat?"

"No, not yet." She had to sit, just sit for a moment and take in the enormity of what she'd done. She'd left Drew. She'd gotten away, and now she had her friend, her oldest and closest friend with her. Closing her eyes, she felt a fresh wave of shame.

"Marianne, I'm sorry, so sorry. I know I haven't returned your calls, I haven't been a friend to you these past months. He wouldn't let me."

Marianne lighted two cigarettes, and passed one to Emma. "Don't worry about that now."

"He even told me that you had—that you had tried to take him away from me."

"In his dreams." She nearly laughed at that, but Emma's face stopped her. "You didn't believe it."

"No, not really. But . . . There were times I believed anything he'd tell me. It was easier." She shut her eyes again. "The worst is, it wouldn't have mattered to me."

"If you'd just called me."

"I couldn't talk to you about it, and I couldn't bear to be around you because I was afraid you'd find out."

"I'd have helped you."

Emma could only shake her head as her hands clasped and unclasped in her lap. "I'm so ashamed."

"What the hell for?"

"I let him do it to me, didn't I? He didn't hold a gun to my head. That's the one thing he never did to me. He didn't have to."

"I don't have the answers, Emma. Or I do have one. You should call the police."

"No. Good God, no. I couldn't bear to . . . to see it spread all over the papers. And they wouldn't believe me. He'd just deny it." Fear came sprinting back, on her face, in her voice. "I can tell you, Marianne, he could make you believe anything."

"All right, we'll hold on the cops and get you a lawyer."

"I—need a few days. I just can't talk to anyone else about this. All I really want is to get as far away from him as I can."

"Okay. We'll plot. Now we're going to eat. I think better on a full stomach."

She bullied Emma into taking a few bites, then pushed the Pepsi on her, hoping the sugar and caffeine would put color back in her friend's cheeks.

"We'll hang around Miami for a few days."

"No." Emma was thinking clearer now, though the nerves were still jangling inside her head. Of all the wild plots and plans that had rushed into her mind over the last two days, only one seemed right. "I can't even stay tonight. It's the first place he'd come looking for me."

"London then, to Bev. She'd want to help you."

"No passport. Drew locked it in a safe-deposit box. I don't even have a driver's license. He tore it up." She sat back because even the few bites of food had made her queasy. "Marianne, I have fifty-five dollars in my purse—I stole fifteen of that from the housekeeping money. I don't have any credit cards. He took them months ago. I have the clothes on my back and that's it."

Because she wanted to break something, Marianne rose and poured another Grand Marnier. All this time, she thought. All this time she'd been sulking in the loft, nursing hurt feelings while Emma had been going through hell.

"You don't have to worry about money. Your credit's good

with me. I'll get a cash advance on my credit card, then call and authorize them to accept your signature. You can have your pick. Visa, MasterCard, or American Express."

"You must think I'm pathetic."

"No, I think you're the best friend I've ever had." Tears burned the back of her eyes. Marianne let them fall. "If I could, I'd kill him for you."

"You won't say anything, to anyone. Not yet."

"Not if that's what you want. But I think your father should know."

"No. Things are bad enough between me and Da without adding this. I think what I need most of all now is a little time. I thought about going into the mountains somewhere, a cabin in the woods, but I don't think I could stand the quiet. I want to lose myself in a big, noisy city. I keep thinking of L.A. Every time I thought about running, I imagined running there. And I've been dreaming about it again, a lot."

"About Darren?"

"Yes. The nightmares started a few months ago, and they won't let up. I feel like I need to be there, and I hope it's the last place Drew would expect me to go."

"I'll go with you."

Emma reached over to take her hand. "I was hoping you would. For a little while."

# Chapter Thirty-three

· · · ·

$\mathcal{J}$T WAS DARK in the bedroom. And filthy. Jane's last day
maid had quit the week before, nipping a couple of silver candle-
sticks on her way out the door. Jane wasn't aware of the theft.
She rarely left the bedroom these days. She made occasional runs
to the kitchen for food, wheezing and panting on the stairs. Like
a hermit, she horded the drugs and bottles and food in her room.

It had once been ornately decorated. She'd had a fancy for
red velvet. It still hung at the windows, heavy creases caked with
dust. But in a rage she'd torn down the curtains that had draped
the plump, round bed. Now, because she was so often cold, she
huddled under them.

The red and silver flocked wallpaper was stained. Jane had a
habit of throwing things at her lovers—lamps, bric-a-brac, and
bottles. Which was why she had such a difficult time keeping
anyone in her bed for more than two nights running.

The last one, a tall, muscular dealer named Hitch, had tolerated her temper fits longer than most, then, philosophically, had
knocked her unconscious, stolen the diamond off her finger, and
had gone off to look for sunnier climes and more sympathetic
company.

But he'd left her the drugs. Hitch, in his way, was a humani-
tarian.

Jane hadn't had sex in over two months. It didn't particularly
bother her. If she wanted an orgasm, she only had to pop the
needle under her skin and cruise. She didn't care that no one
came to see her, no one called. Except during that brief time

after the drug started to wear off and before she craved another fix. Then she would become weepy and full of self-pity. And anger. Most of what she felt was anger.

The movie hadn't done nearly as well as predicted. It had jumped, with almost rude haste, from theater to video. She had been in such a hurry to see the movie made, she had all but signed over the video rights. Her agent had been unhappy with the deal, but Jane had fired him and gone her own way.

The movie hadn't made her rich. A lousy hundred thousand pounds didn't last long with someone of her taste—and appetites. Her new book was being rewritten, again. She wouldn't see the bulk of her advance until the stupid ghost writer had completed the job.

Her oldest source had dried up. There were no more checks from Brian. She'd depended on them. Not only for the money, Jane thought, but because she'd known that as long as he'd been paying, he'd been thinking of her.

She was glad he'd never found real happiness. She was proud that she'd had some part in seeing him denied. If she couldn't have him, she at least had the pleasure of knowing no other woman had held him for very long.

There were still times when she fantasized about him coming to his senses, coming back to her and begging her forgiveness. In those fantasies she saw them making love in the red velvet bed, the hot, frantic sex they had shared so many years before. Her body was curvy and smooth, a young girl's. Jane always imagined herself that way.

She'd grown grotesquely fat. Her breasts, like soggy balloons, hung down to what had been her waist. Fish-white, her belly drooped low and was ringed with row after row of loose flesh. Her arms and thighs were massive and shook like jelly with flab whenever she stirred herself to move them. It had become so difficult to find a vein through the layers of fat that she had taken up freebasing. She could still skin pop, slide the needle under the skin, but mainlining was rare.

She missed it, mourned it like a mother mourns a lost child.

Rising, she turned on the bedside lamp. She didn't like the light, but she needed it to get to her pipe. Her hair hung limply and was blond only on the last few inches. She had wanted to bleach it with Clairol's Bombshell Beige, but had lost the box somewhere in her cluttered bedroom. She wore a black lace nightie the size of a two-man pup tent. When she lit the torch, she looked like some mad, pornographic welder.

The smoke calmed her. She'd been lying in bed planning. She was shrewd enough to know she needed money, a great deal of money if she wanted to pay her supplier. And she wanted pretty clothes again, pretty clothes and pretty boys to come and sink into her. She wanted to go to parties. To have people pay attention.

She smoked, and smiled.

She knew how to get the money, but she'd have to be clever, very clever. The drug made her feel smart. It was time to pull out her ace in the hole.

Scrounging through her dresser, she found a box of stationery. It was pretty, rainbow-colored paper with her name across the top. She admired it for a time, then took another hit from the pipe before searching for a pen, muttering to herself. A little insurance, she thought as she began to write. Of course, she'd have to tear her name off the top. She wasn't a fool.

She wrote like a child, slowly, her tongue caught between her teeth as she formed the letters. When she'd finished she was so pleased with her neatness, she forgot about the letterhead. There were stamps inside the box. She hummed as she attached three of them. They looked so pretty, she added another, then studied her craftsmanship. For a time she puzzled over the address, then began to write again.

> Kesselring, Police Detective
> Los Angeles, California
> U.S.A.

After some thought, she added "Urgent!" in the corner and underlined it.

She took it downstairs with her, thinking she would find some clever hiding place. On a detour into the kitchen, she ate an entire carton of ice cream, shoveling it into her mouth with a serving spoon. Spotting the envelope, she began to mutter.

"Stupid girl," she mumbled, thinking of her last maid. "Can't even post a damn letter. Going to sack her." Indignant, she waddled out, and with considerable effort, bent to push the envelope under the front door. She went back upstairs and smoked herself into oblivion.

It was a week before she remembered her plan. In her mind she remembered writing the letter. The insurance. She'd hidden it. Though she couldn't quite remember where, that didn't worry her. What worried her was that she was nearly out of food, and drugs. Her last bottle of gin had been drained. Jane picked up the phone. After a few hours, she thought, she'd never have to worry about money again.

It was answered on the third ring. "Hello, dear. It's Jane."

"What do you want?"

"Ooh, that's a nice way to speak to an old friend."

There was a sigh, bitten off. "I said, what do you want?"

"Just a chat, luv, just a chat." She giggled. Blackmail was so much fun. "I'm running a bit low on funds."

"That's not my problem."

"Oh, I think it is. You see, when I run low on funds, my conscience starts acting up. Just lately, I've been feeling bad about what happened to Brian's poor little boy. I've been feeling real bad about it."

"You never gave a damn about that boy."

"That's a hard thing to say, dear. After all, I'm a mother. Thinking of my own sweet Emma, a grown-up married lady now, makes me think about that boy. Why, he'd be grown-up himself, if he'd lived."

"I don't have time for this."

"Better make time." Her voice changed, roughened. "I've been thinking that I should drop that detective in the U.S. a note. You remember him, don't you, dearie? Kesselring was his name. Imagine me remembering his name all these years." She smiled to herself. Everyone thought she was stupid. They wouldn't think it for long.

He hesitated too long, and cursed himself. "There's nothing you can tell him."

"No? Well, we'll have to see, won't we? I thought I might write him a letter. They might reopen the case if they had a couple of names to go by. Your name, for instance, and—"

"You stir this up, it's going to come back on you." His voice was still calm, but he was sweating. "You were every bit as involved as I."

"Oh no. I wasn't there, was I? I never laid a finger on that boy." What the hell had the boy been named? Donald or Dennis, she thought. It hardly mattered. "No, I didn't lay a hand on him. But you did. It's murder. Even after all these years, it's murder."

"They've never proven anything. They never will."

"With a little help they might. Want to chance it, dear?"

No, he didn't. She would know that he couldn't chance it. He was exactly where he wanted to be, and intended to stay there. Whatever it took. "How much?"

She smiled. "I think a million pounds would do it."

"You're out of your mind."

"It was my plan," she screeched into the phone. "It was my idea and I never got a frigging penny. It's time to settle accounts, dearie. You're a rich man. You can spare it."

"There was never any ransom to collect," he reminded her.

"Because you screwed up. I haven't got a penny out of Brian in two years. Now that Emma's grown up, he's cut me out cold. We can just think of your payment to me as a retirement account. That much money will keep me for a long time, and I won't have to bother you again. You bring it here tomorrow night, and I won't have to mail my little note."

Hours later she couldn't remember if she made the call or dreamed it. And the letter. Where had she hidden the letter? She went back to the pipe, hoping it would help her think. It seemed the best thing to do was write the letter again. And if he didn't come soon, if he didn't come very soon, she would make another call.

Jane sat down to write, and soon fell asleep.

It was the doorbell that woke her. Ringing and ringing and ringing. She wondered why that damn, stupid girl didn't answer it. It seemed to Jane that nothing got done if she didn't do it herself. Huffing and puffing, she groped her way down the stairs.

She remembered when she saw him. He was standing at the door, his eyes grim, a briefcase in his hand. And she remembered. Yes indeed, you had to do things yourself. "Come on in, ducks. It's been a while." .

"I didn't come to visit." He could only think she looked like a pig, fat, dirty, all of her chins quivering as she laughed.

"Come on, old friends like us. We'll have a drink. The liquor's up in my room. I conduct all my business in my boudoir."

In a coy invitation, she put a hand on his lapel. He tolerated it, knowing he would burn the suit. "We'll conduct business anywhere you like. But let's get it done."

"You always were in a hurry." She started up, mammoth hips swaying. He watched her, seeing the way her hand gripped tight to the banister, hearing her breath puffing. One push, he considered, and she'd go tumbling down. No one would question it as anything but an accident. He nearly reached out, nearly touched her. Then he steadied himself. He had a better way. A surer way.

"Here we are, dear." Red-faced and wheezing, she dropped on the bed. "Name your poison."

The stench almost gagged him. The room was lit by a single lamp, and in the shadows he could see tangles of dirty clothes and dishes, empty cartons and cans and bottles. A fetid odor hung in the room, like the cobwebs in the corners. He could almost see it as he breathed slowly, between his teeth.

"I'll pass on the drink." He was careful not to touch anything. Not just because of fingerprints now, but from fear of soiling himself.

"Suit yourself. What have you brought me?"

He set the briefcase beside her. He would burn that as well. He spun the combination, then flipped the lid. "It's part of the money."

"I told you—"

"It's impossible to raise a million in cash overnight. You'll have to be patient." He turned the case toward her. "But I brought you something else, to tide you over. A sign of good faith."

She saw the bag, plump with white powder on the neat stack of bills. Her heart began to race unsteadily, her mouth filled with saliva. "That's a pretty sight."

Before she could snatch it up, he moved the case out of reach. "Now who's in a hurry?" He enjoyed taunting her. He could see the fine sweat popping out on her face, dribbling down her jowls. He'd dealt with junkies before, and knew just how to handle them. "It's top-grade heroin, the best money can buy. One shot of this and you'll go straight to heaven." Or hell, he thought, if one believed in such things. "You can have it, Jane. All of it. But you've got to give me something back."

Her heart was a trip-hammer in her breast, making her short of breath and giddy. "What do you want?"

"The letter. You give me the letter, and another few days to raise the rest of the money, and the smack is all yours."

"The letter?" She had forgotten about it. All she could do was stare at the bag of white powder and imagine what it would be like to have it swimming in her veins. "There isn't any letter. I didn't write a letter." Insurance, she remembered, and sent him a sly glance. "Yet. I didn't write it yet. But I will. Let me have a hit, then we'll talk."

"Talk first." Oh, it would be a pleasure to kill her, he thought as he studied the flecks of spittle on her mouth. The boy had been an accident, a tragic one, and one he sincerely regretted. He wasn't a violent man, never had been. But it would have given him enormous satisfaction to have choked the life from Jane Palmer with his own hands.

"I started to write it." Confused and anxious, Jane glanced toward the desk. "I started to, but I was waiting for you. I won't finish it, if we have a deal."

She wouldn't lie, he thought as he studied her face. She wasn't clever enough. "We have a deal." He turned the case around again. "Go ahead. Take it."

She grabbed the bag in both hands. For a moment he thought she might tear it apart with her teeth and gobble it like candy. Instead, she moved as fast as her bulk would carry her and began to search through drawers for her works.

He waited, both appalled and fascinated by the procedure she went through. She paid no attention to him now, but mumbled to herself. Her hands shook, so that she spilled a little. Her breath came loud and harsh as she cooked the first spoon. She didn't want to skin-pop it; she didn't want to smoke it. This she would mainline.

Squat on the floor, licking her lips as though she were about to dine, she filled the syringe. There were tears in her eyes as she searched for a vein. Then she closed them, leaning back against the dresser as she waited for the kick.

It did, swelling, speeding, bursting through her. Her eyes popped wide, her body convulsed. She screamed once, riding the enormous crest.

He watched her die, but found he didn't enjoy it after all. It was an ugly process. Jane Palmer had no more dignity in death than she had in life. Turning his back on her, he took the surgical gloves out of his pocket and snapped them on. He picked up the half-written letter first and placed it in the briefcase. Fighting revulsion, he began to search, picking over her things to make certain she'd left nothing else in the house that might incriminate him.

◆ ◆ ◆ ◆

*B*RIAN GROANED WHEN the phone woke him. He tried to sit up, but the hangover screamed through his head like a chain saw. Shielding his eyes with one hand, he groped for the phone.

"What?"

"Bri. I'm P.M."

"Call me back when I'm not dying."

"Bri—I guess you haven't read the morning paper."

"Right the first time. I'll read tomorrow morning's paper. That's when I plan to wake up."

"Jane's dead, Brian."

"Jane?" His mind stayed blank for ten full seconds. "Dead? She's dead? How?"

"OD'd. Somebody found her last night, an ex-lover or a dealer or something. She'd been dead a couple of days."

With the heels of his hands he tried to rid his eyes of grit. "Jesus."

"I thought you should pull it together before the press starts on you. And I figured you'd want to be the one to tell Emma."

"Emma." Brian pushed himself up against the headboard. "Yeah, yeah. I'll call her. Thanks for letting me know."

"Sure. Bri . . ." He trailed off. He'd started to tell Brian he was sorry, but he doubted anyone really was. "See you around."

"Right."

Brian lay in bed a moment trying to imagine it. He had known Jane longer than anyone but Johnno. He had loved her once, and he had hated her. But he couldn't imagine her dead.

Rising, he walked to the window. The sunlight hurt his eyes and churned the hangover up to blinding. Without thought, he poured out two fingers of whiskey and downed it. He was almost sorry that he couldn't feel anything but the pain in his head, dulling now under the coat of whiskey.

She'd been the first woman he'd lain with.

Turning his head, he looked at the brunette sleeping under the rumpled satin sheets of his bed. He didn't have any feelings for her, either. He was always careful to choose women who wouldn't want an attachment, who would be as satisfied as he by a few nights of sex. The dark, dangerous, careless sex that had nothing to do with affection.

He'd made the mistake of choosing a woman who wanted more once. Jane had never let him get on with his life, let him fully enjoy what he had.

Then he'd found Bev. She'd wanted more too, but with her, so had he. My God, so had he. She had never let him get on with his life, either. Not once in seventeen years had a day gone by when he hadn't thought of her. And wanted her.

Jane had shadowed his life by refusing to get out of it. Bev had ruined it by refusing to share it.

So he had his music, and more money than he had ever dreamed of. And he had a succession of women who meant absolutely nothing to him.

Now Jane was dead.

He wished that he could stir his heart, feel some regret for the girl he had known once. The desperate, eager girl who had claimed to love him above all else. But there was nothing to feel. The girl, and the boy he had been, had been dead a long time.

So he would call Emma. It was best that she hear it from him, though he doubted she would feel any true grief. When he had called her, and made certain she didn't need him, he would go to Ireland. To Darren. And spend some quiet days sitting in the tall green grass.

# Chapter Thirty-four

• • • •

"Aʀᴇ ʏᴏᴜ sᴜʀᴇ you're going to be all right?"

"Yes." Emma gave Marianne's hand a squeeze as they walked toward the gate at LAX. "I'm going to be fine. I'm just going to take a few more days to, well, let myself settle."

"You know I'd stay."

"I know." This time the squeeze of a hand wasn't enough. Emma turned and hugged her. "I wouldn't have been able to go through with this on my own."

"Yes, you would have. You're stronger than you think. Didn't you cancel the credit cards, close the bank accounts, and have the accountant play hide the money?"

"Your ideas."

"That's only because you weren't thinking of practical matters. I wasn't going to see that bastard get a penny. I still think you should talk to the police."

Emma only shook her head. She was just beginning to believe she might get her pride back. Involving the police, the press, the public, would only heap humiliation on top of humiliation.

"All right, not yet," Marianne said, though she had no intention of seeing Drew waltz away unscathed. "You're sure the accountant will keep his mouth shut, about where you are?"

"Yes. He's my accountant after all. When I told him I was getting divorced, he went into action." It was almost funny, if such things could be funny. "I suppose after dealing with boring trusts and such all these years, he was excited by a fat, complicated divorce."

Divorce, she thought. It was such a huge word. Such a final one.

Marianne kept silent a moment while they walked. "He's going to find out where you are sooner or later."

"I know." Instantly nerves replaced regret. "I just want it to be later, when I'm sure nothing he can say or do will make me go back with him."

"See the lawyer," Marianne urged. "Get it started."

"As soon as your plane takes off."

Marianne shuffled restlessly, then popped a Lifesaver in her mouth. It was getting so there was no place you could smoke in an airport. "Listen, Emma, it's only been a couple weeks since— since we came out here. Are you sure you don't want me to stay a few more days?"

"I want you to get back to your painting. I mean it," she added before her friend could object. "When a Kennedy commissions your work, your reputation's made. Go finish the painting before Caroline changes her mind."

"You'll call me." Marianne heard the announcement for her flight. "Every day."

"I will." She clung for one last minute. "When this is behind me, I'm going to want my half of the loft back."

"It's yours. Unless I decide to marry that dentist and move to Long Island."

"What dentist?"

"The one who wants me to have my roots planed."

Her lips curved. It was becoming almost easy to smile. "That's certainly a novel, and disgusting, approach."

It was good, Marianne thought, to see Emma really smile again. "Yeah, maybe, but he's got these big brown eyes. Hairy knuckles, though. I don't know if I could fall in love with hairy knuckles."

"Especially since he'd always be sticking them in your mouth. That's your last boarding call."

"You call me."

"Absolutely." She wasn't going to cry. Emma promised herself she wasn't going to. But they both were. With one final hug, Marianne raced off.

Emma waited by the gate, watching through the windows as

the plane taxied back. She was alone now. On her own. Decisions, mistakes, opinions, were hers to make again. And it terrified her. It wasn't so long ago, she thought, she had been on her own in London. That had been such an exciting, such a freeing, feeling. And she'd been in love.

She wasn't in love now. That was one small blessing.

As she started back toward the terminal, she scanned the crowd, watchful, jittery. Moments before, she felt anonymous in the noise and hurry of the airport. Now, now that she was alone, she only felt vulnerable.

She couldn't shake the feeling that Drew might be hidden somewhere in the crowd—there behind the family on their way to Phoenix, or there, among the businessmen waiting to board for Chicago. She kept her head lowered, nerves jumping as she passed a gift shop. He could be in there, idling by the magazine rack, biding his time. He would step out, smiling, saying her name, just before he put a hand on her shoulder in that way he had, fingers digging in, grinding against the bone. She had to force herself to keep moving forward, not to run back to the gate and beg them to stop the plane so Marianne could get off again.

"Emma."

Her breath pushed out of her lungs, her knees buckled as a hand dropped to her shoulder.

"Emma? It is you."

Dead white and dizzy with panic, she stared up at Michael. He was saying something, she could see his lips move, but couldn't hear over the roaring in her head.

The pleasure died out of his face. Eyes narrowed, he pulled her to a chair. It seemed he could almost pour her into it, so boneless were her limbs. He waited until her rapid breathing slowed.

"Better?"

"Yes. Yes, I'm fine."

"Do you always faint when you run into friends at airports?"

She managed what passed for a smile. "Bad habit of mine. You did startle me."

"I could see that." "Startled" wasn't the word, he thought. The word was "terrified." She'd looked the same way when he'd dragged her to the surface of a wave over ten years before. "Will you wait here a minute? I'd better go let my parents know why I ran off on them." When she only nodded, he repeated, "Wait."

"Yes, I'll wait." It was an easy enough promise since she was sure her legs wouldn't support her yet. Alone, she took long and careful breaths. She was already embarrassed enough and didn't want to be a gibbering idiot when he returned. He was gone only moments, but she was confident she was in control again.

"So, where are you going?" she asked.

"Me? Nowhere. My mother's got some kind of convention and Dad's tagging along. I dropped them off because he doesn't like to leave his car at the airport. Did you just get into town?"

"No, I've been here about two weeks. I was just seeing off a friend."

"Here on business?"

"No. Well, yes and no."

A flight had just deplaned. Streams of people marched by. She had to fight down fresh panic as she scanned for Drew.

"I've really got to go."

"I'll walk with you." He didn't offer his hand because he sensed her shying away from being touched. "So, you're here with your husband?"

"No." Her eyes shifted from side to side, ever watchful. "He's in New York. We've . . ." She had to get used to saying it, to meaning it. "We've separated."

"Oh." He didn't grin, at least not on the outside. "I'm sorry." But he remembered her reaction when he'd come up behind her in the airport. "Amicably?"

"I hope so." She shuddered. "Lord, they keep it cold in here."

He opened his mouth to question. It wasn't his place to pry, he reminded himself. Not into her marriage, or the ending of it. "How long do you plan to be in town?"

"I'm really not sure."

"How about some lunch, or a drink?"

"I can't. I have an appointment in an hour."

"Have dinner with me, then."

Her lips curved a little. She would have liked to have had dinner with a friend. "I'm trying to keep a low profile while I'm here. I haven't been going to restaurants."

"How about a backyard barbecue at my place?"

"Well, I—"

"Look, here's my address." Because he didn't want to give her time to say no, he took out a card and scribbled on the back.

"You can come by around seven and we'll throw a couple of steaks on. Very low profile."

She hadn't realized how much she'd been dreading sitting in her room, picking at a room service meal, flipping channels on the television for company. "All right."

He started to offer her a lift, but caught sight of a big white limo at the curb.

"Seven o'clock," he repeated.

She sent him a last smile before they went their separate ways. Michael wondered if he could find a cleaning service at two o'clock on a Friday afternoon. Emma walked past the limo and took her place on line for cabs. Idly, she turned the card over.

DETECTIVE M. KESSELRING
*HOMICIDE*

With a shiver, she slipped it into her bag. Odd, she'd forgotten he was a cop. Like his father.

◆ ◆ ◆ ◆

𝓜ICHAEL STUFFED TWO weeks' worth of newspapers in the bedroom closet. His two twenty-gallon trash cans were already bulging. It was hard for him to believe that one man and one dog could accumulate so much garbage. And he was appalled that in a city like Los Angeles there wasn't a single cleaning service to be had on a Friday afternoon.

He tackled the kitchen first with the bottle of Top Job he'd borrowed from a neighbor. The house smelled like a pine forest, but it couldn't be helped. Then Michael lured Conroy into the bathroom with a slice of bologna. When he stepped naked into the tub and dangled it, the dog hesitated. They both knew bologna was a weakness. The moment the dog leaped into the tub, Michael slid the glass doors closed.

"Grin and bear it, pal," Michael suggested as Conroy bristled with indignation.

It took a half bottle of shampoo, but Conroy bore up like a soldier. He did howl occasionally, but that could have been in response to Michael's singing. When they were both wrapped in towels, Michael searched through the linen closet for his hair dryer. He found it, and a frying pan he'd given up for lost.

He dried Conroy first, though the dog had yet to forgive him. "You ought to thank me for this," Michael told him. "One whiff of you and slut dog's going to crumble like an oatmeal cookie. She won't even look at that stuck-up German shepherd."

It took Michael thirty minutes to mop up the flood of water and dog hair. He was about to try his hand at salad making when he heard a car pull up. He hadn't expected her to take a cab. He'd imagined her arriving in a limo, or some spiffy rental car. As he watched, she passed bills to the driver.

There was a breeze to ruffle her hair and the boxy cotton shirt she wore. Its size and mannish style made her appear smaller and only more feminine. He watched her draw a hand through her hair, brush it out of her face as she looked toward the house. She'd lost weight. He'd noticed that at the airport. Too much weight, Michael thought now. She'd gone from looking slender to almost unbearably fragile.

There was a hesitation in her he'd never noticed before, in the way she walked, in the nervous glances she sent over her shoulder. He'd been a cop long enough to have seen that same kind of controlled panic many times. In suspects. And in victims. Because she looked as though she might bolt, he opened the door.

"So you found it."

She stopped dead, then shielding her eyes from the sun, saw him in the doorway. "Yes." Her stomach muscles slowly unknotted. "You've bought a house," she said and felt foolish immediately. "It's a pretty neighborhood."

Before she could step inside, Conroy raced to the door. He intended to bolt, to roll around in the dirt and grass until he'd rid himself of the undignified and all too human scent of shampoo.

"Hold it!" Michael snapped.

That wouldn't have stopped him, but Emma's soft purr did. "Oh, you have a dog." She crouched to rub his head. "You're a nice dog, aren't you?" Since Conroy was disposed to agree, he sat down and let her scratch his ears. "Yes, such a nice dog. Such a pretty dog."

No one had ever accused him of being pretty. Conroy mooned at her with the one eye that showed beneath his hair, then turned his head to sneer at Michael.

"Now you've done it." Michael took her hand to help her to

her feet. "He'll expect to be complimented on a regular basis now."

"I always wanted a dog." Conroy leaned against her slacks, the picture of devotion.

"I'll give you fifty bucks to take this one." When she laughed, Michael drew her inside.

"This is nice." She turned around the room, comforted by the sound of the dog's nails on the floor behind her.

A big gray chair looked cushy enough to sleep in. The couch was long and low, inviting afternoon naps. He'd tossed an Indian blanket in gray and red stripes on the floor as a throw rug—and as a sop to Conroy. Vertical blinds let in slashes of sunlight.

"I'd imagined you in one of those slick condos near the beach. Oh, *Marianne's Legs*." Delighted, she walked over to the print he'd hung over the couch.

"I picked that up the night of your show."

Emma glanced over her shoulder, one brow lifted. "Why?"

"Why did I buy it?" Thoughtful, Michael tucked his thumbs in his pockets. "I liked it. If you want me to start talking shadows and texture, forget it. The fact is, it's a great pair of legs, shot with a great deal of wit."

"I like your opinion a lot more than a discussion on texture." She turned back, smiling. It had taken them hours to set this shot. Not that it had been so difficult really. They just hadn't been able to agree on the shoes.

It showed Marianne's legs, crossed elegantly at the knee, with a ladylike flounce of hem sliding across them. They'd finally decided on plain black Chucks for her feet.

"You didn't have to buy this. I know the outrageous price Runyun set. I owed you at least a print."

"You gave me one once already."

She remembered the picture she'd taken of him with her father. "But I wasn't a professional then."

"I imagine an early McAvoy would be worth a tidy sum if I ever wanted to sell it." He felt her quick, instinctive jerk when he touched her arm. Gun-shy, he thought automatically. It was natural enough for a woman to be gun-shy right after the breakup of a marriage. "Let's go into the kitchen. I was just getting started on dinner."

The dog followed them in, resting his head adoringly on Emma's foot when she sat at the table. Michael poured wine in glasses he'd borrowed from his neighbor. He turned on the radio, low. Emma recognized Nat King Cole's creamy voice as she idly scratched Conroy's head with her other foot.

"How long have you lived here?"

"Nearly four years." He was glad to have company in the kitchen, a rarity for him unless he counted Conroy. He had fresh vegetables lined up on the counter. Puzzling over them, Michael wished he'd asked his neighbor for a recipe for tossed salad. He remembered to wash the lettuce, then taking up the neighbor's carving knife, prepared to chop it up.

"What are you doing?" Emma asked.

"Making salad." Because of the way she was looking at him, he paused with the knife over the head of romaine. "Maybe you don't like salad."

"I'd rather eat a hot-fudge sundae, but I like it well enough." She rose to inspect the vegetables. She counted four fat tomatoes, slightly underripe, a half-dozen peppers of every color and description, leeks, mushrooms, a gourd of some kind, a full head of cauliflower, and a bunch of carrots. "There's certainly enough of everything," she decided.

"I always make a lot," he improvised. "Conroy's a fiend for salad."

"I see." Emma smiled, then took the knife from him and set it aside. "Why don't you let me do this, while you deal with the steaks?"

"You cook?"

"Yes." Laughing, she began to tear the lettuce leaves. "Do you?"

"No." She smelled like wildflowers, fresh and delicate. He had to fight back an urge to press his lips to her throat. When he smoothed her hair behind her back, she lifted her head, eyes wary. "I never imagined you cooking."

"I like to."

He was standing close, but not so close that she felt afraid. As she scrubbed a green pepper she realized she wasn't afraid around him. Uneasy perhaps, but not afraid.

"You're good at this."

"I took top honors in vegetable chopping five years running." She brushed him away. "Go start the grill."

Later, she carried the salad out to a round wooden table beside a pathetic bed of petunias. A critical glance told her he was handling the steaks well enough, so she went back in. Emma wasn't sure what to make of the giant package of paper plates in the cupboard. A further search unearthed a trio of empty beer bottles, a drawer full of ketchup and mustard packets, and a mother lode of Chef Boyardee pasta meals in a can. She checked the dishwasher, discovered that was where he stored his laundry, and wondered if he had a clothes hamper somewhere full of dishes and flatware.

She found them in the microwave—two pretty china plates with baby roses painted around the edges, matching bowls, and a pair of steak knives and forks.

By the time he'd grilled the steaks, she had the table set as best she could.

"I couldn't find any salad dressing," she told him.

"Salad dressing. Right." He set the steaks down. Now that she was here, looking so right, so simply right smiling at him with one hand resting on the dog's head, he thought it was foolish to try to pretend he knew what he was doing with the meal.

If they were to get to know each other, really get to know each other this time around, she might as well see what she was getting into from the first.

"Make sure Conroy doesn't get any idea about these," he said, then walked to the chain-link fence and swung over. He was back in a few moments with a bottle of Wishbone and a fat blue candle. "Mrs. Petrowski says hello."

With a laugh, Emma glanced over and saw a woman leaning out of the back door of the house next door. Because it seemed natural, she waved before she turned back to Michael.

"Her dishes?"

"Yeah."

"They're very nice."

"I wanted to do better than a burger on the beach this time around."

Cautious, she passed him the salad. "I'm glad you asked me to come. We didn't have much of a chance to talk when you came to New York. I'm sorry I didn't have a chance to show you around."

"Next time," he said and cut into his steak.

They lingered over the meal until twilight. She'd forgotten what it was like to talk about unimportant things, to laugh over dinner with music in the background and a candle flickering. The dog, sated with half of Emma's steak, snored by her feet. Nerves, strung tight for months, smoothed out.

He could see the change. It was a gradual, almost a muscle-by-muscle relaxation. She never spoke of her marriage, or the separation. He found it odd. He had friends, both male and female, who had gone through divorces. During the process, and long afterward, it had been their favorite topic of conversation.

When Rosemary Clooney's seductive voice drifted from the radio, he rose and pulled Emma to her feet. "The old ones are the best to dance to," he said when she took a step in retreat.

"I really don't—"

"And it'd give Mrs. Petrowski such a thrill." Gently, he drew her closer, forcing himself to keep the embrace friendly and undemanding.

Emma moved with him automatically as Clooney crooned out "Tenderly." Closing her eyes, she concentrated on staying relaxed, on ignoring the emotions that were creeping into her. She didn't want to feel anything, unless it was peace.

There was only a flutter of a breeze now as they danced across the grass. The shadows were long. When she opened her eyes on a long, careful breath, she could see the sky in the west glowing in sunset.

"When I was waiting for you to come, I figured out that we've known each other about eighteen years." He brushed a finger over the back of her hand. She didn't jerk away this time, but there was a moment of stillness. "Eighteen years," he repeated. "Even though I can count the days I've spent with you on one hand."

"You didn't pay any attention to me the first time we met." She forgot to be nervous when she smiled up at him. "You were too busy being dazzled by Devastation."

"Eleven-year-old boys can't notice girls. Those particular optic nerves don't develop until the age of thirteen, twelve in some precocious cases."

Chuckling, she didn't object when he brought her a few inches closer. "I read that somewhere. It's fully developed when the young male anticipates the arrival of *Sports Illustrated*'s swimsuit issue as much as he anticipates the football preview." When Michael grinned, she lifted a brow. "It was your loss. I had quite a crush on you."

"Did you?" He skimmed his fingers up her back to toy with the ends of her hair.

"Absolutely. Your father had told me about how you'd roller-skated off the roof. I wanted to ask you how it felt."

"Before or after I regained consciousness?"

"In flight."

"I guess I was up for about three seconds. It was the best three seconds of my life."

It was exactly what she'd hoped he'd say. "Do your parents still live in that same house?"

"Yeah. You couldn't get them out with a howitzer."

"It's nice," she mused. "To have a place like that, a place that's always home. I felt that way about the loft."

"Is that where you're going to live when you go back?"

"I don't know." The haunted look came back into her eyes, and lingered. "I may not go back."

He thought she must have loved her husband very much to be so hurt the marriage was over. "There are some nice places along the beach. I remember you like the water."

"Yes, I do."

He wanted to see her smile again. "Do you still want to learn how to surf?"

She did smile, but it was wistful. "I haven't thought about it in years."

"I have Sunday off. I'll give you a lesson."

She glanced up. There was a challenge in his eyes, just enough of one to hook her. "All right."

He brushed a kiss at her temple in a gesture so easy, she was hardly aware of it. "You know, Emma, when I told you I was sorry about you and your husband . . ." He brought her hand to his lips. "I lied."

She retreated instantly. Turning, she began to gather the dishes. "I'll help you wash up."

He stepped back to the table, putting a hand over both of hers. "It doesn't come as that much of a surprise, does it?"

She made herself look at him. The light was pearly with dusk. Behind him, the eastern sky was deep, deep blue. His eyes were on hers, very direct, a little impatient. "No." She turned and took the dishes inside.

Though it cost him, he didn't press. She was vulnerable, he

reminded himself. A person was bound to be just after the breakup of a marriage. So he'd give her time, as much as he could stand.

She didn't relax again. Couldn't. What kind of a woman was she to be drawn to one man so soon after she'd left another? She didn't want to think about it. Her mind was made up. She would never become involved again. She would never allow herself to be trapped by love, by marriage. Now she only wanted to go back to her hotel, to lock the doors and feel safe for a few hours.

"It's getting late. I really should get back. Can I call a cab?"

"I'll take you back."

"You don't have to. I can—"

"Emma. I said I'd take you."

Stop it. Stop it, she ordered herself and pulled her nervous fingers apart. "Thanks."

"Relax. If you're not ready for the incredibly romantic affair we're going to have, I can wait. It's only been eighteen years so far."

She wasn't sure whether to be amused or annoyed. "An affair takes two people," she said lightly. "I'm afraid I've sworn off."

"Like I said, I can wait." He scooped up his keys. At the jingle of them, Conroy leaped into the air, barking.

"He likes to ride in the car," Michael explained. "Shut up, Conroy."

Knowing a true ally, the dog shuffled over to Emma, head low. "Can he come?" she asked as he rested his head against her thigh.

"I've got an MG."

"I don't mind being crowded."

"He'll shed all over you."

"It's all right."

Conroy followed the conversation, one ear pricked. Michael would have sworn the dog snickered. "You win, Conroy." Michael pointed toward the front door. Sensing victory, Conroy bolted. His waving tail struck Emma's purse and knocked it from table to floor.

When Michael bent to retrieve it, the clasp gave and the contents spilled out. Before he could apologize, he saw the .38. Emma said nothing as he lifted it, turning it over in his hand. It was top grade, the best automatic of that caliber that Smith and Wesson had to offer. It was glossy as silk and heavy in his hand. No elegant ladies' gun, this one was mean and for business only. He pulled out the clip, found it full, then snapped it back into place.

"What are you doing with this?"

"I have a license."

"That wasn't my question."

She crouched down to pick up her wallet and compact and brush. "I live in New York, remember?" She said it lightly, while her stomach churned as it always did when she lied. "A lot of women carry guns in Manhattan. For protection."

He studied the top of her head. "So you've had it awhile."

"Years."

"That's interesting, seeing as this model came out about six months ago. From the looks of it, this gun hasn't been knocking around in your purse more than a couple of days."

When she stood her whole body was shaking. "If you're going to interrogate me, shouldn't you read me my rights?"

"Cut the crap, Emma. You didn't buy this to scare off a mugger."

She could feel the skitter of panic, up her back. It made her throat dry and her stomach roil. He was angry, really angry. She could see it in the way his eyes darkened, in the way he moved when he stepped toward her. "It's my business. If you're going to take me to the hotel—"

"First I want to know why you're carrying this around, why you lied to me, and why you looked so damn scared at the airport this afternoon."

She didn't say a word, but watched him, just watched him with dull, resigned eyes. He'd had a dog look at him like that once, Michael remembered. It had crawled onto the grass at the edge of their lawn one afternoon when he'd been about eight. His mother had been afraid it was rabid, but when they'd taken it to the vet, it had turned out the dog had been beaten. Badly enough, often enough, that the vet had had to put it to sleep.

A sick rage worked inside of him as he stepped toward her. She stumbled back.

"What did he do to you?" He wanted to scream it, but his voice hissed out through his teeth.

She only shook her head. Conroy stopped scratching at the door and sat quivering.

"Emma. What the hell did he do to you?"

"I—I have to go."

"Goddammit, Emma." When he reached for her arm, she rammed back into the wall. Her eyes weren't dull now, but glassy with terror.

"Don't. Please."

"I won't touch you. All right?" It was training that kept his voice calm and quiet. He never took his eyes from hers. His expression was controlled now, carefully blank. "I'm not going to hurt you." Still watching her, he slipped the gun back in her purse and set it aside. "You don't have to be afraid of me."

"I'm not." But she couldn't stop trembling.

"You're afraid of him, of Latimer?"

"I don't want to talk about him."

"I can help you, Emma."

She shook her head again. "No, you can't."

"I can. Did he threaten you?" When she didn't answer, he eased a step closer. "Did he hit you?"

"I'm divorcing him. What difference does it make?"

"It makes a hell of a difference. We can get a warrant."

"No, I don't want to do that. I want it over. Michael, I can't talk to you about this."

He said nothing for a moment. He could all but feel the terror draining out of her and didn't want to frighten her again. "All right. I know places where you can go and talk to someone else, to other people who know what it's like."

Did he really believe there was anyone who knew what it was like? "I don't need to talk to anyone. I'm not going to have strangers reading about—about all of this over their morning coffee. This isn't your concern."

"Do you think that?" he said quietly. "Do you really think that?"

She felt wretchedly ashamed now. In his eyes was something she needed, needed badly if she only had the courage to ask for it. He was only asking for her trust. But she had trusted once before.

"I know it's not. This is my problem, and I'm handling it."

He could see that one nudge too many would cause her to

shatter. So he backed off. "All right. I'd just like you to think about it. You don't have to do this alone."

"He took all of my self-respect," she said quietly. "If I don't do this alone, I'll never get it back. Please just take me to the hotel. I'm very tired."

# Chapter Thirty-five

• • • •

So the bitch figured she could just walk away, Drew thought. She thought she could walk out the door and keep going. He was going to fix her good when he found her. And find her he would. He bitterly regretted that he hadn't beat her more vigorously before she'd gone to Florida.

He shouldn't have let her out of his sight, should have known he couldn't trust her. The only women a man could trust were hookers. They did their job, took the money, and that was that. There was a world of difference between an honest hooker and a whore. And his sweet, delicate-faced wife was a whore, just as his mother had been.

He was going to give her a beating she'd never forget.

Imagine her having the nerve to take off. The fucking gall to transfer her money and cancel the credit. He'd been humiliated at Bijan when the clerk had taken back the cashmere duster Drew had decided to purchase, with the cool comment that his credit card had been canceled.

She was going to pay for that.

Then to have that snotty lawyer serve him with papers. So she wanted a divorce. He'd see her dead first.

The New York lawyer hadn't been any help. Some bullshit about a professional courtesy to another firm. Mrs. Latimer didn't want her whereabouts known. Well, he was going to find her whereabouts all right, and he was going to kick ass.

At first he'd been afraid she'd gone to her father. With the benefit coming up and all Drew's plans to go solo about to bear fruit, he didn't want someone as influential as Brian McAvoy coming down on him. But then Brian had called about Emma's old lady dying. Drew was pleased that he'd been able to cover himself so quickly. He'd told Brian that Emma was out for the evening with a couple of her girlfriends. And he was certain he'd had just the right tone of sympathy and concern in his voice when he'd promised to tell Emma the news.

If McAvoy didn't know where his bitch of a daughter was, then Drew figured none of the other band members knew, either. They were all as thick as bloody thieves. He'd thought of Bev, but he was nearly sure that if Emma had gone to London, her old man would've gotten wind of it.

Or maybe they were all playing with him, laughing at him behind his back. If that was the case, then he'd pay her back, with interest.

She'd been gone for over two weeks. He hoped she'd had herself a high flying time because she was going to pay for every hour.

He hunched his shoulders against the brisk wind as he walked. The leather jacket kept out the worst of the early spring chill, but his ears were ringing from the wind. Or maybe it was fury. He liked that idea better and grinned a little as he crossed the street to the loft.

He'd taken the subway, something he found degrading but safer than a cab under the circumstances. He would more than likely have to do something . . . unpleasant to Marianne. Unpleasant for her, anyway, Drew thought with a laugh. It would be a great pleasure for him.

Emma had lied to him. Marianne had been at the funeral. He'd seen the pictures of them together in the paper. As sure as God made hell, Marianne had been in on the whole thing. She'd know where Emma was hiding. And when he got through with her, she'd be damn delighted to tell him.

He used the key he'd gotten from Emma months before. Inside, he punched in the security code to unlock the elevator. As the doors closed him in, he rubbed the knuckles of one hand against the other. He hoped she was still in bed.

The loft was silent. He moved quietly across the floor and up the stairs with his heart pounding happily. There was disappointment when he saw the empty bed. The sheets were tangled, but cool. The disappointment was so great, he compensated by trashing the loft. It took him nearly an hour to vent his frustration, ripping clothes, breaking glassware, hacking cushion after cushion in the sectional with a knife he'd taken from the kitchen.

He thought of the paintings, stacked up in the studio. Knife in hand, he started up when the phone rang. He stopped, jumping at the sound. He was breathing hard, sweat rolling into his eyes. There was a trickle of blood from his lip where he'd gnawed through while slashing the sofa.

On the fourth ring, the machine picked up.

"Marianne."

Drew bolted down the steps at the sound of Emma's voice. He'd nearly yanked up the receiver before he caught himself. "You're probably still in bed, or up to your elbows in paint, so call me later. Try to make it this morning. I'm going to the beach later to practice my surfing. I can stay up for more than ten seconds. Don't be jealous, but it's going to hit ninety in L.A. today. Call soon."

L.A., Drew thought. Turning, he stared at the mural of Emma on the plaster wall.

♦ ♦ ♦ ♦

WHEN MARIANNE PHONED an hour later, Emma was on her way out the door. She closed it, locked it again before she answered.

"Hi there." Marianne's voice was drowsy and content.

"Hi, yourself. You just getting up? It must be nearly noon in New York."

"I'm not up yet." She snuggled back against the pillows. "I'm in bed. The dentist's bed."

"Having a tooth capped?"

"Let's just say that he's got talents that extend beyond dental hygiene. I called my machine for messages and got yours. So, how are you?"

"I'm doing okay. Really."

"Glad to hear it. Is Michael going to the beach with you?"

"No, he's working."

Marianne wrinkled her nose. If she couldn't be around to look after Emma, she counted on the cop to do so. She could hear the shower in the next room and wished lazily that her new lover would come back to bed instead of heading off to fight plaque. "Tooth decay or bad guys, I guess a man's gotta do what a man's gotta do. Look, I'm thinking of coming out in a couple of weeks."

"To check up on me?"

"Right. And to finally meet this Michael you've been keeping to yourself all these years. Have a good time hanging ten, Emma. I'll call you tomorrow."

◆ ◆ ◆ ◆

𝑀ICHAEL LIKED BEING out in the field. He didn't have any real gripe with paperwork, or the hours it sometimes took talking on the phone, going on door-to-doors. But he liked the action on the streets.

He'd had to ignore a good deal of ribbing in the early years. The captain's son. Some of it had been good-natured, some of it hadn't, but he'd weathered it. He'd worked hard for his gold shield.

In the station now he stole a doughnut from a nearby desk, eating it standing up, while paging through the paper an associate had left next to the coffee maker.

He went straight for the comics. After a night like he'd put in, he needed all the laughs he could get. From there, he went looking for sports, turning the page with one hand and pouring coffee with the other.

### JANE PALMER DIES OF OVERDOSE

Jane Palmer, forty-six, ex-lover of Devastation's Brian McAvoy, and mother of his daughter, Emma, was found dead in her London home, apparently a victim of a drug overdose. The body was discovered by Stanley Hitchman late Sunday afternoon.

Michael read through the rest of the article. It contained only the bare facts, but suicide was hinted at. Swearing, he tossed the paper aside. He grabbed a jacket and signaled McCarthy.

"I need an hour. There's something I have to take care of."

McCarthy put a hand over the phone receiver he held at his ear. "We got three punks in holding."

"Yeah, and they'll hold. An hour," he repeated and strode out.

♦ ♦ ♦ ♦

*H*E FOUND HER AT THE BEACH. It had only been a few days since she had come back into his life, but he knew her habits. She came there every day, to the same spot. Not to surf. That was just an excuse. She came to sit in the sun and watch the water, or to read in the shade of a little blue and white cabana. Most of all she came to heal.

Always she set herself apart from the others who sunned or walked along the beach. She wasn't seeking company but was comforted by the fact that she wasn't alone. She wore a simple blue tank suit, no flighty bikini or spandex one-piece cut provocatively at the thigh. Its very modesty drew eyes toward her. More than one man had considered an approach, but one look from her had them passing by.

To Michael it was as if she had a glass wall surrounding her, thin, ice-cold, and impenetrable. He wondered if within it she could smell the coconut oil or hear the jangle from the portable radios.

He went to her. Her trust in him allowed him to get closer than most. But she'd built a second line of defense that held even friends at their distance.

"Emma."

He hated to see her jolt, that quick, involuntary movement of panic. She dropped the book she'd been reading. Behind her sunglasses fear darted into her eyes, then subsided. Her lips curved, her body relaxed. He saw it all, the change from serenity to panic to calm again, in a matter of seconds. It made him think that she was becoming much too used to living in fear.

"Michael, I didn't expect to see you today. Are you playing hooky?"

"No. I've only got a few minutes."

He sat beside her, in the partial shade. The breeze off the water fluttered his jacket so that she caught a glimpse of his shoulder holster. It was always a shock to remember what he did for a living. He never looked like her image of a detective. Even now when she could see the weapon snug against his USC T-shirt, she couldn't quite believe he would ever use it.

"You look tired, Michael."

"Rough night." She smiled a little. He could see that she thought he was speaking of a heavy date. There was no use telling her he'd spent most of it dealing with four young bodies. "Emma, have you read the paper today?"

"No." She had deliberately avoided newspapers and television. The troubles of the world, like the people in it, were on the other side of her glass wall. But she knew he was going to tell her something she didn't want to hear. "What is it?" When he took her hand, the anxiety quickened. "Is it Da?"

"No." He cursed himself for not coming straight out with it. Her hand had turned to ice in his. "It's Jane Palmer. She's dead, Emma."

She stared at him as though he were speaking in a language she had to translate. "Dead? How?"

"It looks like she overdosed."

"I see." She withdrew her hand from his, then stared out to sea. The water was pale green near the shore, deepening and changing as it stretched toward the horizon. There it gleamed a deep, gemlike blue. She wondered what it would be like to be that far from everything. To float, completely alone.

"Am I supposed to feel anything?" she murmured.

He knew she wasn't asking him so much as herself. Still he answered. "You can't feel what isn't there."

"No, you can't. I never loved her, not even as a child. I used to be ashamed of that. I'm sorry she'd dead, but it's a vague, impersonal kind of sorrow, the kind you feel when you read in the paper that someone's died in a car wreck or a fire."

"Then that's enough." He took her braid, a habit he'd developed, and ran his hand up and down it. "Listen, I've got to get back, but I should have things wrapped by around seven. Why don't we take a drive up the coast? You and me and Conroy."

"I'd like that." When he stood she reached out a hand for his. The contact was fleeting. Then she turned and looked back out to sea.

◆ ◆ ◆ ◆

DREW ARRIVED AT the Beverly Wilshire just after three. It was the first hotel he checked. It both pleased and disgusted him that Emma was so predictable. It was the Connaught in London, the Ritz in Paris, Little Dix Bay in the Virgin Islands, and always the Wilshire in L.A.

He strolled in, an easy, personable smile on his face. He knew his luck was in when the desk clerk was young, female, and attractive. "Hi." He flashed the smile at her and watched her polite expression turn to recognition, then delight.

"Good afternoon, Mr. Latimer."

He put a hand over hers, and lifted the other to place a finger to his lips. "Let's keep that between us, shall we? I'm joining my wife here, but I'm afraid I've been careless and forgotten what room she's taken."

"Mrs. Latimer's staying with us?" The clerk lifted a brow.

"Yes, I had some business to take care of before I joined her. You'll find her for me, won't you?"

"Of course." Her fingers skipped over the keyboard. "I have no Latimer registered."

"No? Perhaps she checked in under McAvoy." He held back his impatience while the computer clicked.

"I'm sorry, Mr. Latimer, we have no McAvoys."

He wanted to grab the clerk by her slender throat and squeeze. With an effort, he fixed a puzzled frown on his face. "That's odd. I'm almost sure I haven't mixed the hotels. Emma wouldn't stay anywhere but the Wilshire." His mind jumped from possibility to possibility. Then he smiled. "Ah, of course. I don't know how I could be so addle-brained. She stayed here with a friend for a bit, probably kept the room in her name. You know how it is when you're trying to slip away for a few days. Try Marianne Carter. It's more than likely on the third floor. Emma's twitchy about heights."

"Yes, here it is. Suite 305."

"That's a relief." Behind his smile, his teeth ground together. "I'd hate to think I'd lose my wife." He waited for the key, struggling to keep his breathing calm and steady. "You've been a big help, luv."

"My pleasure, Mr. Latimer."

Oh no, he thought as he headed for the elevators, it was going to be his pleasure. His great pleasure.

He wasn't disappointed that the suite was empty. In fact, he decided it was that much better. From his bag, he took a small tape recorder and a belt of rich, supple leather. He drew the drapes snug at the windows, then lighting a cigarette, settled down to wait.

♦ ♦ ♦ ♦

"*K*ESSELRING." A YOUNG detective opened the door of the interrogation room where Michael and McCarthy were working in tandem to wear down a suspect. "You got a call."

"I'm a little busy here, Drummond. Take a message."

"Tried. She says it's an emergency."

He started to swear, then thought it might be Emma. "Try not to miss me," he said to Swan as he started out. He sat on the edge of his desk and picked up the phone. "Kesselring."

"Michael? This is Marianne Carter. I'm a friend of Emma's."

"Sure." Annoyed by the interruption, he shoved a hand in his pocket for a cigarette. "You in town?"

"No. No, I'm in New York. I just got into the loft. I—somebody, somebody wrecked it."

He pressed his fingers to his tired eyes. "I think you might be smarter to call the local police. I can't get there for a few hours."

She wasn't in the mood for sarcasm. "I don't give a damn about the loft. It's Emma I'm worried about."

"What does she have to do with it?"

"This place has been torn apart. Everything's slashed, cut up, broken. It was Drew. I'm sure it was Drew. He probably has Emma's key. I don't know how much she's told you, but he's violent. Really violent. And I—"

"Okay. Calm down. The first thing you do is get out, go to a neighbor's or a public place and call the police."

"He's not here." She hated herself for being so scattered she was unable to make herself clear. "I think he knows where she is, Michael. She left a message on the machine this morning. If he was here when she called, or he played it back, then he knows. I tried to call her, but she didn't answer."

"I'll take care of it. Get out of the loft and call the cops." He hung up before she could respond.

"Kesselring, if you've finished talking to your sweetheart—"

"Let's move." Michael interrupted his partner's complaint and started for the door at a run.

"What the—"

"Move," Michael repeated. He was already peeling out when McCarthy jumped in the car.

# Chapter Thirty-six

• • • •

WHEN EMMA WALKED into the lobby of the Beverly Wilshire, it was nearly four. During her long afternoon on the beach, she'd made one decision. She was going to call her father. He would have heard about Jane's death, and Emma had no doubt he would have tried to contact her.

It wouldn't be an easy conversation, but a necessary one. It was time she told him that she had left Drew. Perhaps it was also time to take advantage of the press that was always so eager for gossip. Once the separation was made public, she might break out of her perpetual daze. Maybe she'd stop being afraid.

As she walked down the hall toward her room, she dug in her bag for her key. Her fingers brushed the warm metal of the gun. She was going to stop carrying it, she told herself. She was going to stop looking over her shoulder.

She opened the door of the suite, and frowned. The drapes shut out all but the faintest light. She hated the dark, and silently cursed the maid. Pushing herself forward, she let the door close behind her as she went toward the lamp.

Then the music started. Her fingers froze on the switch. That eerie, unmistakable intro that haunted her dreams. The murdered Lennon began to sing in a crisp staccato.

Across the room the light flashed on. She could only whimper and stumble back. For a moment a face floated into her mind, blurred, but almost, almost recognizable. Then she saw Drew.

"Hello, Emmy luv. Have you missed me?"

She broke out of her trance and raced for the door. He was quick. He'd always been quick. One sweep of his hand knocked her aside and sent her bag flying. Still smiling, he turned the security lock and fixed the chain.

"We want our privacy, don't we?"

His voice, pleasant, quietly loving, sent ice skidding up and down her back. "How did you find me?"

"Oh, we have our ways, Emma. Let's say there's a bond between you and me. Didn't I tell you I'd always find you?"

Behind her the music kept playing. It was a nightmare. She wanted to believe it. She had them often, the music, the dark. She would wake up, sweating cold as she was sweating now. And it would be over.

"Guess what I received, Emma? A petition for divorce. Now, that wasn't very nice, was it? Here I've been worried sick about you for two weeks. Why, you might have been kidnapped." He grinned. "You might have been murdered like your poor little brother."

"Don't."

"Ah, it upsets you to talk about him, doesn't it? The music upsets you, too. Shall I turn it off?"

"Yes." She'd be able to think if he turned the music off. She'd know what to do.

"All right, then." He took a step toward the recorder, then stopped. "No, I think we'll leave it on. You have to learn to face things, Emma. I've told you that before, haven't I?"

Her teeth had begun to chatter. "I am facing them."

"Good. That's good. Now, the first thing you're going to do is call that fancy lawyer of yours and tell him you've changed your mind."

"No." Fear was storming through her system so that she could only whisper. "I'm not going back with you."

"Of course you are. You belong with me. You've had your little snit, Emma, don't make it harder on yourself." When she shook her head, he let out a long, gusty sigh. Then his hand snaked out, quick as a whip, and smashed across her face. Blood filled her mouth as she slammed into a table, sending a lamp crashing to the floor.

Through a haze of pain she saw him coming toward her. And she began to scream. He kicked her full in the stomach, cutting off the screams and her air. When she tried to curl up, he began to hit her, slowly, methodically.

This time, she fought back. Her first blow glanced off his chin, but surprised him enough to give her time to crawl away. She heard pounding on the door, a demand to open it. She managed to struggle to her feet and take a watery step toward the sound, when he caught her again.

"So you want to play rough, Emma?" He began to tear at her clothes, raking his nails down her skin. Her struggles only drove him on. She would be punished this time, in a way she would never forget.

Emma heard someone pleading, begging, promising. She wasn't aware it was her own voice. She hardly felt the blows as he continued to beat her. This time he used his fists, forgetting everything but the need to pay her back.

"Did you think you could walk out on me, bitch? Did you think I'd let you ruin everything I worked for? I'll kill you first."

Her body was a jelly of pain. Even the effort to breathe cut through her like dozens of dull-edged knives. It had never been this bad before. Even at its worst, it had never been this bad. Groggy, she grabbed a chair leg and tried to haul herself up. Wet with her own blood, her fingers slipped off.

She stopped fighting. There was no strength left to hold him off. She felt him lift her, then send her flying. Something snapped in her chest and she screamed again against the sickening pain. Half conscious, she lay sprawled.

"Bitch. Whore bitch." He was panting as he started for her again. Dimly she saw that blood was running from his nose. His eyes were glazed and wild. She knew, looking at his face, that he had crossed some line. This time a beating wouldn't be enough. He would pound on her until she was dead. Weeping, she tried to crawl.

The snap of his belt made her flinch. Her sobs rose up into wails as she pulled herself across the rug. He continued to snap the belt, snap it to the beat of the music as he stalked her. She collapsed. The jolt screamed through her ribs until her vision wavered.

She heard someone calling for her, shouting her name. Splintering wood. Was that the sound of splintering wood or was her body just breaking in two? The first slash of the belt across her back had her arm flinging out. Her fingers brushed metal.

Blindly, she closed her hand around the gun. Choking on sobs, she pushed herself over. She saw his face as he raised the belt again.

She felt the gun jerk up in her hand.

Michael broke in the door in time to see Drew stagger back, a look of puzzlement on his face. Weaving, he lifted the belt again. Michael's weapon was drawn, but before he could use it, Emma fired again, and again. She continued to press the trigger long after it clicked uselessly, long after he was sprawled at her feet. She held the trigger down, aiming at empty air.

"Good Jesus," McCarthy said.

"Keep those people out." Michael moved toward her. Peeling off his jacket, he wrapped it around her. Her clothes were torn to bits and soaked with blood. She didn't move, only continued to fire the empty gun. When he tried to take it, he found her hand convulsed on it.

"Emma. Baby. It's all right now. It's over now." Gently he brushed at her hair. He had to fight to keep his rage buried. Her face was a mass of blood. One eye was already swollen shut. The other was glassy with shock. "Give me the gun now, baby. You don't need it anymore. You're okay." He shifted so that she could see his face. Taking a scrap of what had been her blouse, he dabbed at the blood. "It's Michael. Can you hear me, Emma? It's Michael. It's going to be okay."

Her breath began to hitch violently. Shudders wracked her. He gathered her close, rocking while her body shook. Her hand was limp when he slipped the gun from it. She didn't cry. Michael knew the sound she made as he held her couldn't be called grieving. She moaned, low animal moans that died into whimpering.

"Ambulance is on its way." After a cursory check of Drew's body, McCarthy crouched beside Michael. "Messed her up pretty good, didn't he?"

Michael continued to rock her, but he turned his head and studied Drew Latimer for a long time. "Too bad you can only die once."

"Yeah." McCarthy shook his head as he rose. "The sonofabitch is still holding the belt."

◆ ◆ ◆ ◆

*B*RIAN WATCHED THE clouds race across the sky as he sat beside Darren's grave. Each time he came to sit in the high, sweet grass, he hoped he would find peace. He never had. But he always came back.

He'd let the wildflowers grow where his son was buried. He preferred them to the small marble marker that carried only a name and two dates. The years were pitifully close.

His parents were buried nearby. Though he had known them for decades, he remembered his son with more clarity.

From the cemetery he could see plowed fields, spaces of rich brown cutting through the rich green. And the spotted cows grazing. It was early in the day. Mornings in Ireland were the best for sitting, dreaming. The light was soft and pearly, as he'd never seen it anywhere but Ireland. Dew was glittering on the grass. The only sounds he could hear were the bark of a dog and the distant hum of a tractor.

When Bev saw him, she stopped. She hadn't known he would be there. Through the years she'd been careful to come only when she knew Brian was elsewhere. She hadn't wanted to see him there, beside the grave where they had both stood so many years before.

She nearly turned away. But there was something in the way he sat, his hands resting lightly on his knees, his eyes looking out over the green hills. He looked too much alone.

They were both too much alone.

She walked quietly. He never heard her, but when her shadow fell over him, he turned his head. She said nothing, but laid the spray of lilacs she carried beneath the marble marker. On a sigh, she knelt.

In silence they listened to the wind in the high grass, and the distant purr of the tractor.

"Do you want me to leave?" he asked her.

"No." Gently, she brushed a hand over the soft grass that covered their son. "He was beautiful, wasn't he?"

"Yes." He felt the tears well up and fought them back. It had been a long time since he'd wept here. "He looked so much like you."

"He had the best of each of us." Her voice quiet, she sat back on her heels. Like Brian, she looked toward the hills. They had changed so little in all these years. Life continued. That was the hardest lesson she had learned. "He was so bright, so full of life. He had your smile, Bri. Yours and Emma's."

"He was always happy. Whenever I think of him I remember that."

"My biggest fear was that I would forget somehow, that his face, and his memory, would fade with time. But it hasn't. I remember how he laughed, how it would just roll out of him. I've never heard a prettier sound. I loved him too much, Bri."

"You can't love too much."

"Yes, you can." She fell silent for a time. A cow began to low. Oddly, the sound made her smile. "Do you think it's just lost? That everything he was and might have been just vanished, just went away when he died?"

"No." He looked at her then. "No, I don't."

His answer made all the difference. "I did at first. Perhaps that's why I lost myself for so long. It hurt so much to think that all that beauty and joy had been here for such a short time. But then I knew that wasn't true. He's still alive in my heart. And in yours."

He looked away, toward the distant, shadowed hills. "There are times I want to forget. Times I do whatever I can to forget. It's the worst kind of hell to outlive your own child."

"When you do, you know nothing that happens to you will ever be as painful. We had him for two years, Bri. That's what I like to remember. You were a wonderful father." She reached out for him, took his hands. When his fingers tightened on hers, she held on. "I'm sorry I wouldn't share that pain with you the way I shared the joy. I was selfish with it, as if holding it to myself would make it only mine. But it's ours, the way he was ours."

He said nothing. Tears were clogging his throat. Understanding, she turned to him. Holding each other, they sat in silence as the sun rose higher and dried the dew on the tall grass.

"I should never have left you," he murmured.

"We left each other."

"Why?" He tightened his grip. "Why?"

"I've thought about it so many times. I think we couldn't bear to be happy. That we felt, or I did, that if we could be happy after he was gone, it would be like dishonoring him. It was wrong."

"Bev." He turned his face into her hair. "Don't go. Please don't go."

"No," she said quietly. "I won't."

They walked, hands linked, back to the farmhouse. The sun shone bright through the windows as they went upstairs. They undressed each other, stopping only for long, quiet kisses, gentle caresses.

He wasn't the young man who had once loved her. Nor was she the same woman. They were more patient now. They didn't tumble onto the bed, but lowered slowly, knowing each moment was precious when so many had been lost.

And yet, though they had changed, their bodies moved easily together. When she reached for him the years seemed to vanish. With his mouth pressed against her throat, he drew in the familiar scent, the familiar taste.

Even as passion built, they glided along its edges, unwilling to be ruled by it as they once had been. Her lips curved as she ran a hand through his hair. As her body heated she sighed as much in contentment as desire. With her eyes half closed, she let her hands run over him, remembering every angle, every plane of his body. Passion, released, flowed into them like a fine wine.

She welcomed him, opening and arching. When they joined, she wept. Bringing his mouth to her, she tasted his tears mixed with her own.

Later, they lay quiet, her head tucked in the curve of his shoulder. She wondered that it should be so easy, and feel so right. It had been nearly twenty years. Half of her life had been spent apart from him. Yet they were here, bodies damp from loving. She could feel his heart thud under the palm of her hand.

"It's so much like it used to be," he said, echoing her thoughts. "And yet it's so different."

"I didn't want this to happen. All this time I've worked so hard to stay away from you." She lifted her head, looked in his eyes. "I never wanted to love this much again."

"It's only ever been right with you. Don't ask me to let you go again. I wouldn't make it this time."

She brushed his hair, with its first few sprinkles of gray, away from his brow. "I was always afraid that you didn't really need me, certainly not the way I needed you."

"You were wrong."

"Yes, I know I was." She lowered her head to kiss him. "We've wasted a lot of time, Bri. I'd like you to come home."

They stayed the night there, in the old bed, talking, making love. It was late when the phone rang. Brian answered it only because there was no other way to end the interruption.

"Hello."

"Brian McAvoy?"

"Yes, speaking."

"This is Michael Kesselring. I've been trying to track you down."

"Kesselring." He regretted saying the name the moment Bev stiffened beside him. "What is it?"

"It's Emma."

"Emma?" He sat up quickly, mouth dry as dust. Bev's hand was on his shoulder, squeezing. "Has something happened to her?"

Michael knew from experience it was best to say it all quickly, but he had a difficult time forming the words. "She's in the hospital, here in L.A. She's—"

"An accident? Has she had an accident?"

"No, she was beaten pretty badly. I'll explain when you get here."

"Beaten? Emma's been beaten? I don't understand."

"The doctors are working on her. They tell me she's going to be okay, but she's going to need you."

"We'll be there as soon as we can."

Bev was already up and pulling on her clothes. "What happened?"

"I don't know. She's in the hospital in L.A." He swore, fumbling with the buttons of his shirt.

"Here." Quickly, Bev did them up. "She's going to be all right, Bri. Emma's tougher than she looks."

He could only nod and take a moment to hold her against him.

# Chapter Thirty-seven

♦ ♦ ♦ ♦

$\mathcal{I}$T WAS DARK. There was pain, a dreamy, distant pain that drifted sluggishly through her body. Like a warm red ocean it seemed to cover her, weigh her down, so that she was trapped away from air and light. Emma tried to rise above it, to sink below it, but couldn't seem to outmaneuver the dull ache. She found she could accept that. But not the dark, not the quiet.

She struggled to move. There was panic when she realized she didn't know if she was standing or sitting or lying down. She couldn't feel her arms or legs, just that nagging, somehow fluid ache. She tried to speak, to call out to someone, anyone. In her mind she screamed, but no one answered.

She knew she had been hurt. All too well she could remember the way Drew had looked at her. He'd been waiting for her. He might still be there, watching her, waiting in the dark. This time he would . . .

But maybe she was already dead.

She felt more than pain now. She felt anger. She didn't want to die. Moaning in frustration she strained, using all her strength and will, just to open her eyes. They might have been sewn closed for all the control she had over them.

A hand brushed her hair. She sensed it, just the whisper of a touch that rammed screaming panic against the pain.

"Rest, Emma. It's all right now. You have to rest."

Not Drew. Neither the voice nor the touch was Drew's.

"You're safe now. I promise."

Michael. She wanted to say his name, grateful not to be

alone in the dark. To be alive. Then a dark red wave rolled in and covered her.

She drifted in and out for most of the night. Michael knew the doctors had said she would sleep straight through. But it was fear that had her fighting off the sedatives. He could feel it pumping out of her each time she surfaced.

He talked to her, repeating the same assurances hour after hour. His voice, or the words, seemed to calm her. So he sat, and watched, and held her hand.

He wanted to do something more. None of his training or his years on the force had taught him this kind of patience. To sit helplessly by while the woman he loved waged her own silent battle. Her lovely, elegant face was broken and bandaged. Her slim, soft body, bruised and battered.

They said she wouldn't die. There would be pain, physical and emotional, but she would live. The extent of the trauma could only be judged later. And he could only wait. And regret.

He should have pushed her. Michael cursed himself over and over as he listened to her deep, drugged breathing. If he had applied the right pressure at the right time, he could have convinced her to tell him just how bad things had been for her. He was a cop, for God's sake. He knew how to get information.

But he had backed away. Wanting to give her time, and privacy. Christ. Privacy. He rubbed his hands over his face. He'd given her privacy when she'd belonged in protective custody. He'd given her time when he should have had the New York cops issue a warrant.

Because he hadn't done his job, because he'd let his feelings get in the way, she was lying in the hospital.

He left her only once, when Marianne and Johnno arrived from New York.

"Michael." Johnno gave him a quick nod of recognition and kept a hand on Marianne's shoulder. "What happened?"

Michael rubbed the heels of his hands over his eyes. The lights in the corridor blinded him. "Latimer. Looks like he got into her room at the hotel."

"Oh God." Marianne clutched the little stuffed dog. "How bad?"

"Bad enough." An afterimage of Emma sprawled on the hotel carpet flashed into his brain. "He broke three of her ribs, dislocated her shoulder. She's got some bruised internal organs, I don't know how many contusions and lacerations. And her face . . . They don't think she's going to need any extensive surgery."

Jaw clenched, Johnno stared at the closed door. "Where is the bastard?"

"Dead."

"Good. We want to see her."

Michael knew that the doctors were annoyed enough with him, but he'd used his badge to persuade them to let him sit in her room. "You two go ahead. I'll clear it with the nurse and wait for you in the lounge." Like Johnno, he stared at the closed door. "They've got her sedated."

He gave them time, loitering over a cup of coffee in the visitor's lounge, going over every movement of his day to try to see if there was one thing he could have done differently. It was always timing, he thought wearily. If he had broken in the door five minutes earlier it might have changed everything.

He stood again when he saw them come in. Marianne's eyes were red, but he didn't think she would fall apart. She took the chair Michael vacated. "I shouldn't have left her here by herself."

"It's not your fault," Johnno told her.

"No, it's not my fault. But I shouldn't have left her alone."

Ignoring the signs, Johnno pulled out a cigarette. Once it was lighted, he handed it to Marianne. "Marianne filled me in on what's been going on during the flight over. I assume you're aware that Latimer's been abusing Emma for more than a year."

Michael crushed the empty Styrofoam cup with his fingers. "I don't know the details. I'll take Emma's statement as soon as she's up to it."

"Statement." Marianne looked up. "Why does she have to make a statement?"

"It's procedure." He glanced back toward Emma's door. "Just routine."

"But you'll do it," Johnno put in. "I wouldn't want her to have to talk to a stranger."

"I'll take the statement."

With the ash growing long on her cigarette, Marianne studied him. He'd more than lived up to the promise in the newspaper picture of ten years before. At the moment, he looked tense and exhausted, dark shadows under his eyes, lines of strain beside them. Despite them, she judged him as a man to be depended upon. Whatever Emma had said to the contrary, Michael Kesselring looked precisely like Marianne's image of a cop.

"Did you kill Drew?"

He shifted his gaze and met her eyes. More than anything he could remember, he wished he could have said yes. "No. I was too late."

"Who did?"

"Emma."

"Oh Jesus," was all Johnno said.

"Look, I don't like leaving her alone," Michael said. "I'm going in to sit with her. You might want to check into a hotel, get some rest."

"We'll stay." Marianne reached up to take Johnno's hand. "We can take turns sitting with her."

With a nod, Michael went back into Emma's room.

◆ ◆ ◆ ◆

SHE SURFACED AT DAWN. The light, dim as it was, relieved her. There had been so many dreams, so many strange dreams through the night. Most of them vanished, midnight mirages that slipped away in the sunlight. But she knew she'd had the nightmare again. Almost, she could hear the echo of music and the swish of shadows.

She struggled to throw off sleep, annoyed at first by the heaviness in her limbs. It was frustrating that she could only open one eye. She lifted a hand, found the bandage, and remembered.

Panic. It filled her lungs like smoke, almost choking her. She turned her head, and saw Michael. He was slumped in the chair beside her bed, his chin on his chest. One of his hands covered one of hers. She had only to move her fingers to have him jerking awake.

"Hey." He smiled, tightening his fingers around hers and bringing them to his lips. His voice was rough with fatigue. "Good morning."

"How . . ." She closed her eye again, impatient with the thin whisper. "How long?"

"You just slept through the night, that's all. Any pain?"

She had pain, and plenty of it. But she shook her head. It made her believe she was alive. "It happened, didn't it? All of it?"

"It's over." Wanting the comfort almost as much as he

needed to give it, he kept her hand against his cheek. "I'm going to go get the nurse. They wanted to know when you woke up."

"Michael. Did I kill him?"

He took a moment. Her face was bruised and bandaged. He'd seen worse, but not often. Yet her hand held steady on his. She'd been battered, but she wasn't defeated. "Yes. For the rest of my life I'll regret that you beat me to it."

Her eye closed, but she kept her hand firm around his. There had to be something inside her, something besides the thin rivers of pain and drugged fatigue. "I don't know what to feel. There doesn't seem to be anything, no grief, no relief, no regret. I only feel hollowed out."

He knew what it was to hold a weapon in your hand, to aim, to fire at another human being. In the line of duty. In self-defense. Yet no matter how urgent, how vital the cause, it haunted you.

"You did the only thing you could do. That's all you have to remember. Don't worry about the rest now."

"He had such a lovely voice. I fell in love with it. I wish I knew why it had to be this way."

He had no comfort, and no answers.

Michael left her to the nurse and went to the lounge where Marianne was drowsing against Johnno's shoulder. The room was done in nice pastels, designed, he supposed, to cheer and relax the friends and family who could only sit and wait. There was a color television bracketed to the wall. It was chattering discreetly. A table was set up with pots of water on hot plates and baskets of instant coffee packets and tea bags. There were two telephones at either end of the room and a generous supply of magazines.

"She's awake."

"Awake?" Marianne shot up instantly. "How is she?"

"She's okay." Michael poured another cup of coffee, stirring the instant powder without interest. "She remembers what happened, and she's dealing with it. The nurse is with her, and they're paging the doctor. You should be able to see her pretty soon."

They all fell silent when Emma's picture flashed on the television screen. The report was brisk and brutally concise, interspersed with shots of both Emma and Drew. There was a quick stand-up with the desk clerk of the hotel, and with two of the witnesses who had heard the disturbance and called security.

A middle-aged man, balding and flushed with excitement, spoke into the mike. Michael remembered shoving him aside before he had broken in the door.

"I only know there was a lot of crashing around. And she was screaming, begging him to stop. It sounded pretty bad so I beat on the door myself. I had the room next door. Then the cops came. One of them broke in the door. It was only for a second, but I could see a woman sprawled on the rug, bleeding. She had a gun and she fired it. She kept right on shooting until she ran out of bullets."

Michael was swearing as he strode over to the phone.

On the screen, the news switched to a live remote outside the hospital. The reporter, solemn-faced, announced that Emma McAvoy Latimer was in guarded condition.

"Look," Michael snapped into the phone. "I don't give a damn. You hold them off awhile. I want a uniform outside her door twenty-four hours, to keep out any reporters who try to get in to see her. I'll make a statement myself this afternoon."

"You won't be able to stop it," Johnno said when Michael slammed the phone down.

"I can hold them off for a while."

Johnno rose. There was no use telling Michael that Emma knew the price of celebrity. She'd been paying it all of her life. "Marianne, you go see Emma. I'm going to buy this copper some breakfast."

"I don't want—"

"Sure you do." Johnno cut Michael off. "It isn't every day you get to share scrambled eggs with a legend. Go on, Marianne. Tell Emma I'll be in soon." He waited until Marianne had started down the hall. "The first time I saw Emma she was about three. She was hiding under the kitchen sink in Jane's filthy flat. She'd been kicked around quite a bit already. She pulled out of it. She'll pull out of it this time, as well."

"I should have gotten a warrant," Michael said. "I should have pushed her and gotten a warrant."

"How long have you been in love with her?"

He didn't speak, then let out a long breath. "Most of my life." He walked to the window, jerking it up to let the air hit his face. With his palms braced on the sill he leaned out. "Five minutes. If he'd been five minutes later, or I'd been five minutes faster, I'd have killed him. I had my gun in my hand when I went through the door. I should have killed him for her. That's the way it should have been."

"Ah, the male ego." Johnno kept the same small sarcastic smile on his face when Michael whirled on him. "I have an idea how you feel, but I disagree. I'm glad Emma wasted the sonofabitch herself. There's justice in that. I only wish she'd had the chance before he did this to her. Come on, son." Johnno patted his shoulder. "You need food."

Because he was too tired to argue, Michael went along. They were nearly to the elevators when the doors opened. Brian and Bev rushed out.

"Where is she?" Brian demanded.

"She's right through there. Hold on." Johnno took his arm. "Marianne's with her. You need to calm down before you go busting in there. She'd had enough excitement for a while."

"Johnno's right, Bri." Bev battled back her own nerves to soothe his. "We don't want to upset her. And we need to know what—how she got hurt. Can you tell us what happened?" she asked Michael. "We've been traveling ever since we got the call."

"Yesterday, Drew Latimer found Emma here, in her hotel."

"Found her?" Brian interrupted. "What do you mean? Weren't they together?"

"She's been hiding from him while she set the divorce in motion."

"Divorce?" Because he knew he was punchy from lack of sleep and worry, Brian took a long breath and tried to clear his head. "I talked with Emma only a few weeks ago, she said nothing about wanting a divorce."

"She couldn't say anything about it," Michael told him. "Because she was afraid. Latimer's been abusing her for most of the marriage."

"That's crazy." Brian dragged a hand through his hair. "He dotes on her. I've seen it."

"Yeah." The fury Michael had been holding off bubbled to the surface. "He's been a real loving husband. A fucking prince. That's why she's been terrified. That's why she's lying in there right now, with her face smashed and her ribs broken. The man damn near loved her to death."

Brian's lips trembled open. His hand tightened on Bev's until he rubbed bone against bone. "He beat her? Are you telling me that he's the one who put Emma here?"

"That's right."

Rage flew into him as he grabbed Michael by the shirt front. "Where is he?"

"He's dead."

"Easy, Bri." Johnno rubbed his shoulder, debating the wisdom of stepping between two furious men. "It won't help Emma if you go off."

"I want to see her." He pulled Bev against him. "We want to see her now." He walked to the door as Marianne came out. He didn't speak, only stared for a moment at his daughter lying in the bed.

"Baby." He held tight to Bev as he crossed the room.

Emma looked at them. One hand fluttered to her bruised cheek. Then she lifted both to cover her face. She hadn't wanted him to see her like this. Gently, he drew her hand away.

"Emma." He lowered his head to press a kiss to her forehead. "I'm sorry. I'm so sorry."

She let the tears come then, stumbling over her own apologies and explanations. When she was exhausted, she lay with her hand in his. "I don't even know how it all happened, not really. Or why. I wanted to have someone love me, just me. I wanted a family, and I thought . . ." She let out a long sigh. "I thought he was like you."

He wanted to cry then. It was almost impossible to keep his head from lowering to her breast to weep. But he only brought her hand to his lips again. "You're not to worry about it. You're not to even think about it. No one's ever going to hurt you again. I swear it."

"All that matters is that you're safe now." Gently, Bev brushed the hair back from Emma's bandaged forehead. "That's all that matters to any of us."

"I killed him," Emma murmured. "Did they tell you I killed him?"

Over his daughter's head, Brian's shocked eyes met Bev's. "It's—it's over now." He fumbled for Emma's hand again.

"I wouldn't listen to you. Didn't want to." Curling her fingers into his, she held on. "I was angry and hurt because you thought he only wanted me to get to you."

"Don't." He pressed his lips to her fingers.

"You were right." The words came out on a long, weary sigh. "He never wanted me, or loved me. Not me. And when having me wasn't enough to get him what he wanted, he began to hate me."

"I don't want you to think about it now," Brian insisted. "All I want you to do is rest, and concentrate on getting well."

He was right, Emma thought. She was much too tired to think. "I'm glad you're here. Da, I'm so sorry for pulling away from you all this time. For shutting you out."

"We were both wrong, and it's done." He smiled at her then. "We've all the time in the world now."

"We'd like you to come home when you're better." Bev reached across the bed to touch Brian's cheek. "With us."

"Both of you?"

"Yes." Brian lifted a hand, linked it with Bev's. "We have a lot of time to make up for. All of us."

"When I woke up this morning I didn't think I'd ever have a reason to feel happy again," Emma said. "But I'm happy for you. I need to think about the rest."

"There's no hurry." Bev leaned over to kiss her cheek. "We'll let you get some sleep."

♦ ♦ ♦ ♦

"*K*ESSELRING." IT WAS noon when McCarthy found Michael in the hospital lounge. "Jesus, did you move in here?"

"Coffee?"

"Not if it'll make me look like you." He tossed Michael a bag. "Fresh clothes and shaving stuff. I fed your dog."

"Thanks."

McCarthy changed his mind about the coffee, grumbling about the packaged cream. For the most part, he enjoyed giving his partner grief. At the moment, he thought old Mike had all he could handle. "How's she doing?"

"She's in a lot of pain."

"Dwier wants a statement." McCarthy referred to the acting captain with a sneer in his voice.

"I'll take care of it."

"He knows you're . . . friends with the victim. He wants me to get it."

"I'll take care of it," Michael repeated, dumping sugar in the coffee for energy more than taste. He'd stopped tasting it hours before. "Did you bring a stenographer?"

"Yeah. He's waiting."

"I'll see if Emma's ready." He chugged the coffee like medicine, then tossed the cup away. "How about the press?"

"They want something by two."

Michael checked his watch, then went to change. Fifteen minutes later, he went into her room. P.M. was with her now. Like the rest of them he looked a little worse for wear. Shocked, travel rumpled, and heavy eyed. But he'd made Emma smile.

"P.M.'s going to be a daddy," Emma said.

"Congratulations."

"Thanks." It was awkward, standing beside the bed, trying to think of the right things to say. The things not to say. Stevie had flown over from London with him, and they'd seen the paper at an airport newsstand. They'd barely known what to say to each other, much less what to say to Emma. "I'll be on my way." He kissed her, then paused and kissed her again. "We'll be back around tonight."

"Thanks for the flowers." She lifted a hand to the violas on her tray. "They're lovely."

"Well . . ." Heartsick, he stood for a moment, then left them alone.

"It's uncomfortable for him," Emma murmured. "For all of them." Her fingers worked restlessly at the bedsheets, then moved to brush at Charlie. "It's hard to see their eyes when they first walk in. I suppose I look pretty bad."

"That's the first time I've heard you fish for a compliment." He sat beside her. "People have been going in and out of here most of the day. You haven't gotten much rest."

"I don't really want to be alone. You stayed with me all night." She held out a hand. "I heard you talking to me and I knew I was still alive. I wanted to thank you for that."

"I love you, Emma." He dropped his forehead on their joined hands. There was no response from her as he fought to pull his raw emotions back in line. "Wrong time, wrong place." With a sigh, he rose and paced the room. "I guess you're going to have to think about it since I said it. Anyway, if you're feeling up to it, we'd like to get your statement."

She watched him roam restlessly around the room. There was nothing she could say, not now when she could barely feel. If things had been different . . . She wondered, if things had been different, if she would have reached out, if she could have trusted enough. But things weren't different.

"Who do I have to talk to?"

"You can talk to me." The control was back when he turned to her. "Or I can get a female officer if you'd be more comfortable."

"No." Her restless fingers began to pluck at the violas. "No, I can talk to you."

"There's a stenographer waiting."

"All right. We can do it now. I'd like to get it over with."

It wasn't easy. Somehow she'd thought it would be, with her emotions so deadened. But there were enough left, just enough to bring on the shame. She didn't look at him as she spoke. As time dragged on she told him everything. She hoped that by talking about all the fears, the shames and humiliations, she would be purged of them. But when it was done, she only felt tired.

Michael dismissed the steno with a nod. He couldn't speak, didn't dare.

"Is that all you need?" Emma asked.

He nodded again. He needed to get out. "We'll have it typed up. You can read it over when you're feeling up to it, and sign it. I'll check back later."

He swung out of the room and started for the elevators. McCarthy stopped him. "Dwier wants you back at the station ASAP. The press is foaming at the mouth."

"Fuck the press. I need to walk."

◆ ◆ ◆

*B*ACK IN LONDON, Robert Blackpool read the newspaper report. It amused the hell out of him. The Fleet Street stories were the best. All that murder-of-passion and death-of-a-dream nonsense. They'd gotten hold of a couple of pictures as well. They were grainy, a bit out of focus, but immensely satisfying. Emma being wheeled into an ambulance. Her face was a mess, and that pleased Blackpool very much.

He'd never forgotten the way she'd turned on him.

He thought it was a pity that Latimer hadn't beaten her to death. But then, there were other ways to pay back.

Picking up the phone, he called the London *Times*.

Pete was livid when he read the article the next day. Robert Blackpool, expressing deep sorrow at the death of a talented young artist like Latimer, related an incident that involved himself and Emma. From his slant, she had shown vicious jealousy over his relationship with her roommate. When her attempts at seduction had failed, she had tried to attack him with a pair of scissors.

The headlines were bold.

## THIRST FOR LOVE DRIVES EMMA TO VIOLENCE

It didn't take long for people to gobble up the reports. Opinions were now torn as to whether she had acted in self-defense or in a jealous rage when she had shot her husband.

Grabbing the phone, Pete dialed.

"You fucking lunatic."

"Ah, and good morning to you." Blackpool chuckled. He'd been expecting the call.

"What the hell do you think you're doing, spreading a story like that? I've got enough of a mess to clean up."

"It's not my mess, mate. If you ask me, little Emma got just what she deserved."

"I'm not asking you. And I'm telling you to back off."

"Why should I do that? I can use the publicity. You're the first one to say press sells records, aren't you?"

"I'm telling you to back off."

"Or?"

"I don't care to make threats, Robert. Just take me at my word when I tell you that scrounging up nasty secrets isn't healthy for anyone."

There was a long, humming pause. "I owed her this one."

"Perhaps. That isn't my concern. Your numbers have been slipping the last couple of years, Robert. Record companies are notoriously fickle. You wouldn't want to have to go digging about for a new manager at this stage, would you?"

"We go back, Pete. I doubt either of us wants to break up an old friendship."

"Remember it. Keep stirring things up and I'll drop you like a dirty sock."

"You need me as much as I need you."

"Oh, I doubt that." Pete smiled into the phone. "I doubt that very much."

# Chapter Thirty-eight

♦ ♦ ♦ ♦

*M*ICHAEL PACED THE corridor, stabbed out his cigarette, then paced again. "I don't like it."

"I'm sorry you feel that way." Emma took her breathing carefully. After three weeks, her ribs still tended to twinge if she moved the wrong way. "It's what I want to do, and what I feel is best."

"Holding a press conference the same day you're being released from the hospital is just stupid. And stubborn."

"I'm better off making a formal statement than trying to dodge them." She spoke lightly, but her arms were ice-cold under her linen jacket. "Believe me, I know more about this than you."

"If you're talking about that bullshit Blackpool started, it's already blown over. He did himself more damage than you."

"I don't care about Blackpool, but I do care about my family and what these last few weeks have put them through. And I want to have my say." She started to walk into the conference room, then stopped and turned back. "The police investigation ruled it self-defense. I've spent the last three weeks convincing myself of the same thing. I want my record clear, Michael."

It was useless to argue. He'd come to know her well enough to understand that. But he tried anyway. "The press has been behind you ninety-nine percent."

"And that one percent makes an ugly stain."

He relented enough to cross to her and brush a thumb over

her cheek. "Have you ever wondered why life gets so screwed up?"

"Yes." She smiled. "I've begun to believe that God really is a man. Are you coming in with me?"

"Sure."

The press was waiting. Cameras, lights, microphones at alert. Flashes went off the moment she stepped up to the podium. Murmurs accompanied them. She was very pale so that the healing bruises showed in vivid contrast on her skin. Though no longer swollen, her left eye was a mass of ugly fading colors that spread to cheekbone and hairline.

When she began to speak, they quieted.

She gave them only the facts, and not her feelings. She had learned that much. What she felt inside was hers alone. It was a brief statement, just over eight minutes. As she read, she was grateful that Pete had helped her refine it. She ignored the cameras and the faces that studied her. When she was done, she stepped back from the mike. It had already been established that she would not take questions, but the questions came.

She had turned away, her hand on Michael's arm when one penetrated.

"If he had abused you all those months, why did you stay?"

She didn't intend to answer, but she looked back. They were still hurling questions. Only that one lodged in her mind.

"Why did I stay?" she repeated. The room fell silent again. It had been easy to read the statement. She almost knew it by heart. It was just words printed on paper, and they hadn't touched her. But this, this one simple question drove straight into her heart.

"Why did I stay?" she said again. "I don't know." She fumbled, forgetting not to look at the faces, not to see them. It seemed vital that she answer the question. "I don't know," she said again. "If, two years ago, anyone had told me that I would allow myself to be brutalized, I would have been furious. I don't want to believe that I chose to be a victim." She sent Michael a quick, desperate look. "And yet I stayed. He beat me and humiliated me, but I didn't leave. There were times when I could see myself walking away. Getting in the elevator, going out to the street and walking away. But I didn't. I stayed because I was afraid, and I left for the same reason. So it makes no sense. It makes no sense," she repeated, and turned away. This time she ignored the questions.

"You did fine," Michael told her. "We're going to get you out the side here. McCarthy's got the car waiting."

They drove to Malibu, to the house on the beach that her father had rented. Emma rode in silence, with that one question echoing over and over in her head.

*Why did you stay?*

◆ ◆ ◆ ◆

SHE LIKED TO sit on the redwood terrace in the morning, watching the water and listening to the gulls. If she tired of sitting, she could take long walks along the shore. The outward side of abuse had healed. Her ribs still troubled her occasionally and there was a thin scar just under her jawline. It could have been repaired easily enough. But she discarded the idea of a plastic surgeon. It was barely noticeable. And it reminded her.

The nightmares were another legacy. They came with daunting regularity and were a montage of old and new. Sometimes she walked the darkened hallway as a child. Others as an adult. The music always came, but it was cloudy, as if it played underwater. At times she heard Darren's voice clear as a bell, but then Drew's would layer over it. She would freeze, child or woman, in front of the door. Terrified to open it.

Then as her hand closed over the knob, turned it, pushed, she would wake, sweating.

But the days were calm. There was a breeze off the water, the scent of flowers Bev had planted in tubs and window boxes. And always music.

She'd been given the chance to see her father and Bev start again. That soothed the most raw of her wounds. There was laughter. Bev experimenting in the kitchen, Brian in the shade playing guitar. At night she often lay in bed, thinking of them together. It was as if they had never been apart. How easy it had been once the step had been taken, for them to bridge the gap of twenty years.

And she wanted to weep, for she could never be a child again and fix the mistakes that had been made.

They waited six months, though Emma knew they were both anxious to get back to London. That was their home. She had yet to find hers.

She didn't miss New York, though she did miss Marianne. The months she had lived there with Drew had spoiled the city for her. She would go back, that she promised herself. But she would never live there again.

She preferred to watch the water, to feel the sun on her face. She'd been alone in New York. She was rarely alone here.

Johnno had visited twice, staying two weeks each time. For her birthday he'd given her a pin, a gold Phoenix rising out of a ruby flame. She wore it often, wishing for the courage to spread her wings again.

P.M. married Lady Annabelle, detouring to L.A. on their way to a honeymoon in the Mexican Caribbean. Watching the way the new Mrs. Ferguson doted on her husband nearly restored Emma's faith in the possibilities of marriage. Though plump and pregnant, Annabelle had worn a white leather mini to her wedding. P.M. was obviously delighted with her.

Even now they had company. Stevie and Katherine Haynes had arrived the night before. Long after she'd gone to bed, Emma had heard her father and Stevie playing. Like old times, she'd thought. The music had made her wistful for the days during her early childhood, when, as though she had been Cinderella, Brian had come to take her to a never-ending ball.

"Good morning."

She turned and saw Katherine holding two cups of coffee. "Hello."

"I saw you out here and thought you might like a cup."

"Thanks. It's a beautiful morning."

"Mmmm. I couldn't sleep through it." She chose a chair beside Emma. "Are we the only ones up?"

"Yes." She sipped at the coffee.

"Traveling makes me restless. I imagine you find a lot here to photograph."

Emma hadn't picked up a camera in more than a year, and was sure Katherine was aware of it. "It's a beautiful spot."

"A change from New York."

"Yes."

"Would you rather I went away?"

"No, I'm sorry." Emma's fingers began to tap against her mug. "I didn't mean to be rude."

"But I make you uncomfortable."

"Your profession does."

Katherine stretched out her legs to rest her ankles against the bottom rail. "I'm here as a friend, not as a doctor." She waited, watching a gull soar out to the water. "But I wouldn't be a good friend, or a good doctor, if I didn't try to help."

"I'm fine."

"You look fine. Not all wounds show though, do they?"

Emma looked at her then, calm and passionless. "Perhaps not, but they say time takes care of that."

"If that were true, I'd be out of business. Your parents are concerned, Emma."

"They needn't be. I don't want them to be."

"They love you."

"Drew's dead," Emma said. "He can't hurt me anymore."

"He can't beat you anymore," Katherine agreed. "But he can still hurt you." She lapsed into silence, sipping her coffee and watching the waves. "You're too polite to tell me to go to hell."

"I'm thinking about it."

With a light laugh, Katherine turned her head. "One day I'll tell you about all the rude and revolting things Stevie pulled on me. You might come close, but I doubt you could match him."

"Do you love him?"

"Yes."

"Are you going to marry him?"

Thrown a bit off stride, Katherine lifted one shoulder. "Ask me again in six months. Bev tells me you're seeing someone named Michael."

"He's a friend."

*I love you, Emma.*

"A friend," she repeated as she set the coffee aside.

"A detective, isn't he? The son of the man who investigated your brother's murder." Taking Emma's silence in stride, Katherine continued. "It's strange how life runs in circles, isn't it? Makes us feel a bit like a puppy chasing his own tail. I'd just finished a miserable divorce when I met Stevie. My ego was belly-down, and my opinion of men . . . Well, let's just say I found certain varieties of slugs more attractive. I detested Stevie on sight. That was personal. Professionally I was determined to help him, and get him out of my hair. Now here we are."

Though she no longer wanted it, Emma picked up the mug again and sipped the cooling coffee. "Did you feel as though you'd failed?"

"With my marriage?" Katherine kept her tone easy. It was a question she'd wondered if Emma would ask. "Yes. And I had.

But then people fail all the time. The hard part isn't even admitting it, it's accepting it."

"I failed with Drew, I accept that. Is that what you want me to say?"

"No. I don't want you to say anything unless you need to."

"I failed myself." She sprang up, slamming her mug on the little redwood table. "All those months, I failed myself. Is that the right answer?"

"Is it?"

On an oath, Emma turned to the rail. "I don't want to do this. If I'd wanted a psychiatrist, I could have had a dozen by now."

"You know, you made quite an impression on me the first time I saw you. You were about to storm out of Stevie's hospital room after giving him the dressing-down I'd been dying to give him. He didn't want help, either."

"I'm not Stevie."

"No, you're not." Katherine rose then. She wasn't as tall as Emma, but when her voice grew crisp, she projected total authority. "Would you like me to quote you statistics on how many women are abused every year? I believe it runs about one every eighteen seconds in this country. Surprised?" she asked when Emma stared at her. "Did you want to feel as if you were the only member of an exclusive club? How about how many of them stay with their abusers? It isn't always because they don't have friends or family who would help them. It isn't always because they're poor or uneducated. They're afraid, their self-respect has been shattered. They're ashamed, they're confused. For every one who finds help, there are a dozen more who don't. You're alive, Emma, but you haven't survived it. Not yet."

"No, I haven't." Emma spun around. Her eyes were damp, but there was fury behind them. "I have to live with it every day. Do you think talking about it helps, finding excuses, choosing reasons? What difference does it make why it happened? It happened. I'm going for a walk." She raced down the steps and headed toward the surf.

◆ ◆ ◆ ◆

KATHERINE WAS A patient woman. For two days she said nothing, made no reference to the talk she and Emma had had. She waited, while Emma kept a polite distance.

The days were anything but uneventful. Because it was her first trip to the States, Stevie wanted to show Katherine everything. They spent hours sightseeing, taking in all the tourist spots from the walk of the stars to Disneyland and Knott's Berry Farm. There were clubs in the evening. Sometimes they went alone, sometimes as a group. She liked best the nights they spent at home, with Stevie sitting for hours making love to his guitar.

But she thought incessantly about Emma. Stevie understood —perhaps that was why Katherine had fallen in love with him— that she had to help, even when help was rejected.

She took her chances when she heard Emma go downstairs before dawn one morning. Following her down, Katherine found all the lights shining. Emma was in the kitchen, sitting at the breakfast bar and staring out the dark window.

"I wanted some tea," Katherine said easily and walked to the stove. "I always find it comforting when I wake this early." She didn't comment on the tears drying on Emma's cheeks, but busied herself with cups and saucers. "I admire your mother. The way she adds a few touches and makes the kitchen the coziest room in the house. With mine, I always feel as though I'm standing in someone else's closet."

She measured out tea in a painted pot shaped like a cow.

"Stevie took me through the Universal Studios tour yesterday afternoon. Have you ever been?" She waited only a beat for Emma's response, then continued. "I got a close-up look at Jaws and wondered why the film had terrified me. But then it's all image and illusion." She poured the boiling water into the pot and let the tea steep. "The little tram rode by Norman Bates's house—you know, from *Psycho*? It looks exactly the same, just what you'd expect, but without the terror. It seems when you lift something out of context, even something frightening, it loses power. It becomes just an odd little house or a mechanical fish."

"Life isn't the same as films."

"No, but I've always thought there were interesting parallels. Would you like cream?"

"No. No, thank you." She was silent while Katherine poured the tea. Then the words came out before she could stop them. "Sometimes it's as though the time I spent with Drew was a film. Something I can look at, detached. And then, on mornings like this when I wake up before the light, I think I'm back in New York, in the apartment, and he's sleeping beside me. I can almost hear him breathing in the dark. Then the rest, these last months, are the film. Does that make me crazy?"

"No. It makes you a woman who lived through a terrible ordeal."

"But he's gone. I know he's gone. Why should I still be afraid?"

"Are you?"

She couldn't keep her hands still. She poked and pushed at items on the counter. A wine glass that hadn't been put away from the night before, a bowl of fresh fruit, the sugar bowl that matched the bovine teapot.

"He used to play tricks. After I'd told him about Darren, everything I remembered, everything I felt. He would get out of bed after I was asleep." It was all rushing out now, unstoppable. "He'd put on that song, the one that was playing the night Darren was killed. Then he'd call me, whispering my name over and over so that I'd wake in the dark hearing it. I'd always try to turn on the light, but he would have pulled out the plug so I would just sit there in bed, begging it to stop. Once I started screaming, he would come back. He would tell me it was all a dream. Now when I have the nightmares, I lie there in bed, frozen, terrified he's going to open the door and tell me it was all a dream."

"You had a nightmare tonight?"

"Yes."

"Can you tell me about it?"

"They're always basically the same. It's the night Darren was killed. I wake up just as I did. The hallway's dark, the music playing, and I'm afraid. I can hear him crying. Sometimes I get to the door, and Drew's there. Sometimes it's someone else, but I don't know who."

"Do you want to know?"

"Now I do, when I'm awake and I feel safe. But during the dream I don't. I feel as though I'll die if I do, if he touches me."

"You feel threatened by this man?"

"Yes."

"How do you know it's a man?"

"I . . ." She hesitated. The dark was lightening to gray. Because the window was open she could hear the early gulls, like children crying. "I don't know, but I'm sure it is."

"Are you threatened by men, Emma, because of what Drew did to you?"

"I'm not afraid of Da, or Stevie. I've never been afraid of Johnno or P.M. I couldn't be."

"And Michael?"

She picked up her tea for the first time, drinking it cold. "I'm not afraid he'd hurt me."

"But you are afraid?"

"That I wouldn't be able to—" She broke off, shaking her head. "This doesn't have anything to do with Michael. It's me."

"It's natural to be wary of a physical relationship, Emma, when your last experience brought only pain and humiliation. Intellectually you know that those aren't the purposes, or the usual result, of intimacy, but intellect and emotion run on different tracks."

Emma nearly smiled. "Are you saying the nightmares are a result of sexual repression?"

"I'm sure Freud would," Katherine said mildly. "But then I'm half convinced the man was a lunatic. I'm just exploring possibilities."

"I think we can rule Michael out. He's never asked me to have sex with him."

Not make love with, Katherine noted, but have sex with. She would file that for later. "Do you want him to?"

Now she did smile. Dawn had come, and with it, the safety of morning. "I've often wondered if psychiatrists are just gossips."

"Okay, we'll pass on that one. Can I make a suggestion?"

"All right."

"Get your camera, go out and take pictures today. Drew took a number of things from you. Why don't you prove to yourself that he didn't take everything?"

◆ ◆ ◆ ◆

EMMA WASN'T SURE why she took Katherine's advice. She could think of nothing she wanted to photograph. People had always been her favorite subject, but she'd shied away from them for so long. Still she had to admit it felt good to have the camera in her hand, to toy with lenses, to plan a particular shot.

She spent the morning focusing on palm trees and buildings. The shots wouldn't win any prizes, she knew, but the mechanics of photography were relaxing. By noon she'd used up two rolls and wondered why she'd waited so long to enjoy something she loved.

She wasn't sure why she pointed the car in the direction of Michael's house. It was a beautiful Sunday afternoon, too pretty to spend alone. She hadn't taken a picture of him since that first one years before. Conroy would make an interesting subject. Those were all easy excuses. She settled on them as she pulled up in front of his house.

Though his car was there, he didn't answer for so long she thought she'd missed him. The dog had begun to bark on her first knock and now could be heard howling and scratching on the other side of the door. She heard Michael swear at him and grinned.

The moment he opened the door she knew she'd awakened him. It was past noon, but his eyes were heavy and unfocused. He wore only a pair of jeans, obviously tugged on hastily and still half zipped. He dragged a hand over his face and back into his hair.

"Emma?"

"Yes. I'm sorry, Michael. I should have called."

He blinked against the sunlight. "Is something wrong?"

"No. Listen, I'll go on. I was just out riding around."

"No, come on in." He reached for her hand as he glanced over his shoulder. "Shit."

"Michael, really, it's a bad time. I can just—" She'd stepped over the threshold. The dim light had her narrowing her eyes. "Oh my." She couldn't think of anything else. The living room looked as though it had been run over by a group of particularly vicious elves. "Have you been robbed?"

"No." He was too groggy to worry about appearances and took her arm to drag her back to the kitchen. The dog continued to bark and leap in circles around them.

"You must have had a party," she decided and felt a bit miffed that he hadn't asked her to come.

"No. Please God, let there be coffee," he muttered, pushing through the cupboards.

"Here." She found the can of Maxwell House in the sink with a bag of potato chips. "Would you like me to—"

"No." He brushed her aside. "I can make the damn coffee. Conroy, if you don't shut up I'm going to tie your tongue around your neck." In defense, he took the chips and set the bag on the floor for the dog to enjoy. "What time is it?"

Emma cleared her throat. She decided it would be unwise to point out that there was a clock on the coffee maker. "About twelve-thirty."

He was scowling at the coffee scoop in his hand. Obviously, he'd lost track. As he began to add more, Emma lifted her camera and shot. "I'm sorry," she said when he glared at her. "It's reflex."

He said nothing, but turned to root through the cupboards again. His mouth felt as though he'd dined on chalk. There was a jazz combo jamming gleefully in his head. He was sure his eyes had swollen to the size of golf balls, and, he discovered, he was out of fucking cereal.

"Michael . . ." Emma trod carefully, not because she was intimidated, but because she was deathly afraid she would laugh. "Would you like me to fix you some breakfast?"

"I can't find any."

"Sit down." She had to clear her throat again as she pushed him to a chair. "We'll start with coffee. Where are your cups?"

"In the kitchen."

"Okay." After a search, she found a package of Styrofoam cups, jumbo size. She poured the coffee. It looked as thick as mud and just as appetizing, but he guzzled it. As the caffeine kicked in, he saw her with her head in his refrigerator.

She looked great, absolutely great, with a little cropped blouse and breezy summer pants in pale blue. Her hair was loose. He liked it best loose so he could imagine running his hands through it. But what was she doing with her head in his refrigerator?

"What are you doing?"

"Fixing you breakfast. You have one egg. How would you like it?"

"Cooked." He drained the cup and hobbled back for another dose.

"Your bologna's green, and there's something in here that might be alive." She took out the egg, a hunk of cheese, and a heel of bread. "I've never seen things move in a refrigerator before. Got a skillet?"

"I think so. Why?"

"Never mind." She found it eventually and with a little invention managed to fix him an open-face egg-and-cheese sandwich. She settled on a flat ginger ale and sat across from him as he ate. "Michael, not to intrude, but could I ask how long you've been living this way?"

"I bought the place about four years ago."

"And you're still alive. You're a strong man, Michael."

"I've been thinking about getting it cleaned."

"Think bulldozers."

"It's hard to get insulted when I'm eating." He watched her take a picture of Conroy, who had gone back to sleep with his paws crossed over the bag of chips. "He'll never sign a release form."

She smiled at him. "Feeling better?"

"Almost human."

"I was out—decided it was time to start working again. I thought you might like to tag along for a few hours." She felt shy suddenly. It was different now that he was fully awake, watching her over the remains of the breakfast she'd fixed him. "I know you've been busy the last few weeks."

"Tackling crime single-handed. Conroy, you lazy mutt, go fetch." The dog opened one eye and grumbled. "Go on." He gave what sounded like a very human sigh as he dragged himself up and out. "You've been avoiding me, Emma."

She started to deny it. "Yes. I'm sorry. You've been a good friend, and I—"

"If you start on that friendship-and-gratitude business again, you're only going to piss me off." He took the pack of cigarettes Conroy dropped in his lap, then rose to let the dog out.

"I won't mention it again."

"Good." He turned back. Six months he'd waited, hoping she'd come knocking on his door. Now that she had, he couldn't kick the anger. "Why did you come here?"

"I told you."

"You wanted company while you took some pictures, and you thought about good old Michael."

She set the bottle of ginger ale down and rose stiffly. "Obviously I should have thought again. I'm sorry I disturbed you."

"Walk in and walk out," he murmured. "That's a bad habit of yours, Emma."

"I didn't come here to fight with you."

"That's too damn bad. It's long past time we had this out."

He took a step toward her. She retreated. Nothing she could have done would have infuriated him more.

"I'm not Latimer, goddammit. I'm sick to death of you thinking of him every time I get close. If we're going to fight, it's going to be you and me and nobody else."

"I don't want to fight." Before she'd realized she'd done it, she picked up the bottle and threw it. Glass and ginger ale exploded in the sink. She stood, stunned, as the fizzing died away.

"Want another?"

"I have to go." She reached for her camera, but he moved and laid a hand over hers.

"Not this time." His voice wasn't calm. When she looked up at him, she braced, waiting. "You're not going to walk out on me again, Emma. Not until I've said what I need to say."

"Michael—"

"Just shut up. I've wanted you for as long as I can remember. That day all those years ago, that day on the beach when I took you home, I had such a crush on you I could hardly see. I was barely seventeen and I couldn't think of anyone but you for weeks after. I haunted that beach, waiting for you to come back."

"I couldn't." She turned away, but made no attempt to leave.

"I got over it." Michael shook a cigarette out of the pack, then slammed through the kitchen drawers looking for a match. "I thought I'd gotten over it, and then you came back. There I am minding my own business, cutting the lawn, and you're standing in front of me. I could hardly breathe. Dammit, I wasn't a boy anymore and it wasn't a crush."

She had to struggle to find her voice. It was a different kind of fear now. Dozens of nerves jumping to tangle over each other. "You hardly knew me."

He shifted his gaze to meet hers. "You know better, Emma. There was something there, when we sat on the beach. The first time I kissed you. The only time. I've never forgotten it. I haven't been able to. Then you walked away."

"I had to."

"Maybe you did." He pitched his cigarette out the door and let the screen slam shut. "The time wasn't right, that's what I told myself. Christ, I've been telling myself that for years." He crossed to her. He could feel her tremble when he took her arms, but he didn't let go. Not this time. "When is the time going to be right, Emma?"

"I don't know what you want me to say."

"That's bullshit. You know just what I want you to say."

"I can't."

"Won't," he corrected. "Because of him. Dammit, you broke my heart when you married him, and I had to live with that. It seems like I've spent half my life trying to get over you. Maybe I could have done it, but you came back again."

"I—" She moistened her dry lips. "I couldn't help that, either."

Something came into his eyes that had her holding her breath. "I told myself this time it would be different. I was going to make it different. And then . . . When I found out what he'd done to you I almost went crazy. I've been afraid to touch you, all these months. Give her time, that's what I kept telling myself. Give her time to get over it. The hell with it."

He pulled her close and covered her mouth with his.

# Chapter Thirty-nine
• • • •

IT WASN'T WHAT she expected. She was trapped. There was no denying that she was trapped against him, his body strong and hard and tense, his mouth like a fire on hers. She'd thought she would be revolted, or terrified to find herself held tight by a man again. But those weren't her feelings. What emotions rushed into her came so quickly her head spun. Warmth and pleasure and an ice-edged spear of desire.

She didn't want to give herself to them, or to him. How could she when it meant handing her control over to someone else again? But before she could fight, he was drawing away.

He didn't speak, just looked at her. Wide-eyed, breath quickened, she stood absolutely still. Yes, she was trapped, Emma realized. But it didn't seem to matter. Because she was feeling again, really feeling, in a way she'd long ago accepted she was incapable of.

The anger had drained out of him so that only his needs remained. "I don't want you to be afraid of me."

It would be her choice. She could see that in his eyes. If she was trapped, it was her own longings, her own dreams, that held her prisoner. "I'm not."

His hands had gentled on her shoulders. She didn't protest when he slid them up to frame her face. Nor did she try to pull away when his lips touched hers again. Gently now, and soft. Her muscles went lax even as her pulse scrambled. Her choice, she thought again, and one she'd taken much too long to make.

Then her mind filled up with him so completely there was room for nothing else.

He felt the change, the slow, hesitant response as her lips parted beneath his, as her body seemed to melt against him. He was trembling himself as he skimmed kisses over her face. Then her arms came around him and she found his lips with her own.

He lifted her up. It seemed the only way to love her this first time. He continued to kiss her, light and promising, deep and drugging, as he carried her into the bedroom.

The shades were drawn so that the sun beat against them in yellow waves. He wished it could have been candlelight.

Emma tried not to stiffen when he laid her on the bed. She knew it would go quickly now. She wanted him to go on kissing her, holding her. But she knew better. She thought she knew better.

He was beside her. He didn't roll on top of her and tug at her clothes. His mouth sought hers again, to seduce as much as to reassure. Though her body was taut as wire, she seemed so fragile. Her skin, her mouth, the scent that he could wallow in when he buried his face in her hair. Her fingers brushed hesitantly over his bare chest, nearly driving him mad.

With a little moan of pleasure, he began to tease her tongue with his. Her taste ran through him like a warm river. He moved slowly, confusing her. Seducing her. She waited for him to take, but he continued to give.

His hands ran over her, making her shudder. But there was no fear in it. Here, at last, was generosity. Here, at last, was compassion. A pleasure so deep and dark coursed through her that she moved against him, hands clutching. Greed poured into her. She hadn't known she could feel it, not for a man. Her hands were in his hair, dragging his mouth back to hers so that she could sink into those hot, wet kisses.

When he drew back, she moaned in protest and reached for him.

"I want to look at you," he told her. "I've waited a long time to look at you here."

She could only stare, bewildered and aching as he brushed his hands through her hair, watching the way it fell from his fingers onto the pillow. He continued to watch her face as he slowly unbuttoned her blouse. He could see the confusion in her eyes, and the cloudy haze of desire. It made it easy to be tender.

When she lifted a hand to cover herself, he took it, pressed her fingers to his lips. With her hand still in his, he lowered his mouth to her breast. A groan escaped him. She was small and firm. Sweet. Unbearable.

Her skin fired with the slightest touch. He filled himself with her, the taste, the smooth silky texture. He could hear her breath, as fast and shallow as his own. Her body arched as he peeled the blouse from her.

His mouth was everywhere. She shivered from the heat as he ranged quick, openmouthed kisses over her face, her shoulders, then gently, torturously, down her rib cage. She jolted when he used his teeth, but there was no pain. Only delirium. He drew down her slacks, inch by maddening inch, following the path with his lips.

She wanted. She had never wanted before. Only dreamed. Her body was slick with sweat, writhing with need, but he continued to kiss and caress, making her claw at the sheets as he nibbled on the back of her knee.

The heat was unbearable, yet she wanted more. As his fingers skimmed up her thighs, her body convulsed. She couldn't draw air. A roaring filled her head, bolted through her system, terrifying her. With a wild mixture of pleasure and fear, she reared up. The climax slammed into her, a velvet fist, which had her falling back, gasping.

"My God, you're sweet." He could barely breathe himself as he brought his mouth back to sear hers. Before her shudders had stopped, he was driving her up again. She wanted to scream out his name, but could only whisper it as her hands slid over his damp skin.

"Please." Her breath was sobbing out now. Sensation after sensation poured into her body until it was a mass of fevered pleasure. Yet it wasn't enough. It wasn't nearly enough. "I want . . ." She cried out again, flinging out a hand and sending something crashing.

"Tell me." He was crazed to hear it. The pressure had built to a pitch he'd never experienced. Yet he held back. "Look at me, and tell me."

She opened her eyes. His face was all she could see, and in his eyes, she saw herself. "I want you." Reaching up, she dragged his mouth to hers. She cried out again when he filled her.

◆ ◆ ◆

$S$HE SLEPT FOR an hour, exhausted, across his bed. He'd sat beside her for a long time, stroking her hair and wondering how to keep her in his life. Even being in love with her all that time hadn't prepared him for what it would be like to be her lover. He'd imagined it. Countless times. But whenever he had, he'd had only women as comparisons.

There was no one like Emma.

If he had to beg, he'd beg. If he had to fight, he'd fight. But he wasn't going to lose her again.

When she woke, he was gone. She lay, stomach down, across the bed, trying to adjust her mind to what had happened to her body. It seemed impossible that she had felt all those things, done all those things, without a moment of regret or hesitation. Even hours before, she had been certain she would never want to be touched again. And yet, perhaps today was the first time she truly had been touched. Smiling, she rolled over and thought idly about getting dressed and finding him.

Then she saw his gun. It was still holstered, the strap slung across the back of a chair a few feet from the bed. She had used a gun, Emma remembered. Though much of that last horror with Drew came only in vague patches, she could clearly see those final moments. She could remember how it had felt to wrap her hands around the gun, to pull the trigger. To kill.

To know she was capable of that made her stomach coil into knots. She had loved and married and killed in a little less than two years. Now, she had the rest of her life to wonder how she could have done any one of the three.

When the bedroom door swung open, she groped automatically for the sheet.

"Good. You're up." Michael strolled in carrying a bucket of chicken and a six-pack of Cokes. "I thought you might get hungry."

He'd pulled an LAPD T-shirt on with his jeans. But he was still barefoot. To Emma he looked more like a beachcomber than a man who would fire a gun. Before she could answer, he leaned down and kissed her in a way that had her mind clouding again.

"Figured we could have a picnic."

"A picnic," she echoed. "Where?"

"Right here." He dropped the bucket of chicken on the bed.

"That way the neighbors won't be shocked because you're naked."

She laughed. "I could get dressed."

He sat on the bed across from her and took a long look. "I really wish you wouldn't." Grinning, he twisted the top off a Coke. "Want some music?" He leaned over and punched a button on his clock radio. Linda Ronstadt soared over "Blue Bayou." Getting down to business, he peeled the top off the bucket and dug in. "Aren't you hungry?"

The scent of the chicken was glorious. Emma watched him take a bite and dragged a hand through her tousled hair. "I can't eat naked."

"Sure you can." He held out the drumstick. She shifted, took a bite, then laughed again.

"Really, I can't."

Michael dropped the chicken back in the bucket, then dragged his shirt off. He pulled it over her head. "Better?"

Emma worked her arms through. "Lots." The shirt smelled of him. It amazed her that it made her every bit as hungry as the chicken did. "I've never had a picnic in bed before."

"Same principle as a blanket on the beach. We eat, listen to music, and then I make love with you. This way we avoid the sand."

She took the bottle he offered and drank to ease a dry throat. "I don't know how all this happened."

"That's okay. I'll be glad to run through it all again for you."

"Was it—" She broke off, annoyed with herself.

"You weren't going to ask if it was good for me, were you?"

"No." He was grinning at her. "Sort of." She took another bite of chicken. "Never mind."

Delighted with her, with himself, with everything, he ran a fingertip down her bare arm. "You want like a scale of one to ten?"

"Shut up, Michael."

"Just as well, because you went right off the scale."

He only flustered her. "It's never been like that for me before," she murmured. "I've never . . . I didn't think I could—" She broke off again, then taking a deep breath got the rest out of her system. "I thought I was frigid."

He nearly laughed, but he could see by her face that it wasn't a joke. Latimer again, Michael thought and had to take several seconds to control his voice. "You thought wrong."

His careless response was exactly the right one. Looking up again, she smiled. "If I had followed my instincts that day on the beach when I kissed you, I'd have known differently a long time ago."

"Why don't you follow them now?"

She hesitated. Rising up to her knees, she linked her arms around his neck and kissed him. Michael tossed the half-eaten drumstick over his shoulder. She was laughing when they rolled over the bed.

◆ ◆ ◆ ◆

"STAY TONIGHT."

The sun was going down as she started to dress. "Not tonight. I need to think."

"I was afraid you'd start thinking again." He reached for her, holding her against him. "I love you, Emma. Why don't you think about that?"

Her only response was to close her eyes.

"I need you to believe me."

"I want to believe you," she told him. "I don't trust my own judgment right now. Not so long ago I thought Drew loved me, and that I loved him. I was wrong on both counts."

"Goddammit, Emma." Biting off the words, he moved away to pull up the shade. Twilight crept in.

"I'm not comparing you."

"Aren't you?"

"No." She knew he couldn't understand how far she had come already to be able to go to him and rest her cheek against his back. "It's me I'm not sure of. My problems didn't start with Drew. It would be difficult enough if they had. I have to be sure I know what I want before I ask for it again."

"I'm not going to settle for one day with you."

She sighed and kissed his shoulder. "Da and Bev will be going back to England soon."

He turned at that. She could see the glint of fury in his eyes in the dying light. "If you're thinking about going back with them, think again."

"You can't bully me, Michael. I'm past that." Until she'd said the words, she hadn't realized they were true. "I'm thinking of staying on at the beach house. They need to get on with their lives and I need to decide what I want to do with the rest of mine."

"And you want me to back off?"

"Not too far." She put her arms around him again. "I don't want to lose you, I'm sure of that. I just don't know what to do about it yet. Can we leave things as they are for now, for a little while longer?"

"All right. But understand this. I'm not going to wait forever."

"Neither am I."

# Chapter Forty

• • • •

STRAINING FOR PATIENCE, Michael propped his feet on his desk and studied the ceiling. The high, excited voice in the phone receiver rambled on and on. They would haul the little weasel in as a material witness sooner or later, he knew. He just wanted it to be sooner.

"Listen, pal," he interrupted at length. "I got the impression Springer was your friend. Yeah, well, talk's cheap. He may have been a worthless two-bit bagman, but once we get the stiff, we take a personal interest." He paused, listened to another moment of babbling. No one was more uncooperative than a jumpy witness with a fistful of priors.

"That's fine. You don't want to come in, we'll find you." He glanced up as the sergeant dropped a load of files and mail on his desk. "Take your chances on the street. We've always got room for one more at the morgue." He listened as he pushed through the files. "Good choice. Ask for Detective Kesselring."

Michael hung up and scowled at the paperwork. He'd hoped for five minutes to call Emma, but the odds were against it. Resigned, he tuned out the noise of the squad room and went for the mail first.

"Hey, Kesselring, we need your ten bucks for the Christmas party."

Michael decided if he heard the word "Christmas" again, he'd shoot somebody. Preferably Santa himself. "McCarthy owes me twenty. Get it from him."

"Hey." Hearing his name, McCarthy wandered over. "Where's your holiday spirit?"

"In your wallet," Michael told him.

"Still sulking 'cause his lady's going to spend Christmas in London? Lighten up, Kesselring, the world's full of blondes."

"Kiss off."

McCarthy put a hand over his heart. "Must be love."

Ignoring him, Michael studied the manila envelope. It was odd when he was thinking such dark thoughts about London that he would get a letter from that city. A law firm, he mused, skimming the return address. What would a London law firm want with him? When he opened it, he found a cover letter and an envelope in shades of pink and blue. Turning the envelope over, he saw another return address in fancy script. Jane Palmer.

Though he wasn't a superstitious man, he stared at the envelope for several minutes, thinking about messages from the dead. He slit it open and studied the cramped handwriting. Within five minutes, he was standing in his father's office watching Lou read the letter.

> Dear Detective Kesselring,
>     You investigated the death of Brian McAvoy's son. I'm sure you remember the case. I remember it also. If you're still interested, you should come to London and talk to me. I know all about it. It was my idea, but they made a mess of it. If you will pay for information, we can work out a deal.
>
>                                          Yours truly,
>                                          Jane Palmer

"What do you think?" Michael demanded.

"I think she might have known something." Lou adjusted his glasses and read the letter through again. "She was six thousand miles away when it went down, and we could never tie her to it. But . . ." He had always wondered.

"The first postmark's just a few days before her body was found. According to the lawyers the letter bounced around because of the incomplete address, then ended up with the rest of her papers. Over eight months," Michael said in disgust.

"I'm not sure it would have made a difference if it had been eight days. She'd still have been dead."

"If she was telling the truth and knew who killed the kid, someone could have gotten to her. Someone who didn't know she'd send off a letter. I want to see the report, talk to the investigating officer."

Lou turned the letter over in his hand. There wasn't any purpose in reminding Michael that the letter had been addressed to the investigating officer on the case. "It's possible. It's the first lead we've had on this in nearly twenty years." He remembered the police photograph of a little boy, and looked up at his son. "I guess you're going to London."

♦ ♦ ♦ ♦

*E*MMA ROLLED OUT cookie dough and tried to put her heart into it. She'd always loved Christmas. This year, for the first time since childhood, she would be spending it with her family. The kitchen smelled of cinnamon and brown sugar, carols were playing through the speakers, and Bev was measuring out ingredients for plum pudding. Outside, a light snow was falling.

But her heart wasn't in it. She was afraid it was six thousand miles away, with Michael.

As Emma pressed the cutters into the dough, Bev slipped an arm around her. "I'm so glad you're here, Emma. It means everything to me, and your father."

"And to me." She scooped up a cookie in the shape of a snowflake and laid it on the baking sheet. "You used to let me do this when I was little. If Johnno was around, he'd come in and pinch a few before they were even cooked."

"Why do you think I sent him off with Bri?" She watched Emma sprinkle colored sugar over the tops. "You miss Michael, don't you?"

"I didn't know I would. Not this much." She carried the tray to the oven. "It's silly. It's only two weeks." After setting the timer, she walked back to ball the dough together and roll it again. It felt good to do something with her hands, to feel competent. In charge. "It's probably good for me to get away. I don't want to get too involved too quickly."

"Katherine says you're making wonderful progress."

"I think I am. I'm grateful to her for staying on with me in L.A. for the last couple of months. I wasn't always," she added with a smile. "But talking things out helped."

"You're still having nightmares."

"Not as often. And I'm getting back to work, finally pushing through with the book." She paused with a cookie cutter in her hand. "A year ago, Christmas was a nightmare. This year, it's almost perfect." She glanced over as the kitchen door swung open. The cookie cutter clattered to the floor. "Michael?"

"The housekeeper said I should just come back."

She didn't think. She didn't need to. With a cry of pleasure, she raced into his arms. Before he could speak again, her mouth was on his.

"I can't believe you're here." She pulled back, laughed, and began to dust him off. "I've got flour all over you."

"I'm sure I can find a dozen things to do." Bev wiped her hands on a cloth and slipped out the door.

"You said you couldn't come," Emma began.

"I had a change in schedule." He drew her close again, wanting another taste. Desire rippled through him as her mouth moved warm under his. "Merry Christmas."

"How long can you stay?"

"A couple of days." He glanced over toward the stove. "What's that noise?"

"Oh, my cookies." She dashed over to turn off the timer and rescue them. "I was thinking of you when I made these. And wishing you weren't so far away." Turning, tray in hand, she looked at him. "I'll go back with you if you want."

"You know I want." He ran a hand down her braid. "I also know that you need time with your family. I'll be waiting for you when you get home."

"I love you." The words went through her heart to her mind so quickly it stunned her. The tray clattered as she dropped it on the rangetop.

"Say it again."

His eyes were so dark and intense she lifted a hand to his cheek to soothe. "I love you, Michael. I'm sorry it's taken me so long to get it out."

Saying nothing, he pulled her close and held her. For a moment, everything he'd ever wanted was within the circle of his arms.

"I knew when I saw you in New York, at my showing. As soon as I saw you, I knew." With a combination of relief and pleasure she turned her face into his throat. "It scared me. It seems I've been scared for years. Then when you walked in the door just now, it all fell into place."

"You won't be able to shake me off now."

"Good." She tilted her head up to his. "How about a cookie?"

◆ ◆ ◆ ◆

*H*E MADE EXCUSES. Michael didn't enjoy lying to Emma, but he felt it best that the business that had brought him to London remain his for a while longer. He found his British counterparts polite and tidy. He also discovered that British red tape was every bit as convoluted as American.

It took him two hours to be told he would have to come back the next day for a look at the files.

It was time well spent. Emma was thrilled at the opportunity to show him London, steering him from the Tower to Piccadilly, to the changing of the guards to Westminster Abbey. Though he'd been easily persuaded to stay in the McAvoys' home, he'd kept his hotel room. After the frantic tour, they spent hours in bed.

The files were little help to him. A standard investigation had ultimately ruled death by misadventure. Forensics had turned up no prints other than Jane's, her former maid's, and those of the dealer who had found the body. Both his and the maid's alibis were airtight. The neighbors had nothing good to say about the deceased, but they hadn't seen anything or anyone on the night of her death.

Michael skimmed through the police photographs. And people called him a slob, he mused as he studied the filth in which Jane had lived and died. Frustrated that the scene had long since been cleaned out, he went over the pictures again with a magnifying glass.

Inspector Carlson, who had been in charge of the Palmer investigation, looked on patiently.

"It was a bit of a sty," he pointed out. "To be frank, I've never seen anything quite like it. Or smelled anything like it. The old girl had cooked for a couple of days."

"No prints but hers on the syringe?"

"No. She did the job herself." Carlson removed his horn-rims to polish the lenses. "We debated suicide, but it simply didn't fit. As it says in the report, it appears that she obtained the heroin, was too strung out to remember to cut it down, and took a quick last ride."

"Where'd she get the horse? This guy Hitch?"

The inspector pursed his lips. "He's small-time. Doesn't have the connections to deal anything that pure."

"If not him, then who?"

"We've never been able to ascertain. We assumed she'd made the buy herself. She was a bit of a celebrity in her day and had a number of connections."

"You've seen the letter she sent to my department."

"That's why we're willing to reopen the case, Detective. If indeed we've had a murder here that connects with a murder in your country, you'll have our complete cooperation." He settled the horn-rims comfortably on his hooked nose. "It's been nearly twenty years, but none of us has forgotten what happened to Darren McAvoy."

No, no one had forgotten, Michael thought as he sat in Brian's oak-paneled office and watched the man read his ex-lover's letter.

There was a fire crackling cheerfully in the hearth across the room. Easy chairs were placed cozily in front of it. Awards and plaques and photographs lined the shelves and walls. There were a few cardboard boxes, a testament to the fact he'd only moved in weeks before. His desk looked more like an executive's than a rock star's. Glossy and piled with files and papers. Against the wall was a Yamaha keyboard and synthesizer, along with a huge reel-to-reel tape recorder. There was only mineral water and soft drinks in the bar. Michael waited until Brian looked up.

"My father and I discussed it. We thought you should know."

Shaken, Brian groped for a cigarette. "You think it's genuine."

"Yes."

He fumbled with his lighter. There was a bottle of Irish whiskey in the bottom drawer of his desk—still sealed. It was a test to himself. In the six weeks and three days since he'd tipped a bottle, he'd never wanted a drink more.

"Sweet Jesus, I thought I knew what she was capable of. I can't understand this." He dragged in smoke like a drowning man sucks air. "If she was—why would she have wanted to hurt him?" He buried his face in his hands. "Me. She wanted to hurt me."

"We're still of the opinion that the death was an accident." Hardly words of comfort, Michael thought. "Logically, kidnapping and the ransom you would have paid were the motives."

"I was already paying her for Emma." He scrubbed his face with his hands, then dropped them on the desk. "She would have killed Emma, snapped her neck right before my eyes. She was capable of that in a rage. But to plan something like this." Lifting his face again, he shook his head. "I can't believe she could do it."

"She had help."

He rose then, all but lunged from the chair to roam the room. It was full of the tangible proof of his success. Gold records, platinum records, Grammys, American Music Awards. Signs that the music he had created was important.

Jockeying for space with them were dozens of photographs. Devastation, yesterday and today, Brian with other singers, musicians, politicians he'd supported, celebrities. There was a framed snapshot among them, of Emma and his lost son, sitting on the banks of a little creek and smiling into the sunlight. He had created them as well.

Twenty years dissolved in an instant, and he was back on the sun-dappled grass, listening to the laughter of his children. "I thought I'd put this behind me." He rubbed his fingers over his eyes and turned away from the picture. "I don't want Bev to know, not yet. I'll tell her when I think the time's right."

"That's up to you. I wanted you to know I'm going to reopen the case."

"Are you as dedicated as your father?"

"I'd like to think so."

With a nod, Brian accepted that. Whatever bond had been forged on that horrible night two decades before had yet to be broken. But he had another child to consider. "What about Emma? Are you going to put her through all the questioning again?"

"I'll do everything I can to keep Emma from being hurt."

He opened a bottle of ginger ale. A poor substitute for whiskey. "Bev seems to think you're in love with her."

"I am." Michael shook his head at the offer of a drink. "I'm going to marry her as soon as she's ready."

Brian stood where he was and drank. The thirst was unbearable. "I didn't want her involved with Drew. For all the wrong reasons. I've had the opportunity to ask myself, If I hadn't pushed her, if I hadn't objected so strongly, would she have waited?"

"Latimer wanted you and what you could do for him. I only want Emma. I always have."

With a sigh, Brian sat again. "She has always been the most constant and beautiful part of my life. Something I made thoughtlessly that turned out perfectly right." With a ghost of a smile, so much like his daughter's, he looked at Michael. "You made me nervous the day Emma brought you to that miserable house of P.M.'s in Beverly Hills. I looked at you and thought, This boy is going to take Emma away from me. Must be the Irish," he said as he drank again. "It seems the lot of us are drunks or poets or seers. I've had a chance to be all three."

"I can make her happy."

"I'll hold you to it." He picked up the letter again. "As important as it is to me for you to find who killed my son, it's more important that you make Emma happy."

"Da, P.M. and Annabelle have brought the baby. Oh, I'm sorry." Emma stopped with her hand on the knob. "I didn't know you were here, Michael."

"You were shopping when I got back." He stood, casually taking the letter from Brian and slipping it into his pocket.

"What's wrong?"

"Nothing." Brian came around the desk to kiss her. "I've been grilling Michael. It seems he has ideas about my daughter."

She smiled, on the verge of believing it before she saw her father's eyes. "What is it?"

"I've just told you." He put an arm around her shoulders and would have led her out, but she turned to Michael.

"I won't be lied to."

"I do have ideas about his daughter," Michael countered.

She shrugged off the arm around her shoulder and stood firm. "Will you let me see the envelope that's in your pocket?"

"Yes, but I'd rather do it later."

"Da, would you leave us alone a moment."

"Emma—"

"Please."

Reluctantly he closed the door behind him and left them alone.

"I trust you, Michael," she began. "If you tell me that the only thing you and Da talked about in this room was our relationship, I'll believe you."

He started to. He wanted to. "No, it's not all we talked about. Will you sit?"

It was going to be bad. She found herself gripping her hands together in her lap as she had done since her school days when she was afraid to hear what she had to hear. Instead of speaking, Michael took the envelope out of his pocket and handed it to her.

Ice prickled along her skin as she saw the name on the back of the envelope. A message from the dead, she thought, and wished she could have laughed at the phrase. She opened the letter and sat in silence reading it.

She was so much like her father, Michael noted. Her expressions, the way grief came into her eyes, the quiet way she held herself as she coped with it. Before she spoke, she folded the letter again and gave it back to him.

"This is why you're here?"

"Yes."

Her eyes were dark and wretched when they met his. "I wanted to think you couldn't stay away from me."

"I can't."

She lowered her head again. It was so difficult to think when the ache came this way, marching hard. "Do you believe this letter?"

"It's not up to me to believe," he said carefully. "I'm following it up."

"I believe it." Emma had a flash of her last clear image of Jane, standing in the doorway of the dirty house, her face shadowed with bitterness. "She only wanted to hurt Da. She wanted to make him suffer. I still remember the way she looked at him the day he took me away. I was only a baby really, but I remember."

She took a ragged breath. Tears were useless now. "How is it possible to love and hate a person as she did? How is it possible to take those feelings and distort them so completely that you could play a part in taking a little boy's life? It's been almost twenty years, but she still wants him to suffer."

He crouched beside her and took the envelope that lay in her lap. "Maybe that's true, but she may have started something that will help us find out who killed him, and why."

"I know." She closed her eyes tight. "It's buried somewhere deep inside me, but I know. This time I'm going to dig it out."

♦ ♦ ♦ ♦

*W*HEN THE MUSIC started she was standing in the dark doorway in her favorite nightgown, clutching Charlie. Darren was crying. She wanted to go back to bed, back to her own bed and the glow of the night-light. But she'd promised to take care of him, and he was crying.

She stepped out, but her foot didn't touch the floor. It seemed to float on a dark gray cloud. She could hear the hissing, the dry skittering of the *things* that liked the dark. The things that ate bad little girls, like her mam had told her.

She didn't know which way to go. It was too dark and there were sounds everywhere, under and over the music that wouldn't stop. She walked toward her crying brother, trying to be small, so small no one could see. She could feel the sweat running down her back.

She had her hand on the knob. Turned it slowly. Pushed the door. Open.

Hands gripped her arms, twisting.

"I told you not to run away from me, Emma." Drew slipped a hand around her throat and squeezed. "I told you I'd find you."

"Emma!" Michael caught her flailing arms and pulled her close. "Wake up. Emma, wake up. It's just a dream."

She couldn't get her breath. Even when she realized where she was and who was holding her, it seemed that Drew still had his hands locked around her throat.

"The light." She dragged the words out. "Please, turn on the light."

"All right. Hang on." He shifted, dragging her with him as he hit the switch. "There. Now look at me. Emma, look at me." He put a hand firmly under her chin and held it. She was still shuddering, and in the gleam of the lamp her face was marble-white, sheened with sweat. "It was a dream," he said quietly. "You're with me."

"I'm all right."

He pulled the sheet up around her shivering shoulders. "I'm going to get you some water." When she nodded he slipped out of bed into the adjoining bath. Emma brought her knees close to her chest, listening to the sound of water hitting glass. She knew where she was. In the hotel room with Michael. She'd wanted one night alone with him before he went back to the States. Though she knew it had only been a dream, she lifted a hand to her throat. She could still feel the grip of Drew's fingers.

"Drink a little."

She sipped. It didn't burn as she'd feared. "I'm sorry, Michael."

He wasn't interested in apologies. Nor did he want her to know he was as shaken as she. She'd sounded as though she had been choking in sleep, trying to gasp for air that was trapped in her throat.

"How often do you have these?"

"Too often."

"Is this why you wouldn't ever spend the night with me before?"

She moved her shoulders and looked miserably into the glass.

"You're too beautiful to be a jerk, Emma." He shoved the pillows into place and pulled her back beside him. "Tell me about it."

When she'd finished, he continued to stare into middle distance. She was calm now. He could feel it in each easy breath she took. He was wired tight.

"The letter probably set it off," she murmured. "I used to pray that the nightmares would stop. Now I don't want them to. I want to see. I want to get through the door and see."

He turned his head to press his lips to her hair. "Do you trust me?"

His arm was firm around her, not holding her down. Just holding her. "Yes."

"I'm going to do everything I can to find out who's responsible for your brother's death."

"It was so long ago."

"I've got some ideas. Let me see if I can put them together."

She rested against him, wishing she could go on forever beside him, her head cushioned on his shoulder. "I know I said I'd go back with you if you wanted. But I need to stay. I have to talk to Katherine. I need a few weeks."

He said nothing for a moment, adjusting himself to the idea of being without her. "While you're here, think about whether you could handle being married to a cop." He turned her face up to his. "Think about it hard, will you?"

"Yes." She slid her arms around him. "Make love with me, Michael."

◆ ◆ ◆ ◆

*THE* CLUB WAS noisy, filled with young bodies stuffed into tight jeans. Snug, short skirts barely covered the hips of long-legged girls. The music was hard and loud, the liquor watered. But the club was packed, the dance floor jammed. Colored lights whirled, distorting faces. Couples standing hip to hip had to shout to communicate. Drugs and money exchanged hands as casually as phone numbers.

It wasn't what he was used to. It certainly wasn't what he preferred. But he had come. He squeezed into a small corner table and ordered a Scotch.

"If you'd wanted to talk, you could have picked a better spot."

His companion grinned and downed a whiskey. "What better place for secrets than in public?" He lit a cigarette with a monogrammed gold lighter. "The grapevine has it that Jane slipped something by you."

"I know about the letter."

"You know, and didn't think it was worth mentioning?"

"That's right."

"It won't do to forget that what concerns you concerns me."

"The letter only implicates Jane, not you, or me. Since she's dead, it hardly matters." He paused, waiting until the waitress had set down his drink. "There's something else that may be more pressing. Emma's having troubling dreams."

The man laughed and blew smoke between his teeth. "Emma's dreams don't bother me."

"They should. Since they concern us both. She's in therapy, with the psychiatrist who treated Stevie Nimmons." After sampling the Scotch, he decided it wasn't good enough to water a plant with. "It looks as though she may be starting to remember."

His expression changed. There was a trace of fear, then a flood of anger. "You should have let me kill her years ago."

"It wasn't necessary then." The other man shrugged and sipped his Scotch. "It may be necessary now."

"I don't intend to get my hands dirty at this stage, old man. You take care of her."

"I dealt with Jane." His voice was cool and level. "At the moment, I think Emma only bears watching. If it goes further, it will be up to you."

"All right. Not because you order it, but because I owe her."

"Mr. Blackpool, can I have your autograph?"

He set down his lighter and smiled at the curvy young redhead. "Of course, dear. It would be a pleasure."

# Chapter Forty-one

♦ ♦ ♦ ♦

*T*HROUGH THE PARLOR window, Emma could see the last of the New Year's snow melting from the hedgerow.

"Michael wants me to marry him."

Katherine barely lifted a brow. "How do you feel about that?"

Emma nearly laughed. It was such a standard response, therapist to patient. "I feel a lot of things about that. Surprise isn't one of them. I've known for some time he's only been waiting to ask me. When I'm with him, I start to believe that it could work. A home, a family. It's what I've always wanted."

"Do you love him?"

"Oh yes." That part, it seemed, was quite simple. "I do."

There was no hesitation there, Katherine noticed. "But you're not sure of marriage."

"It works for some people. We could hardly say it worked for me."

"How does Michael compare with Drew?"

"In what way?"

Katherine merely lifted her hands palms up, fingers spread. "They're both men. Attractive, determined men."

"Anything else?"

Emma wandered the room. The house was empty and quiet. It was understood that at three each afternoon she would be left alone to talk to Katherine. She hadn't meant to speak of Michael today, but of the nightmares. But her thoughts had focused on him.

"No, nothing. Even before I realized Drew was violent, I couldn't have compared them. He was careless with people, only able to focus on one at a time. There was no real sense of loyalty. He could be very clever and very romantic, but it was never done out of simple generosity. He always required payment."

"And Michael?"

"He cares. About people, his job, his family. Loyalty is like, well, the color of his eyes. Just part of him. I never thought I'd want to be with a man again. To have sex. When we made love for the first time, I felt things I'd always wanted to feel and hadn't been able to."

"You call it having sex when you refer to Drew. Making love with Michael."

"Do I?" Emma paused and gave Katherine one of her rare smiles. A memory drifted back—Johnno sitting on her bed in her room in Martinique. *When it's with someone you care about, it's almost holy.* "I don't suppose a degree is required to puzzle that out."

"No." Pleased, Katherine leaned back against the cushions. "Are you comfortable, physically, with Michael?"

"No. But it's a wonderful kind of discomfort."

"Exciting?"

"Yes. But I haven't been able to . . . initiate."

"Do you want to?"

"I don't know. I think—I'd like to show him. I suppose I'm afraid of doing something wrong."

"In what way?"

Baffled, Emma lifted her hands and let them fall. "I'm not sure, just that I might do something to annoy him, or . . ." Impatient with herself, she turned back to the window. "I can't shake Drew, and the things he said to me about how stupid, how useless I was in bed." She hated that, knowing she was still allowing him to control some part of her life.

"Have you considered that if you were inadequate in bed, it was due to your partner and the circumstances?"

"Yes. Up here." Emma touched a finger to her temple. "I know I'm not cold and unresponsive. I can feel passion, desire. But I'm afraid to move toward Michael, afraid I might spoil something." Pausing, she picked up a crystal pyramid and watched the colors run through it. "And it's the nightmares. I'm almost as afraid of him now as I was when he was alive. Somehow I think if I could pull him out of my dreams, erase his face and his voice from my subconscious, I'd be able to take that next step with Michael."

"Is that what you want?"

"Of course that's what I want. Do you think I want to go on being punished?"

"For what?"

"For not doing what he wanted quickly enough, or in the wrong way." Agitated, she set the crystal down to wrap her arms around her breasts. "For not wearing the right dress. For being in love with Michael. He knew, he knew I felt something for Michael." She began to pace again, twisting her fingers together. "When he saw us together at the showing, he knew it. So he beat me. He made me promise I'd never see Michael again, and he still beat me. He knew I wouldn't keep the promise."

"A promise made under duress isn't a promise at all."

Dismissing logic, Emma shook her head. "The point is, I tried to keep it, but I didn't. I couldn't. So he punished me."

She dropped into a chair. "I lied," she continued, half to herself. "I lied to Drew, and to myself."

Katherine leaned forward, but she kept her voice very low and mild. "Why do you suppose Drew is there in your dream, your dream of the night Darren died?"

"I lied then, too," Emma murmured. "I didn't keep my promise. I didn't take care of Darren. We lost him. Da and Bev lost each other. I'd sworn to them that I would always look after him. That I'd keep him safe. But I broke my promise. No one ever punished me. No one ever blamed me."

"But you did. Haven't you blamed yourself? Punished yourself?"

"If I hadn't run away—he called to me." For an instant it flashed into her mind. The way his voice had raced after her as she'd fled down the dark hall. "He was so scared, but I didn't go back to him. I knew they were going to hurt him, but I ran. And he died. I should have stayed. I was supposed to stay."

"Could you have helped him?"

"I ran because I was afraid for myself."

"You were a child, Emma."

"What difference does that make? I made a promise. You don't break promises to people you love, no matter how difficult they are to keep. I made one to Drew, and I stayed because . . ."

"Because?"

"Because I deserved to be punished." She closed her eyes on a dull, dreary horror. "Oh God. Did I stay all those months because I wanted to be punished for losing Darren?"

Katherine allowed herself only the briefest moment of satisfaction. This was exactly what she'd been hoping for. "I think that's part of it. You've said before that Drew reminded you of Brian. You've blamed yourself for Darren's death, and in a child's mind, punishment follows guilt."

"I didn't know Drew was violent when I married him."

"No. You were attracted to what you saw on the surface. A beautiful young man with a beautiful voice. Romantic, charming. You chose someone you thought was gentle and affectionate."

"I was wrong."

"Yes, you were wrong about Drew. He deceived you and many others. Because he was so attractive, so loving on the outside, you became convinced that you deserved what he did to you. He used your vulnerability, exploited it and compounded it. You didn't ask to be battered, Emma. And you weren't to blame for his sickness. Just as you weren't to blame for your brother's death." She took Emma's hand. "I believe when you accept that, completely, you'll remember the rest. Once you remember, the nightmares will pass."

"I will remember," Emma murmured. "And I won't run this time."

♦ ♦ ♦ ♦

*T*HE LOFT HAD hardly changed. Marianne had added a few of her own bizarre touches. A full-sized blowup of Godzilla, an enormous plastic palm tree that was still decorated for Christmas though the January white sales were in full swing, and a stuffed minah bird that swung on a perch in front of the window. Her paintings dominated the walls, landscapes, seascapes, portraits, and still-lifes. The studio smelled of paint, turpentine, and Calvin Klein's Obsession.

Emma sat on a stool in a slash of sunlight wearing a sweatshirt that drooped off one shoulder and the sapphire and diamond earrings her father had given her for Christmas.

"You're not relaxed," Marianne complained as she stroked a pencil over her pad.

"You always say that when you sketch me."

"No, you're really not relaxed." Marianne stuck the pencil in her hair. It was a mass of curls now that just skimmed her shoulders. She sat back to drum her fingers on the pad and study Emma. "Is it being here, in New York?"

"I don't know. Maybe." But she'd been tense the last couple of days in London as well, unable to shake the feeling she was being watched, followed. Stalked.

Stupid. She took three deliberate breaths. In all likelihood the tension stemmed from finally acknowledging her guilt and shame, and her anger, which revolved around Darren and Drew. And yet, once she had, she felt relief.

"You want to quit?" Even as she asked, Marianne took out the pencil and began to sketch again. She'd always wanted to capture that quiet, haunted look in Emma's eyes. "We could run uptown, go to Bloomies, or go to Elizabeth Arden's for the works. I haven't had a facial in weeks."

"I've been meaning to mention how haggard you look." She smiled so that the dimple winked at the corner of her mouth. "What is it, vitamins, macrobiotics, sex? You look wonderful."

"I think it might be love."

"The dentist?"

"Who? Oh, no. Talk of root canals destroyed our relationship. His name's Ross. I met him about six months ago."

"Six months ago." Emma arched a brow. "And you never mentioned him."

"I thought I might jinx it." With a shrug, Marianne turned the pad and started a new sketch. "Shift a little, would you? Turn your head. Yeah."

"Serious." Emma glanced out the window. Her stomach did a little loop so that she had to inhale slowly. People were hurrying along below, chased by a chill wind that threatened rain or sleet. There was a man standing in the doorway of the deli, smoking. She would have sworn he looked right at her. "What?" she said when she heard Marianne's voice.

"I said it could be. I'd like it to be. The problem is, he's a senator."

"As in U.S.?"

"The gentleman from Virginia. Can you see me as one of those classy Washington wives?"

"Yes," Emma said and smiled. "I can."

"Teas and protocol." Marianne wrinkled her nose. "I can't imagine actually having to sit through a speech on the defense budget. What are you staring at?"

"Oh. Nothing." With a quick shake of her head, Emma shifted her gaze. "There's just a man standing down on the street."

"Imagine that. In downtown New York. You're tensing up again."

"Sorry." Deliberately she looked away and tried to relax. "Paranoia," she said, hoping for a light touch. "So, do I get to meet the politician?"

"He's in D.C." In two strokes Marianne penciled in Emma's brow. "If you weren't in such a hurry to get back to L.A., you could go down with me next weekend."

"It is serious then."

"Semi. Emma, what is so fascinating out there?"

"It's just this man. It's almost as if he's looking right at me."

"Sounds more like vanity than paranoia." Pushing herself up, Marianne walked to the window. "Probably waiting to make a drug deal," she decided. She moved away again to pick up her long-neglected coffee cup. "In the serious vein, what about Michael? Are you going to give the man and his dog a break?"

"I want to take my time."

"You've been taking your time with Michael since you were thirteen," Marianne pointed out. "What's it like to have a man carry a torch for you for over ten years?"

"It's not like that."

"It's exactly like that. In fact, I'm surprised he managed to stay on the Coast when you told him you were going to visit here for a couple of days before flying back."

"He wants to get married."

"Well, you could knock me over with a twenty-foot crane. Who'd have guessed it?"

"I suppose I haven't wanted to think about what happens next."

"That's only because you've blocked the M word out of your vocabulary for a while. So what are you going to do about it?"

"It?"

"The two *M*s. Marriage and Michael."

"I don't know." She looked out the window again. He was still there, standing patiently. "I'm going to wait until I see him again. We both may feel differently now that things have settled down, and our lives are getting back to normal. Dammit."

"What?"

"I don't know why I didn't realize it before. Da's hired a bodyguard again." She turned her head quickly, eyes narrowed. "Did you know about this?"

"No." Marianne stirred herself to go to the window and look out again. "Brian never said a word to me. Look, the guy's just standing around. Why automatically assume he's there for you?"

"When you've lived with it most of your life, you know when you're being watched." Annoyed, she moved away from the window. On an oath, she whirled back and yanked the window open. "Hey!" Her sudden shout surprised her as much as the man on the street. "Go call your boss and tell him I can take care of myself. If I see you down there in five minutes, I'm calling the cops."

"Feel better?" Marianne murmured at her shoulder.

"Lots."

"I'm not sure he could hear you all the way down there."

"He heard enough," Emma said with a satisfied nod. "He's leaving." A little dizzy, she pulled her head in. "Let's go get a facial."

◆ ◆ ◆ ◆

*M*ICHAEL PORED OVER the printout. It had taken him days to correlate lists and cross-check. In the past weeks he'd found himself just as caught up in Darren McAvoy's murder as his father had been twenty years before. He had read every inch of every file, studied every photograph, checked and rechecked every interview that had been compiled during the original investigation. From his own memory he pulled out the visit to the house in the hills with Emma, making his own notes from her descriptions and recollections.

From his father's meticulous investigation and Emma's recollections, he was able to re-create, in his mind, the night of Darren's death.

Music. He imagined Beatles, Stones, Joplin, the Doors.

Drugs. Everything from grass to LSD cheerfully shared.

Shop talk, party talk, gossip. Laughter and intense political discussions. Vietnam, Nixon, women's liberation.

People coming and going. Some invited, some just showing up. No one questioning unfamiliar faces. Formal invitations had been for the establishment. Peace, love, and communal living the order of the day. It sounded nice enough, but for a cop in the first year of the nineties, it was frustrating.

He had the guest list his father had compiled. It was, of course, woefully inadequate, but a place to start. Playing a hunch, he spent days verifying the whereabouts on the night of Jane Palmer's death of every name on the list. He'd turned up sixteen people who had been in London, including all four members of Devastation, their manager, and Bev McAvoy. Michael ignored his tendency to cross them off, and spent several more days checking alibis.

His printout now had twelve names. He liked to think if there was indeed a connection between two murders, twenty years apart, it was on that list.

"It gives us something to work with," Michael said. He leaned over his father's shoulder so that they could both study the printout. "I want to dig a little deeper, find any and all of the connections between these twelve people and Jane Palmer."

"You've got the McAvoys on the list. You don't think they killed their own son?"

"No. It's the connection." He pulled over a file and opened it. He had a list of names connected with broken lines. It resembled a family tree, headed by Bev, Brian, and Jane. Below were Emma's and Darren's names. "I've been hooking them up, using interviews and file information. Take Johnno." Michael slid his finger down. "He's Brian's oldest friend, his writing partner. They formed the group together. He remained friends with Bev during her long estrangement from Brian. He also knew Jane the longest."

"Motive?"

"Money or revenge is all we've got," Michael went on. "We can easily apply both of those to Jane Palmer, but it's a stretch for anyone else on the list. Blackpool." Michael moved his finger down. "He was more of a hanger-on at the time Darren was killed. His big break came several months later when he recorded a song Brian and Johnno had written. And Pete Page became his manager." He ran his finger over the lines connecting Blackpool with Brian, Johnno, Pete, and Emma.

"No connection with Palmer?" Lou asked.

"I haven't found one yet."

With a nod, Lou leaned back. "There are several names on your list that even I recognize."

"A rock-and-roll countdown." Sitting on the edge of the desk, Michael lit a cigarette. "I know when you figure the main motive for kidnapping is money, most of these names don't fit. That's where Jane comes in. If she planted the idea, she could have used blackmail, sex, drugs, or any other kind of hook to pressure someone into getting to Brian through Darren. She tried to get to him once through Emma, and all she got out of it was money. She wanted more. What better way than through his son?"

He pushed away from the desk to pace the office and try to figure it out. "If she could have gotten into the house, she would have done it herself. But she was the one person who wouldn't have been welcome that night. So she found someone else, used whatever lever worked best, and got what she wanted."

"You sound like you understand her very well."

Michael thought of his brief, destructive affair with Angie Parks. "I think I do. If we take her at her word that the kidnapping was her idea, then we have to find the connection. She used someone on this list."

"There were two people in the nursery that night."

"And one of them had to know their way around the house. He had to know the layout of the rooms upstairs, the McAvoys' private space. He had to know the kids, the routine. So we look for someone connected to both Jane and Brian."

"You're forgetting something, Michael." Lou leaned back to study his son. "If you penciled your name on this page, how many lines would connect you? Nothing clouds an investigation quicker than personal involvement."

"And nothing motivates more." Michael tapped out his cigarette. "I'm not sure I would be a cop today if it hadn't been for Emma. She came to the house that time. You remember, it was around Christmas. She came to see you."

"I remember."

"She was looking for help. There wasn't a lot anyone could give her, but she came to you. It started me thinking. It wasn't all filling out forms, making lists. It wasn't all shoot-outs and collars. It was having people come to you because they knew you'd know what to do. We went to the house in the hills, and I walked through it with her. I understood that there have to be people who know what to do. Who care enough about one small boy they've never met to keep trying."

Touched, Lou looked down at the papers on his desk. "It's going on twenty years, and I haven't figured out what to do about this one."

"What color were Darren McAvoy's eyes?"

"Green," Lou answered. "Like his mother's."

Smiling a little, Michael rose. "You've never stopped trying. I've got to pick Emma up at the airport. Can I leave this stuff with you? I don't want her to see it."

"Yeah." He fully intended to go over every word in his son's report. "Michael." He glanced up as Michael paused at the door. "You've turned out to be a pretty good cop."

"So have you."

# Chapter Forty-two

#### ♦ ♦ ♦ ♦

$\mathcal{E}$MMA HAD CONVINCED herself to ease back. Her relationship with Michael was moving too quickly. She would gently pull their relationship back a few notches. Her book was about to be published. It was time to open her own studio, perhaps have another showing.

How did she know her own feelings in any case? Her life had been in too much upheaval. It was easy to mistake love for gratitude and friendship. And she was grateful to him. Always would be. He had been her friend, a constant if distant one for most of her life. Her decision to back off was best for both of them.

She took a firm grip on her camera case as she walked through the gate.

There he was. He saw her the same instant she saw him. All of the practical decisions she'd made over the last three thousand miles vanished. Before she could say his name, he had swooped her off her feet. To the amusement and annoyance of other passengers, he greeted her in silence, blocking most of the gateway.

When she could breathe again, she touched a hand to his cheek. "Hi."

"Hi." He kissed her again. "It's good to see you."

"I hope you haven't been waiting long."

"I think it's over eleven years now." He turned and started toward the terminal.

"Aren't you going to put me down?"

"I don't think so. How was your flight?"

"Smooth." With a laugh, she pressed a kiss to his cheek. "Michael, you can't carry me through the airport."

"There's no law against it. I checked. I guess you've got luggage."

"Yes, I do."

"You want to pick it up now?"

She answered his grin, then settled back to enjoy the ride. "Not particularly."

♦ ♦ ♦ ♦

*T*WO HOURS LATER they were in her bed, sharing a bowl of ice cream.

"I'd never developed the habit of eating in bed before I met you." Emma scooped out a spoonful and offered it. "Marianne and I used to hoard Hershey bars in our room at school. Sometimes we'd sneak them into bed after lights out, but that was as decadent as it got."

"I always figured girls snuck guys into their room after lights out."

"No. Just chocolate." She slid the ice cream into her mouth and closed her eyes. "We only dreamed about boys. We talked about sex all the time, looking up with envy to any of the girls who claimed to have lived through the experience." She opened her eyes and smiled at him. "It's better than I imagined it would be." She offered him another spoonful and the strap of the tank top she wore slithered off her shoulder.

Reaching out, Michael toyed with it. "If you let me move in, we could practice a lot more."

He was looking at her, waiting. Wanting an answer, Emma thought. And she didn't know which one to give him. "I haven't decided whether I'm going to keep this house or look for another one." That was true enough, but they both knew it was an evasion rather than an answer. "I need studio space, and a darkroom. I think I'd like to find a place where I could have it all."

"Here, in L.A.?"

"Yes." She thought of New York. It would never be her home again. "I'd like to try to start here."

"Good."

She set the bowl aside, certain he didn't know what she meant by starting. "I need to concentrate on getting ready for another show. I have a number of contacts out here, and I think if we could tie it in with the book—"

"What book?"

She smoothed the sheets and took a deep breath. "Mine. I sold it about eighteen months ago. On Devastation. Early photographs from when I was a child up to the last tour I went on with Da. It's been delayed a couple of times because . . . because of what happened. But it's due to come out in about six months." She glanced toward the window. The wind had picked up from the sea and brought with it a rush of rain. "I have an idea for another one. The publisher seems to be interested."

"Why didn't you tell me?" Before she could make an excuse, he cupped her face in his hands and kissed her, long and hard. "All we have is a bottle of mineral water to celebrate with. Uh-oh."

She'd nearly relaxed, and now braced again. "What?"

"My mother's going to kill me if you don't give her first dibs on autographing sessions."

And that was it? she thought, staring at him. No demands, no questions, no criticisms. "I . . . the publisher wants me to tour. It's going to mean a lot of traveling for a few weeks."

"Do I get to watch you on *Donahue*?"

"I—I don't know. They're setting stuff up. I told them I'd be available for anything they wanted during the month of publication."

It was her tone that had him lifting a brow. "Is this a test, Emma? Are you waiting for me to grow fangs because you're telling me you've got a life?"

"Maybe."

"Sorry to disappoint you." He started to rise, but she laid a hand on his arm.

"Don't. If it's not fair, I'm sorry. It's not always easy to be fair." She dragged both hands through her hair. "I know better than to make comparisons, but I can't help making them."

"Work on it," he suggested flatly, then reached over for his cigarettes.

"Dammit, Michael, he's all I have to compare. I never lived with another man, I never slept with another man. You want me to pretend that that part of my life never happened. That I never let myself be used or hurt. I'm supposed to forget and pick up and go on so that you can take care of me. Every man who's ever been important to me has wanted to take over because I'm too weak or stupid or defenseless to make the right choices."

"Hold on."

But she was scrambling out of bed to pace the room. "All of my life I've been tucked into corners, all for my own good. My father wanted me to forget about Darren, not to dwell on it, not to think of it. I wasn't supposed to worry about what he was doing to his own life, either. Then Drew was going to take care of it all. I was too naïve to handle my finances, my friends, my work. And I was so bloody used to being pointed in a direction, I just went. Now I'm supposed to forget all of that, just forget it, and let you click into place so I'm protected again."

"Is that why you think I'm here?"

She turned back. "Isn't it?"

"Maybe that's part of it." He blew out smoke, then deliberately crushed out his cigarette. "It's hard to be in love with someone and not want to protect them. But let's just back up, okay? I don't want you to forget about what happened between you and Latimer. I want you to be able to live with it, but I hope to Christ you never forget it."

"I won't."

"Neither will I." He stood then to cross to her. Outside the rain was whipped by the wind, battering windows. "I'll remember everything he did to you. And there'll be times when I'll wish he was still alive so I could kill him myself. But I'll also remember that you pulled yourself out of it. You took a stand, and you survived. Weak?" He lifted a fingertip to trace the faint scar under her jawline. "Do you really believe I think you're weak? I saw what he did to you that day. I'll always be able to see it. You didn't let him plow you under, Emma."

"No, and I won't let anyone take control of my life again."

"I'm not your father." He spit out the words as he gripped her shoulders. "And I'm not Latimer. I don't want to control your life, I just want to be part of it."

"I don't know what I want." She lifted her hands to cover his. "I keep coming back to you, and it's frightening because I can't stop. I don't want to need you this way."

"Dammit, Emma—" When the phone rang, he swore again.

"It's for you," she said, holding out the receiver.

"Yeah?" He picked up his cigarettes, then paused. "Where?

Twenty minutes," he said and hung up. "I've got to go." He was already pulling on his jeans.

She only nodded. Someone was dead. She could see it on his face.

"We're not finished here, Emma."

"No."

He shouldered on his gun. "I'll be back as soon as I can."

"Michael." She didn't know what she wanted to say. Instead, she went with instinct and put her arms around him. "Goodbye."

She couldn't settle once he'd gone. The rain was coming in sheets now. She could barely see the ocean through it, but she could hear the waves crashing. She found it soothing, the gray light, the sound of water. It was cool enough to start a fire from the stack of split oak in the woodbox. Once it was blazing, she called the airport to arrange for her luggage to be delivered.

It occurred to her that it was the first time she was completely alone in the house, a house she was considering making her own. After brewing tea, she wandered through it, sipping. If she did buy it, remodeling would be essential. There was a room off the kitchen that could be enlarged for a studio. The light was good. Or was, she thought, when there was sun.

There were three bedrooms upstairs, all large and lofty. An impractical amount of space perhaps, but she liked having it. She could make it her own. Thoughtful, she glanced at her watch. It would be worth a call to the real estate agent. Before she could pick up the phone, it rang.

"Emma?"

"Da." She sat on the arm of the sofa.

"I just wanted to see if you'd gotten there."

"Everything's fine. How are you?"

"A little crazed at the moment. We're recording. We'll be breaking off to come out to the Coast."

"Da, I told you, I'm fine. It really isn't necessary for you to come all this way."

"I'd like to see you for myself, plus we're up for three Grammys."

She broke off her objections. "Of course. Congratulations."

"We figured we'd show up in force. You'll come along, won't you?"

"I'd love to."

"I thought you might like to ask Michael. Pete's arranging the tickets."

"I will." She remembered the way he'd looked when he'd strapped on his gun. "He may be busy."

"Check it out. We'll be coming in at the end of the week for rehearsals. Pete got a request for you to be one of the presenters. He asked me to pass it along."

"I don't know."

"It would mean a lot to me, Emma, having you make the announcement if Johnno and I cop song of the year."

She smiled. "And if you don't, I can read your names anyway."

"That's the way. You'll take care of yourself, won't you?"

"Yes, and that's something I wanted to speak to you about." She shifted the phone to her other ear. "Da, I don't want the bodyguard. I fully intend to take care of myself, so call him off."

"What bodyguard?"

"The one you hired before I left London."

"I didn't hire anyone, Emma."

"Look I—" She broke off. He often hid things from her, but he never lied. "You didn't arrange for someone to follow me, look out for me?"

"No. It didn't occur to me that you'd need it. Has someone been bothering you? I can break off earlier and come out—"

"No." Sighing, she pressed her fingers to her eyes. "No one's been bothering me. Marianne was right, it's just paranoia. I guess I haven't gotten used to coming and going as I choose, but I intend to." To prove it, she made her decision quickly. "Tell Pete I'd be delighted to be a presenter at the Grammys. In fact, I'll start hunting up a dress tomorrow."

"Someone will contact you about the rehearsals. Keep a night free. Bev and I would like to take you and Michael out to dinner."

"I'll ask him. He's . . . Da," she said on impulse. "What is it that makes you so comfortable with Michael?"

"He's steady as a rock. And he loves you as much as I do. He'll make you happy. That's all I've ever wanted."

"I know. I love you, Da. I'll see you soon."

Maybe it was just that easy, she thought as she hung up the phone. She had a man who loved her, and who could make her happy. She'd never doubted Michael's feelings, or her own. The doubts came from whether she would be able to give anything back.

Bundling into a slicker, she raced into the rain. The least she could give Michael when he returned was a hot meal.

She enjoyed pushing the cart up and down the aisles of the market, choosing this, selecting that. By the time she checked out, she had three bags loaded. Drenched, she settled back into the car. It was only three, but she had to turn on her lights to cut the gloom. Jet lag had set in, but the fatigue was almost pleasant, and suited to the rain.

The road was all but deserted. Other shoppers had planned more carefully, or were waiting for the storm to pass. Perhaps that was why she noticed the car behind her, turning where she turned, always keeping two lengths behind. Turning up the radio, she struggled to ignore it.

Paranoia, she told herself.

But her eyes kept flicking to the rearview mirror, and she could see the twin headlights glowing steadily behind her. Emma increased her speed, a little more than safety allowed on the slick roads. The headlights paced her. She eased off the gas. The trailing car slowed. Catching her lip between her teeth, she swerved into an abrupt left turn. Her car fishtailed, skidded. Behind her, the car swung left, then slid across the road.

Fighting for control, Emma punched the gas and managed to pull her car out of the skid. On a burst of speed, she turned toward home, praying the few moments' lead was all she would need.

She had her fingers around the door handle before she hit the brakes. She wanted to get inside, to safety. Whether it was her imagination or not, she didn't want to be caught outside and defenseless if the other car cruised up. Leaving the groceries, she sprinted out of the car. Then screamed when a hand clamped on her arm.

"Lady!" The young driver jumped back and nearly overbalanced into a puddle. "Jeeze, get a grip."

"What do you want?"

The rain was dripping off a cap onto a blunt, freckled nose. She couldn't see his eyes. "This your house?"

She had her keys, balled in her hand. Emma wondered if she could use them as a weapon. "Why?"

"I got three pieces of luggage, American flight number 457 from New York, for Emma McAvoy."

Her luggage. Emma nearly laughed as she ran a hand over her face. "I'm sorry. You startled me. You were behind me when I left the market, and I guess I got spooked."

"I've been waiting here for the last ten minutes," he corrected and shoved a clipboard at her. "Want to sign, please?"

"But—" She looked over in time to see a car drive slowly toward the house. The figure behind the wheel was lost in the sheeting rain and shadows as it cruised down the street. "I'm sorry," she said again. "Would you mind waiting until I get the groceries in?"

"Look, lady, I've got other stops to make."

She pulled a twenty out of her purse. "Please." Without waiting for his agreement, she went back to her car to unload.

Inside she double-checked all the locks. With the fire, the lights, the warmth, she'd all but convinced herself that she'd made a mistake. When she didn't see the car reappear during the next twenty minutes, she was almost sure of it.

Cooking relaxed her. She liked the scents she created, the low murmur of music. As the hour grew later, the gray simply deepened. There was no twilight, just the steady fall of rain. At ease again, she decided to go upstairs and unpack.

The sound of a car swishing through the rain outside had panic streaking up her spine again. She stood frozen at the base of the stairs, staring out the wide, dark window. It hadn't occurred to her until that moment how exposed she was, with all the lights burning. She could hear a brake set, a door slam.

She was on the way to the phone when she heard the footsteps in front of the door. Without hesitating, she ran to the fireplace and grabbed the brass poker. The knock had her grip tightening.

She was alone. He knew she was alone, Emma thought frantically, because she'd been foolish enough to wander through the house with the lights burning and the shades drawn up. She inched her way toward the phone. She would call for help. If it didn't get there in time, she would help herself.

Her heart tattooed against her chest as she lifted the receiver.

"Emma! I'm drowning out here."

"Michael?" The phone slipped out of her fingers and fell to the floor. She let the poker drop as well as she rushed to the door. Her fingers weren't steady as she fumbled with locks. She could hear him swearing. By the time she pulled open the door and threw her arms around him, she was laughing.

"Sorry, I don't get the joke."

"No, I'm sorry. It was just that I—" But when she drew back, she saw something in his eyes she hadn't seen before. Despair. "Here, let me help you. You're soaked through." She helped him peel off his jacket. "I've got some tea. I wish I'd thought of brandy, but there's probably a bottle of whiskey somewhere." She nudged him over by the fire, then went into the kitchen. Moments later, she returned with a cup. He hadn't moved, she noted. He just stood there, looking down at the flames.

"It's a nice Irish tea, heavy on the Irish." She handed it to him.

"Thanks." He sipped, grimaced, then downed it.

"You should get out of those wet clothes."

"In a minute."

She started to speak again, then changed her mind and went quietly upstairs. When she came back, she simply took his hand. "Come on. I'm running you a bath."

He couldn't find the energy to argue. "Do I get bubbles?"

"All you want. Go ahead." She gestured toward the door. "Relax. I'll get you some more tea."

He pulled off his shirt and let it fall with a wet splat to the floor. "Make it straight Irish this time. Two fingers, no ice."

She hesitated while he unsnapped his pants. She had to stop looking for ghosts in bottles, as well. Not everyone who wanted a drink wanted to get drunk. "All right."

When she came back, the water had stopped running. She paused at the door, then feeling foolish, set the glass on the table by the bed. Though they were lovers, she couldn't see herself waltzing in while he was bathing. Whether it was a matter of intimacy or privacy, she couldn't cross the line. She sat on the window seat, watched the rain and waited.

With a towel slung low on his hips, he stepped out. The light was behind him and she could clearly see the tension and withdrawal in his face.

"I started dinner."

He nodded, but only picked up the glass. He thought he

could hold the whiskey down. Food was another matter. "Why don't you go ahead?"

"I can wait." She wanted to go to him, take his hand, smooth the lines away from his brow. But he was brooding into the glass as if she weren't even there. Rising, she walked into the bath to tidy the wet clothes and towels.

"You don't have to pick up after me." He was standing in the doorway now. An anger, deep and raw, came through in both his voice and his eyes. "I don't need a mother."

"I just—"

"Latimer wanted to be waited on, Emma. It's not my style."

"Fine." Her own temper rose up to meet his. She let his shirt fall to the floor again. "Pick it up yourself then, not everyone likes to live in a sty."

He snatched up the shirt and hurled it into the tub. Emma retreated two steps before she could stop herself. "Don't look at me like that." He whirled on her, furious with her, himself, with everything. "Don't ever look at me like that. I can get pissed off at you without throwing a punch."

She started to check the venom that burned her tongue, but it poured out. "I'm not afraid you'll hit me. No one will ever hit me again and walk away. I'm through being victimized by anyone. That includes you. If you want to sulk, then go ahead and sulk. If you want to fight, fine. I'll fight, but I'm going to know what I'm fighting about. If you're acting like this because I won't do what you want, be what you want, and say what you want, then tough. Shouting isn't going to change my mind."

He held up a hand before she could storm by. Not to block her, but to ask her to wait. The subtle difference was enough to make her hold back the next burst of temper.

"It has nothing to do with you," he said quietly. "Nothing at all. I'm sorry. I shouldn't have come back here tonight." He looked down at his wet clothes. "Look, can we throw these in the dryer or something so I can get them back on and get the hell out of here?"

It was there again, she noted. Not just anger, but a deep, dark despair. "What is it, Michael?"

"I told you it has nothing to do with you."

"Let's sit down."

"Back off, Emma."

He turned away and walked back into the bedroom. He'd

been wrong, he decided as he put the whiskey aside. He couldn't keep that down, either.

"Oh, I see. You want to be a part of my life, but I'm not to be a part of yours."

"Not this part."

"You can't section off pieces of yourself and tuck them away. I know." She moved to him, touched a hand to his arm. Until that moment, she hadn't realized how much she loved him. With a kind of wonder it came to her that the need wasn't all hers after all. "Talk to me, Michael. Please."

"It was kids," he murmured. "Jesus, babies. He just walked over to the playground at recess and let loose." Michael had to sit. Groping his way to the bed, he sat on the edge, pushing the heels of his hands into his eyes. He could still see it. What terrified him was that he knew he always would.

Bewildered, Emma sat beside him, rubbing a hand over his shoulder to try to ease the tension from the muscles bunched there. "I don't understand."

"Neither do I. We found out who he was. He'd had a history of mental illness. Been in and out of institutions all his life. Turns out he went to that school, that same school, through first and second grades before they put him away the first time. We'll find out more, for what it's worth."

"Who? Who are you talking about?"

"Just a loser. Some sick, pitiful loser who got his hands on a forty-five automatic."

And she began to see. A sickness welled up to her throat. "Oh my God."

"He drove to the school. Walked right up to the playground. Kids were playing ball and jumping rope. It hadn't started to rain yet. So he opened up. Six kids are dead. Twenty more are hospitalized. They won't all make it."

"Oh, Michael." She put her arms around him, rested her cheek against his.

"Then he just walked away. By the time the black and whites got there, he was gone. When McCarthy and I drove up—" But he couldn't describe it, not to her. Not even to himself. "We got a make on the car and found it a couple of blocks away. He was right there, eating lunch in the park. Just sitting on a bench in the fucking park eating a sandwich in the rain. He didn't even bother to run when we moved in. He picked up the gun and stuck the barrel in his mouth. So we'll never know why. We'll never even know why."

"I'm sorry." She could think of nothing else to say. "I'm so sorry."

"We're supposed to make a difference. Goddammit, we're supposed to make a difference. Six kids dead, and there's nothing you can do. You couldn't stop it, and you couldn't fix it. All you can do is walk away and try to convince yourself that there was nothing you could do."

"But you don't walk away," she murmured. "That's why you make a difference. Michael." She drew away, to study his face. "You couldn't have stopped this. I won't tell you you shouldn't grieve over something you couldn't prevent, because that makes you who you are."

"You never get used to it." He dropped his brow on hers. "I used to wonder why my father would come home sometimes and close himself off. When he did, I'd hear him and my mother talking after I went to bed. For hours."

"You can talk to me."

He pulled her close. She was so warm, so soft. "I need you, Emma. I wasn't going to come back here with this. I needed to hold on to something."

"This time, you hold on to me." She lifted her mouth to his. His response was so strong, almost desperate, that she no longer tried to soothe. If he needed to burn out despair in passion, she was there for him.

She took control as she hadn't known she could, pulling him down with her, letting her hands excite, her mouth demand. He had always loved her before, gently, patiently. There was no room for that now, and no need. If his passion was dark, hers could equal it. If his desire was urgent, she would match it.

This time she would chase away his demons.

She rolled with him, over him, dragging the towel aside, giving herself the pleasure of driving him, feeling his body tremble and heat and tense as she raced over it. No hesitation, no fears, no doubts. To pleasure herself as much as him, she stroked with fingertips, slow circles, teasing lines.

The lamplight glowed over his skin, tempting her to taste with quick flicks of her tongue, with long strokes of her lips.

Power, just discovered, rocked through her like thunder.

He felt himself pulse, wherever she touched him. Though his

hands weren't idle, she shifted away. Wait, she seemed to tell him. Let me show you. Let me love you. Linking her hands with his, she slithered down his body, her mouth burning frantic arrows of pleasure into his flesh.

He could hear the patter of rain on the glass, feel the sheet heat under his back. In the slanted light he saw her, long, pale hair streaming down her shoulders. Her eyes dark, depthless as they met his.

Rearing up, he dragged her close until they were thigh to thigh. With the need pumping through him, he tugged at buttons, wanting to see her, desperate to feel her.

Her teeth nipped into his shoulder as he ripped her blouse. Here was a violence she could understand, and relish. Savage without brutality. And the turbulence in him was a storm within her. Equal. Interchangeable. She found that love and lust could tangle gloriously.

As he tore at her clothes, her low-throated moan had nothing to do with surrender. How could she have known that all of her life she had waited to be wanted this way? Desperately, exclusively, heedlessly. Nor had she known that she had waited to feel this same wild recklessness.

He wasn't gentle now, and she reveled in the furor. He wasn't controlled, and she pushed him further to the edge. When his fingers dug into her hips, she knew he wasn't thinking of her as frail and fragile and in need of defending. When her name tore from between his lips, the need was there, for her. And only for her.

She rolled over him, arching her back with both triumph and release as she took him into her. The first stunning climax ripped through her, but didn't weaken. It was his hands that slid from her, that groped blindly for hers. With their fingers linked, she set the pace, fast and frantic.

Even after she felt him explode inside her, she rode him, driving him, demanding more. She brought her mouth back to his, insatiable, until his lips grew hungry and his breathing shallow. Her tongue slid along his throat where his pulse began to throb. He murmured something, dazed and incoherent. But she could only moan as she felt him harden inside of her again.

Half mad, he reared up, gripping her arms in tense fingers, covering her mouth with hot, crushing kisses. Then she was beneath him and his body was like a furnace, pumping and plunging into hers.

Long and limber, her limbs linked around him. Her eyes were open and on his. He could see them begin to glaze. Watch her lips begin to tremble. Pleasure rippled through him as he felt her body shudder over a new peak. Then he saw her lips curve, slowly, beautifully.

It was the last thing he saw before passion dragged him under.

# Chapter Forty-three
• • • •

*I*T INFURIATED EMMA that she kept looking over her shoulder. Almost a week had passed since she'd settled back into the house on the beach—since Michael and Conroy had unofficially settled in with her. A rehearsal, she sometimes thought, for the future she was beginning to believe in. Living with Michael, sharing her bed and her time with him, didn't make her feel trapped. It made her feel, at long last, normal . . . and happy.

Yet no matter how content she was, Emma couldn't shake the sensation of being watched. Most of the time she ignored it, or tried to, telling herself it was just another reporter looking for a new angle. Another photographer with a long lens looking for an exclusive picture.

They couldn't touch her, or what she was building with Michael.

But she kept the doors locked and Conroy close whenever she was alone.

No matter how often she told herself there was no one there but her own ghosts, she kept watching, waiting. Even walking down Rodeo Drive in bright sunshine she felt the tension in the back of her neck.

She was more embarrassed than afraid, and wished she had called a limo rather than driving herself.

She'd thought she would enjoy looking for just the right outfit, trying on both the outrageous and the classic, being pampered and cooed over by the clerks. But it was only a relief to have it over, to tuck the dress box into her car and drive off.

It was pitiful, she told herself, this persecution complex. Emma thought Katherine would lift her psychiatrist's brow and make interested noises if she told her. Poor Emma's gone off the bend again. Thinks she's being followed. Wonders if someone's been in the house when she goes out. What about those odd noises on the phone? Must be tapped.

Christ. She rubbed a finger against her temple and tried to laugh. The next thing she'd start doing was checking under the bed at night. Then she'd be in therapy for life.

Well, she'd chosen L.A., hadn't she? Before long she'd have a personal trainer as well as a therapist. She'd be worried about her polarity or she'd start channeling for a three-hundred-year-old Buddist monk.

And then she did laugh.

After she stopped at the auditorium, she picked up her camera. Buddhist monks would have to hold off, at least until she'd dealt with the business at hand. Acts and presenters for the awards show would already be inside. It would be like the old days, she mused. Watching rehearsals, taking pictures.

It was a satisfying feeling to know that her past and her future had found a way to meld.

When she stepped from the car, Blackpool stood blocking her path.

"Well, well. Hello again, Emmy luv."

It infuriated her that he could still make her cringe. Without speaking, she started to skirt around him. He simply shifted, trapping her against the car as easily as he had once trapped her in her darkroom.

Smiling, he stroked a fingertip down the back of her neck. "Is this any way to treat an old friend?"

"Get out of my way."

"We'll have to work on those manners." He gripped her braid and tugged hard enough to make her gasp. "Little girls who grow up with money always end up spoiled. I'd have thought your husband would have taught you better—before you killed him."

It wasn't fear, she realized as she began to shake. It was fury. Hot, glittering fury. "You bastard. Let go of me."

"I thought we might have a chat, just the two of us. Let's take a ride." He kept his hand on her hair, pulling her along. She swung back, bringing her camera case hard into his midsection. When he doubled over, she stepped back, and into someone else. Without thinking, she whirled and nearly caught Stevie in the face.

"Hang on." He threw up a hand before her fist could connect with his nose. "Don't hit me. I'm just a poor recovering addict who's come to play guitar." He put a hand on her shoulder, gave it a quick squeeze. "Is there a problem here?"

Almost carelessly, Emma glanced back at Blackpool. He'd recovered his wind, and was standing, fists clenched. Emma felt a quick surge of pleasure. She had taken care of herself, and very well. "No, there's no problem." Turning, she walked toward the theater with Stevie.

"What was all that about?"

There was still a smile on her face. Pure satisfaction. "He's just a bully."

"And you're a regular Amazon. Here I was loping across the lot, trying to play white knight. You stole my thunder."

She laughed and kissed his cheek. "You'd have flattened him."

"I don't know. He's a lot bigger than I am. Better all around that you punched him yourself. I'd hate to have gone on the telly with a black eye."

"You'd have looked dashing, and rakish." She slipped an arm around his waist. "Let's not say anything about this to Da."

"Bri's very handy with his fists. I'd fancy seeing Blackpool with a shiner."

"I'd fancy it myself," she murmured. "At least wait until after the awards."

"I never could resist a pretty face."

"No, you couldn't. Have you convinced Katherine to marry you yet?"

"She's weakening." They could hear one of the rehearsing acts playing before they entered the theater. Rough, unapologetic rock blasted through the walls. "She stayed in London. Said she had too many patients to take the time for this. But she also stayed behind to see if I could deal with this business on my own."

He stopped near the rear of the theater, just to listen.

"And can you?"

"It's funny, all those years I took drugs because I wanted to feel good. There were some things I wanted to forget." He thought of Sylvie, and sighed. "But mostly because I wanted to feel good. They never made me feel good, but I kept right on taking them. In the past couple of years, I've started to realize what life can be like when you face it straight." He laughed, his shoulders moving restlessly. "I sound like a bloody public service announcement."

"No. You sound like someone who's happy."

He grinned. It was true, he was happy. More, he'd begun to believe he deserved to be. "I'm still the best," he told her as they walked toward the stage. "Only now I can enjoy it."

She saw her father being interviewed offstage. He was happy too, she thought. Johnno was stage right harassing P.M., who was trying to show off baby pictures to any technician he could collar.

The group onstage had broken off rehearsing. They were young, Emma noted. Six smooth young faces, under masses of hair, who were up for Best New Group. She could feel the nerves from them, and she could see, with a sense of pride, the way they glanced toward her father from time to time.

Would they last so long? she imagined them asking themselves. Would they make so deep a mark? Would another generation be touched, and moved by their music?

"You're right," she said to Stevie. "You are the best. All of you."

She didn't think of Blackpool again. She didn't look over her shoulder. For hours she indulged herself, taking pictures, talking music, laughing at old stories. It didn't even bother her to make an entrance, and stand at the podium reciting her lines to a near-empty theater. She sat, sipping a lukewarm Coke, as some of the musicians jammed centerstage on old Chuck Berry tunes.

Only P.M. left early, anxious to get back to his wife and baby.

"He's getting old," Johnno decided, plopping down beside her to play some blues on a harmonica. He glanced back to study the seventeen-year-old vocalist who was already an established star. "Christ, we're all getting old. Before long, you'll commit the ultimate insult and make us grandfathers."

"We'll just push your rocking chair up to a mike." She tipped up the bottle.

"You're a nasty one, Emma."

"I learned from the best." Chuckling, she draped an arm

around his shoulders. "Look at it this way, there hasn't been anyone else onstage today who's lived through two decades of rock-and-roll hell. You're practically a monument."

"Truly nasty," he decided and cupped the harmonica. "All this talk about lifetime achievement awards," he muttered between chords. "Rock and Roll Hall of Fame."

"They have their nerve, don't they?" She laughed and hugged him. "Johnno, you're not really worried about age."

He scowled and began to blow more blues. Behind him, someone picked up the rhythm on bass. "See how you like it when you're cruising toward fucking fifty."

"Jagger's older."

He shrugged. The drums had fallen in, a brush on the snare. "Not good enough," he told her and continued to play.

"You're better looking."

He considered that. "True."

"And I've never had a crush on him."

He grinned. "Never got over me, did you?"

"Never." Then she spoiled the solemn look with a chuckle. She began to sing, improvising lyrics as she went. "I've got those rock-and-roll blues. Those old, old, rocking blues. When my hair is gray, and you ask me to play, I say don't bug me, Momma, my bones they're aching today. I got them rock-and-roll blues. Them old man rocking blues."

She grinned at him. "Did I pass the audition?"

"Pretty bloody clever, aren't you?"

"Like I said, I learned from the best."

While he continued to play, she slid off the edge of the stage and framed him in. "One last shot before I go." She snapped, changed the angle, and snapped again. "I'll call it *Rock Icon*." She laughed when he called her a nasty name, then packed the camera in her case. "Shall I tell you what rock and roll is, Johnno, from someone who doesn't perform, but observes?"

He gestured with the harmonica, then cupped it again to play softly as he watched her.

"It's restless and rude." Walking back, she laid a hand on his knee. "It's daring and defiant. It's a fist shaken at age. It's a voice that often screams out questions because the answers are always changing."

She glanced up to see her father standing behind Johnno, listening. Her smile swept over him. "The very young play it because they're searching for some way to express their anger or joy, their confusion and their dreams. Once in a while, and only once in a while, someone comes along who truly understands, who has the gift to transfer all those needs and emotions into music.

"When I was three years old, I watched you"—she looked back up at Brian—"all of you, go out onstage. I didn't know about things like harmony or rhythms or riffs. All I saw was magic. I still see it, Johnno, every time I watch the four of you step onstage."

He toyed with the copper column at her ear, then sent it spinning. "I knew there was a reason we kept you around. Give us a kiss."

Her lips were curved as they touched his. "See you tomorrow. You're going to knock them dead."

It was dusk when she walked to her car. Sometime during the afternoon it had rained again. The streets were shiny, and the air was cool and misty. She didn't want to go home to an empty house. Michael was working late, again.

When she started the car, she turned the radio up loud, as she liked it best on aimless drives. She would entertain herself for a couple of hours, look at houses in the glow of street lights, try to decide if she wanted the beach, the hills, or the canyons.

Relaxed, she set the car at a moderate pace and let the music wash over her. She didn't check her rearview mirror, or notice the car that fell in behind her.

◆ ◆ ◆ ◆

MICHAEL STOOD IN front of the pegboard in the conference room and studied his lists. He'd made another connection. It was slow work, frustrating, but each link brought him closer to the end of the chain.

Jane Palmer had had many men. Finding them all could be a life's work, Michael thought. But it was particularly satisfying when he turned one up whose name was on the list.

She had used Brian's money to move out of her dingy little flat and into bigger, more comfortable quarters in Chelsea, where she'd lived from 1968 to 1971, until she'd bought the house on King's Road. For the better part of '70, she'd had a flatmate, a struggling pub singer named Blackpool.

Wasn't it interesting, Michael thought as he rubbed eyes

dead-dry with strain, that while the McAvoys had been living in the hills of Hollywood, Jane Palmer had been playing house with Blackpool? Blackpool who had been at the McAvoys' party that night in early December?

And odd, wasn't it just a bit odd, that Jane hadn't mentioned the connection in her book? She'd dropped every name that could have made the slightest ring, but Blackpool, an established star by the mid-seventies, didn't rate a footnote. Because, Michael concluded, neither of them wanted the connection remembered.

McCarthy stuck his head in the door. "Christ, Kesselring, you still playing with that thing? I want some dinner."

"Robert Blackpool was Palmer's live-in lover from June of '70 to February of '71."

"Well, call out the wrath of God."

Michael slapped a file in McCarthy's hand. "I need everything there is to know about Blackpool."

"I need red meat."

"I'll buy you a steer," Michael said as he walked back into the squad room.

"You know, partner, this whole business has ruined your sense of humor. And my appetite. Blackpool's a big star. He does beer commercials, for Christ's sake. You're not going to tie him to a twenty-year-old case."

"Maybe not, but I'm down to eight names." He sat at his desk and pulled out a cigarette. "Somebody stole my damn Pepsi."

"I'll call a cop." McCarthy leaned over. "Mike, no fooling around, you're pushing this too hard."

"Looking out for me, Mac?"

"I'm your goddamn partner. Yeah, I'm looking out for you, and I'm looking out for myself. If we have to go out on the streets while you're strung out like this, you're not going to back me up."

Through a veil of smoke, Michael studied his partner. His voice, when he spoke, was dangerously soft. "I know how to do my job."

It was a tender area. McCarthy was well aware of the razzing Michael had taken his first years on the force. "I'm also your friend, and I'm telling you, if you don't ease off for a few hours, you're not going to do anybody any good. Including your lady."

Slowly, Michael unclenched his fists. "I'm getting close. I know it. It's not like it was twenty years ago. It's like it was yesterday, and I was there, right there going over every step."

"Like your old man."

"Yeah." He braced his elbows on the desk to scrub his hands over his face. "I'm going crazy."

"You're just overcharged, kid. Take a couple hours. Ease off."

Michael stared down at the papers on his desk. "I'll buy you a steak. You help me run the make on Blackpool."

"Deal." He waited while Michael shrugged into his jacket. "Why don't you give me a couple other names? Marilyn's on a new kick and we're getting nothing but fish this week anyway."

"Thanks."

◆ ◆ ◆ ◆

EMMA STOPPED THE car and looked at the house through the rising mists. She hadn't consciously decided to drive to it. Years before she had sat in the car with Michael and studied the house. It had been sunny then, she remembered.

There were lights in the windows. Though she could see no movement, she wondered who lived there now. Did a child sleep in the room where she had once slept, or where Darren's crib had stood? She hoped so. She wanted to think that more than tragedy lived on. There had been laughter in the house as well, a great deal of it. She hoped there was again.

She supposed Johnno had made her think of it, when he had talked of growing older. Most of the time she still saw them as they had been in her own childhood, not as men who had lived for nearly a quarter of a century with fame and ambition, with success and failure.

They had all changed. Perhaps herself most of all. She no longer felt like a shadow of the men who had so dominated her life. If she was stronger, it was because of the effort it had taken to finally see herself as whole, rather than as parts of the people she'd loved the best.

She looked through the gloom to the house nestled on the hill, and hoped with all her heart she would dream of it that night. When she did, she would open that door. She would stand, and look, and she would see.

Releasing the brake, she started down the narrow road. Six months before, she knew, she wouldn't have had the courage to come alone, to open herself to all those feelings. It was good, so good not to be afraid.

The headlights flashed into her rearview mirror so close, so fast, they blinded her. Instinctively she threw a hand up to block the glare.

Drunk and stupid, she thought and glanced for a place to pull over and let the car pass.

When it rammed her from behind, her hands clamped automatically on the wheel. Still, the few seconds of shock cost her, and had her veering dangerously close to the guardrail. Dragging the wheel back, she heard her tires squeal on the wet pavement. Her heart jackhammered to her throat as she slid sideways around the next turn.

"Asshole!" With a trembling hand she wiped a smear of blood from her lip where she'd bitten it. Then the lights were blinding her again, and the impact of the next hit had her seat belt snapping against her breastbone.

There was no time to think, no room for panic. Her rear fender slapped against the metal guard as her car shimmied. The car behind backed off as she fought her own out of a skid. She saw the tree, a big leafy oak, and used every ounce of strength to jerk the wheel to the right. Panting, she concentrated on maneuvering around an S turn, pumping her brakes to slow her speed.

He came again. She caught a glimpse of the car, burned the image into her brain before the lights glared against her mirror again. Though braced for the impact, she cried out.

He wasn't drunk. And he wasn't stupid. In one part of her mind the terror screamed out. Someone was trying to kill her. It wasn't her imagination. It wasn't leftover fears. It was happening. She could see the lights, hear the crunch of metal against metal, feel her tires skid as they fought for traction.

The car came up on her left, punching hers toward the drop. She was screaming; she could hear herself as she laid on the gas and tore around the next turn.

She wouldn't outrun him. Emma blinked the glaze out of her eyes and tried to think. His car was bigger, and faster. And the hunter always had the advantage over the hunted. The road cut through the hills gave her no room to maneuver, and there was no place to go but down.

He pulled up again. She could see the dark shape of the car, creeping closer, and closer, like a spider toward a victim in the web. She shook her head, knowing at any moment he would ram her and send her crashing over the edge.

In desperation, she jerked her car to the left, surprising him by taking the offensive. It gave her an instant, hardly more. But even as he approached again, she saw the headlights gleam from the other direction.

On a prayer, she took her last chance and poured on the speed. The oncoming car swerved, brakes high and shrill, horn blasting. She caught a glimpse of the car behind her veering back to the right at a dangerous speed.

For a second, she was alone, around the next turn. Then she heard the crash. It echoed with her own screams as she hurtled down the winding road toward the lights of L.A.

◆ ◆ ◆

$\mathcal{M}$CCARTHY HAD BEEN right. Not only did Michael feel better after a meal and an hour's break, but he thought more clearly. As a second-generation cop, he had not only his contacts to call on, but his father's. He made a call to Lou's poker buddy who worked in Immigration, to his own contact in the Motor Vehicle Administration, used his father's name with the FBI and his own with Inspector Carlson in London.

No one was particularly pleased to be called on after hours, but the meal had made it easier for him to use charm.

"I know it's irregular, Inspector, and I'm sorry to bother—oh, Lord, I totally forgot the time difference. I am *really* sorry. Yes, well, I need some information, background stuff. Robert Blackpool. Yeah, that Blackpool. I want to know who he was before 1970, Inspector. I should be able to connect the dots after that." He made a note to himself to contact Pete Page. "Everything you can find. I don't know if I've got anything, but you'll be the first—"

He broke off when he saw Emma running in, glassy-eyed, with a trickle of blood on her temple.

"Please." She collapsed into the chair in front of his desk. "Someone's trying to kill me."

He cut Inspector Carlson off without a word. "What happened?" He was beside her, taking her face in his hands.

"On a road up in the hills . . . a car . . . tried to run me down."

"Were you hit?" He began to search frantically for broken bones.

She heard other voices. They were crowding around her. A phone was ringing, ringing, ringing. She saw the lights revolve. The room followed it before she slid out of the chair.

There was a cloth against her head. Cool. She moaned, reaching a hand to it as she opened her eyes.

"You're okay," Michael told her. "You just passed out for a minute. Drink a little of this. It's only water."

She sipped, letting her head rest against his supporting arm. She could smell him—her soap, his sweat. She was safe again. Somehow she was safe again. "I want to sit up."

"Okay. Take it easy."

She stared around, waiting to settle. She was in an office. His father's office, she thought. She'd seen it when she'd stopped by earlier in the week, wanting to see where Michael worked. It was very plain. Brown carpet, glass walls. The blinds were closed now. His desk was ordered. There was a picture of his wife on it. Michael's mother. Looking beyond, she saw another man, thin, balding.

"I'm sorry. You're Michael's partner."

"McCarthy."

"I met you a few days ago."

He nodded. She might have been concussed, but she was lucid.

"Emma." Michael touched her cheek to make her look at him. "Tell us what happened."

"I thought I was imagining it."

"What?"

"That someone was after me. Could I have that water?"

"Sure." Because her hands were shaking, he closed his over them on the cup. "Who was after you?"

"I don't know. Before I left London, I . . . maybe it was my imagination."

"Tell me."

"I thought someone was following me." She glanced over at McCarthy, waiting to see the doubt, or the amusement. He only sat on the edge of the captain's desk and listened. "I was almost sure of it. After so many years with bodyguards, you just know. I can't explain it."

"You don't have to," Michael told her. "Go on."

She looked at him and wanted to weep because he meant it. She would never have to explain to him. "While I was in New York, I saw someone watching the loft. I was sure Da had hired someone to look out for me. But when I asked him, he said he hadn't, so I decided I'd been wrong. The first night I was back, a car followed me home from the market."

"You never mentioned it."

"I was going to, but . . ." She trailed off again. "You were upset when you got back. And then I more or less forgot about it. I didn't like thinking I was going crazy. I would think someone had been in the house when I'd go out, that the phone was making noises. Like it was tapped." She closed her eyes. "Typical paranoid behavior."

"Don't be stupid, Emma."

She nearly smiled. He never let her feel sorry for herself for long. "I can't prove it had anything to do with tonight, but I feel it."

"Can you talk about it now?" He'd given her time. Now her hands were steadier and the glassy look had faded.

"Yeah." Taking a deep breath, she related everything that she could remember about the incident on the road. "I just kept going," she finished. "I don't know if anyone was hurt. That other car. I didn't even think about it until I was nearly here. I just kept going."

"You did the right thing. Check out her car," he asked McCarthy. "Emma, did you get a look at the driver?"

"No."

"At the car?"

"Yes." Calm again, she nodded. "I made a point of looking, of trying to pick out whatever details I could. It was dark—blue or black—I can't be sure. I don't know much about makes and models but it was good-sized. Not a small car like mine. It could have been a . . . Cadillac, I think, or a Lincoln. It had L.A. plates. MBE. I think those were the letters, but in the mist I couldn't catch the last numbers."

"You did great." He kissed her. "I'm going to have someone drive you to the hospital."

"I don't need the hospital."

He traced a fingertip over her temple. "You've got a major-league bump on your head."

"I didn't even feel it." Though she could now, with more

clarity than was comfortable, she stood firm. "I won't go, Michael. I've had enough of hospitals to last me a lifetime."

"All right. We'll get someone to take you home and stay with you."

"Can't you?"

"I've got to check this out," he began, then glanced up when McCarthy came back in.

"You must be a hell of a driver, Miss McAvoy."

"Emma," she said. "I was too scared to be a bad one."

"Mike, I need you a minute."

"Just sit. I won't be long," he told Emma as he rose. Recognizing the look on his partner's face, he shut the door behind him. "Well?"

"I don't know how the hell she managed to get through it in one piece. Car looks like she took third place in the Demolition Derby." Casually, he laid a hand on Michael's arm. He didn't think his partner was quite ready to take a look at it himself. "I had one of the guys check the hospitals before I took a look at her car. They just got an admission, car wreck up in the hills. Cut the guy out of a brand-new Cadillac. Blackpool," he said and watched Michael's eyes narrow. "He's in a coma."

# Chapter Forty-four

♦ ♦ ♦ ♦

$\mathcal{A}$RE YOU SURE you're up to this?" Johnno took a careful study of Emma as she came to the bottom of the stairs.

"Don't I look up to it?" She did a slow model's pivot. The deep blue dress left her shoulders bare and dipped low at the back before it slid down her body, sparkling with hundreds of bugle beads.

Her hair was scooped up in intricate tiny waves and clipped with two glittery combs. On the lapel of the silver jacket she carried was pinned the phoenix he had given her.

"I'd best not comment what you look up to." Still, he crossed to her to stroke a thumb over the bruise on her temple which she'd camouflaged with makeup. "You had a rough time a couple days ago."

"But it's over." She walked to the table to pour him a glass of wine. After a moment's hesitation, she poured another for herself. "Blackpool can't harm me from a hospital bed." She offered Johnno a glass. "I know Michael believes he was involved with Darren's murder, and I certainly won't rule him out, but until he comes out of the coma—if he comes out—we won't be sure. I've tried to picture him in Darren's room that night, but I just can't remember."

"There was someone else there," he reminded her.

"Isn't that why I have the hottest escort in town for the awards tonight?"

He grinned over the rim of his glass. "I doubt if I make up for Michael."

She set down the glass, barely touched, and picked up her evening bag. "You don't have to make up for anyone. And he'll get there if he can. Ready?"

"As I'll ever be." He offered his arm, formally, and led her outside to the waiting limo.

"Don't try that shy, retiring stuff on me. I happen to know that no one loves the spotlight better."

It was true enough. He settled back against the cushy seat, enjoying the scent of leather and fresh flowers. But he worried. "I thought I knew the bastard," he said half to himself. "I didn't like him particularly, but I figured I knew him. One of the biggest pissers is I helped write his first hit."

"It's a bit foolish to beat yourself up over that now."

"If he had anything to do with Darren . . ." With a shake of his head he pulled out a cigarette. "That should keep the tabloids going for years."

"We'll deal with it." She laid a hand over his. "It's all going to come out anyway. Jane's part in it, and Blackpool's. We'll just have to learn to live with it."

"It's rough on Bri. Like going through it a second time."

"He's stronger now." She fingered the pin on her jacket. "I guess we all are."

He brought her hand to his lips. "You know, if you threw Michael over, I might just might consider changing my . . . style."

She laughed, then picked up the phone as it began to ring. "Hello. Michael."

Johnno sat back and watched her smile spread.

"Yes, I'm sitting here thinking over a proposal from an incredibly attractive man. No, Johnno." She put a hand over the receiver. "Michael wants you to know he's got an in with the Department of Motor Vehicles and can make your life a living hell."

"I'll take the bus," Johnno decided.

"Yes. We're due at the theater at four. The early award ceremonies should have already started."

"I'm sorry I can't be there," Michael told her. He glanced down the hospital corridor toward ICU. "If things change here, I'll meet you."

"Don't worry about it."

"Easy for you to say. I miss my chance to ride in a limo and rub elbows with the rich and famous. If you married me, I could do it once a week."

"All right."

He caught a glimpse of a doctor coming down the corridor. "All right what?"

"I'll marry you."

He ran a hand through his hair and shifted the phone. "Excuse me?"

She grinned foolishly at Johnno and squeezed his hand. "Have we got a bad connection?"

"No, I . . . Shit, hold on." He put a hand over the speaker to listen to the doctor. "I've got to go, Emma. He's coming out of it. Listen, don't forget where we left off. Okay?"

"No, I won't." She hung up just as Johnno popped the cork on the champagne.

"Do I get invited this time?"

"Hmmm? Oh, yes. Yes." A little dazed herself, she stared at the glass he handed her. "It was so easy."

"It's supposed to be when it's right." Feeling a bit misty, he touched his rim to hers. "He's the luckiest man I know."

"We can make it work." She sipped, letting the wine explode on her tongue. "We will make it work." Dreamily she settled back and didn't give a thought to Blackpool.

◆ ◆ ◆ ◆

*M*ICHAEL THOUGHT OF him. He stood at the foot of the bed and studied the man who had tried to kill Emma. He hadn't come out of it well. His face was ruined. If he made it, he would need a series of operations to reconstruct it. His survival didn't look promising with the internal damage he'd suffered in the crash.

Michael didn't give a damn whether he lived or died. He only wanted five minutes.

He had the background report on Blackpool. It was still sketchy, but it told him enough. The man swimming toward consciousness in ICU had been born Terrance Peters. As a juvenile he'd racked up a record of petty theft, vandalism, possession. He'd graduated to assault, usually on women, dealing, and larceny before he'd changed his name and tried his hand at singing in clubs. He'd let London swallow him, and though he'd been under suspicion for a handful of robberies, he'd always slid his way out.

His luck had turned when he'd hooked up with Jane Palmer.

For the worse as it turned out, Michael thought. It's taken twenty years, you sonofabitch, but we've got you.

"He won't be in any shape to talk," the doctor pointed out. "He needs to stabilize."

"I'll keep it brief."

"I can't leave you alone with him."

"Fine. We can always use a witness." He stepped to the side of the bed. "Blackpool." He watched the eyes flutter, still, then flutter again. "Blackpool, I want to talk to you about Darren McAvoy."

Blackpool dragged his eyes open again. His vision wavered and pain ice-picked into his head. "You a cop?"

"That's right."

"Fuck off. I'm in pain."

"I'll bring you a get-well card. You took a bad ride, pal. It's touch and go."

"I want a doctor."

"I'm Dr. West, Mr. Blackpool. You're—"

"Get this bastard out of my face."

Ignoring him, Michael leaned closer. "It's a good time to clean out your conscience."

"I haven't got one." He tried to laugh and ended up gasping.

"Then maybe you'd like to stick it to someone else. We know about you, how you screwed up the boy's kidnapping."

"She remembered." When Michael didn't respond, he shut his eyes. Even through the pain, he could feel hate and fury. "It figures the bitch would remember me and not him. Supposed to be a nice smooth job, he told me. Take the kid, pick up the ransom. He didn't even want the money. Then when it was all fucked, he just walked away. Told me to clean it up. Like that guy in the kitchen who was ordering pizzas. All I had to do was whack him and keep cool and I'd have everything I wanted."

"Who?" Michael demanded. "Who was with you?"

"Gave me ten thousand pounds anyway. Nowhere close to the million we were going to ask for the kid, but a nice tidy sum. Just had to keep cool and let him handle it. The kid was dead, and the girl didn't remember. Traumatized, he called it. Little Emma was too traumatized to remember. Nobody would ever know and he was going to see I made it to the top. On McAvoy's coattails."

He laughed again and fought for breath.

"You'll have to leave now, Detective."

Michael shook the doctor off. "A name, goddammit. Give me a name. Who set it up?"

Blackpool opened his eyes again. They were red and watery and still malicious. "Go to hell."

"You're going to die for this," Michael said between his teeth. "Either here in this bed, or breathing in a lungful of poison gas, nice and legal. But you're going to die. You can go alone, or you can take him with you."

"You'll take him down?"

"Personally."

With a smile, Blackpool closed his eyes again. "It was Page. Pete Page. Tell him I'll see him in hell."

◆ ◆ ◆ ◆

*E*MMA WATCHED GRIPS raise and lower the sliding doors at the rear of the stage. In a few hours, she realized, she would walk through the one on the right and go to the microphone. "I'm nervous," she told Bev. "It's silly. All I have to do is stand there and read the cue cards and hand out the awards."

"Hopefully to your father and Johnno. Let's go into the dressing room. They're too busy to use it."

"Don't you want to go out front?" Emma glanced at her watch. "They'll be starting in ten minutes."

"Not yet. Whoops, sorry, Annabelle."

Emma cursed herself for not having brought her camera. It was quite a sight, Lady Annabelle tucked into hot pink silk that dripped with sequins, changing a diaper.

"Don't worry. He's nearly decent." She picked young Samuel Ferguson up to cuddle. "We just nipped in here for a quick feed and change. I couldn't leave him with the nanny. It didn't seem fair that he should miss his papa's big night."

Emma looked at the baby's sleepy eyes. "I don't think he's going to make it."

"Just needs a little nap." She nuzzled again, then laid him on the sofa. "Would you mind standing guard for a few minutes? I need to find P.M."

"You could twist our arms," Bev murmured, bending down to stroke the baby's head.

"I won't be more than ten minutes." Annabelle hesitated at the door. "Are you sure? If he wakes up—"

"We'll entertain him," Bev promised.

After one last look, Annabelle shut the door quietly behind her.

"Who would have imagined the ditsy Lady Annabelle as a devoted mother?" Emma mused.

"Babies change you." Bev sat on the arm of the sofa watching Samuel sleep. "I've been wanting to talk to you alone."

Automatically Emma lifted a hand to the bruise on her temple. "There's nothing to worry about."

Noting the gesture, Bev nodded. "I wanted to touch on that as well, but there's something else. I'm not sure how you'll feel about it." One deep breath, and she plunged. "Brian and I are going to have another baby."

Emma stared, lips parted in surprise. "A baby?"

"I know. It surprised us too, though we have been trying." She lifted a hand to her hair. "After all this time—I suppose it's crazy. I'm almost forty-two."

"A baby," Emma repeated.

"Not to replace Darren," Bev said quickly. "Nothing could. And it isn't that we don't love you as much as it's possible to love a daughter, but—"

"A baby." With a laugh, Emma dragged Bev up and hugged her. "Oh, I'm so glad. I'm so happy for you. For me. For all of us. When?"

"Near the end of summer." She pulled back to study Emma's face. What she saw had tears rushing to her eyes. "We were afraid you might be upset."

"Upset?" Emma brushed the back of her hand over her own cheeks. "Why would I be upset?"

"It brings back memories. Brian and I have had to deal with ours. I didn't think I would want another child, but, Emma, I want this one so badly. I want it so much, for me, for Bri, but—I know how much you loved Darren."

"We all loved him." As she had more than twenty years ago, she laid a hand on Bev's stomach. "I already love this one. He's going to be beautiful, and strong, and safe."

As she finished speaking, the lights went out. The instant fear clicked in, making her grope for Bev's hand.

"It's all right," Bev said. "They'll have it fixed in a minute. I'm right here."

"I'm okay." She was going to beat this too, she told herself. This hideous, hateful fear of the dark. "Maybe it's just the backstage lights. I'll go see what's going on."

"I'll go with you."

"No." She took a step toward the door. She could barely see the outline of it. Only a shadow in the dark. A rustling noise had her jolting. The baby was stirring, she told herself as her mouth went dry. There were no monsters, and she wasn't afraid of the dark.

She found the knob, but instead of relief, she was struck by a wild, unreasonable fear. She could see herself opening it. Opening it and looking in. The baby was crying. Dizzy, she tried to understand if it was the baby behind her, or the one in her mind.

Instinctively she snatched her hand away. She wasn't to open it. She didn't want to see. Inside her head the echo of her heart pounded like a musical rhythm. An old song—one she couldn't forget.

Not a dream, Emma reminded herself. She was wide awake. And she had waited most of her life to see what was behind the door.

With rigid fingers, she opened the door, in reality and in her mind. And she knew.

"Oh my God."

"Emma." Bev, soothing the baby on her shoulder, reached out. "What is it?"

"It was Pete."

"What? Is Pete in the hall?"

"He was in Darren's room."

Bev's fingers closed over Emma's arm. "What are you saying?"

"He was in Darren's room that night. When I opened the door, he turned and looked at me. Someone else was holding Darren, making him cry. I didn't know him. Pete smiled at me, but he was angry. I ran away. The baby was crying."

"It's Samuel," Bev murmured. "It's not Darren, Emma. Come sit down."

"It was Pete." On a moan, she pressed her hands to her face. "I saw him."

"I'd hoped you wouldn't remember."

When she lowered her hands she saw him standing in the doorway. He held a flashlight in one hand. And in the other a gun.

Clutching the baby, Bev stared at the shadow of the man in the doorway. "I don't understand this. What's going on?"

"Emma's overwrought." Pete spoke quietly, his eyes on Emma's. "You'd better come with me."

Not again, Emma told herself. It wouldn't happen again. Before she could think, she hurled herself at him. The flashlight popped out of his hand, sending the beam in crazy arches over the walls and ceiling.

"Run!" She screamed to Bev as she struggled to get up and away. "Take the baby and run. Get someone. He'll kill him." She shouted, kicking out as Pete grabbed for her. "Don't let him kill another baby. Get Da."

With the baby wailing, Bev fled toward the confusion on-stage.

"It's too late," Emma said when Pete hauled her to her feet. "They'll catch you. They'll be here any second."

Already spotlights were glowing onstage. Shouts and running feet closed in. Desperate, he dragged her onward. Emma stopped struggling when she felt the barrel of the gun under her jaw.

"They know it's you."

"She didn't see me," he muttered. "It was dark. She can't be sure." He had to believe that—had to. Or it was all over.

"She knows." Emma winced when he dragged her up a flight of stairs. "Everyone knows now. They're coming, Pete. It's finished."

No, it couldn't be. He'd worked too hard, planned too carefully. "I say when it's finished. I know what to do. I can fix it."

They were above and behind the stage now. Far below she could see the lights and confusion. Taking her hair, he wrapped it tight around his wrist. "If you scream, I'll shoot you."

He needed to think. Confused, he continued to drag her along. She stumbled, and as he pulled her up, she yanked the pin from her jacket and let it drop. Seizing a chance, he shoved her into a freight elevator. It was time, time that he needed.

It was supposed to have been so easy. In the dark, while

everyone was confused, he should have been able to get to her. He still had the pills in his pocket he had planned to force her to take. It would have been easy, smooth, quiet.

But nothing had gone easily.

Just like the first time.

"Why?" Sick with vertigo, Emma sunk to the floor. "Why did you do that to Darren?"

Sweat was running off him, drenching his crisp linen shirt. "He wasn't supposed to be hurt. No one was. It was just a publicity stunt."

She shook her head to clear it. "What?"

"Your mother gave me the idea." He looked down at her. He doubted she'd give him much trouble. She was white as a sheet. She'd always had trouble on planes, elevators. With heights. He glanced at the buttons on the panel. Why hadn't he thought of it before?

The opening act would be starting. The show must go on, he thought. Illusion was the first order of the day. While millions of people around the country were watching the record industry pat itself on the back, a few confused guards were looking for Emma backstage. Up here he had time to think. And to plan.

She felt the elevator shudder and bump to a halt. "What are you talking about?"

"Jane—she was always pressuring for more money, threatening to go to the press with this story, or that story. She worried me at first until I began to see that the publicity about you equaled a boom in record sales." He pulled her up. She was limp with nausea and clammy with icy sweat. So much the better. With his arm around her neck, he dragged her up another flight of stairs.

She had to keep him talking. Emma bit back the sickness and the fear. Bev had gotten away, and the baby. Someone would come looking for her.

He didn't worry about her screaming now. She could yell her lungs out and no one would hear. Shoving open a door, he pushed her out on the roof. The wind slapped across her face, tore at her hair. And cleared her head.

"We were talking about Darren." She kept her eyes on his as she backed away. The sun was still bright. One part of her mind wondered how it could be day when she'd been in the dark for so long. "I need to know why—" She backed into the low wall, then swayed at the dizzying view below. Clenching her teeth, she looked back at him. "Tell me why you were in Darren's room."

He could afford to indulge her. And himself. He'd nearly lost control for a moment, but he could feel himself leveling now. He'd find a way out. "Everything was fine for a while. Then it started to flatten out. We were having some internal troubles with the group, as well. They needed something to shake them up. Jane came to me with Blackpool. She wanted me to make him a star, a bigger star than Brian. And she wanted a cut. She got drunk." He waved his hand. "In any case, she offered me a solution. We planned to kidnap Darren. The press would eat it up. A lot of sympathy, a lot of sales. The band would pull together. Blackpool and Jane could keep the money and everyone would be happy."

She wasn't worried about the height any longer, or about the gun. With the wind in her hair and the sun dropping lower at her back, she stared at him. "You're telling me my brother was killed to sell records?"

"It was an accident. Blackpool was clumsy. You came in. It was a poor set of circumstances."

"A poor set . . ." She did scream then, loud and long as she struck out at him.

# Chapter Forty-five

• • • •

*B*ACKSTAGE OF THE auditorium was in chaos when Michael rushed in. In the audience a cheer rose up as another winner was announced.

"Where is she?"

"He took her." Bev was clinging to Brian's arm. She was still out of breath from her race down the hall with the baby. "He had a gun. She held him off so I could get the baby away and find help. Pete," she said, still dazed. "It was Pete."

"It hasn't been more than a couple minutes," Brian told him. "Security's already after him."

"Get this building blocked off," Michael shouted to McCarthy. "Call for more backup. We need a floor-by-floor search. Which way?"

Drawing his weapon, he headed down the corridor. He flashed his badge to a uniformed guard.

"This floor secured. He didn't come out onstage with or without her. We figure he took her up."

"I want two men." Back to the wall, Michael started up the stairs. He could hear the music pumping from behind him. As he climbed, it took on a hollow, echoing tone. His palms were wet. Making the first turn, he checked his grip, then swept the area with his weapon. At the clatter on the stairs, he whirled and swore when he saw the four men grouped together. "Get back downstairs."

"She's ours, too," Brian said.

"I haven't got time to argue." Bending, Michael retrieved the phoenix pin, a swatch of silvery material caught in the clasp. "Is this Emma's?"

"She was wearing it tonight," Johnno told him. "I gave it to her."

Michael stared at the elevator, then slipped the pin into his pocket. "She's using her head," he murmured. "Seal off this area," he shouted to the security guards. "And keep up the floor-by-floor." He punched the button on the elevator and watched the numbers light up above the door. "Tell McCarthy he took her all the way up." Listening to the rumble of the elevator, he began to pray.

"We're going with you," Brian said.

"This is police business."

"It's personal," Brian corrected. "It's always been personal. If he hurts her, I'm going to kill him myself."

Michael shot a grim look at the four men behind him. "You'll have to get in line."

◆ ◆ ◆ ◆

PETE SHOVED EMMA back, sending her sprawling while he tried to catch his breath. "That's not going to do any good. I don't want to hurt you any more than I must, Emma."

"He was a baby." She pushed herself up. "You bought him a silver cup after he was born, with his name on it. For his first birthday you rented a pony for his party."

"I was fond of him."

"You murdered him."

"I never laid a hand on him. Blackpool got too rough, pan-icked. I never wanted to hurt that boy."

She dragged her wind-tossed hair out of her face. "You just wanted to use him, to use him and my father's fear and pain for some bloody publicity. Oh, I can see it," she added. 'Brian McAvoy's son stolen from his crib. Rock star pays a king's ransom for safe return of beloved child.' That's what you had in mind, didn't you? Lots of print, lots of film at eleven. Reporters crammed on the front yard waiting for a statement from the terrified parents. Then more of the same when the baby was returned to loving arms. But he was never returned, was he?"

"What happened was tragic—"

"Don't talk to me about tragedy." Too anguished to be afraid, she turned away. The gun was trained on her, she knew it. It didn't seem to matter. After all these years, she remembered and it left her hollow. But worse, much worse, was to know it had been for nothing. "You were there at his funeral with the rest of us, your eyes down, your face solemn. All the while, you were getting just what you wanted. A boy had to die, unfortunately, but you got your press, didn't you?" She turned back. "You sold your bloody records."

"I've devoted nearly half my life to them." Pete took a long, calming breath. "I shaped and I molded, I made deals, listened to their problems. Solved them. Who do you think made sure they got everything that was coming to them? Who made certain that the record company didn't play any games with royalties? Who fought so that they would reach the top?"

She took a step toward him. There was enough of a need to survive to stop her when he motioned with the gun. "Do you think they needed you?" she spat out. "Do you really believe that you mattered?"

"I made them."

"No. They made you."

Saying nothing, he reached in his pocket. "Be that as it may, even what happens tonight will add to the legend. Brian and Johnno are odds-on favorites for Song of the Year. With a bit of luck, the group will pick up a couple more for Best Performance, Rock, and Best Album. I'd thought it a nice touch for you to hand out the award. Brian's daughter, and the tragic widow of Drew Latimer. Tragedies sell," he said with a shrug. "We'll have one more tonight." He held out two pills. "Take these. They're very strong. It'll make it easier."

She looked down at them, then back into his face. "I won't make it easier."

"Very well." He put them back in his pocket. "It's a very long fall, Emma." He grabbed her, holding her against him at the edge. "By the time you hit, I'll be on my way down." He had it worked out now, calm and precise. "I came to see if you were all right when the lights went out, but you went wild. I chased you up here, concerned. You were hysterical, and I was too late to save you. All these years, and you still blamed yourself for your brother's death. You finally couldn't live with it anymore." He forced her around to face the fall. One of her combs came loose and spun off into empty space. "No one knows but you. And no one but you will ever know."

She clawed at him, fighting her way back from the edge. Her strength threw him off balance, and for an instant, she was free. Then he clamped an arm around her waist and began to heave.

She lost her footing, teetered, then threw her weight back against him. Screaming, she saw the sky and ground revolve.

Michael broke through the door at a run. He shouted, but neither of the two locked in a life-and-death struggle heard. He saw Pete raise his gun, and fired his own.

The wall caught Emma at the waist, stealing her breath. Hands grabbed at her, dragged at her until half her body tilted over the edge. Dazed, she saw Pete's face below her, his eyes wide and terrified. The fingers on her wrist slipped, and released. Then he was falling, falling. Momentum had her sliding toward him.

Hands were dragging her back, pulling her away from the wall. Her feet left the floor again, but there were arms around her, squeezing, holding her safe and close. Through the ringing in her ears, she heard her name repeated over and over.

"Michael." She didn't have to look, but let her head drop on his shoulder. "Michael, don't let go."

"I won't."

"I remembered." She began to sob then. Through the tears, she saw her father standing beside her. "Da. I remembered." She reached out for him.

♦ ♦ ♦ ♦

EMMA WATCHED THE flames from the fire Stevie had built in the hearth. He stood beside it, hands in his pockets, saying nothing. They had all come home with her, her father, P.M. and his family, Johnno. Bev made endless pots of tea.

Though no one spoke, she sensed the shock was wearing off into bewilderment. There were questions that could never be answered, mistakes that could never be rectified. Regrets that would never completely disappear.

But they had survived, Emma thought. The odds had been against them, individually and as a group, but they had survived. Even triumphed.

Rising, she walked out to the terrace where Brian was alone, watching the sea. He would suffer, Emma thought. It was his nature to pull problems into his heart and mourn, whether they were his or the world's. Then somehow, he would turn them into something to be played on guitar or keyboard, with flute and violin. Moving to him, she rested her head on his shoulder.

"He was one of us," Brian said after a moment. "He'd been with us since the beginning."

"I know."

"When I saw him with his hands on you, I wanted to kill him myself. And now . . ." He watched the play of the early moon on the water. "I can hardly believe it all happened. Why?" He turned, taking her into his arms. "For God's sake, why did he do it?"

She pressed hard against him, listening to the ebb and flow of the sea. How could she tell him? If he knew the reasons, he would never be able to make music again. "I don't know. We could ask ourselves forever, but it wouldn't change." She drew back. "Da. We have to set it aside. Not forget, but set it aside."

"A new beginning?"

"God no." She smiled. "I wouldn't want to begin again. Not for anything. Finally I know where I am and where I want to go. I don't have to be afraid anymore. I don't have to wonder. And I can stop blaming myself, because I didn't run this time."

"You were never to blame, Emma."

"None of us were. Come inside." She drew him into the light and the warmth. In the silence, she walked to the television and switched it on. "I want to hear them say your name."

As she watched the set, P.M. touched her arm. "Emma." Unable to find the words, he brought her hand to his cheek.

"Here we go, mates." Johnno laid a hand on Brian's shoulder as the nominees for Song of the Year were announced.

Emma held her breath, then let it out on a laugh when she heard Brian McAvoy and Johnno Donovan. "Congratulations." She swung her arms around both of them. "Oh, I wish I could have handed it to you."

"Next year," Johnno said, giving her a quick, hard kiss.

"It's a promise. It's important," she said, squeezing Brian's hand. "It means something. Don't let what happened spoil this for you, or for me."

"No." He relaxed, and when he smiled she watched it reach his eyes. He threw an arm around Johnno's shoulder. "Not bad for a couple of aging rockers."

"Mind your adjectives, Bri." Johnno winked at Emma. "Jagger's older." He lifted a brow when he heard the knock on the door. "Ah, the call of the gray-eyed, infatuated copper."

"Shut up, Johnno," Emma said pleasantly as she hurried to answer with Conroy at her heels. "Michael."

"Sorry it took so long." He dragged on the dog's collar to keep him from leaping. "Okay?"

"Sure." She leaned down, the beads of her evening dress glinting, to rub between Conroy's ears. "We were just passing out congratulations. Da and Johnno won Song of the Year."

"No, we were just leaving." Bev was already picking up her wrap. If ever she'd seen a man who wanted to be alone with a woman, it was Michael. "There's a pot of tea in the kitchen," she added, flicking a glance over her shoulder to get the others moving. Before Emma could protest, she pulled her close. "Time's too precious to waste," she murmured. "Michael." She put her arms around him. "Thank you," she said quietly. And pulling back, smiled. "Welcome to chaos."

They made their way out, one at a time, while a disinterested Conroy sniffed around, then went to sleep in the corner.

"They're quite a group," Michael stated when the door finally closed. "No pun intended."

"Yes, they are. You're not going to mind having dinner with the lot of them tomorrow, are you?"

"No." He didn't give a hang about tomorrow. Only tonight. The way she looked, the way she smelled, the way she smiled at him. "Come here." He held out his arms. When she was in them, he found he couldn't let go. In the hours that had passed, he'd thought he'd calmed himself. But now, holding her, it all crashed down on him.

He'd almost lost her.

She could feel his rage building, degree by degree. "Don't," she murmured. "It's over. It's really over this time."

"Just shut up a minute." He brought his mouth to hers, hard, as if to convince himself she was whole, and safe, and his. "If he had—"

"He didn't." She lifted both hands to his face. "You saved my life."

"Yeah." He backed away, digging his hands into his pockets. "If you have to be grateful, could you get it over with fast?"

She tilted her head. "We haven't had much of a chance to talk."

"I'm sorry I couldn't come back with you."

"I understand. Maybe it worked out for the best, gave us both a chance to settle."

"I haven't been able to pull that off yet." He could still see her, teetering on the edge of the roof. Wanting to block the image, he turned to pace the room. "So, how was your day?"

She grinned. It was going to be all right. It was going to be just fine. "Dandy. Yours?"

He shrugged, kept moving, picking up little odds and ends and setting them down again. "Emma, I know you're probably tired."

"No, I'm not."

"And the timing sucks."

"No." She smiled again. "It doesn't."

He turned back. She looked so beautiful, the dress shimmering down, the light from the fire catching in her hair, glowing on her skin. "I love you. I've always loved you. We haven't had a lot of time to let things just happen. I'd like to say that I'm ready to give you that time." He picked up a crystal butterfly, then set it down. "I'm not."

"Michael, if I wanted time, I'd take it." She stepped toward him. "What I want is you."

After a long breath he took a small box out of his pocket. "I bought this months ago. I'd wanted to give it to you for Christmas, but I didn't think you'd take it then. I'd figured on being traditional, having a candlelight dinner, music, the works." With a half-laugh, he turned the box over in his hand. "I guess it's a little late to start being traditional now."

"Are you going to give it to me?"

With a nod, he held it out.

"I'd like to say something before I open it." Carefully, she studied his face, every inch, every angle. "If this had happened five or six years ago, I wouldn't have appreciated it, or you, the way I can tonight."

Her hands weren't steady. She let out a frustrated breath as she fumbled with the lid. "Oh, Michael, it's lovely." She looked up from the ring. "Absolutely lovely."

"Be damn sure," he told her. "You take it, and that's it."

She strangled on a laugh. "That's the most romantic proposal a woman could possibly dream of."

"I've already asked you too many times." He cupped the

back of her head in his hand. "How's this?" The kiss was soft, gentle, and promising. "No one's ever going to love you more than I do. I only want a lifetime to prove it."

"That's good." She blinked back a film of tears. "That's very good." Taking the ring from the box, she studied it. "Why three circles?" she asked, running a fingertip around the trio of linked diamond spheres.

"One's your life, one's mine." He took it from her and slipped it onto her finger. "And one's the life we'll make together. We've been connected for a long time."

She nodded, then looking up, reached out to him. "I want to start on that third circle, Michael. Right away."

Look for another Nora Roberts favorite,
available now from Bantam Books


# BRAZEN VIRTUE


Please turn the page for a riveting preview of

## Brazen Virtue

GRACE HEARD THE low, droning buzz and blamed it on the wine. She didn't groan or grumble about the hangover. She'd been taught that every sin, venial or mortal, required penance. It was one of the few aspects of her early Catholic training she carried with her into adulthood.

The sun was up and strong enough to filter through the gauzy curtains at the windows. In defense, she buried her face in the pillow. She managed to block out the light, but not the buzzing. She was awake, and hating it.

Thinking of aspirin and coffee, she pushed herself up in bed. It was then she realized the buzzing wasn't inside her head, but outside the house. She rummaged through one of her bags and came up with a ratty terry-cloth robe. In her closet at home was a silk one, a gift from a former lover. Grace had fond memories of the lover, but preferred the terry-cloth robe. Still groggy, she stumbled to the window and pushed the curtain aside.

It was a beautiful day, cool and smelling just faintly of spring and turned earth. There was a sagging chain-link fence separating her sister's yard from the yard next door. Tangled and pitiful against it was a forsythia bush. It was struggling to bloom, and Grace thought its tiny yellow flowers looked brave and daring. It hadn't occurred to her until then how tired she was of hothouse flowers and perfect petals. On a huge yawn, she looked beyond it.

She saw him then, in the backyard of the house next door. Long narrow boards were braced on sawhorses. With the kind of easy competence she admired, he measured and marked and cut through. Intrigued, Grace shoved the window up to get a better look. The morning air was chill, but she leaned into it, pleased that it cleared her head. Like the forsythia, he was something to see.

Paul Bunyan, she thought, and grinned. The man had to be six-four if he was an inch and built along the lines of a fullback. Even with the distance she could see the power of his muscles moving under his jacket. He had a mane of red hair and a full beard—not a trimmed little affectation, but the real thing. She could just see his mouth move in its cushion in time to the country music that jingled out of a portable radio.

When the buzzing stopped, she was smiling down at him, her elbows resting on the sill. "Hi," she called. Her smile widened as he turned and looked up. She'd noticed that his body had braced as he'd turned, not so much in surprise, she thought, but in readiness. "I like your house."

Ed relaxed as he saw the woman in the window. He'd put in over sixty hours that week, and had killed a man. The sight of a pretty woman smiling at him from a second-story window did a lot to soothe his worn nerves. "Thanks."

"You fixing it up?"

"Bit by bit." He shaded his eyes against the sun and studied her. She wasn't his neighbor. Though he and Kathleen Breezewood hadn't exchanged more than a dozen words, he knew her by sight. But there was something familiar in the grinning face and tousled hair. "You visiting?"

"Yes, Kathy's my sister. I guess she's gone already. She teaches."

"Oh." He'd learned more about his neighbor in two seconds than he had in two months. Her nickname was Kathy, she had a sister, and she was a teacher. Ed hefted another board onto the horses. "Staying long?"

"I'm not sure." She leaned out a bit farther so the breeze ruffled her hair. It was a small indulgence the pace and convenience of New York had denied her. "Did you plant the azaleas out front?"

"Yeah. Last week."

"They're terrific. I think I'll put some in for Kath." She smiled again. "See you." She pulled her head inside and was gone.

For a minute longer Ed stared at the empty window. She'd left it open, he noted, and the temperature had yet to climb to sixty. He took out his carpenter's pencil to mark the wood. He knew that face. It was both a matter of business and personality that he never forgot one. It would come to him.

Inside, Grace pulled on a pair of sweats. Her hair was still damp from the shower, but she wasn't in the mood to fuss with blow dryers and styling brushes. There was coffee to be drunk, a paper to be read, and a murder to be solved. By her calculations, she could put Maxwell to work and have enough carved out to be satisfied before Kathleen returned from Our Lady of Hope.

Downstairs, she put on the coffee, then checked out the contents of the refrigerator. The best bet was the spaghetti left over from the night before. Grace bypassed eggs and pulled out the neat plastic container. It took her a minute to realize that her sister's kitchen wasn't civilized enough to have a microwave. Taking this in stride, she tossed the top into the sink and dug in. She'd eat it cold. Chewing, she spotted the note on the kitchen table. Kathleen always left notes.

*Help yourself to whatever's in the kitchen.* Grace smiled and forked more cold spaghetti into her mouth. *Don't worry about dinner, I'll pick up a couple of steaks.* And that, she thought, was Kathleen's polite way of telling her not to mess up the kitchen. *Parent conference this afternoon. I'll be home by five-thirty. Don't use the phone in my office.*

Grace wrinkled her nose as she stuffed the note into her pocket. It would take time, and some pressure, but she was determined to learn more of her sister's moonlighting adventures. And there was the matter of finding out the name of her sister's lawyer. Kathleen's objections and pride aside, Grace wanted to speak to him personally. If she did so carefully enough, her sister's ego wouldn't be bruised. In any case, sometimes you had to overlook a couple of bruises and shoot for the goal. Until she had Kevin back, Kathleen would never be able to put her life in order. That scum Breezewood had no right using Kevin as a weapon against Kathleen.

He'd always been an operator, she thought. Jonathan Breezewood the third was a cold and calculating manipulator who used family position and monied politics to get his way. But not this time. It might take some maneuvering, but Grace would find a way to set things right.

She turned the heat off under the coffeepot just as someone knocked on the front door.

Her trunk, she decided, and snatched up the carton of spaghetti as she started down the hall. An extra ten bucks should convince the delivery man to haul it upstairs. She had a persuasive smile ready as she opened the door.

"G. B. McCabe, right?" Ed stood on the stoop with a hardback copy of *Murder in Style*. He'd nearly sawed a finger off when he'd put the name together with the face.

"That's right." She glanced at the picture on the back cover. Her hair had been styled and crimped, and the photographer had used stark black and white to make her look mysterious. "You've got a good eye. I barely recognize myself from that picture."

Now that he was here, he hadn't the least idea what to do with himself. This kind of thing always happened, he knew, whenever he acted on impulse. Especially with a woman. "I like your stuff. I guess I've read most of it."

"Only most of it?" Grace stuck the fork back in the spaghetti as she smiled at him. "Don't you know that writers have huge and fragile egos? You're supposed to say you've read every word I've ever written and adored them all."

He relaxed a little because her smile demanded he do so. "How about you tell a hell of a story?"

"That'll do."

"When I realized who you were, I guess I wanted to come over and make sure I was right."

"Well, you win the prize. Come on in."

"Thanks." He shifted the book to his other hand and felt like an idiot. "But I don't want to bother you."

Grace gave him a long, solemn look. He was even more impressive up close than he'd been from the window. And his eyes were blue, a dark, interesting blue. "You mean you don't want me to sign that?"

"Well, yes, but—"

"Come in then." She took his arm and pulled him inside. "The coffee's hot."

"I don't drink it."

"Don't drink coffee? How do you stay alive?" Then she smiled and gestured with her fork. "Come on back anyway, there's probably something you can drink. So you like mysteries?"

He liked the way she walked, slowly, carelessly, as though she could change her mind about direction at any moment. "I guess you could say mysteries are my life."

"Mine too." In the kitchen, she opened the refrigerator again. "No beer," she murmured and decided to remedy that at the first opportunity. "No sodas, either. Christ, Kathy. There's juice. It looks like orange."

"Fine."

"I've got some spaghetti here. Want to share?"

"No, thanks. Is that your breakfast?"

"Mmmm." She poured his juice, gesturing casually to a chair as she went to the stove to pour her coffee. "Have you lived next door long?"

He was tempted to mention nutrition but managed to control himself. "Just a couple of months."

"It must be great, fixing it up the way you want." She took another bite of the pasta. "Is that what you are, a carpenter? You have the hands for it."

He found himself pleasantly relieved that she hadn't asked him if he played ball. "No. I'm a cop."

"You're kidding. Really?" She shoved her carton aside and leaned forward. It was her eyes that made her beautiful, he decided on the spot. They were so alive, so full of fascination. "I'm crazy about cops. Some of my best characters are cops, even the bad ones."

"I know." He had to smile. "You've got a feel for police work. It shows in the way you plot a book. Everything works on logic and deduction."

"All my logic goes into writing." She picked up her coffee, then remembered she'd forgotten the cream. Rather than get up, she drank it black. "What kind of cop are you—uniform, undercover?"

"Homicide."

"Kismet." She laughed and squeezed his hand. "I can't believe it, I come to visit my sister and plop right down beside a homicide detective. Are you working on anything right now?"

"Actually, we just wrapped up something yesterday."

A rough one, she decided. There'd been something about the way he'd said it, the faintest change of tone. Though her curiosity was piqued, it was controlled by compassion. "I've got a hell of a murder working right now. A series of murders, actually. I've got . . ." She trailed off. Ed saw her eyes darken. She sat back and propped her bare feet on an empty chair. "I can change the location," she began slowly. "Set it right here in D.C. That's better. It would work. What do you think?"

"Well, I—"

"Maybe I could come down to the station sometime. You could show me around." Already taking her thought processes to the next stage, she thrust her hand into the pocket of her robe for a cigarette. "That's allowed, isn't it?"

"I could probably work it out."

"Terrific. Look, have you got a wife or a lover or anything?"

He stared at her as she lit the cigarette and blew out smoke. "Not right now," he said cautiously.

"Then maybe you'd have a couple of hours now and again in the evening for me."

He picked up his juice and took a long swallow. "A couple of hours," he repeated. "Now and again?"

"Yeah. I wouldn't expect you to give me all your free time, just squeeze me in when you're in the mood."

"When I'm in the mood," he murmured. Her robe dipped down to the floor but was parted at the knee to reveal her legs, pale from winter and smooth as marble. Maybe miracles did still happen.

"You could be kind of my expert consultant, you know? I mean, who'd know murder investigations in D.C. better than a D.C. homicide detective?"

Consultant. A little flustered by his own thoughts, he switched his mind off her legs. "Right." He let out a long breath, then laughed. "You roll right along, don't you, Miss McCabe?"

"It's Grace, and I'm pushy, but I won't pout very long if you say no."

He wondered as he looked at her if there was a man alive who could have said no to those eyes. Then again, his partner Ben always told him he was a sucker. "I've got a couple hours, now and then."

"Thanks. Listen, how about dinner tomorrow? By that time Kath will be thrilled to be rid of me for a while. We could talk murder. I'm buying."

"I'd like that." He rose, feeling as though he'd just taken a fast, unexpected ride. "I'd better get back to work."

"Let me sign your book." After a quick search, she found a pen on a magnetic holder by the phone. "I don't know your name."

"It's Ed. Ed Jackson."

"Hi, Ed." She scrawled on the title page, then unconsciously slipped the pen into her pocket. "See you tomorrow, about seven?"

"Okay." She had freckles, he noticed. A half dozen of them sprinkled over the bridge of her nose. And her wrists were slim and frail. He shifted the book again. "Thanks for the autograph."

Grace let him out the back door. He smelled good, she thought, like wood shavings and soap. Then, rubbing her hands together, she went upstairs to plug in Maxwell.

She worked throughout the day, skipping lunch in favor of the candy bar she found in her coat pocket. Whenever she surfaced from the world she was creating into the one around her, she could hear the hammering and sawing from the house next door. She'd set up her workstation by the window because she liked looking at that house and imagining what was going on inside.

Once she noticed a car pull up in the driveway next

door. A rangy, dark-haired man got out and sauntered up the walk, entering the house without knocking. Grace speculated on him for a moment, then dove back into her plot. The next time she bothered to look, two hours had passed and the car was gone.

She arched her back, then, digging her last cigarette out of the pack, read over a few paragraphs. "Good work, Maxwell," she declared. Pushing a series of buttons, she shut him down for the day. Because her thoughts drifted to her sister, Grace got up to tidy the bed.

Her trunk stood in the middle of the room. The delivery man had indeed carried it upstairs for her, and with the least encouragement from her would have unpacked it as well. She glanced at it, considered, then opted to deal with the chaos inside it later. Instead she went downstairs, found a top-forty station on the radio, and filled the house with the latest from ZZ Top.

Kathleen found her in the living room, sprawled on the sofa with a magazine and a glass of wine. She had to fight back the surge of impatience. She'd just spent the day battling to push something into the minds of a hundred and thirty teenagers. The parent consultation had gotten her nowhere, and her car had begun to make ominous noises on the way home. And here was her sister, with nothing but time on her hands and money in the bank.

With the bag of groceries in her arm, she walked over to the radio and switched it off. Grace glanced up, focused, and smiled. "Hi. I didn't hear you come in."

"I'm not surprised. You had the radio up all the way."

"Sorry." Grace remembered to put the magazine back on the table rather than let it slide to the floor. "Rough day?"

"Some of us have them." She turned and walked toward the kitchen.

Grace swung her feet to the floor, then sat for a minute with her head in her hands. After taking a few deep breaths, she rose and followed her sister into the kitchen. "I went ahead and beefed up the salad from last night. It's still the best thing I cook."

"Fine." Kathleen was already lining a broiling pan with foil.

"Want some wine?"

"No, I'm working tonight."

"On the phone?"

"That's right. On the phone." She slapped the meat onto the broiler pan.

"Hey, Kath, I was asking, not criticizing." When she got no response, Grace reached for the wine and topped off her glass. "Actually, it crossed my mind that I might be able to use what you're doing as an angle in a book."

"You don't change, do you?" Kathleen whirled around. In her eyes, the fury was hot and pulsing. "Nothing's ever private where you're concerned."

"For heaven's sake, Kathy, I didn't mean I'd use your name or even your situation, just the idea, that's all. It was simply a thought."

"Everything's grist for the mill, your mill. Maybe you'd like to use my divorce while you're at it."

"I've never used you," Grace said quietly.

"You use everyone—friends, lovers, family. Oh, you sympathize with their pain and problems on the outside, but inside you're ticking away, figuring out how to make it work for you. Can't you be told anything, see anything without thinking how you can use it in a book?"

Grace opened her mouth to deny, to protest, then closed it again on a sigh. The truth, no matter how unattractive, was better faced. "No, I guess not. I'm sorry."

"Then drop it, all right?" Kathleen's voice was abruptly calm again. "I don't want to argue tonight."

"Neither do I." Making an effort, she started fresh. "I was thinking I might rent a car while I'm here, play tourist a little. And if I was mobile, I could do the shopping and save you some time."

"Fine." Kathleen switched the broiler on, shifting her body enough so that Grace couldn't see her hand wasn't steady. "There's a Hertz place on the way to school. I could drop you off in the morning."

"Okay." Now what, Grace asked herself as she sipped her wine. "Oh, I met the guy next door this morning."

"I'm sure you did." Her voice was taut as she slid the meat under the flame. She was surprised Grace hadn't made friends with everyone in the entire neighborhood by now.

Grace sipped her wine and worked on her temper. It was usually she who lost it first, she remembered. This time she wouldn't. "He's very nice. Turns out to be a cop. We're having dinner tomorrow."

"Isn't that lovely." Kathleen slammed the pot on the stove and added water. "You work fast, Gracie, as usual."

Grace took another slow sip, then set her glass carefully on the counter. "I think I'll go for a walk."

"I'm sorry." With her eyes closed, Kathleen leaned against the stove. "I didn't mean that, I didn't mean to snap at you."

"All right." She wasn't always quick to forgive, but she only had one sister. "Why don't you sit down? You're tired."

"No, I'm on call tonight. I want to get this done before the phone starts ringing."

"I'll do it. You can supervise." She took her sister's arm and nudged her into a chair. "What goes in the pan?"

"There's a package in the bag." Kathleen dug in her purse, pulled out a bottle, and shook out two pills.

Graced dipped in the grocery bag and took out an envelope. "Noodles in garlic sauce. Handy." She ripped it open and dumped it in without reading the directions. "I'd just as soon you didn't jump down my throat again, but do you want to talk about it?"

"No, it was just a long day." She dry-swallowed the pills. "I've got papers to grade."

"Well, I won't be able to do you any good there. I could take the phone calls for you."

Kathleen managed a smile. "No, thanks."

Grace took out the salad bowl and set it on the table. "Maybe I could just take notes."

"No. If you don't stir the noodles, they'll stick."

"Oh." Willing to oblige, Grace turned to them. In the silence, she heard the meat begin to sizzle. "Easter's next week. Don't you get a few days off?"

"Five, counting the weekend."

"Why don't we take a quick trip, join the madness in Fort Lauderdale, get some sun?"

"I can't afford it."

"My treat, Kath. Come on, it'd be fun. Remember the spring of our senior year when we begged and pleaded with Mom and Dad to let us go?"

"You begged and pleaded," Kathleen reminded her.

"Whatever, we went. For three days we partied, got sunburned, and met dozens of guys. Remember that one, Joe or Jack, who tried to climb in the window of our motel room?"

"After you told him I was hot for his body."

"Well, you were. Poor guy nearly killed himself." With a laugh, she stabbed a noodle and wondered if it was done. "God, we were so young, and so stupid. What the hell, Kath, we've still got it together enough to have a few college guys leer at us."

"Drinking sprees and college boys don't interest me. Besides, I've arranged to be on call all weekend. Switch the noodles down to warm, Grace, and turn the meat over."

She obeyed and said nothing as she heard Kathleen setting the table. It wasn't the drinking or the men, Grace thought. She'd just wanted to recapture something of the sisterhood they'd shared. "You're working too hard."

"I'm not in your position, Grace. I can't afford to lie on the couch and read magazines all afternoon."

Grace picked up her wine again. And bit her tongue. There were days she sat in front of a screen for twelve hours, nights she worked until three. On a book tour she was on all day and half the night until she had only enough energy to crawl into bed and fall into a stuporous sleep. She might consider herself lucky, she might still be astonished at the amount of money that rolled in from royalty checks, but she earned it. It was a constant source of annoyance that her sister never understood that.

"I'm on vacation." She tried to say it lightly, but the edge was there.

"I'm not."

"Fine. If you don't want to go away, would you mind if I did some puttering around in the yard?"

"I don't care." Kathleen rubbed her temple. The headaches never seemed to fade completely any longer. "Actually I'd appreciate it. I haven't given it much thought. We had a beautiful garden in California. Do you remember?"

"Sure." Grace had always thought it too orderly and formal, like Jonathan. Like Kathleen. She hated the little stab of bitterness she felt and pushed it aside. "We could go for some pansies, and what were those things Mom always loved? Morning glories."

"All right." But her mind was on other things. "Grace, the meat's going to burn."

Later, Kathleen closed herself in her office. Grace could hear the phone ring, the Fantasy phone, as she'd decided to term it. She counted ten calls before she went upstairs. Too restless to sleep, she turned on her computer. But she wasn't thinking of work or of the murders she created.

The contented feeling that had been with her the night before and most of the day was gone. Kathleen wasn't all right. Her mood swings were too quick and too sharp. It had been on the tip of her tongue to mention therapy, but she'd been too aware of what the reaction would have been. Kathleen would have given her one of those hard, closed-in looks, and the discussion would have ended.

Grace had mentioned Kevin only once. Kathleen had told her she didn't want to discuss him or Jonathan. She knew her sister well enough to realize that Kathleen was regretting her visit. What was worse, Grace was regretting it herself. Kathleen always managed to point out the worst aspects of her, aspects that under other circumstances Grace herself managed to brush over.

But she'd come to help. Somehow, despite both of them, she was going to. But it would take some time, she told herself for comfort, resting her chin on her arm. She could see lights in the windows next door.

She couldn't hear the phone ring now with the office door closed and her own pulled to. She wondered how many more calls her sister would take that night. How many more men would she satisfy without ever having seen their faces? Did she grade papers between calls? It should have been funny. She wished it were funny, but she couldn't stop seeing the tension on Kathleen's face as she'd pushed her food around her plate.

There was nothing she could do, Grace told herself as she rubbed her hands over her eyes. Kathleen was determined to handle things her way.

❦

It was wonderful to hear her voice again, to hear her make promises and give that quick, husky laugh. She was wearing black this time, something thin and flimsy that a man could tear away on a whim. She'd like that, he thought. She'd like it if he were there with her, ripping off her clothes.

The man she was talking to barely spoke at all. He was glad. If he closed his eyes, he could imagine she was talking to him. And only him. He'd been listening to her for hours, call after call. After a while, the words no longer mattered. Just her voice, the warm, teasing voice that poured through his earphones and into his head. From somewhere in the house a television was playing, but he didn't hear it. He only heard Desiree.

She wanted him.

In his mind he sometimes heard her say his name. Jerald. She would say it with that half laugh she often had in her voice. When he went to her, she would open up her arms and say it again, slowly, breathlessly. Jerald.

They would make love in all the ways she described.

He would be the man to finally satisfy her. He would be the man she wanted above all others. It would be his name she said over and over again, on a whisper, on a moan, on a scream.

Jerald, Jerald, Jerald.

He shuddered, then lay back, spent, in the swivel chair in front of his computer.

He was eighteen years old and had made love to women only in his dreams. Tonight his dreams wer' only of Desiree.

And he was mad.